CURSED ON THE PRAIRIES

PRAIRIES

A SACRED LAND STORY

ALSO BY TANYA REIMER

SACRED LAND STORIES
LEGENDS ON THE PRAIRIES
GHOSTS ON THE PRAIRIES

FROM THE DARK CHRONICLES
CAN'T DREAM WITHOUT YOU

CURSED ON THE PRAIRIES

A SACRED LAND STORY

TANYA REIMER

Elsewhen Press

CONTENTS

For Mom.

She believes in impossible things, even me.

-Prologue-

Russ shut his book and leaned back with his feet on the windowsill. With a big stretch, he glanced at his pocket watch. Two in the morning wasn't far off, which meant Cal's turn to be the lookout approached.

Russ took one last peek out the window and smirked at what he saw. Finally, something happened. A ghostly shadow paced by the haystack, talking to someone… If he stared close enough, he could make out a girlie silhouette, but at this distance, Russ couldn't be sure. He leaned in for a better look. Dang. Cal was right, some strange girl hung around their haystack, talking to a ghost. Not any ghost—Silver.

He rushed to wake Cal. With an evil-brotherly smirk, Russ prepared to wallop him on the head with his book.

Cal rolled out of the way before Russ made contact and sneaked behind him. He tightened an arm around Russ' neck.

"I saw him," Russ choked out. "Silver. He's talking to the girl you saw sitting on our barn. What the hell, Cal! Let's get out there and find out what's happening."

Cal's grip loosened and he rushed to the window to see for himself. "Come on." He slid the window open and hopped out. Cal leapt down the roof and ran through the field before Russ caught his breath.

Their sister Bernadette sat up and rubbed her glistening blue eyes from her bed along the far wall.

Pretending not to notice, Russ took the lantern and headed out the window after Cal.

"May I come?" Bernadette asked all sleepy. At eight years old, she was a whole year younger than Russ and much too young to be running around in the dark.

He paused with a foot out the window. "Not tonight." He

didn't want her to tell Ma so Russ added, "Tonight is for the guys, but if we don't get busted, I'll ask Silver if you're allowed to come next time."

"Are you scared of him?"

Was he scared of Silver? He'd never talked to him before, but Cal said he'd haunted these prairies since Pa was a wee gaffer.

"He's our grandpa." That didn't answer her question though, because Russ wasn't sure if he was scared of him. Should he be? Cal called him a see-through *Cîpay* warrior. Of course, Cal figured earning the title *Cîpay* was every warrior's dream. Russ thought of the title more as a promotion of some sorts that sounded like a whole bunch of danger and fun all rolled into one. Besides, if there was a strange girl chatting with him, they could handle a ghost, too.

"Why can't I see Silver?" Bernadette asked.

"Pa says you have to be in touch with the earth to see its spirits." He took off.

Bernadette was a bit of a tattletale, which meant he'd better run full speed in case she woke Ma and ended their evening with Silver early.

At the haystack, Russ stumbled, shocked. Silver looked no older than Pa. Heck, maybe younger. This guy was their grandpa?

Cal already sat cross-legged. Silver nodded to Russ. "*Russ, how old are you?*"

Russ blurted out, "How old are you?"

Silver chuckled. "*My soul has seen a few more years than it would appear.*"

The girl snuggled in the straw and Russ didn't give her more than a glance. Cal remained very still, which was unlike him. He spoke for Russ, "He will be ten summers old."

Russ was nine going on ten and prepared to tell his brother to talk like a normal person when Silver blurted out, "*Ten?*" He studied Russ harder. "*You're much too smart for ten.*"

The one thing Russ wanted was to be smart. Only he was called a dummy most days.

"*Well, we have serious business to discuss tonight, sit by your brother, and listen closely to my story because legends say brothers are destined to end a curse plaguing our land, a curse I started. Kit's vision proves this might be you. She came to me immediately, and seeing you together, I have to agree that your destinies are written."*

End a curse? Cal sat taller but Russ didn't want the hassle. He liked living a quiet life like Pa. He didn't appreciate someone telling him his destiny was written, either. He glared at the girl in the straw who'd gotten him involved with this. Kit sat up. She was older than Cal, and even this late at night, she looked alert and ready to cause trouble. Troublemaker was all she was. Russ made a face at her. She shot to her feet and sat by him. Her face stayed expressionless. Her eyes sparkled in the dim light with thoughts that made him curious and he decided she might fit right in with them, *if* she wasn't a troublemaker.

"We don't know anything about a curse," Russ told them politely so they didn't get their hopes up. "And I make my own destiny."

For once, Cal nodded in agreement with him.

Even though Silver seemed solid enough when Russ first arrived, now a white horse blew to life inside him, then he became less and less solid and more and more see-through as if he might wisp away at any moment.

"Are you a ghost?" Russ asked.

Cal nudged him and gave him a dirty glare. Russ placed the lantern in front of them and waited for an answer. He was sure Silver was a ghost, and bet Cal was too chicken to hear the truth.

Silver sat in front of them. *"At the heart of the world is land so sacred, all life is born and returns in that spot. A sacred connection to this land allows Cîpay to be born, reborn, and to live forever. Under our feet is the energy of our existence. Without Sacred Land, there is no Cîpay. Without Cîpay, there is no life."*

"How are we connected to the ground?" Russ demanded, needing to understand everything. He glanced at Kit in case she thought he was a dummy for asking but she looked eager for answers, too, so he relaxed.

Silver thought about the question. *"Imagine Mother Earth pushes energy into the world and makes life."* He plucked a dandelion weed from the grass. *"Like a forbidden flower. Its roots hide in the soil but the beautiful bloom is vulnerable. The ground protects the roots, but nothing protects the rest. The flower will die, returning to the earth and the cycle of energy will continue.*"

"So the earth spawns life yet only protects half?" Cal sounded skeptical, and Russ understood his doubt. They had a mare who'd given birth, and dang, she protected her baby just fine. Ma was protective of her baby, too. Pa told them that came with being a ma, and Russ believed him.

"*Her protection is to curse those who disrespect this energy she transfers.*" Silver bowed his head. Kit and Cal copied him, but Russ was curious about the horse in Silver's soul so he kept his head up to watch the shadow rear up and bow.

So far, his story sucked and Russ wasn't interested in the tale at all. Rumours claimed that Silver was the greatest *Cîpay* warrior of their tribe, yet he shared a story about a flower cursing people. Talk about boring. Where was the danger, the fun, the anything else?

Silver lifted his head again. "*The flower has many enemies who don't understand her importance. They interrupt the cycle of energy and pay with a curse. We must protect all life.*"

"I will," Cal and Kit said instantly, which ticked Russ off. He could protect things, too. Even stupid flowers.

Russ laughed before Cal could brag about his speed and strength or before this girl could show off how smart she was. "You'll protect a flower?"

"It's a symbol, stupid." Cal whacked him.

"Oh. So what are we protecting for real?" Russ stressed the 'we' so Silver knew he was as committed. "Don't speak in symbols, teach me truth."

"*The truth is, if we fail,*" Silver continued, "*the earth will suck us into it to reset the balance.*"

Silence dropped on them.

Finally, Russ asked, "You mean, a mud monster will eat us?" He knew the stories about mud monsters on the prairies, he just didn't think they were true.

Silver sighed. "*I didn't mean to scare you, but take your destiny seriously. Because if this flower—*"

"Stop calling it a flower. What is it really?" Russ demanded.

Kit whispered, "Sacred Land."

"If Sacred Land is destroyed, everything will die: the plants, the animals, and all the people. The energy will not be balanced, and Mother will do everything possible to reset her livelihood."

"So how does the curse work?" Cal asked.

"The land surrounding Sacred Land, your land, is the Cursed Lands. Its purpose is to protect Sacred Land. I did something that brought an ancient curse back to life..."

Kit slid in closer to Russ as if they could protect each other from a curse. Russ glanced around in case the haunted land might show him these spirits coming and going.

Cal asked, "Why would someone destroy Sacred Land?"

"Your father wishes for you to discover the truth with your own eyes. There are many dangers."

"So? Tell us anyway," Russ said, always annoyed when someone told him he couldn't do or learn something. He could do anything he wanted. "He won't care. We're always learning things he doesn't need to know about."

Cal whacked him on the arm so Russ punched Cal's leg.

"Tell us," Kit whispered.

"The dangers are fear, greed, even the misguided." He bowed his head. *"The curse I wish to discuss with you, the one that is my doing, happened on the day I disrupted the balance."*

They listened carefully.

"This young boy, well, he was probably close to your age, Russ, he killed someone. His own father."

"By accident?" Russ asked, curious how something so horrible might happen.

"No. His father had been cursed by greed."

Russ couldn't imagine killing his pa because of some curse; there had to be a better way of handling a curse.

"His father's soul clung to his, a shadow threatening him and his learning. My sister tried to help. She took this shadow in her soul. The maleficent spirit just about killed her."

Russ glanced at Kit, proud of his family's strength.

Kit ignored him.

"*I brought her to the Healing Chamber under the Cursed Lands and vexed the evil to the land under us.*"

Russ wasn't sure what a Healing Chamber did but if this place lurked under his land, he'd find it.

"*This shadow found the boy's uncle Bellecoeur and latched on, not as a shadow but as a cursed soul infecting his every breath.*" Silver bowed his head and Kit and Cal copied him.

Russ thought about the horrible twist this story had taken while they were silent. He asked, "So that made his uncle Bellecoeur go nuts, right?"

Silver nodded. "*Nuts. Yup, you could say that. Bellecoeur sought me out and killed me. He tried to take our land.*"

"Holy haystacks!" Cal leapt up, his knife out, ready to kill this Bellecoeur guy.

Kit pulled him back. "Listen, Silver is telling us that he can't move on because he's tied to this Bellecoeur fellow."

So his grandpa didn't want to be a ghost but was cursed to live as one? Weird.

Sadness washed through his ghostly form in a rainy mess. "*It did not end there. I have doomed us. Unleashing a curse is like unleashing a cougar in a herd of buffalo. Panic spreads and a stampede is unavoidable.*

"*Bellecoeur has worked his entire life to destroy Sacred Land. At first, greed pushed him. As his enemy, I taught him this was not the way. Then he sought balance, taking my life for his brother's. But I died on Cursed Lands and shadow him. As his shadow, I have taught him that revenge is but a breath from regret. Now he lives with a new fear; that we hide witches among us. His teachings affect many, mostly because of the curse. He has made his quest one to scare us and I have nothing left to teach him.*"

"We don't scare easily," Cal pointed out and Russ nodded in agreement.

Cal's jaw firmed as he gripped his knife. He carried that thing everywhere. "I will tell everyone how important Sacred Land is and others will understand even if he doesn't."

Russ had never seen Cal this upset. The horse in Silver stopped to listen. Russ thought about what Cal said.

"You can't, Cal," Russ complained. "Weren't ya listening?

If you start yapping about this type of power, things will get worse and everyone will be cursed."

"*What?*" Silver raised a hand to silence Cal who looked ready to beat on Russ for telling him he was stupid. "*Explain this to me, Russ. What do you know about the curse? Do you understand how such a thing spreads?*"

"I understand how being cursed works, sure. Pa told me not to touch the baby bird, but as soon as he wasn't looking, this weird need to touch it came over me. The bird died 'cause of me." Russ took a deep breath and Kit grabbed his hand. When their fingers touched, a strange warmth comforted him, as if he had nothing to worry about. He yanked his hand from her, giving her a dirty glare. She stuck out her tongue at him.

"I felt bad," Russ admitted, talking mostly to Kit. She focused on him, which made confessing things to her easy. The bright moon made the streaks of filth on her cheeks and gobs of mud in her hair stand out. He'd never seen a gal so dirty. "I can't explain why I touched the bird after he made it clear I shouldn't. I was cursed without wanting to be. If Cal goes around and tells everyone to leave our land alone, they'll line up to take Sacred Land thinking it's magical or something. Everyone will be cursed."

Silver ran a shaking hand in his long hair. "*Your Pa is storming this way. Best be off with ya.*"

Kit leapt up and ran off. Russ took one last glance at her as she vanished in the dark. "Where is she going?" he asked Cal. A part of him wanted to run with her to learn how she got so dirty.

"Home." Cal nudged him. "She came from far to share her vision. Neat, eh?"

"But she never told us anything."

Cal pushed him. "Sometimes, Russ, people talk without speaking. Learn to listen with your soul, your heart, everything but your ears."

Russ followed Cal home trying to figure out how he could hear without his ears. Had she said things without words? He studied his hand. A smear of mud marked her touch.

"Cal, he never told us what exactly is cursed, did he?"

PART ONE

SEVEN YEARS LATER

"You asked if I was a ghost, but really, aren't we all?"

–Silver

–ONE–

June 1928—

Russ was almost seventeen when Pa sent him to face his first cougar. She'd scared the horses and killed one of their cows. Normally, Cal took care of the wildlife, but Pa and Cal were having some sort of weird fight that involved a lot of sighing and glaring.

Still, determined to impress them both, Russ planned to do a good job.

He'd followed her tracks along the creek and crossed over to the other side before the banks grew too steep to climb. Meant he'd left the safety of Dubois' land and travelled Kaplain's, but he needed a better view of her den, which would be across the creek. He knew exactly where she headed.

The banks grew sharper until he stared about twenty feet down to the creek. They called this place The Cliffs and since Russ hadn't ever seen actual cliffs, he believed they were such. Over the ledge on the other side stood three maple trees with a bunch of large boulders. The land between the trees was sacred and the rocks had carvings on them with prayers for brave warriors. Dubois' land ended there on that side, but on this side, Russ stood on Kaplain's land. He found a quiet place across from the trees so he could see the face of the rocks and the ledge properly on the other bank.

Along the face, a thin path led to the cave embedded in the side of the cliff, overlooking the drop to the creek. It took a leap to reach the cave and felt like a dangerous journey, even though the drop wasn't far to the water. Russ supposed that was because he was used to living on solid land that didn't just vanish and drop. Of course, the ledge proved to be a safe enough place for a cougar to hide. He and his friend Kika used to play there when they were younger and pretended they were cave people. They practiced all sorts of rituals and once they even called on a mud monster with a ceremony that didn't work, but was fun.

Russ prepared his shotgun and took aim. Safe across the creek, he'd get a good shot. Of course, he'd have to fire and run, because he didn't want Kaplains catching him on their land and he couldn't cross to Dubois' land for about half a mile because The Cliffs were too steep.

Patience was his strongest quality and he wriggled in the grass so no one could see him. Enjoying the sun on his neck and the breeze coming off the land, Russ listened to the water rippling below. He decided this was the perfect place. He would never ask for more than this moment.

Movement caught his attention and he prepared to shoot.

Out of the den rolled a cub with spots. Another joined her. They caught each other's ears and the play was so adorable, Russ relaxed his finger on the trigger.

The mother walked in the sun, moving on the ledge with ease. Monstrous, she paused to stare directly at Russ. His heart picked up as his finger curled around the trigger. The cubs stopped their playing to watch him, too.

The world stood still for a moment and didn't restart until Russ rested the gun on the long grass.

-Two-

Two days later, Russ came home from another afternoon out by the cougar den. Pa chatted with Ma by the garden and he rubbed his pants with his left hand, which was a weird thing Russ had never seen him do.

When Pa saw Russ enter the barn, he left her and stormed toward him. Arms crossed he waited for Russ to store the gun.

Russ avoided his glaring but his rage filled the entire barn.

"I just lied to your mother for you."

That was a new one. Pa wasn't one to lie to Ma.

"Why?"

He almost pounced on Russ and dragged him behind the barn. He tossed him to his knees and Russ fell in the dirt by a fallen horse. Ma's best mare laid mangled. One glance told him a cougar had attacked. Dang.

"You told me you found her."

"I did, but she has two cubs with her, so I didn't shoot her." Russ placed his hands on the mare's head. She'd been expecting. They couldn't afford the loss. She was a damn good horse, too.

Now she was dead because he didn't pull the trigger.

"Cubs?" Pa sighed. "Son." He knelt beside Russ. "Sometimes we have to do things to protect ourselves, to protect those who count on us. I don't enjoy killing either, but lying to your Ma is worse. She's counting on us to protect our farm. She invested a lot of work into this horse. We all did. We let her down. I told her the mare died foaling. She was crushed but my lie will buy you time to finish your job. I expect you to kill the cougar and her cubs. Chances of them surviving are slim anyhow. If you can't, tell me now, and I'll have Cal kill 'em."

Russ couldn't meet his eyes. "I thought if I brought the horses in at night, they'd be safe. Sometimes there are other solutions."

"Yet you didn't."

No, he hadn't. He'd been busy last night with Isabelle in the haystack but couldn't very well tell Pa a girl had distracted him with cookies. But dang. She made good cookies.

"Russ, sometimes there are no other solutions." Pa left Russ to clean up his mess. By suppertime, he had the mare buried so Ma wouldn't see the truth.

He sat quietly at the table between his brothers, facing his three sisters. Pa sat at the head of the table. He wouldn't glance at Russ. Ma fussed at the stove and they waited for her to join them before they could eat.

When she finally did, Russ looked at his food with a knot in his stomach. Knowing he had to hunt the cougar tomorrow had him sick, but the deed had to be done if he was to face Pa again.

Cal nudged him and dumped peas on their plates. He hardly had anything on his plate either, which was weird for Cal; he usually liked eating. Russ glanced at Pa. His plate stayed full since he hadn't taken a bite.

His brother shifted.

The tension around the table wasn't something they were used to and Russ prepared to confess everything to Ma to clear the air.

"Ma, I'm sorry about your mare," he said.

"Thank you for burying her."

Pa shot up before Russ could come clean. "You hear that?" he asked Cal, then remembered their fight, so he looked at Russ, but he was disappointed in Russ so he asked his youngest son Samuel instead. Sammy shook his head and dropped his forkful of potatoes.

The tension tripled. Even the girls stopped eating to stare at Cal. He kept his head down and asked, "Do you need me?"

Cal had just turned eighteen. In the muscle department, he was broader than Pa and Russ together. He was so strong that when Jessie Kaplain showed up in Eau Claire to beat on Russ for looking at his horse the wrong way, Cal just had to stand beside Russ to make him back off. Of course, Jessie was so stupid he called Cal a French Savage as he walked away, which cost him his two front teeth.

Pa pushed his chair back and left his food to get cold. He motioned for Cal to stay seated with a mean glare unlike his usual playful way.

Cal ground his teeth, his eyes focused on his plate, not eating.

The minute Pa shut the front door, Russ and Cal bolted for the window to see what the heck was important enough for Pa to let his food go cold.

"Russ, shove over. Give me room." Cal crowded him, even though he hogged the window.

"Bernadette, grab Pa's plate, we'll warm his food in the oven." Ma added wood to the stove as if Pa might flip on her if his food went cold. He was weird about his food and all, but he was the dumbass who'd left during one helluva good meal. Even Russ was brave enough to point that out to him if he complained about his food being cold when he returned.

"Damn, it's Montague," Cal said. Montague was Cal's hero. His face normally lit up when he shared the gory stories about the hell the chief of the Ghosts of the Earth ravaged on the prairies. Given that some tribals were see-through and kinda ghostly, the name of their tribe fit. Even though Russ was a descendant from the tribe, he didn't know the location of their secret town. Maybe they lived everywhere. They were always around—underfoot, in the shadows, by the creek—not harming anyone. A normal guy got used to seeing them and left them alone.

Of course, Cal was not a normal guy.

"Aw man." Cal moaned, glancing in the distance at Silver. He had his arms crossed and watched the powwow Pa had with Montague. "Great. Even Silver knows what I did." Cal banged his head against the glass with a heavy sigh. "Pa is gonna have my hide for sure," Cal whispered to the pane.

Russ wasn't too worried, Cal and Pa fought a lot, but they were always tight. Still, he was curious as heck what Cal had done to get everyone so wild. With a chance to figure out a mystery, Russ smirked, excited. He knew better than to ask

Cal for details, that would just get him a whack on the back of the head.

Pa talked to this fellow as if they were old friends. Montague wore pants, something like Pa's work pants. He kept a knife along his back and didn't wear a shirt, but men from the Ghosts of the Earth tribe never wore shirts in nice weather, and since Russ wasn't outside in bad weather, he didn't know their bad weather habits. Cal said their muscles were too big for shirts. Watching Montague, he decided Cal was serious.

Pa stood in his tie, like a guy about to tell a joke, but Montague stayed planted like...well...like a guy no one would be dumb enough to tell a joke to. He gripped a tomahawk, ready to bash Pa's skull in if the joke sucked. Russ wasn't too worried, because he'd be dead before he swung that tomahawk. Silver wouldn't let anyone hurt his son, not even Montague.

Montague was taller, but not much older than Pa. They were related for sure, but Russ wasn't sure how. He wore the same tattoo on the back of his hand as everyone in their family. The silver arrow caught the eye, even from the window. He had many more markings running up his arm and across his shoulder, which was kinda neat. Pa said tribals earned tattoos so Russ wondered what Montague had done that was so special. Russ glanced quickly at his own tattoo, proud.

They shared a few words, then Montague ran toward the chicken coop and plum vanished in the bushes around the shed.

Moments later, Pa burst in for his hat and jacket.

The boys rushed to their seats and pretended to eat.

Pa glanced in, his cap on. He wore his suit on Sundays since Ma washed his work clothes every Sunday and he had nothing else to wear. He wore his suit with pride, and if Russ owned clothes that fine, he would, too.

"I'm going to Dubois' for a spell. Just sit tight."

Russ sat up taller when Pa said Dubois, which caught Pa's attention. He told Russ, "No running off tonight, Russ. Lock up the windows, the doors, *everything*." He stressed the 'everything', which tightened a knot in Russ' stomach.

Would he ever let him live down the fact that he'd forgotten to bring the horses in?

Then Pa grinned at the three girls. His shoulders relaxed, proving he wasn't mad or disappointed in them. "Study hard, girls. I'm quizzing you tomorrow. Ask Russ if you need help. We'll read in the morning."

Pa loved to read to them. Like supper, he never missed his time with them. Gerard the pharmacist kept a box at the drug store with almost a hundred books. Russ called the big wooden box a travelling library. They were welcome to read them as long as they brought them back. Come June 1st, someone exchanged the big box for a new one—like magic. Russ had stopped by today and grabbed four books he itched to read.

Samuel was ready to jump from his chair when Pa glanced his way. He stared at Samuel long and hard before saying, "Samuel, I'm leaving you in charge of feeding the geese, dogs, and you'd better give a bit of milk to the cats." Sammy nodded as if this was serious work, which made Russ roll his eyes.

"Supper was excellent, *mon amour*, but I lost my appetite." He winked at Ma as if he always did things like this and his strange behaviour was a bit of fun they were having. But until that day, Pa had never missed a meal. He was weird about his food all right, but, in a way, his dedication to meals was nice 'cause no matter what dirt the day brought, come supper, they'd all be at the table together. Well, 'cept tonight. Tonight something so important went down he left so he could go off by himself to check things out.

Pa was Russ' hero, more so than Cal. Cal was tough with a wild streak in him Russ envied, but Pa, he was right out smart. If there's one thing Russ knew: brains—working brains, that is—could outsmart muscles any day of the week. When a guy is built like a twig and always up to his ass in trouble, being smart came in handy.

Still, Russ had to wonder, even if Pa was smart, how the heck had he heard a warrior in them there bushes while at the supper table? A bloody mystery. Yet nothing became more mysterious than what he said next.

Pa stood around the corner, probably with his hand on the

doorknob, but he had a distinctive croak in his voice when he said, "And Cal, bring in the horses before you pack up your things. I don't want to see you at this supper table again."

A long silence followed. Not those good silences, but the painful kind that makes an idiot jump up and say a bunch of stupid things so everyone laughs and forgets how mean they're being.

The longer they sat in the horrible silence, the more Russ suspected the idiot might be him because the idea of Cal no longer at the table made him sick to his stomach.

Normally, Cal would argue or yell something wild and stupid, but he kept his head down. He wiped his nose along his sleeve. Was he crying? Russ tilted his head to check and Cal kicked him under the table. Dang.

Russ decided Cal was probably praying not crying. Still, he shifted uneasy because if Cal cried, Russ would probably cry, too.

Ma made a terrible sound that reminded Russ of a mouse caught in a trap. She said to Pa, "Do not let this come between you and your son."

The silence killed him so Russ checked if Pa was alive on the other side of the wall. Pa had his head against the door and when he turned to see who watched him, tears glistened on his cheek but he wiped at 'em quickly.

Russ was speechless. He'd never seen his pa cry.

"I meant not alone. I don't expect you back at our table alone. These secrets are not how we do things and I'm disgusted that you assumed she's not welcome."

Not alone? Russ was baffled. What gal would Cal bring to the supper table? The kitchen was crowded enough.

From his spot in the doorway, Russ glared at Cal, shocked he'd actually made Pa cry. Plus, if he brought a girl to supper from now on, Russ wanted to have Isabelle over every now and again. Of course, he couldn't ask anything, not with Pa so upset.

Pa opened the door and left.

Russ went back to the table, too shaken to talk. Cal let out his breath and pushed his plate away with a half smirk.

A gloss haunted his eyes as if he might lose his composure at any moment. Which was hard to believe 'cause Cal hadn't cried since he was ten and he'd run his sled off the roof, ramming it into a tree, breaking his arm. Even then, he'd claimed he wasn't crying 'cause of the pain but because he broke the sled he'd worked so hard on. Of course, that made sense; the sled had been a beauty, all right.

Cal said, "At least he's talking to me again. Could be worse, I could be dead. Thanks, Ma."

Ma stood at the stove, gripping her apron. "Bernoit." Bernoit was Cal's real name since they'd named him after Pa, who was named after Grandma Lacey Bernoit-Montague. Cal was actually the name of a wild stallion. When he died, Cal announced he was taking his name. Made sense, a guy like Cal should be named after a wild horse and not his grandma. So everyone called him Cal. Well, except Ma, but like Cal, no one questioned her unless they wanted to do their own laundry and eat soap for supper.

Cal didn't peek at Ma, as if doing so might make them tears he hid jerk forth.

"I should meet her," Ma announced in her you-can't-refuse-me way.

Thing about Ma was that she always expected the worst, and well, when they delivered, she took the bad news much better than Pa.

Ma was the definition of uptight, and Russ counted his lucky stars Pa was around to lighten the mood. She always talked as if the boys were loose cannons, Pa included, yet Russ had never seen Pa throw anything at her but kisses. He did that a lot.

Despite the fact that she never saw the good in anything, she loved her family something fierce, and Pa claimed they were a hard bunch to love.

Now, she studied Cal as if she'd expected him to disappoint Pa and it was about time he'd proved her right.

Cal nodded and bit his lip, but wouldn't face her.

"I'll talk to your father." She sighed, proving such a discussion would be a chore and a half.

Cal stood. "What about you, Ma, you disappointed?"

Ma said something that got Russ thinking he'd missed something important about what had happened, "It's a father's job to be disappointed in a son when he slips, but a mother's joy is seeing her boy slip into a man prepared to love enough to be disappointed himself."

Cal's eyebrows shot up as if she'd given him ice cream, but Russ didn't get why he was so happy. If he let Pa down, this was serious. Pa let them get away with just about anything as long as their dumb ideas followed the law of the land: *respect nature, respect yourself, respect others.*

"Now hit the fields. He gave you all jobs. He's seen enough disappointment from you children this week."

Russ nodded. He wasn't sure what the others had done, but he'd done plenty to disappoint Pa.

—THREE—

After Russ finished watching Sammy do his chores, he headed up to his room. Well…it wasn't just his room, these days he shared a room with Cal and Sammy. The girls had their own room—thank you, Ma.

He tossed his books on the bed and stared out the window. He wasn't staying home tonight, but the question was, should he risk pissing Pa off more and follow him or head over to see Isabelle and forget about Pa?

Ah Isabelle.

Either way, he was headed to Dubois Farm. Russ respected Pa enough to listen to him, he did, but they hadn't locked windows or doors since he was born, so that sounded like a waste of time. The horses were all in for the night and he had no reason to sit around being bored when something exciting was going down.

Russ grabbed a book in case Pa caught him. Then he could claim he headed to teach Isabelle to read. Sounded innocent enough, Pa might let it go. Of course, Ma was a different story, so Russ opted for climbing out the window and heading out that way.

He stayed in the untrimmed hedges outside Dubois' house, low to the ground. Pa and Skinny were along the side of the house talking. Guys like Pa and Skinny were known in Western Canada as adventurers and pioneers, which wasn't the case since they were born before Eau Claire. Their roots weren't something either bragged about, but others respected them.

Skinny's real name was Michel Dubois and he was French Canadian. Russ wasn't sure he spoke English or knew what his nickname meant so he was sure to call him Monsieur

Dubois whenever he was caught sneaking about Dubois Farm, which was about twelve more times than he needed to be caught this week.

Every time Skinny caught him, he'd say, "Always nice to see you with your pants on." Russ didn't ever want to be caught without 'em on because Skinny was a tall angry bear with a daughter Russ planned to marry. Not a doubt in his mind. His love for her wasn't some foolish schoolboy fantasy. She was his best friend since a day way back when they were ten, when Russ did something selfish that made him look like a hero to her.

Of course, Monsieur Dubois wasn't the only threat. Isabelle had two brothers. Thomas had more muscle than Cal. He promised Russ that if he didn't keep his pecker in his pants he'd find boot marks on it. Every time Russ changed his pants he remembered the promise, but the joke was on him 'cause what Thomas didn't know was that Russ would suffer daily beatings to see Isabelle. *Heck yeah. Bring 'em on, macho man.*

Their families couldn't be more different. Everyone in her family had different coloured skin, kinda like at Cousin Antoine's. Which to Russ was neat. At their place, they looked pretty much the same. Sure Ma's skin was a touch paler and Bernadette's eyes were a blue like Grandma Lacey's, but they were still from the same clan, that's for sure. At the end of the day, Russ wasn't sure those things mattered, but he did like to know which family he was tied to and by looking at them, he knew where he belonged, sure as mud.

Unlike the Dubois family, Russ' family wasn't the best-looking crew. They had long bumpy noses and matted hair that made them look like a messed up bird. But Ma made sure they were always clean. She washed them a lot. Cal used to complain that she couldn't wash the savage out of them, which would get Pa chuckling. Still, Ma believed cleanliness was clothes to God in a mess or something weird like that, which made no sense to Isabelle and Russ, but they quoted her anyway because pretending they were that smart was exciting.

The Dubois family were a good-looking bunch. They might

blow over if the wind picked up because they were so skinny, but they were so bloody tall, Russ would get stomped on for sure if one of them found him unfit for hanging around Isabelle. Cal came in handy when pricks were stupid, but when Russ was the dumbass, Cal just crossed his arms and watched him get the boot imprint.

Now Pa said in French to Skinny, "Antoine talked to Kaplain about Sacred Land. Explained real nice-like how important it is to our people and how to respect the land. He asked if we could hunt or even pray on our land again because if we could just walk it, maybe divert some of Kaplain's negative energy…"

"And?"

"And no. Montague says a group are headed this way to make his 'no' stick," Pa answered. "Montague will stand with us. I thought he came to kill my son, but he called him one of his warriors." Pa sounded proud. "I always wanted to be like Montague."

"Not sure why when you can be you like no one else can. Glad he sees that we're on his side. I was worried when he snapped a few months back."

Pa nodded. "That was a big loss. He feels responsible, but doesn't blame us."

Russ paid closer attention. What did they lose?

"I'll have to thank Cal myself for getting Montague focused again. I always liked that *one* boy of yours." The way Old Skinny stressed the 'one' made Russ cringe. Dang.

"Now about Cal," Pa lowered his voice. "Montague has it in his head that Cal's the Ghost Hunter *Cîpay* legends speak about." Pa sighed. "I'm afraid the truth is somewhat more real world." He slouched forward. "You called that one. I should have talked to Cal before he caved."

Caved? Stubborn like he was, Russ couldn't see Cal caving to anyone. Russ moved in for a better view but stayed on his belly, under the bushes. His feet stuck out along the back, but Pa wouldn't be able to see them.

Skinny slapped Pa on the back. "Well, he's your first. I have two boys. Trust me, when they start disappearing you have to get on 'em like a maggot. You'd better make damn sure Russ behaves because I'd hate to have his death between us."

A large lump formed in the back of Russ' throat.

Pa chuckled and Russ stole a breath, relieved they were joking even if he saw nothing funny in what Skinny had said. Pa glanced back at their farm, then at the bushes where Russ hid. Despite his hiding spot, Russ felt vulnerable. How the heck did Pa know he was there?

Pa said, "We'll share horror stories later. We have to beat these guys to the church and end this."

"We planning to try this Silver's way or Montague's way?" Skinny's voice croaked.

"I just told Russ to do whatever it takes to protect us." Pa ran the palm of his hands against his forehead. "Feels like I'm a fraud, seeing I can't do much with the weight of our ancestors on me."

Skinny seemed to agree. "You have your own curse to bear. My boys and I will take care of this. Last time, Montague's way cost us the Trading Lands. We can't afford to mess this up anymore. We'll do this Silver's way then we'll go home and pray. We'll pray hard, because these guys are cursed and everyone we take out will haunt us until they destroy us. Best you give me your gun and your knife before we head out there. I can't risk having one haunt you. Not when our past and future rest within you."

Pa handed over his knife and picked up the shotgun he'd had resting against the wagon. He handed it over, too. "Are you sure you're up for this?" Pa asked.

"Yup. You?"

Pa studied his hands, looking at the palms then the backs of them. "I have no choice. The screams are a little painful tonight. Do you really think Kit can help me?"

Feet shuffled nearby and Russ realized Skinny's boys were there. "I'll talk to her," Francis, Isabelle's brother, said as he walked by. "She helped me handle the cursed shadowing me. Until then, if you feel the urge to blow something up, keep your hands in your pockets holding that amulet I gave you and breathe through the fear. Oh, and chew on this." He handed Pa some type of leaf.

Why were Francis and Thomas in on this? Sure, they were older than Cal and Russ, but weren't they smarter? Then again, Russ hid in a bush with no clue what caused Pa pain or why that troublemaker Kit could help him, so maybe not.

Pa jumped in the wagon to leave with Skinny and his sons. Russ prepared to run after them when out of the bushes by the house hopped Isabelle. Her dark skin was dirty as usual, but she was lovely just the same.

"What ya doing out here?" Russ scolded her. This gal of his was bloody determined to break every rule he knew. He grabbed her hand. "Come on."

She ran with him down the road, not saying anything. Probably what Russ liked best about her. His sisters never shut the hell up and that got annoying fast.

Russ told her everything and she nodded thoughtfully, working things out in that genius brain of hers.

They ran smack into Cal on the road by their place before she could tell him what she thought was happening. Cal had brought his own posse with him. A group of Natives.

Kika stood with them so Russ waited by him. Russ and Kika never talked much, some friends were more for adventures than gossip, but Russ couldn't remember a time when he wasn't friends with Kika. They were so tight that when they were about nine, Kika had followed Russ to class. Miss Penelope—or as Russ liked to call her, Old Cracker Jack—had sent him home and told him there was no place for boys like Kika in her school. Which was ironic because no one believed the school belonged to her, and for sure no one believed there were other boys like Kika kicking around.

When Russ told Pa what had happened the next day, Pa walked them to school with a determination that amused them, because really, Kika didn't care if he went to school, he just wanted to hang with Russ. Pa had brought in a desk from the attic and arranged it for Kika. Russ handed Kika a book from his desk that he hated and a pencil he loved, to make up for the crappy reading material. Then, to their shock, Pa stood at the back of the one room classroom all day watching Cracker Jack teach. She didn't dare send Kika home a second time. She didn't say anything weird that day either.

Russ stayed back to hear Pa yell at her. Instead, what he heard was her demanding a raise if she had to educate savages or she'd be reporting the lot of 'em to the superintendent for insisting she teach in French. Russ wasn't sure what language she wanted to teach in, but Pa paid her from his own pocket, well, not in cash, he handed her a flask. After all that fuss, Russ told Kika he'd better go to school every day and do real well, too. And so he did.

Now, standing by Kika, Russ felt like he belonged and copied his relaxed stance.

Cal rubbed the new tattoos on his upper arm while he glared at Russ. What the heck had Cal been up to this last bit while Russ had his head stuck in a book? Clearly, he'd lied to Ma about going to college.

Before Russ could tease him, Isabelle walked up to one of the gals to Cal's right and got right in her face. The gesture was intimidating and the gal pulled a knife on Isabelle and held the blade under her chin.

Pa taught Russ to let women fight their own battles, but no one pulled a knife on his gal. He dived for her.

Cal caught him mid-flight and knocked Russ on his ass.

Isabelle's dog, Beast, growled.

"What the heck, Cal?" Russ scrambled to his feet, ready to fight them all with his bare hands.

Isabelle hadn't moved, but she opened her hand, which shut the dog up.

Cal ran an arm around this girl real protective like, and pushed her knife down. He mumbled in her ear in her language, "Ease up, she's kinda slow."

Isabelle was not slow and if she studied this gal, the reason would be important.

Still, Cal had touched this woman at his side as if she were his wife. Russ mimicked his actions, running his arm around Isabelle, in case he could appear tough like Cal. Russ liked to think he was grownup like Cal, capable of making his own manly decisions.

Cal's gal put the knife away so maybe he knew how to talk to her and she was the slow one.

Isabelle whispered against Russ' neck, "This is the woman your ma wants to meet."

Russ chuckled, 'cause what the heck would Ma say—in her frilly apron and with flour on her nose—if Cal walked in with a tall Native dressed in pelts with a knife in her skirt and markings all over her arms?

"These are Montague's warriors from the Trading Lands. Silver brought them here when they lost their land," Cal said as if that explained why he was on the road with 'em, his arm around one. Russ was about to ask how an entire tribe lost their land when he added, "Meet Kika's cousin, Desire." He pronounced her name in French so the word rolled out, sounding like Dezeerr. "She has a bit of a protective streak. She'll make a great mother, wouldn't ya say?"

She glared at Russ with piercing black eyes. He wasn't sure about her making a great mother. She wasn't the type of plump pessimistic mother he knew.

"Don't you ever pull a knife on her again," Russ said in her language even though he was sure she'd kill him for talking to her.

Desire ruffled his hair as if he were a little boy. She wore a bead bracelet with small feathers dangling from it. The beads made a familiar jingling sound.

"You were in my room last week," Russ blurted out and pulled Isabelle behind him, wishing he were brave enough to mark his skin up, pull knives on strangers, or walk through houses he didn't own.

"She was with me, moron. Relax. Listen up, little brother. Remember how Silver told us the Cursed Lands would protect Sacred Land when danger showed? This is happening."

Russ glanced at Isabelle. He didn't like Cal talking about curses in front of her and worried about that when he should have paid attention, because that was Cal's subtle way of asking for help.

"You were right. The more Antoine tells them how important the land is, the more they stake their claim. Now one of them stole a bright idea from Bellecoeur to come covered up."

Cal spoke Bellecoeur's name with a rage that made Russ instantly dislike the bloke.

"Covered like a ghost?" Russ asked. "Why?"

"So they can make a point that they aren't afraid of haunted land and maybe they're the ghosts haunting Sacred Land."

Russ chuckled. This is what they were worried about? That

wasn't scary at all. "I'm not afraid of idiots in sheets or of a curse for that matter."

"These men have a cursed soul attached to theirs," Cal spoke low. "I don't see souls, but I imagine having a shadow latched onto you would suck. Don't you?" Cal fell to his knees and tossed dirt on his arms and on his feet. Once Isabelle had caught Pa doing this and asked if he'd gone mad, but blessing was a perfectly natural thing for Pa to do so Russ had said no. She'd asked if he did such things, too. Russ lied and said no. He didn't want her asking if he'd gone mad.

When the others joined in, Isabelle knelt and blessed herself with sacred soil, too. She invited Russ to join her, as if this was her secret to share and not the other way around. Russ mumbled the prayers with her, surprised that she knew them. Then again, maybe everyone knew them.

When they returned to their feet, Russ proudly stood with them, Isabelle at his side.

"So what'll Pa say when he catches us running around when we're supposed to move you out?" Russ was dumb enough to ask.

"He'll probably say thanks." Cal grinned and ran off with his new friends.

They ran toward town, headed for the bushes by the slough on Dubois land. Russ glanced at Isabelle in case she wanted to follow. When he looked back, they were gone. Not a trace of them. Dumbfounded, he wondered if maybe this magical land had gobbled them up.

Standing on the prairies at sunset, Russ felt the mystery and the hugeness of the world. Opened skies promised long endless fields with bumps of fences. Strange sounds reminded him that it grew late. Bushes and shrubs lined the horizon.

They stood on the road. Isabelle about twenty feet from him. Between their homes, they were at a crossway. Her mutt of a dog paced beside her—he followed her everywhere. Cal had vanished. Pa ran off with her pa and Russ had no clue what happened. They should have headed home or to their happy spot to read. Heck, he should have kissed her or something neat like that. Of course, they didn't do anything that smart. They gawked at each other, silent, lost in thoughts, neither caring about the world around them.

Something moved in the distance. Russ was used to locals running on their land, but this was a shadow of a man. Silver watched them, which was weird. He didn't usually appear when Isabelle hung around with him. Silver's long hair blew behind him, free. His arrow aimed for something behind Russ. Russ didn't realize how focused he'd become on his ghostly grandpa until Isabelle cried out. He wanted to reassure her that Silver was safe but she wasn't looking his way.

If he'd glanced to his right instead of at Silver, he would have seen them.

A wagon full of morons in sheets pulled between Russ and Isabelle.

Shocked, his legs refused to move.

On countless occasions, Isabelle had told him about nightmares she had of ghosts snagging her. He'd promised her these things were bad dreams, yet he watched her imagination become a reality as they stole Isabelle from right in front of him. He'd told Cal he wasn't afraid of men hiding under a sheet, but he suddenly was. He was afraid because he had no idea who lurked under the cloaks and the unknown terrified him.

They pulled Isabelle into the wagon, and rode off with her.

–FOUR–

Watching the veiled jerks haul off his gal was the exact moment Russ turned into a man. Until that point, being a man meant moments of him copying his brother or his pa and congratulating himself for looking like them, or for kissing Isabelle without being slapped or caught.

He ran home and fetched his horse and the gun from the barn. He filled his pockets with ammunition and headed into town, cursing himself the entire way, 'cause he'd end up dead, then what?

Twice the panic of a young boy gripped him, forcing him to slow his horse, but then the invincible feeling of a young man washed over him and he picked up the pace.

About halfway, something on the road got him off his horse.

It was Beast.

Russ dropped to his knees beside the dog.

Beast lay in a pool of blood. His throat cut.

Had they killed Isabelle's dog in front of her? What the heck was wrong with these people? And they were people, he promised himself. Cowards in sheets hiding their faces as they destroyed his life.

Russ loaded the gun with no other thoughts. He rode, pulling the trigger in his mind, over and over again, hoping he was brave enough to actually do it, then hoping to hell no one pushed him to that point.

The sudden responsibility drowned him. Some other fool would have gone in and got himself shot, ending things. But he had a simple plan: *save Isabelle and don't get dead*. If he kept this mission simple, what could go wrong?

He left his horse in a safe place between the livery barn and the school. She wandered off without him tying her up. She was smart that way—knew how to keep safe. He was the moron running into the line of fire.

With the loaded gun in front of him, Russ advanced, his finger hot on the trigger. He held it against his shoulder because the sucker packed a kick. Eau Claire was only two streets, one running north-south, and one running east-west. He came from the west and planned to turn north toward the church.

With a glance around, he saw that town folk kept low: lanterns were off, doors were shut. The schoolhouse stood by the church and from the second storey where Old Cracker Jack slept, a dim light gleamed. She probably busied herself making him homework.

The crew had gathered out front of the church. Two jerks strapped Isabelle to a wooden makeshift pole they'd planted in front of the church. Another two piled wood on the steps of the church around her. The idea of flames engulfing his love pushed him forward.

Panic gripped Russ and he roared, "What do you want?" Russ stepped closer cautiously, keeping to the shadows. They were surrounded by light and he noticed Isabelle's jaw shake when she saw him.

Russ kept one of them in the crosshairs, ready to shoot.

The guy held wood and dropped the logs to raise his hands.

Russ had expected them to offer a deal: Isabelle for Sacred Land. He'd sworn to protect his land, but he would have handed over every grain of dirt for Isabelle. Having Pa mad at him made more sense than losing Isabelle. He couldn't lose Isabelle.

The priest stormed out of the church with a shotgun. They ignored him, everyone searching for Russ in the shadows so they could get a decent shot. Russ doubted the priest posed much of a threat to these guys. Not as much as him at this point, but Russ was wrong. The priest shot before Russ could and dropped the one who'd raised his pistol. The man he shot wasn't dead though because he turned on the priest and tackled him. They vanished along the side of the church.

Gunshots erupted and someone tossed a torch toward Russ to light up the area. He stepped to the side and away from the light.

Russ shot.

He hit the guy carrying wood. The bullet found a home in this guy's right leg causing him to drop the wood and crumble. He crawled toward the side of the church where the priest had vanished.

A shot hit the torch and made a poof that Russ ignored.

A shadow moved along the other side of the church and Russ ran toward the spot ready to shoot, too late. The man hiding under a sheet was pinned to the building by an arrow. Russ only knew one guy who could make such a clean shot—Cal. He glanced over his shoulder and nodded to the dark field, sure his brother was close.

Shotgun ready, Russ marched around the corner of the church. The torchbearer let out a cry. A rock bounced off his head and he dropped. A rock square to the forehead that takes down a man meant Cousin Antoine lurked in the dark. He had a nasty arm on him and rocks were always his weapon of choice. Still, arrows and rocks against guys with guns and torches, didn't give Russ much confidence.

He held his gun, scanning the remaining men. Three stood. The priest remained out of sight and he hoped he was alive.

"Let her go," Russ ordered, as if he were the boss of things.

Someone appeared to his right: Isabelle's brother, Francis. He gave Russ a quick nod, standing so they were shoulder to shoulder. He aimed his handgun, but his stink assaulted Russ' senses. He smelled like basil and…marigolds?

The sheets who were busy with Isabelle, stopped tying her to the pole to take care of Russ and Francis.

A bullet vibrated the air around Russ. Dizzy from the strange smell emanating off Francis, Russ stumbled.

Isabelle cried out. Her scream tore through him and Russ met her eyes so she knew they'd be fine.

Grounding himself, Russ pulled the trigger and hit a sheet who tumbled into another. Their sheets caught in the flames. Russ didn't wait around to see what would happen. He dove toward Isabelle with his knife out.

Her waist was tied, so, from behind her, Russ slid his knife through the thick ropes, then she frantically scrambled out of them. Free.

Before he could scoop her up, someone tackled him. Russ

threw wild punches, managing to tear the sheet off his attacker. If he died, he should know by whose hands. His muscles burned when Russ recognized Jessie Kaplain. He refused to die by the hands of a jerkface Kaplain. Jessie's long black hair flew around like a wild mess as he hit Russ in the gut and jaw.

A bit of vomit sneaked up the back of Russ' throat. He shoved Jessie off but Jessie came back and wailed on him something harsh. Russ curled up, taking the hits, remembering what Cal had said about how a guy could take a lot of hits, but he only had to give one to make his point. Trouble was getting in that one.

Determination swelled in him as Russ breathed between the pains of each hit. Relief smashed into him so sudden; Russ had no idea when Jessie had stopped hitting.

He glanced up to see what had happened. Isabelle had dropped a burning log on Jessie. He swatted at his clothes, swearing about witches. She knelt beside Russ but he sat quick, pretending he could handle a beating that bad because he didn't want her to see him weak. She brought a hand to his chest and he squeezed it, meeting her eyes briefly to reassure her that he was fine.

The priest appeared from around the corner and swore, which ticked Russ off. He'd made Russ do six rosaries when Ma told him he had a dirty mouth, and here he cursed to Satan's delight.

No one moved to help Jessie. He slipped his suspenders down and removed his shirt as flames swarmed up his clothes. Jessie tossed the shirt aside and flames ate at the crumpled mess.

Francis hollered to his sister, "Isabelle, run to me."

Russ was sure she'd leave, but she helped him to his feet. "I'm fine. I'm with Russ."

All Francis needed to hear, because he vanished.

Only jerk left standing was Jessie. Russ winced at the scars on his body. He'd been whipped. The fire had done damage, leaving his chest red and Russ wondered how he'd survived.

The priest had his shotgun up again, pointed at Jessie. "On your knees, boy. I don't know what you're high on tonight but I promise you, you're not invincible."

Victory was brief. In rode another wagon full of sheets. This one only had three guys but bullets whipped by the priest. He ducked into the church, leaving Russ out front with Isabelle and Jessie who leaned forward, half-naked. A door slammed across the street, surprising Russ. A man left the schoolhouse. Who the heck would be hiding away in there with Miss Penelope?

The man ran to the wagon and talked to them. They handed him a gun and he vanished into the shadows by the livery barn.

"Did you see who that was?" Russ asked Isabelle. Her eyes were far better than his.

"Jessie's pa," she whispered.

Russ pulled Isabelle behind him and away from Jessie. They needed the shelter of the dark so he brought them to the side of the church.

Pa stood like a god between him and the fields. His hands were up like a shield. "Duck."

Russ tossed Isabelle to the ground and glanced up at Pa. A fool in a sheet had been behind Russ and Isabelle. His head exploded off, blowing pieces of him all over Pa and Russ. Russ used his body to shield Isabelle so she couldn't see what had happened. Not that he could explain it. He'd never seen anything that could blow a guy's head right off and stared at his pa wondering how he'd made that guy's head explode when he had no weapons.

Russ glanced at the field. Someone had to be out there with a shotgun...

Slowly, Pa wiped at the mess on his nice tie and moved along the side of the church to check on the guy with the arrow in his neck. "Get her home. Don't let her out of your sight." Pa walked past, then paused to give Russ a glance over his shoulder.

The house suddenly felt far. How many others were out in the night?

Shadows rushed past, cutting them off from town. Russ kept Isabelle behind him.

"What do you see?" she whispered against his shoulder as Russ peeked around the church.

What he saw was chaos. Warriors circled the wagon in the

dark. "Townspeople. Your brothers. Pa. Cal." The town was lit up by flames dancing in front of the church, making the scene that much more surreal.

Jessie stumbled against the side of the church. He had an arrow in his arm. Among the whip marks on his chest were deep purple bruises that made Russ think he'd taken one heck of a beating.

"Help me," Jessie pleaded, holding his arm, his missing teeth not so funny all of a sudden.

Russ had no intention of helping him and leaned against the church to wait for a moment when they could run to the wagon.

Jessie fell around the corner right into Russ' arms, struggling for air. Russ doubted he'd live and released him so he fell to the ground. Jessie groaned, rolling into the pain.

Isabelle dropped to her knees beside him. "Roussel!" she scolded. "Give me your hanky."

"What? You're gonna help this asswipe?"

She didn't repeat herself, just waited for Russ to give her the hanky, so Russ bent with her and tied the hanky around Jessie's arm to cut off the blood to the wound. He pulled out the arrow with a bit of satisfaction when Jessie screamed and passed out.

Isabelle ripped a chunk from her skirt and wrapped his arm. Kindness like this was more than he deserved but Russ watched her work with new eyes.

"Why you helping this jerk?"

"Someone beat him." She traced around the whip wounds on his chest and Russ grabbed her fingers. He didn't want her touching the jerkface more than she had to. "He's infected by a cursed spirit. Look at his eyes." She pulled Jessie's eye open wide and Russ moved in to check. Black consumed them, which was weird.

"His father hurt him. We have to help him. How would you feel if your father treated you this way?"

Russ couldn't imagine his pa lifting a finger to hit anyone. He had the best pa ever. "I doubt his pa did this. He's got a big mouth, probably deserved each swat." Russ brushed her hand to stop her, and placed the shotgun on the ground. "Isabelle, do you know why they took you?"

She glanced up and he wanted to sit in the moment forever and gaze into her kind eyes. "They want Pa's land. They said our land shouldn't belong to witch-folk."

Russ whacked Jessie. "Wake up."

Jessie stole a quick breath and pulled back, shocked to see Russ in his face.

"Do you want the Cursed Lands? Why?"

Jessie mumbled, "You're with the witch? You make me sick." Then much to Russ' shock, Jessie shoved him and snagged Isabelle's throat. Jessie flipped her to the ground. A flash of a knife caught in the dim light and instinct rushed over Russ. He knocked the blade from Jessie's hand, and brought his own knife to Jessie's throat. Without hesitation, Russ sliced his throat and shoved him off Isabelle. When he glanced down at Jessie, Russ was shocked to see Isabelle's knife jabbed in him. Russ pulled the blade out, cleaned it off, and handed it back to her. "Anyone asks, I did him in first."

Their eyes met.

She opened her mouth to say something, then didn't. Russ stared at Jessie, horrified that they'd killed a man. Not a good one, but he was alive a moment ago and now he was not.

He helped Isabelle to her feet, and wiped at the blood on her. They were a filthy mess. "You hurt?"

She shook her head.

"Let's get out of here."

Russ peeked around the church again, suddenly afraid of how quiet things were.

Cal stepped in front of him.

"Shit, Cal! You scared the dirt right off me."

"We're picking up the bodies." He glanced at the knife in Russ' blood covered hand. "Next time, roll your sleeves up or loosen the shirt. Explaining the blood to Ma gets hard. Last week, I had to tell her I wrestled with a cougar, so good-luck topping that one."

"Next time? What the hell, Cal? They attacked us and tried to burn Isabelle. What's going on?"

"She hurt?"

"She'll live."

Cal pushed past Russ. "We have something they want, and damn if I can figure out what. Silver thinks he's to blame for them being nuts, but Antoine says he's seen this before and it wasn't no cursed spirits. He believes this is drugs, the priest agrees with him. So if you figure out what they want, let me know." He hauled Jessie into his arms and tossed him on the wagon around the corner.

Cal faced them. "He was dead anyway. We left them alive last time and survivors babbling about ghosts and warriors is worse. If no one lives, we can pretend no one stopped by."

Isabelle stayed tight behind Russ. She dug her fingers into his arm.

Cal loaded the guy whose head had exploded, and finally the one pinned to the side of the church with the arrow.

Then he rode off through the field, taking the light with him.

Darkness surrounded them, and Isabelle held Russ' hand. The comfort was welcome.

"You were brave," he told her. "My sisters would have screamed bloody murder."

"I knew you'd come."

How did she know that?

"They were here before." Her voice shook with the realness of what had happened.

Light came on by the livery barn and shadows gathered out front, hauling in the wagon. "You saw these guys before? Is this what the nightmares are about?"

"They hurt Mama."

Her Ma had died months ago. Isabelle looked a lot like her. Her nose was tiny, her cheeks round, her chin delicate, but overall, her brown eyes made him forget everything except her. Especially those long eyelashes.

Her mother had a rough life, or so Ma told the story. She'd lived as a slave across the border. Monsieur Dubois and Russ' Great Aunt Sacri sneaked her into Canada. Freeing slaves was in their blood, or so Silver promised him.

"Did they touch you when they hurt your ma?"

"Yes." She let his hand go and curled up in the shadows of long grass by the church. She clutched her skirt tight against her legs as if it might blow off. "Do you hate me?"

Russ sat with her, pulling her into his arms. "Never. I did this because I love you."

"We can't say that. Papa said that those we love will be taken from us. Love is our weakness. We must never say that."

Russ frowned, but he nodded. "I won't say the words, but I'll be thinking them. I didn't feel weak. I felt strong." Besides, his pa had a love for everything and he was the strongest guy Russ knew. Maybe not physically, but dang, who else could stand in front of a guy who got his head blown off and not even flinch?

Isabelle curled up in a tight ball against him and he wiped the nightmare from her mind with gentle kisses.

Then she said something that made his heart stop. "I didn't see Jessie's pa in that wagon of bodies. What kinda trouble will he cause when he finds out Jessie ain't coming home tonight?"

Ah shit.

—FIVE—

From their spot along the side of the church, Russ watched lanterns dance in the field as the crew buried the bodies. He should have taken his good hanky back. Isabelle had hand-stitched his name on the corner and it was important to him. Dang.

"Are the stories true about your pa stealing your ma from a prick slaving her?"

"Miss Penelope said I shouldn't talk about that."

"So? Who cares what the old crow thinks?"

She pulled away from Russ, ticked. "I have to care. She said coloured folk won't finish in her school but you want me to. It's impossible to please everyone."

"What?" Russ had no idea Cracker Jack wasn't giving her the grades because she was black. "Why would she say that to you? That doesn't seem like something a teacher should say. Not at all." He frowned.

"She hates me, told me as much the day she made me stay late. The day your brother got in the fight with Jessie."

"You came out with a bruise on your cheek." Russ tightened his fist. "You told me you fell." She didn't usually lie, and he didn't like this at all.

"I did fall." Her voice expressed shock that he'd think otherwise.

"Tell me what happened, leave nothing out."

"Miss Penelope yelled at me for being such a dummy that I wouldn't pass my exams and she'd look the fool, when in stormed a man."

"Who?"

"Mister Kaplain, Jessie's pa. He has a scar on his lip." She traced a finger in a zigzag from her lip to her nose. "He explained that he couldn't be seen in town, but needed to go out there and get his loud-mouth son out of trouble. She helped him and forgot all about me. I tried to sneak past them but I slipped on a pencil and fell into the desk and hit my cheek." She held her cheek as if the memory was suddenly real.

She'd told him everything except the part about Jessie's pa.

"I wish you would have told me his pa acted all weird."

"You were too mad with Jessie, I couldn't talk to you. Miss Penelope smells like Mister Kaplain a lot. He comes to see her, you know. I spied on them a few times."

Spying.

Isabelle and Russ had read a few spy novels and the idea that they might be caught in a government conspiracy was very intriguing. Not that he knew what a government was but Pa said the best way to fight a government was to get educated and slip among them. Russ looked forward to working for this government as a spy; turning a few heads in the mud for pissing on his pa and the school he'd built. He didn't understand Pa's plan back then, but the mission sounded like a party he wanted in on.

Having done her own thinking, Isabelle added, "Miss Penelope and Mister Kaplain were sharing the sacred vision plants last time. The one I used for my coming of age ceremony."

"What?"

"I'm sure of what I saw."

"I wasn't questioning you," he reassured her. "I'm just surprised they got their hands on sacred plants." Plus, he was a little insulted that she hadn't told him about her coming of age ceremony. Ceremonies were different for girls and boys, and Bernadette was pretty dang secretive about hers, too, but he thought Isabelle told him everything.

He decided to change the subject. "So did Jessie take a drug? Is that what was wrong with his eyes?"

Isabelle remained silent, so Russ tried a different question. "Did Miss Penelope catch you spying on her? Did she hurt you?"

She stared straight ahead, her way of avoiding a lie.

Russ wouldn't stand for anyone harassing Isabelle, no

matter the reason. "It's over. I won't let her hurt you again. You have to tell me these things." He kissed Isabelle's forehead.

She shot to her feet.

"Isabelle, where did you find this sacred plant you used for your ceremony? Maybe it's all they want and has nothing to do with a curse my grandpa unleashed." Guys after drugs he could handle. Curses would be a different mission.

Isabelle said, "Or maybe Miss Penelope is a spy and told Mister Kaplain about Sacred Land and he thought sacred meant money and he wants the land for profits."

Russ swatted at a skeeter. "Money?" Money did curse some people. "Explains why Pa asked me to stay in school another year. He wants someone to keep an eye on Old Cracker Jack. I'm his little spy. Wait until I tell him all this."

"She said I was evil," Isabelle told him.

"I watched you help someone who did you nothing but harm. Evil people don't forgive or care that easily."

She grabbed his arm, sending tingles right through him. "She said I was evil because I'm too much like my ma. Do you think my ma had evil in her?"

"Nope. It's a good thing you're like her, your pa is one scary bear. And your ma was nice to me. Always gave me one more cookie than Cal."

"Are people saying my ma was evil?"

"None who I would talk to."

"Do I frighten you? Think I'll be evil? Am I a witch?" she asked.

Russ held her hand. All this talk made him nervous. What the heck kinda dirt had Cracker Jack filled her head with? "Most girls annoy me, but not you. When I was young, this girl Kit held my hand, making me feel safe. When you hold my hand, the connection we share reminds me of that feeling. I love the happy you give me inside."

"Kit? You held her hand?" Isabelle studied her own hands.

"No, she held mine. I was upset and she was brave. Like you."

"They wanted to burn me alive. That's what they do to evil witches. We read about witch hunts."

Russ hadn't thought about why they'd wanted to burn her

in particular. "They plucked you off a road, Isabelle. Could have been me or anyone else."

"They said—"

He cut her off with a rough kiss right on her lips, pouring passion and promises of safety in it. He didn't want to hear about others filling her head with negative thoughts about herself. He pulled away slowly and she touched his cheek. Russ whispered to her lips, "You're perfect. Others will have their own ideas and they can have them, as long as they don't steal you away, we'll let them be." Gloomy fear filled him.

"Isabelle?" Thomas called to her from the livery barn. "You better not be kissing the twig." He'd unhitched the horses from the second wagon and had stopped to glare at them. Isabelle ran to her brother, leaving Russ alone by the church.

Francis walked out of their uncle's hardware store. Russ debated helping her brothers dismantle the wagon, since that was clearly what they were about to do.

The curtain blew in the room over the school, catching his attention. The window had been closed earlier and now the curtain blew in the wind.

Russ slipped away unnoticed. Anger pushed him toward the schoolhouse. He marched in as if he owned the place. Desks were lined up, ready for happy children to burst in at any moment. Only the school was never a happy place.

The stove was cold and Russ didn't see any traces of food. A deathly silence resonated up the steps and he found it hard to believe Miss Penelope had slept through the chaos.

Ripping through her desk, he pushed around a few books and letters. He wasn't searching for anything in particular, but a nice big clue as to what went on would be helpful.

He opened the stove carefully and gently rested the heavy lid aside. The stove hadn't been lit in a while so he shut it up.

He raised his lantern to get a better view around the room. Dang. His hands were covered in ashes and blood. Russ wiped the soot on his shirt. He was sticky and it smeared into the fabric. Cal had a good point, blood and soot would be hard to explain to Ma.

Russ climbed the steps slowly, not sure what he'd say to his teacher if she found him in her place, but he had to make the rules clear that Isabelle was to be treated with the same respect as everyone else in that class. That wasn't asking for much.

Old Cracker Jack slept in her bed with the blankets up to her chin.

A man's belt was discarded on the floor. Left as if he'd run off and hadn't had time to dress properly. Russ peered out the window. He had a perfect view of the church steps and he doubted she would have slept through that ruckus.

Her feet peeked out from the blankets. Much to his horror, undergarments hung off them.

Mosquitos hummed around her. A metal case like Ma stored medicine in was by an empty bottle of wine from their place. He'd helped Pa fill this bottle himself.

A flat plant he'd never seen before was in the metal case. Russ sniffed the leaves and shoved the case in his pocket. Cal might know about the plant. Maybe Isabelle would.

Teachers weren't allowed to drink. Or so her contract stated. Russ knew Pa slipped her booze. Maybe he needed to talk to Pa. Was he hoping to get her fired? Well, with this evidence it'd be easy. Plus, she'd messed around with Mister Kaplain. Missus Kaplain wouldn't like that.

On top of all that, she had a strange plant in her room. Sounded like a great Sunday night for their teacher.

Russ sat beside her, waiting for her to wake up screaming at seeing him in her room, but she slept harder than Cal.

He moved in closer to her face. "Wake up!" he shouted, to scare her, but she didn't move. He watched her chest, to see if she was even alive, and when she didn't breathe, he decided she was dead to begin with.

He sat beside her not sure what to do. A morbid silence crept up on him. Russ never thought he'd miss her, yet a weird emptiness and fear settled in him. Maybe unsettled business haunted him. If she was gone, he'd missed his chance to tell her something that weighed on him. Only problem was, he didn't know what he wanted to tell her.

When Russ stood, Silver appeared in the doorway with his arms crossed. He glanced around as if Russ might have a crew with him.

"Isabelle is asking for you." Silver peeked at Cracker Jack.

"She's dead," Russ told him.

"*I see that. You do this?*" Silver shot back.

"Me? No. She was just resting here not moving… I thought I'd freak her out, but she didn't do anything."

Silver knelt. "*Yeah, too much of your father's wine will do that. He wanted her fired, not dead.*" He sniffed the bottle and pulled away shaking his head as if he were real. "*Damn it. This wine is drugged. You do this?*"

"I helped make the bottle of wine, but I didn't add nothing bad. Is her dying my fault?"

Silver sighed. "*I don't know. I thought souls only shadowed when they were killed on Cursed Land.*" He stared at something to Russ' left. Russ glanced around as if he might see her shadowing him. The curtain blew in the breeze. Still, Russ fought a chill. Was he implying that Old Cracker Jack had latched her soul onto his and would follow him around?

Dread filled him.

"*Maybe I was wrong. What do I know about dying? I couldn't even do that right.*" Silver frowned. "*You sure you didn't kill her?*"

Russ stared at her body. "I wished her dead a lot of times."

"*What were you doing in here?*" Silver demanded.

"Eric Kaplain…" Russ met Silver's eyes, uneasy. "He was here, I saw him, but he ran off before he was busted with the others. He won't be happy that I killed Jessie."

"*Hmm. You didn't kill Jessie, but this I'm not so sure about.*"

Russ glanced at Miss Penelope, a strange sadness wisped into him. "I didn't do her in, Silver. Believe what you want, I know."

Silver dismissed him so Russ ran down the steps. As he shut the front door to the schoolhouse, he could have sworn he saw Cracker Jack sitting at her desk, frowning at the mess he'd made of her things.

–Six–

The sun touched the horizon behind them as they headed to their farms. Isabelle and Russ walked his horse home, following their families down the road. Russ had never been on such a long, silent walk. He grabbed Isabelle's hand and held it for dear life.

Francis carried Beast's body and he stepped beside them. "You think he's in heaven with Mama?" he asked Russ.

Russ nodded. He wasn't an expert on heaven but Silver told him dogs had souls and all souls had an afterlife and if a guy can't trust his see-through grandpa, really whom could he trust? "I'll miss him growling at me every time I kiss you," Russ told Isabelle.

"Me, too." Yet she didn't cry.

Francis ignored the exchange, not bothered by Russ draping himself all over Isabelle. Proud to walk beside him, Russ promised himself to always be there for this guy.

Russ whispered to Isabelle "Cry if you want. I'll hold ya."

She shook her head. "Ma said we don't cry when someone brave passes on. We honour their death with no tears. Ma said there is no heaven, we come right back."

"Maybe it's both and we stop off in heaven to get ready then we come back and live a decent life. I like that. You're smart about things."

She always beamed when Russ called her smart and this time was no different. Probably because Russ didn't lie about things like people being stupid.

He didn't much worry about getting a whopping for holding her hand while they talked about afterlife and this life.

His horse waited at the gate while Russ walked Isabelle to

her front door. He was about to leave her but Pa walked up to them. He studied them long and hard. "You didn't see nothing. Not a thing. Anyone asks, they drove right through our town and set up shop down the road. Not our problem. And we have no idea why they passed us by, but others will heed the warning."

"Pa, Jessie's pa slipped away, left his belt behind at Miss..." Russ couldn't very well tell Pa he'd paid the teacher a visit. "He'll know we're lying. He won't be none too happy about us burying his son, either."

Pa rubbed his hands over his face as if his dreams shattered, but, as far as Russ knew, his dreams were to farm with Ma. The problem with a guy like Pa was that he was too smart to live a simple life. He saw things others didn't. He knew how to talk, to lead, and to dig himself in so deep he was the only one smart enough to dig himself out.

Not wanting to disappoint him more, Russ agreed to shut his mouth. If Pa wanted them to shut up about what they saw, really, that plan was good enough for him.

Isabelle's Pa joined them and Isabelle said, "I saw a bunch of things and Beast died 'cause of 'em."

Pa gave Russ a glare as if Isabelle questioning him was his fault. "No one will ask us anything, Pa, and if they do, I'll handle all the questions."

"Why wouldn't I say what happened?" Her eyelashes moved extra slow as she peeked up at Pa and damn if Russ didn't slip both her hands in his and explain things to her real sweet like, right there in front of his pa and hers, their lips so close they breathed the same air.

"Because one sneaked away, and he'll be doing enough chatting. If word gets out that I killed Jessie, I could be hauled to prison or worse: shamed."

She promised, "I won't tell a soul what I heard or saw. Tonight won't ever be discussed again."

Her pa raised his hand, and for a moment, Russ thought he might smack her so Russ pulled her behind him, ready to tackle the skinny prick to the ground. Skinny paused and his hand dropped on Russ' shoulder.

"Russ and I need to talk, Isabelle. You have chores to do before you head in," he reminded her.

Russ shifted, suddenly uneasy. What would they discuss?

"No, she's tired," Russ said, as if this was his wife and not this man's only daughter, or the woman running his farm. Talking this way was dumb on his part but he didn't feel like a little boy anymore. "I'll do her chores. She needs sleep. She's been through a lot. She can't be tired if you expect her to do your slaving."

Slaving was the wrong word choice. Given what Ma had told Russ about Monsieur Dubois' wife, that was probably the worst word Russ could have use with Skinny's hand gripping his shoulder. When Pa whacked Russ on the back of the head, it proved he was an ass for using such a forbidden word.

"Well then, you go in, Isabelle. Seems the young Monsieur Roussel and I will have a long chat about his place around here and the difference between slaving and helping out when your family is in need."

Isabelle rushed up the steps but she didn't go in the house.

His sons appeared out of nowhere, taking steps until they were even with Monsieur Dubois. Towering over Russ like unhappy gods. Thomas had blood on his sleeve, too, and some smeared into the mud on his face. He looked like a monster to Russ. Pa must have sensed his terror 'cause he stepped in behind him so Russ didn't run like the coward he was.

Russ glanced at Isabelle as she stood on the stoop, pure horror on her face. "Pa, you be good to him. He's taken a wallop for me before, and he was brave tonight. No one asked him to come after me."

Her pa's eyebrows crept up but he didn't turn away.

The only way to keep face was to meet his eyes, so Russ did. Meeting his eyes was harder than pulling the trigger had been earlier. But a guy can't say much to his girl's pa when his ears are red.

"Any jerk who comes along and takes advantage of her simple ways is on my needs-a-shit-kicking list."

Isabelle was not simple and Russ prepared to let him have it when Pa said, "Russ teaches her to read when they're alone. Stole a bunch of my good books, too. Their time together was harmless, Michel. He's helping her learn

English. My boy speaks five languages fluently and reads in a few, too. He has a gift for words, is all." Fact that Pa used his real name meant Russ was in over his head, so he kept his yap shut.

"Words? He never says squat."

Russ let him finish yelling at him. Sometimes taking your punishment was easier than fighting.

"Read? What the heck she need to read for? She's a good cook, keeps a clean house, and wards off more cursed souls than any spirit hunter I know." He squinted and sidled up to study Russ. "I don't like you alone with her. From now on her brothers tag along."

Russ studied Thomas. He had a black eye. Francis had a rag tied around his arm dripping in blood. Dread washed over Russ that he might vanish one night if he didn't say something brilliant right then and there.

"They can tag along. I'll teach them to read, too. In fact, I offered last week. Not my fault they didn't wanna come. Said they had better things to do than beat on me."

Thomas laughed, much to Russ' relief. But her pa whispered in his face. "You keep your pants on with her."

Nervous, Russ wasn't sure if that was a question or an order so he blurted out all stupid-like, "Yes sir, 'cept when we swim in the creek. I always let her slip in first so not to see anything I shouldn't. I mean, we wouldn't have gone yesterday but no one was around—and with the hot weather and all—and we had a bunch of skeeters after us since we were making out in the loft and you know how once you roll in the—"

Pa whacked him on the back of the head, which was a good cue to shut the hell up.

"My boy would never disrespect her. He's teaching her to read. Trust that and forget the other crap he doesn't know anything about. I've been watching them."

"Yeah, we both know how well you watch."

Russ clenched his fist. Not sure which one of them deserved a good punch. Monsieur Dubois called his pa lazy but Pa right out called Russ a dumbass in his fancy-pants way.

Russ relaxed when he noticed Pa rubbed his leg with his

left hand, as he'd done when he'd lied to Ma about the cougar.

Pa had no clue if Russ planned to marry her or if he'd kept his pants on, but Pa stood there and lied his ass off to his best friend to keep his son safe. Russ was impressed.

They walked off in one piece and when Russ glanced back, Isabelle waved from a window and held up three fingers. Russ nodded. He'd meet her at three this afternoon instead of seven. He'd probably be out cold by seven anyway.

It closed in on five-ish when Pa and Russ walked up to their farm with the horse in tow. The sun was already hot, and they had a full day of work ahead of them.

"So you sneak off with Dubois' daughter every night?"

Russ nodded. "Days, too."

"Didn't you see her brothers? You trying to get killed?"

Russ shrugged. "Figured some things are worth the risks. You should understand since Ma has more brothers than Isabelle does."

He nodded. "Only takes one to kill you. You keeping your pants on or should I be worried? 'Cause I won't be able to cover for you if she shows up heavy."

She was as light as a kitten. Russ carried her around all the time. "I must admit, I'm getting mighty curious what might happen if I slip 'em off."

Pa chuckled. "Well, don't be. God will punish you if you do that before you're married so you keep your hands out of her blouse. I have enough problems. I don't need Michel killing you. I respect him far too much. He taught me everything I know." He kept talking but Russ wasn't listening. He was stuck on *her blouse*.

Russ glanced at Pa. Why wasn't he allowed under her blouse? Where the heck did that rule come from?

Russ considered things. The way Pa had said it implied Russ would have to be stupid not to have gotten under her blouse, and Pa knew he wasn't stupid. So why tell him not to?

His words nestled in his thoughts until Russ decided he meant more than her blouse. Because slipping his hands under her blouse really hadn't led to much until a few days ago when she slid her hand down his pants at the same time.

Now that was dangerous territory.

Giving up his pants for life had actually entered his mind.

"So you'll respect her," Pa stopped walking and stared at him, finished with his speech and ready to hear Russ' side of things.

"She wanted to learn to read, but that didn't go well so we gave up and I read her stories instead. Mostly we sit in silence and think. She likes to share stories from her imagination that I write in my notebook." Russ wasn't so sure they sprang from her imagination anymore. Many of her stories involved ghosts and Russ saw the world with paranoid and not-so-innocent eyes. "You know the notebook you bought me for Christmas? She tells great stories. So far, we have ten of 'em."

"She doesn't say much. What's wrong with her?"

"Nothing." Russ smacked Pa on the arm, annoyed. "She's my friend, and I will marry her one day." Being with her was his only goal. "So you'd better be nice to her." Russ glared, and wasn't sure when it happened, but they stood eye to eye.

Pa chuckled as if they were two friends out for a stroll and they hadn't just witnessed a man's head blown off in front of them or that they hadn't faced off with a lunatic wanting to rip him to pieces for teaching his daughter to read while exploring under her blouse.

"Pa?"

He waited.

"Do they come by often?"

"I told you we don't talk about these attacks."

"That's fine to tell some girl you don't trust, but between us, I wanna know what's going on. 'Cause Pa, I stood in the open with her just twenty feet from me and they right out stole her in front of me. There are a whole bunch of things not right with what went down tonight. And one of them is what blew that guy's head off?"

He nodded. "They're hoping to scare us off land we grew up on."

"Why?"

His face scrunched up. "Silver believes these fools are a bunch of cursed souls that can't move on and have surfaced to leech on good people, driving them mad. Cal says they are a bunch of drugged up cowards. The Healing Ghosts from up north warned us that they might be after a rare plant that grows in our tunnels. Everyone has a different theory, even your ma has ideas."

"And you? What do you think?"

Pa sighed. "I've never seen any plant or anything really to get excited about. Because they keep targeting families like Dubois, I'm wondering if maybe these men are from a hate group settling in Saskatchewan. I know it's not good, I feel it inside me, and that panic builds up and... I haven't slept in three days," he confessed. "What do you think?"

"Me?" Russ thought about his question. It wasn't often Pa asked his advice and he wanted to come off intelligent. "You might all be right, you all might be wrong. It doesn't matter why they come, they need to stop taking my girl."

"I agree. You remember the politician who went missing about three weeks back?"

Russ nodded. He'd read about a hunting accident or something in the paper.

"His wife said he went missing while on a duck hunting trip but we had him in Dubois' barn, chilling, hoping he'd explain what they wanted. And believe me, we didn't find him out here hunting any ducks. Someone covered his misadventure up. Why? Why not say them savage buggers scalped him? I don't understand, Russ. Why are they doing this?" He winced.

Russ thought about all the reasons why they might cover up him being missing and decided the answer was probably something simple. "Maybe no one knew where he'd gone. I mean if I planned to ride around the prairies with a bedroom sheet on like some fool, I'd probably tell my wife I planned on duck hunting so she didn't think I'd gone mad."

Pa chuckled and led the horse through the gate. "Possibly. So a ring leader convinced him to have fun and they ended up caught?" He wiped his nose on his sleeve. "Guys we don't know causing trouble I can live with but that was Eric Kaplain's boy." He shook his head as he locked the gate. "He's one of us."

"Jessie was never one of us, Pa. When you talk about hate groups, he would fit right in. Those missing teeth of his, Cal did that. He had nasty ideas and believed he was better than others because of his money."

Pa shook his head. "Eric was a good guy, but you're right, ever since he bought that section of Cursed Land north of us, the entire family went nutso. Eric won't stand for us killing his boy." Pa's face was a real mess, covered in mud. The spark left his eyes. He was a man wearing a new serious face and this wasn't a side Russ ever got to see.

"So we're back to people being cursed by evil spirits," Pa said.

They stopped walking and peered out at the field. Ma had already let the horses out. She loved being outside.

While watching the horses graze the field, believing in curses was too easy.

"I find it hard sometimes," Pa confessed, "to see where the lines between my two lives begin. I stand in this blurry spot and stare at my house. A house I built with my bare hands, even though I vowed to Silver when I was your age that I would never own a house. That I would be the perfect example of a warrior. Then I study this field. A field I walk with my bare feet even though I wear shoes and swear to the banker in Moose Jaw that I'm a settler. It's important for me to be a part of both worlds, yet I don't fit into either. Both confuse me and both make a bunch of sense. I believe in this curse Silver talks about, and I believe that men would come in sheets and ruin our lives for something they want that we don't even know exists. Both make sense and both sound so stupid."

"I heard Skinny tell ya that you carry the weight of our ancestors. What did he mean?"

He looked at his hands. "Until you understand what having a shadow means, I won't burden you with my destiny. I just think sometimes that being like Cal would be easier. He knows his path and it's simple."

"Easier? You kicked Cal out. Where the heck is he gonna live? Don't you want him to farm with us?"

"Cal lives at one with the earth, now. He has accepted the path." Pa sighed. "You're actually not in control of your life. You assume you are, because you think you're making your own decisions and that you have your life all figured out, but the more you fight your destiny, the harder life gets."

"You believe that garbage?"

"I know the truth. Once I embraced the needs of those haunting me, things went better. What would you say, Russ, if I told you that Silver sees your soul and everything you have planned won't happen? That every day you spend with the Dubois girl will be a struggle? What would you say, if I told you spirits talk to me and promise me that you will have a great life with someone else?"

Russ frowned. "I don't have much for plans, Pa. I want to go to college, marry Isabelle, and have us a bunch of children. Boys I can teach to farm. Tell me that's not my destiny all you want, I'll prove you wrong."

"I understand what you're feeling, Russ. Pay attention because when I met your mother, all my plans crashed around me. I drowned in a life I could no longer endure. She told me to give her a couple years so her father could find a housekeeper, but I had no idea how I'd even survived for so long without her. Her voice of reason is all I need sometimes to ground myself."

Russ supposed if he heard spirits demand things from him, having Ma there to smack him on the back of the head would help regain focus.

"It's like there was my first life, a life where I was me, then my second life where I was really me. She helped me understand my destiny and how these spirits want me to teach them something. They know how to be warriors in the past, but they don't know how to be them today."

Russ liked the idea of teaching spirits things. "You have the perfect life here."

"Back then, I had nothing. Imagine asking a woman to marry you and having nothing to offer her. Thankfully, my mother understood. She trusted what Silver saw in my soul, even if I'd been determined to prove to him that I could live at one with the land. She knew I would eventually find my way and start a family. She'd kept me cash. She'd bought me land." He smirked. "She was probably the smartest woman I've ever met. And you know what? She couldn't talk. Her arsehole father had smashed in her vocal cords when she was young." He looked right proud of his ma, and that rubbed off on Russ. They came from a family of stubborn and strong souls. "Gosh, your ma fell in love with her. She said that my mother spoke with her soul and eyes. It was the most beautiful voice she'd ever heard. Took me two weeks to get my destiny moving back toward the right pasture and Silver never once said, 'Told you so'. Things got easier for me after that."

"Things were not easy tonight."

Pa stared at Russ. "That's not my fault. Tonight, when you walked into town pointing that gun, I knew the look on your face. You're fighting against your destiny, Russ, and you're sucking us all in."

"So now you're blaming me for those idiots showing up?"

Pa shook his head. "Your fate has been decided and not a fool alive controls that." He winced.

"Sorry, Pa." Russ hated to disappoint him. "But I'd do that hell all over again for her." He tightened his jaw. "I'm not taking the blame for things Jessie Kaplain did."

Pa took a deep breath. "Sucks to see my boy making such hard choices. I suddenly understand why I upset Silver so many times. Can you…maybe let Isabelle go?"

"Go where?"

He winced. "Never mind. Just…when things get bad, remember that I'm here for you and I understand, probably more than you think. Let's get cleaned up. Be sure to tell Sammy that Cal will be by for supper."

"So you forgive Cal?" The relief lightened the pressure around him.

"I was insulted by the lying. I don't want him hiding anymore. I want the truth. Plus, he owned up to things like a man. It's not up to me to forgive anything, he's on his own path now, and fate will lead him where he needs to go."

Pa talked as if Russ knew what caused the tiff between him and Cal, so he pretended he did, but he'd said a bunch of things that had him confused. Where was he supposed to let Isabelle go? What was his destiny? Why could Pa hear spirits? And what the heck had Cal done?

Maybe Isabelle knew the answers.

"You're growing up fast," Pa said.

"You too," Russ said solemnly, which didn't make any

sense yet Pa nodded, so maybe the statement did mean something to him.

"It's time to buy you land to work."

Russ prepared to ask if buying land had to do with his destiny when Cracker Jack appeared behind Pa, all freaky and see-through and not at all who he wanted to see right now.

–Seven–

Ma had breakfast ready but Russ couldn't eat. Cracker Jack had followed him around all morning. She hadn't said a word. No one else acknowledged her so Russ hoped she'd vanish and move on or something.

But she didn't move on and Pa's comments about a shadow were making him nervous.

Pa rested his gun by the huge wanted poster of Louis Riel they kept in the front room, and she stood to watch him clean up for a spell, leaning against the poster.

The poster was Pa's pride. He'd often tell stories about Louis Riel as if he knew the bugger himself. Russ usually ran to the poster if Pa planned to smack him, 'cause Pa always calmed when the big ass picture of Louis Riel eyed him up, promising him a better life. He was Pa's hero, and Russ understood heroes since Pa was his. The poster grew to be family and the fact that Pa settled his gun by it, meant something only he understood, but this truth was something important just the same.

Pa washed the mud off his face and from under his nails. He placed the tie Ma had scrubbed clean on the rack for next Sunday. Hard to believe the thing was covered in brains earlier that night.

By this time, Russ had rinsed off the shovel. He'd shaken out his pants that reeked like smoke, which he'd slipped on quickly so Cracker Jack wouldn't see anything.

Cal was missing, but no one asked why.

Russ got ready for school like every Monday but when he swung by Isabelle's, she said she wasn't up for school, so he led his family down the road, not sure how far they'd make it before they were sent home. Turns out, they went all the way, which was a waste of time, but necessary just the same.

At school, Antoine met them, "Go home. The teacher ain't feeling well."

Russ glanced at Miss Penelope who had followed him. She crossed her arms. She looked fine to him. Sure she was see-through, but he couldn't very well say that.

"I'll teach 'em," Russ offered. "We walked all this way. Why not?"

Antoine smirked, amused, but he agreed. Much to Russ' relief, Miss Penelope vanished up to her room.

The parents kicking around didn't see any harm in Russ teaching for the day so he taught the lessons she'd left on the desk and invented a few. Russ promised everyone that if they worked hard they'd head home early before the day was too hot.

He led his crew home before lunch and they were excited, sharing stories. Maybe his sisters weren't so bad.

Much to his shock, at home, his chores were done. Pa met him at the chicken coop. "Why you not in school?"

"Teacher was sick so I taught the lessons and they're so smart I let them out early." Russ glanced around in case Cracker Jack had followed him home, but they were alone.

Pa smirked. "What's wrong with the lush now?"

"We weren't told." Which was true enough.

"If you guessed?"

"She drank too much of the sleepy-wine you slipped her and told Kaplain she'd go to his wife about them messing around. He tucked her in real nice-like and held a pillow over her face. Then some fool-boy showed up and she was a lost soul freaking out so she latched onto him because she's stupid that way." That was the best explanation Russ had for the entire affair.

Pa's eyes wandered up and down Russ but the rest of him didn't move. Then he checked the area as if he might see her. "So I need to find a new teacher?"

"School is almost done. I'll teach the rest of the year. I love teaching."

Pa's jaw tightened and he bit his tongue as he stormed off.

Antoine arrived later that day. He was on the schoolboard with Pa and he spit dirt he was so ticked. Russ stayed along the barn to listen to what he told Pa. "Miss Penelope was found upstairs, dead. Doc says she died peacefully in her sleep from drinking too much, but you and I don't believe those lies, do we?"

"I didn't tell her to drink the wine," Pa said.

"Yeah, but if you poisoned the bottle, she'll shadow you. Don't you have enough shadows?"

"So be it."

"This isn't a joke, Bernoit. Did you go through with your stupid plan? If you won't tell me what happened, I'll bring Hoolie over to give me a detailed report of what he sees in your soul."

Like Silver, Hoolie had the gift of Sight and could see souls and spirits all the time, which Russ thought sounded like a curse. Russ found it annoying enough seeing spirits haunting the land, he couldn't imagine seeing everyone's. Hoolie was pretty awesome about his gift, though. He taught Russ how to speak Chinese for a bunch of reasons. He'd told Pa that Russ had a gift for languages and wanted to make sure he was ready when he met the gal he'd linked to. Russ understood the importance in learning the language even if he didn't understand what being linked to a gal meant. And frankly, he was too afraid to ask. Hoolie was a damn good teacher and Russ respected everything he taught him.

"It's not my soul that's the problem. Seems I have a son who can't kill a cougar but…well… I'll handle him."

Nervous, Russ checked over his shoulder in case Cracker Jack hovered behind him. He felt a chill. What if she stuck to his soul and everyone thought he killed her? Would she make him nuts like Jessie had been? The idea freaked him out and Russ ran to the haystack.

Silver appeared while Russ leaned against the stack. He watched Russ with a serious face.

"I don't want Pa thinking I killed her," Russ told him.

"Sleep. I'm not sure what's going on, but he'll believe me when I explain what I see. You're safe."

His words rested on Russ like a warm blanket and he fell asleep in the straw enveloped in peace.

When he woke, later that afternoon, Isabelle had snuggled in tight, her leg wound around his. His hand gripped her ass as if she were a lifeline and he drowned. Keeping his pants on was suddenly impossible. 'Cause yeah, they seared against his skin. He needed out of them and fast.

Without a word, Isabelle helped. When she slipped her clothes off, too, about as fast as he had, Russ suspected she'd been waiting forever for him to come up with this idea.

Russ sat there speechless.

Getting out of his pants was so important that it never dawned on him she'd go naked, too.

So there they were as naked as newborns snuggled in an itchy haystack. Dang. He was a dead man if one of her brothers wandered over, but in moments like this, the risk made breaking the rules better. Russ ran his hands over her slender body all nice-like, her tight against him, thanking God for not lighting him on fire.

He didn't do much exploring of her body. They were naked together for about two minutes, which was hardly enough time for him to sort through the emotions swirling in him. Breathing was impossible at points.

Holding her was about all he could stand 'cause every time her skin touched him, things happened in him that reminded him of Pa's cave-in expression. He was about to cave into something and the punishment would be big. Anything this exciting, that no one talked about was forbidden, sure as mud in the spring. Yet touching her skin with his made every part of him come alive.

Holding her for those two minutes or so made the rest of the night and day feel like a fog. A nightmare that must have not happened.

"Was any of that real?" Russ asked, his head against hers.

"I didn't see anything. I usually come and smooch with you. Not naked though. This is a first and I like being naked with you."

"Gosh, I love it. Best idea we ever had."

She pulled away and her long hair fell lazily against her chest. He gazed at the tips of her strands and marvelled at how they rubbed her breasts. Wow. Tickling her like her hair did tempted him something fierce. He brushed her hair aside so he could see her. "You're beautiful. Makes me hope that maybe you'd let me explore you inch by inch. Being naked with you is exciting yet terrifying. I feel so innocent all of a sudden." She made him feel foolish and happy.

She nodded but before she said what was on her mind, a shadow loomed over them. He was tall and bulky. Thomas?

Russ didn't dare look. He glanced around for something to cover her up with but his heart stopped when a hand hauled him up.

-EIGHT-

Much to Russ' relief, Thomas wasn't hovering over them. Cal yanked Russ to his feet. Russ snagged Isabelle's dress and tossed it to cover her up. Her knickers flew up and off in the wind. What the heck kinda wind was *that*?

Cal said, "There's a bloody tornado headed our way." Cal always dished out the worst news possible at the worst moments ever. Still, Russ was glad Cal found them and not Thomas 'cause even though she was worth getting a beating for, he didn't want one if he could avoid it.

Isabelle pointed out the dark clouds before Cal's words even made sense in Russ' terrified brain. For a moment, Russ was just happy to be alive. When he peered over the haystack, nasty black clouds rolled toward them on a mission.

"Dang it all." They would never make the half mile to the storm shelter. He slipped on his pants, and grabbed her hand. She wore her dress half-assed but was covered. The wind stopped. Russ didn't want to glance up. Hail would be next and where would they hide in the field with only a haystack for cover?

He squinted at the farm. Sammy paced by the chicken coop. Pa gathered the horses in the barn. When a storm rolled in, they were each responsible for those younger. Pa took care of the horses. But Samuel hovered in the open, the girls were in the house, and Russ would die in a field, half-naked.

"Come on," Cal said as a chunk of hail fell between Isabelle and Russ. Not a pellet, but a chunk of ice the size of his fist. It splattered on the ground and left a large ball of ice behind. Dying from hail didn't sound like a good idea so he followed Cal to the back of the haystack in case he had a brilliant plan.

This was what Pa meant about God punishing him for taking off his pants. Russ couldn't imagine the smack he'd get for causing a tornado or angering God.

Cal wasn't wearing a shirt either so Russ didn't feel naked now that his pants were on. He pulled his shoulders back, bravely. "Straw ain't gonna save us in a bloody tornado!" A twister headed right for the farmhouse. Samuel was too far and the hail pounded around him. He'd be stuck in the chicken coop.

Ma led the girls to the storm cellar. They held pots over their heads like helmets and if he wouldn't have felt responsible for this mess, Russ might have laughed at how stupid they looked.

"Samuel," Russ screamed, sure the boy would never hear him, but fear heightened his senses and Samuel glanced at him.

"Roll into the bushes," Cal screamed to him, rolling his hands, then pointing to the bushes. Another chunk of ice fell inches from them.

"What the heck is wrong with you?" Russ yelled at Cal, but hell, Samuel rolled into the bushes and vanished. Cal dropped to the ground, too. He rolled toward the haystack and disappeared under the straw. Russ got down with Isabelle and once on the ground something surprised him. A plank sheltered a hole. He should have guessed the haystack covered something. Over the years the stack never moved, just got fresh straw. At first, he thought Pa kept the stack nice for him, so he had a place to hide out when he needed a quiet place to think, but now he understood the purpose behind this straw. It covered the entrance to an underground room. With no time to question the madness, Russ was happy someone— probably Pa—thought to do something this genius.

They rolled into the entrance like Cal and landed in a tiny square room. Cal lit a lantern and Desire hung out in the dark like a weirdo bat woman. She wasn't wearing much, which made him wonder if maybe Cal was down here with his pants off when he peeked out and realized he had to save his brothers.

Desire turned on a lantern she held to get a good look at them.

"Samuel was at the coop. We have to get to him." Cal ran. The others followed like fools, no clue where they headed in the underground cave. Or were these tunnels?

Russ glanced at Isabelle to make sure she was fine. Her arm bled a bit so he stopped to help her. He searched his pocket for his hanky forgetting they'd buried it with Jessie. So he stopped running and used her skirt to clean the blood. Russ wiped her arm tenderly when Cal returned with the lantern and held the light between them.

"Keep moving, lover boy, or you'll get lost."

Cal travelled these strange earthy tunnels as if he lived in them. Heck, maybe he did.

They found Samuel in a ball sobbing which made Russ feel even worse.

Pa had told them to talk to Sammy like an equal, 'cause one day, he'd be a man. Russ had never seen Cal do anything other than that, until that moment. He fell to his knees and pulled Samuel into his arms. "You're safe, little one. You're safe. I'll take you to Mama. Bernoit has you. You're safe."

"Papa was in the barn." Samuel sobbed.

"Pa has a hole to hide in. He's fine. We're safe."

Now, hearing him say those words was the comfort Russ needed. He could have been lying, he probably was because Russ did plenty of exploring in their barn and never came across a hole, but he relaxed and pulled Isabelle against his naked chest and breathed with her, 'cause until Cal told Samuel they were safe, he hadn't thought they would be.

"Cal, you'll make an excellent pa." Her words made the truth click in with Russ. She was smart about things like that.

"Holy shit, man. You're gonna be a pa?" Russ asked in disbelief.

"Watch your language in front of my wife, moron." Cal glared. Desire walked off with the lantern, leaving them in the dark.

"Your wife? What the heck, Cal? I mean what in all this dirt is going on with you?"

"You get lessons on how to talk from Pa? Get over it. I got married, this is what guys do."

"Yeah, but why didn't you invite me?" Russ felt cheated and didn't know why.

Russ expected Cal to tell him to grow up but he mumbled a sorry instead and Russ doubted he'd ever apologized to him before so he let the issue go.

They followed Cal down the tunnels. Well, tunnels were being generous. They were natural fissures in the earth. Like the cave along the edge over the creek where the cougar lived, only some walls looked like someone had chipped away to make room for big guys like Cal. By the looks of things, there were a dozen ways in, very few ways out. Every time they passed such an entrance or exit, the airflow changed making things...*draughty?* Russ paused. Along the wall, a glowing plant grew. He knelt beside the plant. "It glows."

"It's a weed." Cal shoved him and ordered him to keep moving.

"You sure? What kinda weed grows underground? Desire, you live here, you know what this is?" Russ asked Desire.

She didn't give him a straight answer, but Russ listened closely, used to how Silver skirted around the truth. She told a tale about how the passages formed so they could travel in the snow and survive the hard winters and the wild storms of the prairies. She told them about how her tribe had lost their tunnels and moved here, about how they had all this room for many more tribes to join them. She talked about how she liked the feel of Sacred Land and how the ceremonial chambers out by Antoine's were full of family, but Russ got the impression they weren't living and breathing family but spirits like Silver. She was excited about talking to them, but really, Russ talked to Silver all the time, and he could be right out boring and annoying.

Desire was a talker and Russ was sorry he'd asked her anything.

Cal cut her off when he stopped abruptly. "Sammy, I'll put you down. I want you to crawl through the passageway at my feet. Mama is on the other side of this wall. Russ will go first 'cause he's brave, right Russ?"

Russ grumbled but they did as Cal instructed. He joined them last. Ma and the girls sat on the bunk they crawled out from underneath. The girls were traumatized by the entire affair but Ma was calm as usual, expecting the worst.

Ma studied them in the dim lantern light and never once asked where they came from. "Thank heavens you made it. Where is your shirt, Roussel?"

"Storm blew it away," he told her.

"Took my knickers, too," Isabelle said in her innocent way. "And them were my only pair."

Russ laughed 'cause the look on Ma's face was worth giving up land for and he was sure he'd be smacked. Considering they were in a storm and Ma never displayed interest in anything Cal or Russ did, her sudden attention to these gals of theirs was weird. But that was Ma. Russ never knew what she'd do or say. The next words out of her mouth were as shocking to him as everything else she'd ever said. "Every Wednesday when my young men visit Father to learn Latin, you young women will sew with me." Used to running things her way, Ma didn't make requests people could refuse. She waited until everyone nodded.

Ma stared so hard at Isabelle, Russ thought she might blame her for the tornado and despite his better judgement, he confessed everything as quickly as possible. "I knew better, Ma, but taking my pants off was a righto plan in the moment. God sent a tornado to set me straight and nothing happened. I knew the risks, and will be sure to do like Cal and hide underground next time."

Ma didn't flinch or even glance his way. She stepped away from Isabelle who smirked so innocently and started her staring contest with Desire. Russ relaxed because that was Cal's problem.

His sisters talked quietly with Isabelle.

Ma wasn't so quiet. "You must be Desire." She touched Desire on the arm and ran a hand along her naked belly, the spot between her top and skirt.

In the storm cellar with them crowded together, while God sent a tornado to tear through their farm because Russ thought with his pants off instead of on, Ma smiled. Her meeting a gal Cal married without telling them made her smile. Confused him, that woman.

"Bernoit glows because of you." Ma was happy from the inside out. "You know, Desire, I used to fear my boys would be dead before they gave me grandchildren, but here you are, so beautiful and full of life. It's a miracle." She wrapped her in her arms as if she was one of her children and Russ expected Desire to pull away or panic but she hugged her back and the ground under his feet warmed. Something inside him relaxed as if everything might be fine.

Maybe a tornado bringing them together was a good thing. Somehow, Russ doubted Pa would see the disaster this way.

Ma never asked where they lived or nothing. She was just happy for the first time ever. Damn, she was weird.

The girls gathered around Cal with their questions so Russ pulled out from the clump of people and Isabelle followed him to the corner. They curled up to wait out the storm. No one was supposed to open the cellar door except Pa. So they waited.

Isabelle and Russ held each other, worried about how bad things were overhead. Finally, he asked, "You gonna learn to sew from my ma?"

"I have nothing that fits."

"You're always dressed nice."

"I'm wearing Ma's old things and they're too big around the chest and too tight around the hips."

She always dressed the same to him. Only now, she sat beside him with no knickers and wouldn't have any until Wednesday. Weird but the thought teased his brain and became the only one worthy of any consideration.

When Pa flung open the cellar door, Russ was sleeping. Cal woke Russ long after the others left.

He'd sent Isabelle home to help her family and pushed Russ up against the cold wall made of earth. Russ' back was naked and rocks poked into him.

"Now you listen to me, and you listen closely."

Russ nodded. Cal's hand tightened around his throat. His feet couldn't touch the ground, as Russ dangled, at his brother's mercy. "If you mess around with her, she'll get pregnant." He pushed into him and explained how things worked, with him planting a seed and all, and how his pecker belonged in his pants and not in her. Which was blunt, but Russ listened regardless. He understood the basics anyway since Ma taught him how to breed the horses.

"It isn't God punishing you. He's saving your ass. You

understand what could have happened?"

Russ nodded, the best he could pinned like that.

"You ready to be a father at sixteen?"

He was almost seventeen and was about to point that out but Cal used a fist on his pecker making Russ cry out instead. Really, next time he prayed for Pa to smack him instead. "I didn't invite you to my wedding because the marriage was imaginary. Something I pretend happened 'cause Pa was being an ass about this and Desire doesn't care about his stupid ceremonies. She chooses me, and that's all that matters." Cal got right in his face. "You have a choice. Wait until you're married. I don't want to ever have this conversation with you again."

He let him go and Russ fell to the cellar floor like a dishrag.

"Shit, Cal. I mean damn, ever hear of talking to me?"

"Be a boy for a few more breaths and let me worry about being the man around here."

"So the tornado wasn't my fault?"

"Oh this mess was your fault all right. Come see how much God wants you to keep that pecker in your pants."

Cal left him in the cellar, on the cold floor. Something he said didn't make sense. Had he messed around with Desire and oops, he had to marry her? Even Cal was a mystery. Guess Russ' days of living with his head in a book were done.

Russ climbed out of the cellar more afraid to be alive than dead, 'cause he couldn't see himself hanging with Isabelle and not taking his pants off. Yet he was not ready to be a pa, worse, clean up after a tornado every day. Not even close. When he saw the fear in Cal's eyes a moment ago, he wasn't so sure his tough brother was ready to be a pa either.

The mess the storm left was monstrous. Half the barn had blown into the chicken coop. When Russ saw the damage, he actually picked Samuel up and held him. He should be dead. Fact that Russ held him was a miracle and he thanked Cal a dozen times for saving him. He repeated what Isabelle had said about him making a great father. Cal grinned once when he'd said the words, and he might have believed Russ.

The house stood, which was a good thing. The outhouse at

Dubois' was gone. They never found any of the walls, and a tree leaned against their house, roots and all, but the house was fine. Russ asked Monsieur Dubois who he blamed for the tornado.

"We should count ourselves lucky to be alive, ain't no one to blame, these things happen." If he wanted to believe that, Russ planned to let him.

Dubois decided clean-up would be easier and faster if they helped each other, so that's what they did. Took them a week to get their lives back and in the meanwhile, Russ caught Pa sneaking out in the dead of the night twice.

Russ headed to Isabelle's to make sure she was safe on those nights, and he kept his pants on so as not to anger God or Cal. He wasn't sure which one scared him more sometimes. A tornado they could hide from, but if Cal was ever after him, he wasn't so sure he'd be able to vanish.

PART TWO

LATER THAT WEEK

"Destiny has a way of setting you straight. Doesn't mean you'll listen."
—Silver

–Nine–

Come Wednesday, Isabelle was thrilled to spend the evening sewing with Russ' ma. It never occurred to Russ that she missed her ma until she bounced toward his house without a second glance his way. Cal stood with Russ, watching Desire join them. She glanced at Cal as if he might save her from this hell.

"I see you have her knife," Russ said with a smirk.

"She's nervous as heck, but I told her to bring things she's working on, you know, in case they impress Ma and gives them something to talk about. Think they'll have fun?" he asked, worried enough for the both of them.

Russ was about to say, "Sure" but Cracker Jack waited by the house for Isabelle. She followed her in, flashing him the bird as the door shut behind her. Shit. Russ didn't know what to do. Why was she following Isabelle? "Maybe we should go with them," he offered.

"Yeah, you wanna explain us learning to sew to Ma?"

Russ frowned, torn, but he was more afraid of Ma than a ghost.

Frustrated, Russ blurted out what bothered him all week. "Where the hell are you living?"

Cal let out a long puff of air. "Everywhere. Nowhere. We sneak in and sleep in your bed sometimes, since you're never home, and it used to be mine. She has a room underground by the creek."

"Don't you want a house?"

He shrugged. "It's complicated. I'm between two worlds and she don't believe in owning land. These things take time. I'll get there." Cal always got what he wanted.

"Oh yeah, Pa said you owe the land. What does that mean?"

Cal looked like Silver when he sighed as if the world was on his shoulders and he had no idea how he'd survive the weight of his new responsibility. Russ decided Cal's destiny of freedom was actually a burden he might need help with.

Cal gave him a gift. He gave Russ the freedom to be a young foolish boy for a few more breaths. So Russ included Cal in his dreams because that's what brothers did. "Well, I'll build a house with an extra part on the back for you to live in when you decide your choices are too complicated. I'll make enough room for you and your family. You won't have to sneak in 'cause my place will be yours. I'll do that. I will 'cause you scared my pecker back in my pants, but mostly, I'm gonna do this 'cause you saved Samuel and you'll be a great pa and need a place to raise that brat of yours."

"My warning didn't come too late, did it?"

"Nope, I was close though to doing what you said and I dreamed about doing those things with her last night. I woke up shocked by what the idea did to me."

They raced to town for their Latin lessons, being boys for one night with no acting like grownups.

The next few days, Russ took his mind off things by searching around for a dog for Isabelle. A few in the area needed a home, but none were as loyal as Beast, so he was left with a dreadful feeling that her birthday would come and go and he still wouldn't have the perfect dog for her.

–Ten–

Further north—

Kit studied Julien. For a grown man, he suddenly looked the part of a boy being forced to apologize for something he was not at all sorry for.

"Why this desire to marry me so suddenly?" Kit demanded. "Our friendship is strong. You're my teacher. You challenge me, but there is no fire between us, and I see no desire in your stance. I know where your heart lies."

He glanced away from her, his face glowing as red as it had two nights ago when she'd caught him kissing another. He tightened his jaw. His short hair and clothes reminded her of how the men dressed in Moose Jaw, but she knew he was a warrior. He was strong and determined. Perhaps too arrogant at times, but he could afford to be. He had a reputation as the best healer among her people. He'd taught her many things but this question of marriage hung between them, making an awkward silence.

He held her hands as if her question was very important. "I need a wife."

Kit pulled her hands away from him. "Why me? Many women wait for ya to share their mats. Go bother them."

"I need a wife to lead with me, not a mate. You are the only choice, Kit. I won't be settling down with children, and this is what other women will want. You are different. You don't question my knowledge. Your faith in me has made me the leader this tribe needed. You are a warrior like me and others will respect that. You travel to Sacred Land. If I brought you with me, you could help me bring the last of the tribes together. This is my destiny. This is all I see."

"I only visit there because they have a Healing Chamber," Kit snipped. "I have a friend there, Francis. He teaches me different ways to heal. He protects this." She showed him the sacred plant she'd brought with her. The leaves were dried and withered in her hand.

Julien raised an eyebrow, suddenly intrigued as he took the plant from her and studied the leaves. "This is good. I could bring you there and offer you in marriage in hopes that this will unite our tribes." He looked excited.

"That would still leave you without a wife." She shook her head. "Julien, I wish to marry someone who captures my heart and soul. He should love me and want to grow with me. I care for Francis as I do for you. He is my teacher and friend. But I had a vision I cannot deny."

"I must take a wife who can lead with me."

"Sit and explain why this sudden need for a wife has ya so crazy you'd even marry me." She sat on her mat. Julien had given her the buffalo hide many years ago. Everything she owned, Julien had given her. He was an incredibly kind leader.

He sat beside her, bringing a comfort. Family was important to her and she rested her head on his shoulder, needing a friend, a brother, a leader.

"I don't ask to share your mat. I need you as my wife." He sighed. "This should be an honour to you. I don't understand why you turn me away."

She couldn't believe he made such an impossible offer. "We are hiding things from each other, Julien. How can either of us understand what is in our hearts. Perhaps if I share a secret, you will share yours."

"My heart is of no importance."

He laced his fingers through hers and rested his head against hers. Sadness washed over Kit.

"What I am about to tell ya, used to fill me with hope, but this destiny I see terrifies me, because I can't make this choice real."

"I understand the feeling." He gently caressed her hands.

"My mother had a vision when I was born. Perhaps the pain of childbirth drove her mad, but she liked to believe magic was in the air that night. She said that in the light while she pushed me into the world, she saw the symbols for great warrior swirl at her through a tunnel. And a gentle hand caught them and cradled them, resting them by a single flower. A sacred plant."

"These are powerful images that complement my vision and my need to marry you."

"Let me finish. Because I too had a vision during my coming of womanhood trials. In this vision, brothers pulled out the flower, roots and all. The symbols for warrior that were resting by the flower tumbled into the hole. The younger of the two gathered the plant in his hands and knelt before me, offering me this symbol of life. I plan to marry this warrior. If he is brave enough to get on one knee and offer me life from roots to blooms."

Julien held her chin in his rough hands and peered deep in her eyes. "If this is your destiny, even marrying me won't keep you from the path. Do what is right for your people in this moment."

Silver had told her the same thing.

Julien spoke low. "Last night, I visited our Healing Chamber and a vision came to me as they do there. In this one, I am to marry you. This will bring us closer to Montague's tribe and the Healing Ghosts will be at one with the Ghosts of the Earth. Do not deny me my vision. Our tribe is weak. We are healers and need the protection of the warriors from the south."

Kit understood that there used to be seven Ghosts tribes but only two remained; the Ghosts of the Earth led by Montague and the Healing Ghosts led by Julien. Any warriors from those tribes could earn the right to be *Cîpay* if they connected their soul to Sacred Land for eternity, giving of themselves to bring the world life.

"But my vision—"

Julien cut her off. "Such sight is not images of marriage, merely a gift of life. This vision might mean that in your lifetime you will see leaders crumble but Sacred Land will flourish. You can't deny me something so important based on a vision that could mean many things."

She trusted his wisdom when it came to reading visions but she was troubled, because in her heart she knew it meant more. She'd felt love when she'd looked down at the young man presenting her the flower. She'd felt safe. Hope.

Only one made her feel that way and Silver promised her the link between their souls held firm.

"The legends from the Ghosts of the Earth speak of brothers. They say they will be family to Silver. I spoke to Silver—"

Julien grabbed her arm. "You speak to *Cîpay*?"

She nodded.

"This confirms my plan even more. As my wife, you will bring our people to greatness. They need a leader like you. You heal, you fight, you see spirits. *I* need a leader like you. Perhaps this is what your vision speaks of. This boy, he gives you a flower because he trusts you to lead him now that the great warriors have crumbled into the earth."

This was not how the vision made her feel. What she felt mattered. It frustrated her that Julien wasn't listening to her. Still, if Julien insisted they marry, she would have to make a choice: marry him or leave.

"I cannot answer without first speaking to..." She didn't want to give him Russ' name for fear he'd go to him before her. "I hope ya understand."

"It is fine. I care not about your visits or those sharing your mat."

"You should care if you're serious about marrying me."

His jaw tightened. "I only wish to marry a warrior of your skill. I promise you a title. I promise my people a leader." He was his cold self again and she hated it when he closed up around her.

"Julien."

He left.

She loved him like family, but Kit stayed on her mat, to think about his offer. Julien always confused her.

–ELEVEN–

It took Kit a couple days to travel to Eau Claire. She loved the area. The skies were so unlike her world further north. Things here were closer to the earth. They didn't use the tunnels much, anymore, but they didn't have to. The people had a way about them that suggested they were one with the earth no matter what.

She'd said her good-byes to Francis after visiting their Healing Chamber and walked through his yard when his sister came out to meet her. She had a big grin. "You again. Francis fancies you, ya know."

"Isabelle, right?"

The girl nodded. She had a fun energy to her. Kit liked her right off. "I'm Kit."

"I know who you are. Francis goes on about you after you leave for days. Come in for supper. He'd love that."

"I can't." Kit glanced toward Russ' farm. "I'm not here for your brother. He's a good friend and teacher." Kit sat on the steps, needing to talk to a woman. Men were only adding to her problems. "I had a leader ask me to marry him."

"Did you tell Francis that? Did you agree?"

"Francis freaked and asked me himself. Your brother is a much better match for me and we get along great."

"Good then, you'll marry him." Her face lit up.

"We'd probably be happy, but the other chose me because he wants me to lead our people with him."

"Oh. That would be hard to refuse, but Francis is a good boy. This is a difficult choice."

Kit nodded. She was right. "Trouble is I don't see myself marrying either. The one I see as my forever, he doesn't even know me, yet. I saw him in a vision."

Isabelle listened closely. "You'd give up two good, real warriors, for one who might not even want you? One you might not like once you met him properly? One who could be a total bust?"

"Put it like that and I sound crazy. But ya have to understand, Isabelle, something connects us. Every time I go in your Healing Chamber, I get the same vision. His eyes…gosh. I can't marry anyone else until I at least tell him."

"You never met him? Not once?" Isabelle's eyes were huge.

"I met him years ago. He probably doesn't remember but I held his hand. We shared a connection, even back then." Kit studied her hand. "I've never felt that with anyone else. Almost a spark drawing us together. I can't imagine how strong our connection would be now. But you're right, I need a good reason before I say no. I should talk to him, tell him everything. Just let destiny take its course."

"Maybe get to know him. I plan to marry my best friend. I wouldn't marry someone I didn't learn every little secret about. I don't care what my vision said, I know who'll make the bestest husband ever." Her shoulders went up high and sunk with her content sigh. Kit almost envied her. If only things could be that easy.

"I suppose, if I remove him from the equation, I would pick Francis, there's something magical about him. But how do I remove my destiny from the choices?"

"It's like saying my dead mama came to me in a dream and told me not to marry my best friend. Do I trust my dead mama in a dream or do I trust my awake alive thoughts and brain?"

"Did your mama come to you in a dream?"

Isabelle stared off, not answering.

Kit would place faith in that dream. It didn't come out of nowhere. Yet she didn't say that because clearly Isabelle didn't want to hear that this boy she fancied wasn't the one. "Imagine if you knew your best friend was your one forever, yet everyone else told you this path would never happen, even your dead mama in a dream. What would ya do?"

Isabelle sat taller and something flashed in her eyes that

intrigued Kit. Maybe she understood. "I would make him cookies," she whispered as if that was pure evil.

Kit smirked at the joke. She liked Isabelle. "I have no desire to lead, but Julien chooses me. Whatever his reasons may be, I trust them."

"So a sense of duty would make you marry him?"

Kit nodded again.

"Now pretend that sense of duty wasn't there and you could choose between someone as wonderful and happy as Francis and do something as important as guarding Cursed Lands with him or this guy you hardly know haunting your visions."

Kit closed her eyes. She imagined holding Francis, so warm and full of love. Then she imagined Russ looking up at her on one knee with life in his hands… "There is no choice to make, the feeling I get is that my destiny is fulfilled. My purpose is greater than leading or protecting. He needs me and I need him."

Isabelle smirked. "Sounds romantic. If you want, I could burn leaves for you, to see if he's really your destiny."

Kit kept her face emotionless, but any rituals she wasn't aware of got her excited. "How does this work?"

Isabelle shrugged. She stood and Kit followed her behind the house. She almost passed out when she saw Isabelle's garden. "It's incredible. What are all these herbs for?" She walked them, recognizing many herbs she needed for healing. "I could use a garden like this."

"You're welcome to anything. Any time. My mother knew many things about herbs. If you burn two of these," Isabelle pulled a basil leaf from a plant and showed her, "over hot coals and watch the reaction, the burn will tell you if you'll have a happy marriage."

"Show me."

"Two for me, six for you." She handed Kit the leaves and walked to the end of her garden. There she had a cooking hole in the shelter of apple trees and raspberry bushes.

"Do others know ya have these herbs? This burning hole?"

Isabelle met her eyes. Her jaw firmed but she didn't answer.

She lit coal and sat by the pit. Kit sat across from her.

While they waited for the coal to warm, Kit glanced around uneasy. She divided her leaves in sets of twos. Rituals that weren't for healing but for vision paths were usually performed underground. Julien was very clear that outsiders wouldn't understand and call them witches, burning them at the stake. They were well-sheltered but she felt trapped. "Your mother…she used these herbs to help people?"

"Of course. Mama was a healer like you. She used the Healing Chamber, but preferred to sit back here with the sun on her and the smell of her plants nearby. She taught me how to cook with them, to burn them." She bowed her head. "I had much left to learn."

Kit had assumed Francis knew all those things from his father not his mother. "She brought in new ways and mixed them with the ways of the Ghosts tribes. This is interesting. How many of her teachings have you and your brother adapted to our rituals?"

Isabelle smiled. "I just do what feels right."

Kit studied the ritual area. Under the bushes were earthenware pots. This was amazing. By bringing this knowledge back to her people, they would learn so much.

"Now meditate on your chosen one. One thing you love most about him and place the leaves together like so." She dropped them with a wicked smirk on the coals. They seared quickly. "If they burn peacefully like that, you will have a happy marriage. Of course, how long the leaves burn is the length of the marriage."

Kit studied Isabelle. She had her eyes closed. Her lips were drawn tight, curled up slightly to the left. Kit felt Isabelle's worries. "You love him, but you wonder sometimes how serious he is about you?"

"He loves me. The leaves never lie. He never lies, not to me. We will be happy. It might not last long but happiness rarely does." Her smile grew. "I keep him hooked with cookies just to be sure."

Kit chuckled. "Good for you. I can't cook."

"I'll show you how. The caraway seeds must be prepared on the coals with prayers."

Kit's smile faded. She'd drugged his cookies with a love potion? "You're serious? Isabelle, ya shouldn't use this knowledge to alter destinies. This is powerful energy you're transferring and doing so has a price."

"We will be happy. You saw the truth in the leaves."

"What if he's to be with another? What if you are?" Kit was too flustered to toss her leaves. She needed focus for a ritual to work, even one she wasn't familiar with.

Isabelle pulled her skirt around her. "You think I'm evil?"

"No. You misunderstood. I would love to teach ya. If you teach me what ya do with these herbs."

Isabelle nodded so Kit drew a circle, prepared to teach. "Every time you use energy from things Mother provided, life must return to her, creating a circle." Kit inserted the stick at a point in the circle. "This stick represents the leaves you use today in your ritual. You place them on hot coals and they leave you with a knowledge of your destiny." She inserted another stick at another point in the circle. "You will take this information and apply what you believe to your life, creating another point, yet unknown, where Mother will ask for something." Kit planted another stick. "This will in turn bring your energy back to Mother. This is a circle every transfer of energy must do. Each stick must balance around the circle. So if ya do something like use this energy to change someone's destiny using cookies laced with caraway seeds, the thing Mother will ask of you is much bigger and will change your destiny. This is why we always balance out what we do. Why we reflect before we use Her energy."

Isabelle sat perfectly still while she taught. "I understand. I can't undo what is done."

"No, you can't, but you can prepare, because only you know what Mother will require of you to keep the balance. And if you altered this boy's destiny with your love spell, you will have to set his path straight again or expect your destiny to be altered. I can't tell you how, but the answer will reveal itself to you in good time."

Isabelle nodded. "Will you burn the leaves?"

"I will but I need a moment to pray before. I must prepare myself for I am asking Mother to confirm whose destiny I am linked to."

Kit returned to the garden and walked, thinking. Had she forgotten to tell her something? Did Isabelle understand how serious playing with destinies could be? Kit paused. "When I travelled the road, I noticed many plants of dill and mustard line the sides of the roads."

Isabelle answered from where she stayed in the sacred area. "They keep evil spirits from our place. We live on Cursed Land. We have to protect ourselves. Evil spirits don't like the smell of them."

She walked in to see that Isabelle hadn't moved. Kit sat by the leaves and picked up two. She thought about Francis and his kind, happy energy. She tossed the leaves on the coals. They simmered slowly, peacefully and suddenly sizzled and flew apart. "What does that mean?"

"Your marriage will end in tragedy."

Tragedy. She didn't need leaves to tell her this. She felt this loss when she visited with Francis. He was happy, but a darkness loomed around him, like Isabelle. They were cursed by something she would never understand, even though he'd said her rituals gave him comfort.

Kit sat breathing.

Julien. She thought of his gentle touch. Of his guiding hands. She dropped them. They floated to the coals far apart and crackled and jumped. They refused to burn. Finally, they jumped from the coals. Kit picked them up and prepared to burn them again but Isabelle grabbed her arm to stop her.

"You only get the one try. This marriage will never happen. It is so improbable that the thought tires Mother." Isabelle rubbed her eyes. "Can you feel how this has drained our energy?"

Again, Kit didn't need leaves to tell her this. Being with Julien was a comfort, but his confusion exhausted her. He was never on the same page as her. One minute he held her hand asking her to marry him and the next she found him rolling on his mat, lost in the embrace of a man not from their tribe.

Kit bowed her head. Maybe she was destined to be with no one. She had never seen this ritual, but her lack of experience in darker arts didn't mean the magic was less powerful than the rituals she knew.

Kit dropped the last leaves. This one was for Russ and her. All her life she just assumed her destiny was set with his, that there would be no choice to make. She saw his eyes looking up at her from in the vision and still felt this way.

The leaves smoldered, slow and peaceful, snuggled tight together, feeding off each other. She watched them intently as they simmered over the coals. "Are they cold?" Kit asked, moving her hand over them.

"That is the sign that your marriage will last long and be peaceful. He is the right choice, Kit. Was this burn my brother?" Isabelle asked.

Kit bowed her head. "It is my secret."

Isabelle sat beside her. "It looks like you didn't get the answer you were hoping for. I'm sorry."

Kit wiped tears. She knew this all along, but to have a ritual confirm her vision was such a relief, they were tears of joy.

Kit bowed her head. "I should talk to him tonight. Get our destiny on track. I already waited too long."

Isabelle stood. "Yes, then come, I will prepare you a bed. You can stay the night."

Kit shook her head. That wasn't a good idea. "I shouldn't be around Francis until after I talk to Russ."

Isabelle frowned. "Russ? Why would you…" Her eyes ran up Kit thoughtfully and her hands flew to her mouth. "I must go." She ran off.

What was that all about?

-Twelve-

Kit sneaked on Russ' farm and climbed the roof of the barn. From there she had the perfect view of Russ' room. She'd sat here many nights over the years and watched him. Wondering what he was like. Like usual, he had his feet on the windowsill and he read by the lantern. What hid in them books that had him so enthralled? Kit couldn't read, had never been to school, but the idea intrigued her.

She waited for him to dim his lantern, then she'd sneak in his room to talk to him. She planned to tell him everything: her vision, Julien's offer to marry her. Everything. He could decide. He could hold her hand and peer in her eyes and tell her what she needed to hear.

His light never did dim. She thought he must have dozed off when his window opened and he sneaked out. Curious, she followed him. He rushed from the window and ran to the haystack, where she'd met him after her womanhood ceremony.

Kit followed him, the dark her cover, only the Northern Lights for a guide.

Voices floated in the night, making her pause. A woman giggled. Kit listened closely.

"Damn, these cookies are good. I'm gonna marry you just to get them every day."

Giggling.

"I want to find you a dog, Isabelle. Something to protect you when I can't."

Russ fancied Isabelle? Kit stumbled back as if hit with a sack of flour.

"Francis told me you were talking to Silver," Isabelle said. "He said he saw you, but Silver is dead. How do you do this?

Can you teach me how to talk to spirits?"

"There are different stages of dead." Russ answered her in a very teaching way that calmed Kit. She didn't know he taught, but Kit should warn Russ that showing Isabelle such things might lead to dark rituals. Who knew what she was capable of? Like Francis, her knowledge of plants, healing, and spiritual things surpassed anything Kit had seen. Their mother was clearly a gifted healer. But without guidance these rituals were often misused.

"Silver's body died, but his soul continues to live."

Was Russ her teacher? Kit relaxed, understanding. Teaching others was very common in the Ghost of the Earth tribe.

"You ever see him?" Isabelle asked.

"Yeah. I see him all the time."

"I'd like to see him."

"Push your hands in the dirt."

Kit did as he instructed, even if his instructions were meant for Isabelle.

"Close your eyes."

"Silver," Kit whispered. He appeared before her instantly, cross-legged in the grass by the straw.

Silver said, "*Russ is distracted. End this curse I started, Kit. He needs focus.*"

Kit prepared to open her mouth, but Russ said, "Mmm, you taste as good as your cookies."

"Do you feel a spark when we touch, Russ?"

"Of course. You get me all hungry inside."

Kit leapt to her feet and ran. She ran all the way to the train and didn't look back.

–THIRTEEN–

About two weeks after the storm, Pa announced they were headed to Moose Jaw to settle Russ' land with the government. Moose Jaw was an amazing and terrifying place, among the biggest towns Russ had ever seen, the city was an entire new world from Eau Claire. A world he couldn't understand. The unknown wasn't one detail; it was all of it. Everything confused the dirt right off him.

Russ stood in wonder on the platform of the train station and studied the crowd. Pa knew he hated crowds and he'd given Russ a tip. He said to look at one person at a time and not the cluster. So Russ picked out a woman. She wasn't dressed like Isabelle or Ma and most definitely not like Desire. Her dress flowed rich and fluffy. His sisters would call it a gown. This woman held a fan she used as if it were too hot. Perhaps with all those layers on, she was roasting. Russ tilted his head to study the dress from afar, no clue how she got in the getup or even why she'd wear something that warm. The sun beamed, making for a warm June. Her hair was up and covered by a fancy hat with lace and beads. Would Isabelle like a weirdo hat like that? She might. It'd be fun to surprise her with one.

A man followed the woman around as if she was a lord, carrying her things, and loading them into a wagon. He wore shoes. Russ glanced at his bare feet, then at Pa's. He could hear Jessie calling them French Savages. They looked the part and there would be no blending in here. No one was like them in Moose Jaw. No one talked like them. No one even smiled like them and Russ suddenly understood what Pa had meant about not fitting in to either world.

Odd but Russ stood alone in the crowd, even with Pa at his side.

A roofless automobile pulled up. Built like a carriage without a horse. Now, the idea might seem neat, but travelling long distances without a horse wasn't smart and Russ planned to compare the two.

Their first stop was a hospital-type brick building. Pa walked in as if he knew the place. Russ should have read the sign. Had there been a sign?

"What we doing here?" Russ asked as they stood in the too clean entrance. The place had a strange stink to it. Like rancid clean. His stomach turned and without meaning to, he stepped closer to Pa.

"Monsieur Bellecoeur is someone you should meet." He asked the nurse for his room number and Pa navigated the way easily.

The door to room 118 was closed. Screaming erupted from the inside. Pa stormed in. An older man flipped out in the bed and much to his surprise a ghostly figure hovered over him. Grandpa Silver glanced up when they walked in. Seeing him smile made Russ relax.

"Why's the old guy screaming?" Russ asked his ghostly grandpa.

"Silver, cut that out," Pa snapped at Silver, but Pa was fun, and even though he said the words gruffly, he still smirked as if ready for a good joke.

The screaming stopped. Russ took a closer look. The man was probably in his eighties. He wasn't shaven. Oozing sores bubbled on his skin. Russ backed up when he saw the black ghost tattoo on the back of his hand. "My cousin Charlie has that tattoo. What does the marking mean?" Russ instinctively rubbed his hand. He wasn't sure why but the tattoo on his cousin's hand always made him uneasy.

"The tattoo means he was marked for judgement by *Cîpay*. The one Charlie wears wasn't made by *Cîpay*, and we don't talk about that."

Marked for judgment meant *Cîpay* vexed you. But Charlie was a Depaix, and if anyone cursed people and was not a curse, it was him. Once when his sister fell sick, he told Russ while rubbing his gold cross that he'd steal the good energy from Cracker Jack and make his sister better. Sure enough, she was at school the next day, and Cracker Jack was out sick. He sat smug all day and Russ was too 'fraid to ask how the heck he pulled off a curse like that. He was just glad Charlie was family.

"Who is this?" Russ demanded.

Neither answered right off, they were too busy laughing at each other with their silent glares.

Finally, Pa said, "This is Monsieur Bellecoeur. He's the reason Silver can't move on."

What did one have to do with the other?

Silver explained much better, *"He killed my body because he wanted Sacred Land."*

"Why?"

"The tunnels," Silver continued. *"I didn't know it at the time, but he'd hid something in them he wanted. Really, it was that simple. I would have given him his things back, had he asked. Instead, he thought he'd bribe us with ideas of making money, or scare us with veiled idiots he hoped would get us off the land. Now, he's sick and has no idea how out of hand things have gotten. This crew he has working for him want us off the land so they can tear the soil up to get in our tunnels and find this thing he hid."*

"How can he still influence anything when he's sick?" Russ gripped his blade, filtering thousands of questions he suddenly had, by importance. Why were they standing there? The only solution for someone who had killed his family was death.

"Money," Pa said as if that explained everything. "Notice how well-off Kaplain is suddenly?"

Silver took Russ' silence as understanding and continued to explain, *"Plus, the curse has them corrupt with hate and greed."*

"Well. If this is the guy giving them these ideas about our land, maybe getting this bloke out of the picture would help."

"When Bellecoeur ripped my soul from my body, his action linked me to him. The only way for me to move on is when he dies. I torment him but I can't kill him. I was reborn his shadow."

"I can," Russ offered, but stepped back when Cracker Jack appeared by Silver.

Was she his shadow? Was this why Pa brought him here?

To teach him about the shadows?

Pa whacked him on the back of the head. "See the tattoo on the back of his hand?"

Russ nodded but looked at Miss Penelope.

"The black ghost is a warning that it's forbidden to kill him. He has a spirit trapped to his soul that needs to move on," Pa said.

Russ glanced his way. Pa studied Old Cracker Jack, too, and Russ wondered if he could see her. He felt the weight of Pa's words.

Pa continued, "If you kill Bellecoeur, then Silver's and Monsieur Bellecoeur's souls will be tied to yours and Silver will be stuck longer."

He understood why Pa brought him here. He thought he'd messed up like Monsieur Bellecoeur. Russ met his father's eyes. It angered him that he thought Russ did her in, but he wasn't about to defend himself when he'd just thought about killing this old man suffering in front of him. "Is there a way to undo the link? Will I get a tattoo?" Russ was terrified. He didn't want *Cîpay* to disgrace him, he wanted to be one.

Silver shook his head. "*There's no danger of our warriors killing you, so no. But you are stuck with the shadow, and I don't understand why she chose you. She is not Cîpay. She is not cursed. Yet she shadows you.*"

"Only the one?" Russ checked, wondering if Jessie lurked around, too.

"*One is enough. She has the power to make your life hell. Just ask Monsieur Bellecoeur how entertaining I am to have around.*" Silver tightened his fists and Bellecoeur screamed as if he were on fire from the inside.

"Don't give her ideas." Russ frowned. "What am I supposed to do about this?"

"*Learn to live with her. Find out why she shadows you. Teach her. Let her teach you.*"

Pa said to Silver, "He has to learn on his own like the rest of us. Otherwise, it's just our beliefs. He has to make them his own. You taught me this."

Silver shook his head and vanished. Russ followed Pa outside. Once the fresh air hit him he felt much better, but he didn't like Old Cracker Jack haunting him for his entire life.

"So you ever hear of anyone losing their shadows?" Russ asked Pa.

"Well...yes, Antoine did but his wolf taught him an important lesson then disappeared. Hoolie says many lose their shadows right before death or before they are reborn."

"Yet Silver believes we should teach the shadow things so it leaves? I mean really, what does a guy like Silver need to learn?" Russ didn't like the idea. "I don't want Miss Penelope Jack teaching me squat and I have no idea what I could teach her."

Pa bowed his head, tragically. "I should have told you before so you knew what you were getting into, but I never thought you capable of such a thing."

"I won't tolerate anyone hurting Isabelle, but I never killed her, and it pisses me off that you think I did."

"Shh. Don't tell her your weakness."

He gave Pa a doubtful look, sure a spirit dumb enough to shadow him knew his weaknesses. It wasn't a big secret. "So where did Jessie end up? Hell? Heaven?"

"Well. Many years ago, Silver cursed Bellecoeur's brother to the earth in a very powerful ritual that means he haunts this land until he finds a soul worthy of moving on with. He leeches on, turning his host wrathful and if they die at our hands after having dishonoured our lands, he drags them down with him. Now they are many, bound to the soil, searching for hosts to torment in hopes that one will lead them to afterlife."

"You believe Jessie is underground with them?"

"I saw the cursed. You'll have to get Cal or Silver to show you. I'm not allowed under Cursed Land anymore."

"Why not?"

Pa gave him a playful grin. "Silver will tell you that if a guy spends too much time under the land he protects, when he stands on the surface, he doesn't blend in anymore." The explanation was probably the best he ever gave. It made sense to Russ because he saw the difference between Cal and Pa. Cal spent too much time underground and unlike Pa, Cal couldn't pass unnoticed in this crowd.

"But truth is, I was a bit wild as a child and when I destroyed the Sacred Oak, Aunt Sacri forbade me to go underground. Uncle Alex calmed her so she didn't kill me. He made me promise to plant a new oak tree every year by the creek out by Antoine's and if anything should happen to me, that's where I'm to be buried. I won't go under the land again until I'm dead, at one with Sacred Land."

Russ had a bunch of questions for Pa but Pa pointed out a streetlight. "Look, now the stars and moon aren't bright enough." Pa sounded proud yet disgusted all at once, but that was Pa. Russ was never sure which world he lived in but that was his polite way of ending a horrible discussion.

They didn't have one outhouse in Moose Jaw and since he had to go, this was Russ' biggest concern. They found washrooms with running water from taps. Russ spent time monitoring the water as it poured from the faucet.

Pa waited, watching him as if he was broken and he had no idea how to fix his son.

"Think we could do this at our place?" Russ followed the pipe under the sink into the wall. "It's a pipe running to the well." Of course, water needed pressure to travel those pipes. What pumped it?

As if reading his thoughts Pa asked, "How would we get the water to pump from the well?" He acted curious, as if Russ might be smart enough to figure this out. Well, if someone else could figure this contraption out, they could. He needed to think on it.

Russ flicked the light switch and the lights went out. He flicked it again and they were bright again. A lantern in the ceiling.

"What you thinking, Russ?"

"We could do this." Russ planned to figure it out.

"Without electricity?"

"I like them lights coming on when I flick this, but we'll try a few things; hand pumps, gravity feed. I could even fill a tank in the house with water and we could pump from in the house." He could see the plans in his mind and couldn't wait to try them out.

Pa nodded and showed him a paper he'd scribbled on. "This is what I want to do. We need a generator. We'll pick up the supplies today and send them back by train."

A generator? He wanted to bring power to the farm? Russ

loved the idea and studied the picture so he could help.

English was the common language in the city, but the words sounded different from their English. Russ tried speaking like them, 'cause they had an accent, or maybe Russ pronounced his T's like D's. He listened closely. His R's were too long and smooched into the rest of the word. He planned to make them cleaner. What the heck was wrong with them that they weren't talkin' like the rest of the world?

"Don't worry about it, you talk fine," Pa said while they were shopping for nails. But of course, he'd think that, he talked like him.

They did all sorts of weird things that day. They rummaged through a bunch of women's hats, since Pa wanted to buy Ma something. At the pharmacy Pa bought a bottle of whiskey he said they could drink later, then Pa handed him a box of Cracker Jack.

"I can't eat this." Russ held the box, horrified.

"Why not?" He smirked, but Russ couldn't tell him why.

"I'll save it for the girls."

Pa thought Russ was amusing but he bought him three more so he could give Samuel one, too.

On their way to the bank, Pa tapped strange flyers hanging around and mumbled swears at them. Russ stole one because he didn't get why they ticked Pa off, but Isabelle would. He slipped the flyer in his pocket.

They met with a pompous banker who wouldn't shake Russ' hand when Pa introduced them. He talked to Pa as if giving him money might prove they were flakes.

Russ wasn't listening though, because Silver was with them in the bank and Russ was curious why. Silver leaned against the file cabinet cleaning his nails with his knife, grumbling about things the banker said. Once he threw the banker's papers on the floor and the banker gaped at them wondering how the heck they ended up on the floor while they talked all nice-like. The entire scene was funny and Russ had to force his lips downward so he didn't smile.

When the banker left to 'fill out papers', Russ faced Pa. "Do we need a loan from this arrogant asswipe?"

Silver chuckled.

"Shh. A loan is great for you. The debt will give you value

in this world. Make you look smart. Plus, owing on your own land will give you a sense of responsibility and teach you to handle money. I'm not gonna give you everything. Did you understand what he told you about paying the cash back? You have to make one payment a year, after harvest, around November would be best."

"And what the heck happens if I can't pay this moron back? You know as well as me that sometimes we get bum crops. He gonna sit on me if that happens?"

Pa chuckled. "No, I already have the money. After Antoine almost lost Sacred Land to a bunch of debts, I felt it was safer to keep ahead of the bills. The cash is tucked safely in the storm cellar behind the jam, but he doesn't need to know that because well, I didn't necessarily make that money, I kinda found it." As far as Russ knew, they didn't have a bunch of cash, but why in all this dirt did they need any money? Mosquitoes bit the rich as often as the poor, or so Pa'd tell the tale. Russ didn't know a rich bloke from a poor one. He knew a smart one from a dumbass, and this banker was on the short list of dumbasses.

Pa added, "This is for show and makes you look like everyone else."

"I'm not like everyone else?"

Pa sighed but Silver chuckled and mumbled, *"No, you most certainly are not."*

Russ liked to hear Silver laugh, and he smiled with his grandpa, pleased about being different even if he didn't know why.

Pa rubbed his forehead. "No, for starters, not everyone sees spirits. Sammy can't see Silver. Neither can your ma or Bernadette." Pa smirked. "You're a *Cipay* warrior. You might not run around in tunnels like your crazy brother but you were born to protect Sacred Land. It's in your blood. We're just a new type of warrior. One who blends in. This banker sees a farmer †and that's what we want. He doesn't understand the difference and he sure as heck doesn't need to know about cash we keep handy. You pay what he asks until your loan is paid off which will take two crops. We keep what he doesn't ask for."

"Cash? So we have money?"

"Money is a curse brought to our land. We need the cash to fit in. The real value of who we are lives in the soil beneath our feet and how we respect Mother. You can't buy any of that, you have to get out and live the path She delivers."

Russ nodded, thinking a bit of money might be nice just the same, especially if it would save him having to deal with idiot bankers.

"You'll use the profits to pay for next year's crops and no one will ask questions. This is how they do things. Sit straight and pretend you care."

Russ frowned. Trouble was, he didn't care about money. Only bit of money he ever saw was a nickel from his uncle. He said the coin was a reward for getting Jezebel home safe when Jessie decided she should walk home with him and she didn't want to have anything to do with his stupid ugly mug. Russ had given the coin to Isabelle. She'd slipped it in her apron without as much as a thank you.

"I'm not sure we should do this. Silver doesn't like this guy."

Pa glanced at Silver and back at Russ. "Shh. Don't talk about such things in here. You'd better not screw this up because he's the only banker who'll talk to me."

For a minute, Russ thought Pa spoke to him, but Silver answered, "*Just curious if this will work. You remind me a lot of your uncle Alex when you do dumb things.*" He vanished into the floor leaving behind a pile of dust but his voice echoed over them, "*Never sure if that's a good thing or not.*"

–FOURTEEN–

During that trip, Russ discovered how big the world really was. A guy reads about all this magic, but until he sees the people on their elegant porch swings and on their streets, wearing their uncomfortable shoes, or acting important, a guy hasn't seen nothing but crops and school.

He couldn't wait to show this to Isabelle.

They had a lot to do while in the city and Pa paid for a room at a hotel so they could spend the night. He said that tomorrow they'd take the train to Regina. Russ was excited, 'cause Regina was bigger than Moose Jaw. That was impossible for Russ to imagine.

With only one bed in the room, Russ would bunk with Pa, but Pa went to church for a spell. He left the whisky out and said Russ could have a snort if he wanted. Russ had no desire to taste Pa's whiskey. Since Cal and Russ had gotten ripped on Monsieur Dubois' stash, Russ had no interest in being that stupid again. That hell burned like drinking fire. It charred his brain and turned his thoughts to mush he had to throw up. He didn't like seeing his brains all over the ground. He needed 'em if he was to be smart.

Besides, Russ had better things planned for that night. A draught flowed by the armoire that he wanted to investigate. Growing up on the prairies meant wind, air, things like that, talked to him in a way he was familiar with. The break in the airflow meant tunnels. He was on the second floor in the hotel, and so an entrance or an exit to a tunnel sounded mighty unlikely, but he'd snoop around just the same, 'cause he saw the world with new paranoid grownup eyes.

He investigated the armoire from top to bottom and never found an entrance. Yet with his ear right up against the back of the armoire, a dog growled from the other side.

So he moved the heavy oak cabinet. Waiting for Pa to return would have probably been smart, but in his mind, it was wiser to do this without him. Using his muscles, he slipped the unit back. An old lantern stayed on the dresser for emergencies, so he lit it and ran the light behind the armoire.

The wall was covered in paper decorated with big ugly flowers. Russ held his ear up against it, and sure enough, a dog growled on the other side. Maybe the sound came from another room and he was being stupid, but his bare feet felt a draught. Determined to find the source, Russ pulled out the bed and the dresser. Behind the dresser, he discovered a hole in the wall surrounded by bricks. On his knees, Russ moved the lantern inside, excited.

—FIFTEEN—

Russ went on an adventure as he slid in the entrance. This space wasn't built for big men, that's for sure. Standing felt cramped. He made his way about twenty feet inside the wall before the passage led him to a dead end where he stood perfectly still to listen. His lantern showed no signs of anything, yet cool air from the tunnel hit his bare feet again.

Russ dropped on all fours. Along the floor was another hole in the wall, surrounded with bricks, like the entrance. He peeked in, thinking the path might lead to another room.

A slobbering, angry, growling beast appeared in his face. Russ pulled back and sat on his heels breathing madly. Just a dog, he promised himself and peeked again. He was still there. The hole was big enough for the dog to come through yet he didn't, which meant he protected someone, and well, Isabelle could use a dog like this.

Russ placed the lantern between them and talked to the growling mutt as Isabelle always talked to Beast. He could have gone back, a man probably would have, but in the moment, they were alone and Russ felt like a fool, not a man.

Suddenly, a girl spoke in English from the other side, "You a runner?"

He asked, "What's that?"

"Ya know, a tunnel runner, them mice kicking around who have these tunnels memorized."

He was in a tunnel? Russ touched the cement wall. "Gee, no, I'm a farmer," he mumbled wondering if maybe these passages led to tunnels.

"Ya know how to make a stitch, farmer?"

"I suppose I could if push came to shove." He sounded more convinced than he felt.

"I... I could use a hand. I thought I'd die then I heard you talking to my dog like a happy boy. Something about the way you talked made me relax, so if you're game, I could use a hand or two."

Russ thought about Cal and Pa. He wanted to be like them, not some happy boy. "I'm almost seventeen. I'm almost a man."

"You sound real sure, ya do. Leave me alone if you're nothing but a coward."

Of course, them were fighting words, girl or not. Russ wriggled right through the hole, ready to prove her wrong. "What you need help with?" he demanded, acting the hero, until he saw her. She needed more than his help. Heck, she needed...Ma.

They were in a stairwell. She crowded in the corner by a broom and pail. The dog paced beside her, sleek, black, and monstrous. He showed his fangs but didn't growl, since the gal kept a hand on him. She was a mess, as if she'd been beaten senseless and left for dead. He'd seen Cal in bad shape a few times and Ma had nursed him back to health, but this was a gal. Who beat on women in Moose Jaw? And why the heck hang out in a secret passage?

Her dress was ruined but had been fancy; something like Isabelle would wear to church. The pleats were torn and muddy. A soft blue with a gold flower sewn along the side but that was all messed up now. He guessed the dress was pretty at one time. Isabelle hated to dirty her good dress, and Russ imagined other gals were no different.

He placed the lantern beside her to study the blood soaked hanky on her side, the bruises on her arms, and finally the scratches on her face. On a first glance, he thought she might be Chinese, but her cheeks were higher like Desire's. Maybe not all Chinese, no, she had local in her, but which tribe? Her lips were thin, like his. His overall impression was that he really wanted to make those lips happier.

Her eyes were closed as she rested her head against the cement wall. "If you plan to kill me, do it quick."

In Chinese he said, "Killing you might be a last resort. How about I wash you, see if there's a woman under this blood and mud? Your family around here?"

She opened her eyes and stared at him when he spoke Chinese.

"Family is not important," she answered in Chinese.

How could she say family wasn't important? He knelt beside her. The dog growled so he stole a closer look at her face, careful not to touch her. Damn, she was familiar but he couldn't place where he knew her from.

She had a cut on the cheek that had stopped bleeding but he heard Ma say in his mind that cleaning a wound was more important than gawking at the blood, no matter how neat the cut was.

"Family might be annoying, and sure they make it hard for a guy to find a quiet place to think, but at the end of the day, when I glance around the supper table, seeing people who want to share everything with me, even moments like you're living, is kinda nice. Family is not only important; the bond you share is eternal and linked through the soil. I give mine a hard time, but I'd kill for every single one of them."

She held her side, blood oozed from between her fingers, seeping through the hanky.

Russ handed her his hanky when she let out a long puff of air. "Today was my wedding day, and I lost my family."

"All of 'em?" He checked her legs, careful not to touch her, so the dog didn't freak out.

The dog shoved him back, but she snagged his hand suddenly and held it. "Russ, are you really here or am I hallucinating?"

He stared at her hand around his, shocked by the familiar feeling. He hadn't felt that strange tingle in a long time. "Kit?" he breathed her name.

Her chest went up, filling her lungs with air. Russ found himself doing the same.

She sniffed and peeked past Russ as if a bunch of ghosts waited for her to die. "Go. I should die alone." She let his hand go.

Russ couldn't imagine dying alone. Frankly, the idea terrified him. "No." He could have said a bunch of stupid things, but really, there was no need.

"You ever watch someone die?" Kit asked. "I don't want you to see me like that."

Russ used the lantern to get a better look. Her long hair hung around her in a knotted mess. Her fingers had blood smeared on them and his new hanky was ruined.

"You look like the devil beat you with a stick, but I've seen worse. You're not dying."

"The devil I can handle."

He tried to lift her hand off the wound so he could see how bad things were, but she held firmly. The dog growled.

"Don't touch me."

He whispered, "Do you feel that strange tingle when we touch? What causes that…energy between us?"

She looked away from him and wiped tears with her free hand.

"Take one breath," Russ encouraged her. "You're safe with me. I'll help you."

"It hurts to breathe."

Silver materialized from the wall beside them. "*Sometimes it does,*" he said with a love to his voice that made her grin.

Silver normally appeared when his family needed him or when someone died on blessed land. That was pretty much the rule about being Silver—as far as Russ could tell. Well, this wasn't blessed land and Russ didn't need him, so he was nervous when Silver knelt beside her and rested a hand on her shoulder.

"*I'm here with you, Kit,*" he announced as if that was perfectly normal.

"I'm cold," she told him.

He blew on her and the ground around them warmed. "*Be strong, this is your path. Ready?*" He tenderly touched the air in front of her as if feeling fabric.

She winced. Her grunts were like someone fighting pain, and Russ needed the suffering to end.

"Stop that." He pushed Silver back. "I'll help her. You're hurting her."

"*I'm numbing her pain. Go get supplies. Find Bernoit.*"

"I'll be right back. Grandpa Silver will watch you while I'm gone. Don't move. I'll be a minute, and I won't be far."

"Russ?" she mumbled.

As he pulled away, she grabbed his hand and a familiar warmth overwhelmed him from that night long ago when they were children. He looked at his hand as shocked by her touch now as he had been then. Would he ever get used to that?

This time, instead of pushing her away, he squeezed her hand gently. "I'm here, Kit." Such a simple gesture but he found himself planting roots around her. Their connection was solid and nothing would destroy it. "I'll get things to help you."

He hoped Pa was in the room, but he wasn't. Russ was on his own, and disappointing Silver was the last thing he wanted to do.

He grabbed a towel, the whiskey, and the jug of water for washing up. Russ searched the drawers and came up with a sewing kit that would do in a pinch. He made his way back. She hadn't moved and studied him as if he were a hallucination. Silver was gone, but the area stayed warm with the love Silver always left behind. Russ was confident he could do this even if he had no idea how.

"I'll help but you have to let me touch you. No matter how weird our touch feels."

"It's not weird," she snapped. "I just don't like men touching me."

"I'm just a boy. I won't hurt you," he reminded her.

She rested against the wall, beat.

He offered her the whiskey to numb her brain so she didn't feel the pain. She shot it back like she downed hooch all the time, then she poured a bit on her side wound and reached with her free arm to grip his shoulder while she winced through the pain.

Letting out a long breath, she rested the bottle beside her. Head back, she closed her eyes and let him check the wound on her side since he made the injury his first order of business.

The knife wound was a clean slice to her side, right through her dress. He took out his blade, ready to cut her dress so he could get a better look.

The dog growled.

Russ dropped the knife. "I have to cut your dress. Calm him."

She rested against her dog, using him like a pillow, on her

side so Russ could work on the wound.

A type of levelheadedness grounded him as he pulled the fabric back in the dim light. He never felt so in control of his hand as he prepared to make those stitches. He'd seen Ma give Cal and him enough of them. He gently cleaned the wound.

"I was thinking about the jerks who killed my family. Should I make their deaths painful?" she asked, breaking the silence.

"Killing someone in vengeance will backfire." He explained to her about how he just had to think about killing his teacher and now she shadowed him.

"How do I make them suffer if I don't kill them?" she asked.

"When I want to torture my brothers I usually convince my sisters to talk to 'em. I could ask them if they want to talk to these blokes for you."

She let out a chuckle that surprised him. Her laughter was so unlike Isabelle's he actually paused to watch her lips, wondering how she made that crisp and fearful sound. The defiance in her jaw told him she thought she might get a smack for smiling but she'd be happy anyway.

"You always do that?" she asked.

"What?" Russ wondered.

"Answer questions as if your family is all you know."

He didn't know much else.

Russ wiped a tear off her cheek and rubbed the salty drop into the cement wall since their tradition called for them to return tears to the soil that gave them life. The cement was as close as he'd get to dirt in this stairwell.

"I haven't laughed in a long time," she admitted. "Thank you."

"Your husband, he didn't make you laugh?"

"No." She took in a deep breath. "Julien was serious. He had a big burden to swallow as every *Cîpay* does."

"Julien was your husband? The chief of the Healing Ghosts?" his voice shook with the news.

"We weren't married yet. He chose me to lead his people, and now we have no one to lead."

"I'm sorry."

"This is my punishment."

"For what?"

"I ignored the path given to me by Mother because I had a sense of duty to my people." She tightened her jaw, then admitted, "And because I felt rejected and hurt. As a Healing Ghost, I studied with ancients and with *Cîpay*." She swallowed her pain. "I should trust my destiny, yet I let the choices of others stand in my way. You sit with me, a stranger, yet in my death I find comfort knowing our destinies can't be ignored. Thank you for talking with me as I die."

"You're not dying, and I'm not much for talking. But I'll make you a deal, I won't leave until you get off this floor, and if you let me stitch this up, I'll tell you a story."

She nodded into the dog's fur.

He tried to come up with a funny story to share, but everything in his life was suddenly very serious. So he settled on a story about Isabelle while he started the first stitch.

Her skin puffed around the wound and he wasn't sure where to start so he went from one end and planned to work his way to the other.

"You want to hear how my Isabelle stole a book from the teacher shadowing me?" He probably shouldn't have admitted to having a shadow so he added, "She made me look like a hero."

Kit lifted her head and winced. "*Your* Isabelle? You married her?" She sounded shocked and he scuffed, insulted. He was old enough to marry if the fit should take him.

"She's my everything, but no, we ain't married yet."

"So you plan to marry her?"

"Of course."

"What if you're not destined to marry her?" Air filled her lungs as she lay on the dog again. The wound went up and down in front of him.

"I'll tell you my story and you'll see that things like destiny don't matter. This story starts with our teacher. I had no idea where they'd dug her up, but the bottom of a Cracker Jack box was a safe bet. She was a prize, all right. She walked around with her hair in a bun and acted as if she might say something bril—eee—ant but she'd say, 'Russ, is that you making the squatting sounds? I will tell your father if you do not take these classes seriously.'"

Kit's lips curled up, and if she wasn't dying in front of him, she might have laughed, but Russ wasn't sure what had amused her. He stopped working to let her enjoy the happy.

"To this day, I have no idea what a squat sounds like, but I betcha anything it wasn't like the farting I did to annoy my cousin Jezebel. And really, my pa had bigger problems than me farting in school."

She groaned and shifted. The dog didn't move. Russ waited for her to get comfortable again, then started the second stitch.

"So one day, Miss Cracker Jack went outside to yell at my cousin Charlie for being late. He wasn't in any real danger. A Depaix handles himself just fine, so I focused on Isabelle. She walked up to Cracker Jack's desk, pretended to sharpen her pencil but stole a book and shoved it in her apron. I continued to watch her closely. I mean, she was an angel with her long black curls and if she was gonna walk about the room stealing books, I had nothing better to watch on my desk."

Kit winced as he pulled the needle through for the second stitch.

"You have thoughtful eyes," Kit mumbled, but her eyes were still closed so he guessed the booze made her yappy and he kept working. "Thoughtful eyes I want to draw. Capture the thinking going on while they watch me walk about the room."

He ignored her strange mumbling. "To this day, I have no idea why she stole the book. Maybe it was hers; maybe she wanted to annoy the teacher. Maybe she was a thief and that's what she did. She never stole any of my things, 'cept my kisses, so I don't much care. Don't matter. She stole the book. I saw her theft as plain as day. It made me even more curious about the thinking going on in her noggin.

"When the time came to fess up, she stared straight ahead and didn't say a word. Miss Cracker Jack leaned over her desk. She hated Isabelle, and as far as I could tell, Cracker Jack deserved to have her book stolen by her. She passed her over quickly though and settled on my friend Kika who she hated more. Come to think about it, there wasn't one of us she liked. But we knew he'd get the first and best beating 'cause he was Kika."

She opened her eyes. "And now this woman shadows you. Is the link painful? Has she spoken to you? Can I see her?"

Russ stopped telling his story to rinse off the wound again. "Idea freaks me out, but I'm trying to be brave. So far she hasn't done much, and she kinda appears to me when she wants."

"Is she here now?"

He looked around. "Nope. Just us." He stared at the cut. A couple more stitches were needed. The bleeding had stopped, leaving the skin swollen and a weird colour. "You need a doctor."

"I'm from the healing tribe." She rubbed the dog's fur, relaxed.

He wasn't sure why that meant she wouldn't need a doctor.

"Get my bag," she ordered.

He snooped around and found a heavy brown bag about three feet away on the top step. He brought it to Kit and dropped her bag in front of her. She undid the latch and stuck her hands in. Russ peeked. The bag toppled full of dirt. Black soil. She prayed softly to the dirt while he waited, listening to the prayers.

When she stopped, she let her shoulders fall back relaxed, almost asleep so Russ whispered in a soothing voice while starting the next stitch. "When Old Cracker Jack told us we were each getting a whipping until someone came clean about who stole the book, I had to end the punishment session. Not 'cause I was a hero, because truth was, we probably deserved a whipping for something or another."

He pulled the needle through for the fourth stitch.

"I had plans with Cal I couldn't miss. So I stood up to take the beating. She eyed me up and I told Old Cracker Jack that I tossed the book in the wood stove 'cause her corny English books sucked and we needed real French literature to liven the place up."

A laughing-sigh escaped Kit and her lips curled up in a quick smirk. Her soul laugh made him smile.

"Your words are like a blanket," she said.

He went back to stitching. "I even pulled out one of them forbidden books from my desk and offered to read it aloud to the class since I doubted she read in French. Then I read a passage from *Les Misérables*. Well. She was not so happy with Jean Valjean and me. She gave me a whopping with her thick leather belt. The belt snapped toward my shoulder but I caught it with my hand as Cal had taught me and absorbed the hit on the better part of my arm.

"She... She stank like wine, which threw me off a bit 'cause she wasn't supposed to be drinking. I suspect Pa gave her wine laced with something in the hopes she'd get herself fired since the contract she signed meant she had a job until she broke one of the rules." Russ wasn't used to sharing his thoughts aloud and expected her to tell him that his pa would never do that but she brought a fist of soil to her heart and held it there.

"Everyone else had scattered by the time I left, so they took my word for it that I left laughing and not crying, despite the two welts on my arm. Those things sting for days, too."

Her breathing was shallow. Russ felt her fevered head. The stitches were clean though and he bet even Ma would have been proud.

Russ lifted her dress to check her legs again for more damage. She was dirty and bruised. He grabbed some of her earth and rubbed the soil on her legs whispering the prayer she'd said. Then he held her right hand in his to check her arms and fingers. She winced so he kept sharing his story while he searched for what was wrong. Whenever their skin touched, he found focusing hard. Was she magical?

"My oldest sister Bernadette waited for me on the road, and when she saw I was alive she ran home to tattle on me. Isabelle met me by the livery barn with a wet hanky for my arm. I was glad I laughed, too. Nothing worse than looking like a crybaby in front of an angel like her.

"Silently, she walked with me for a spell. I liked that. Most gals chat your ear off as if silence is a bad thing, but she never does that. She likes thinking as much as me, I guess."

Russ wrapped Kit's hand and wrist so her finger didn't move. She preferred keeping her fingers straight so he used his suspenders and strapped her hand to the book he had in his back pocket.

"Isabelle slid this book I'm using from her apron and into my hands. I held the book like it might light itself on fire. It's a book the young ones use to learn to read. I didn't want to insult her theft, or her gift, and so I offered to read it to her.

"She told me Miss Penelope didn't give her a copy because she was a French dummy not worth her time to educate." Russ stopped working on her hand, too angry to continue.

"Ticks ya off when people tell you that you can't do things, too, eh?" Kit seemed fascinated with him.

"Every Wednesday I study Latin with the priest. Not 'cause I want to learn, but 'cause he'd told Pa he had no problems teaching Cal but he wasn't interested in wasting his time on someone slow like me. I was so pissed that he thought I was a dummy that I studied hard to set him straight and make him eat those words. Turns out Latin was the easiest of the languages and I took to learning it like nothing. I doubt I'll ever have much use for Latin, but I'm glad I proved him wrong."

"I fight because Julien told me I should not."

They were silent for a moment.

"Pa told me I wasn't following my destiny. Ticks me off. I make my own destiny."

She shifted, uneasy. "Ya don't believe that these legends and visions are true?"

"I plan to make my life my own. People who make decisions based on legends or visions are foolish."

"What about what ya feel?" She looked at his hand. "That connection between us. Do you believe in what you feel because that's real? Very real."

He studied his hand. "I don't understand the energy we share. What causes this?"

The dog paced around them. Russ sat so Kit could rest her head on his lap and he rubbed her temples. "What if you had an image haunting you?" she whispered. "Like this touch, this connection between us, only every time you closed your eyes, you saw me. What would you do then?"

His heart beat incredibly fast all of a sudden and he warmed up deep inside, as if fire escaped him.

"I'd push the image, the feeling, down, and see what was

right in front of me. I have a bunch of good things in my life, no need to ignore them based on something so uncertain."

She mumbled, "Like me, one moment changed your life, only yours was a good change. Thank you for the story. It…clears things up for me." She sounded so sad; he wanted to steal her pain.

"Didn't feel too good to get the whipping, but things turned out all right in the end, I suppose. I like your dog. I wanted to get Isabelle one for her birthday in a few days, but I never found one quite nasty enough. You know? I need one willing to tear a ghost in two."

"Yeah, good old Fangs comes in handy. He's the reason I escaped. Best dog in the world if you ask me."

He agreed.

Russ pulled a strand of hair off her cheek that stuck to her with dried blood. His hand lingered against her too long, but he enjoyed the comfort of the connection.

"Do you know about this curse everyone is talking about? Sounds like something a guy like me should be in the know about."

She shivered so Russ removed his shirt and wrapped her in it. He sat up taller because the wall teased cold against his skin. She was warm though, despite her shivering.

Russ took a fistful of her soil and piled dirt under each shoulder and along her side that was cut. He could hear Ma telling him to get that dirt out of here because wounds needed to be clean. Everything needed to be clean with Ma. But he could also hear Pa telling him that life comes from the earth and they had to respect that. So he kept the cuts clean and used fistfuls of earth around her to balance out both beliefs.

Suddenly, the dog let out a low growl and a lantern appeared out of the hole. "What the heck you doing in here half naked with a girl, drinking my booze?" Pa squirmed through the hole as Russ had.

Kit gripped her knife †and tensed.

Russ stopped her. "That's my pa. He's safe. Pa, she don't like men much, her dog even less so you best stay back. Or fetch her a blanket, she's shivering."

Pa watched them. Finally, he picked up the bloody hanky and his bottle of booze.

"Where is your husband?" he asked the girl in French. "Where is Julien?"

"*Mort.*" The one word—dead—was all she needed to say to get Pa studying her with his grey eyes. He knelt beside her instantly and the dog growled.

"Where are the others?"

Kit's jaw tightened and she opened her eyes. "If any survived they are deep underground where I couldn't find them. I remain burdened to avenge them."

Pa touched the floor and the walls as if they might tell him something. He sighed. "The earth suffers." Then he stood silent for a second. Russ didn't move, giving him a moment to get a grip on whatever the walls had told him. Plus, he was tempted to touch them, too, yet Russ didn't because if he didn't feel what Pa felt, he'd be right disgusted with himself.

Pa forcefully banged a fist in the wall. "Damn it." He kept his back to them. "Julien and Montague gather *Cîpay* to reclaim blessed lands. Some said they are the warriors of legends." Pa removed his cap, pushed his hair down, and forced his cap back on as if the news wouldn't sink into that brain of his.

"Do you believe these guys were the ones destined to end the curse?" Russ asked him, understanding why Pa was so upset.

He looked crushed when he turned around. "They were good people. All of them." He winced. "Damn. I'm sorry, Kit."

He knew her name? "What's going on, Pa?"

He glared at Russ. "We have access to a Healing Chamber if you need one, Kit."

Kit didn't answer and Russ thought she might be asleep on his lap. He stroked her hair, lost in thought.

Pa watched his fingers while he spoke, and Russ pulled his hand off her. What was wrong with him, touching her like that?

"Hopefully more of her tribe survived and they'll join us on Sacred Land."

"The tribes will be stronger as one," Russ told him. "Change isn't always bad."

Kit mumbled, "It isn't always good."

"I need to talk to Cal," Pa said.

Russ wasn't sure what Cal could do that they couldn't. "I'm not leaving her until she finds the strength to get off this floor and face her life again. If what you say is true and these tribes are vanishing, she's needed. You can't let your tribe die, Kit."

"We won't leave," Pa agreed. "You're always welcome on our lands, Kit. I can't believe we're losing ground."

They were silent for a bit and sitting with her brought him comfort. Russ felt better knowing they'd bring her home with them.

Pa shared his thoughts. "Her grandfather was one of the Chinese workers who helped build the train tracks. The Healing Ghosts adopted her mother Shuang when she was an infant. Kit has a wonderful ancestry that is a part of our history, but her teachings are from the ghost tribes." He grinned proudly. "She looks a lot like Shuang. She was a great friend when we were growing up, and I am honoured to sit with her daughter."

Kit met his eyes and actually smiled. Not her sad half smirk, but a powerful one that lit her entire dirty face.

"Want me to sit with her?" Pa offered. "Run and get her something to eat and drink."

Kit tensed, so Russ told him that he could stay. He didn't want her to feel threatened when they were here to help. "Just teach us, Pa."

Pa's voice was usually reassuring and full of love when he talked about the land and his family. Tonight he looked beaten. "Mother gave us the tunnels as protection. The earth is what feeds us and what absorbs our soul when we die. I suppose, in a way, all land is blessed, Russ, but not all land is Sacred Land. It's like saying each horse is the same. You know this isn't true, some work well with children, others do not. Some need to get out and do things or to work, while others make great mothers. Every part of the earth at our feet has a purpose, as does every living creature. Just because we don't know this truth, doesn't mean it stops being true. This land we protect is at the center of the world, where the first man was raised and the last one will die. Such a place is where heaven and hell meet. Under our land is a world you can't even imagine."

His words were a challenge. He wanted Russ to discover the magic on his own and Russ itched to bring Kit home and do exactly that with her and Isabelle. Russ bet the three of them would have fun exploring those tunnels.

"Why were we chosen to own Cursed Land?"

"No one owns land. That's a sham so others pass it by. At first Silver was against us claiming this land but Uncle Alex taught him how important blending in is. We pretend we own land, when the truth is, we owe this land our every breath, even our last."

Kit blinked half-asleep when Pa said this, yet she ran her hand along her arms and smeared dust on them.

"But Cal can't pretend to own any like we do?" It bothered Russ that Cal would miss out on this.

"To live on Sacred Land, you must be prepared to kill for every grain of dirt, to teach and learn from shadows, to be haunted by ancestors and lost souls. To live as *Cîpay* do, at one with Sacred Land, you must be prepared to die as the life leaves it. Cal has promised to make this sacrifice. As I did. Sounds like the same thing, but this sacrifice is nothing like protecting it. This ensures the energy Sacred Land needs will always be fed." Pa sat with them. "Remember the Sacred Oak I told you I destroyed as a boy? Well, I can plant 80 new trees but that loss won't be replaced until I become one with them, because when the Sacred Oak died, each of the spirits haunting that tree shadowed my soul, and they wait for me to die so they can once again give energy to the world."

He had a bunch of spirits from a tree shadowing him? Russ had questions but the first one to come out was, "You'll merge your soul with a tree when you die?"

He nodded.

"You have our ancestors shadowing you?"

He nodded again. "Sometimes the voices drive me mad. I can't see them, but I hear them all the time. It's relentless. Annoying. Tiresome…and feels like a curse. The only relief I get is when your mother is near. Not sure how, but she shuts them up."

Kit mumbled. "All spirits respect *Cîpay*."

They ignored her.

Russ said, "But if Sacred Land is lost, your soul will be, too."

"But I will finally be worthy." He closed his eyes, relaxed.

Russ let it go. If Pa wanted to be a tree in his next life, really, who could stop him?

Kit fell asleep. Russ watched her until her fever broke, then he fell asleep, too, while Pa watched over them, listening to his spirits.

–Sixteen–

When he woke, Kit was gone with the dog. Russ waited for her, thinking she might come back, impressed as hell that she'd left. She'd taken her soil, the bottle, his suspenders, and his book.

The silence settled around him, heavy. Then he heard a sob in the stairwell. He crept down the steps to see if Kit hid.

Much to his surprise, Miss Penelope crouched in the corner crying.

"What's wrong?" he asked.

She quickly wiped her nose and tears on the hanky she always had up her lacy sleeve. "*Nothing.*" She waved him off.

Russ leaned against the wall beside her, arms crossed, wondering what would make a dead woman cry. "Doesn't seem like nothing."

"*I thought I'd found love. I was foolish.*"

Russ thought about those drugs and the wine… "Did you do yourself in because old Kaplain didn't want you?" Perhaps he should have had more compassion because he felt horrible when she burst into tears.

He got down with her and offered to hold her while she cried. She crumpled against him. For a ghost, she suddenly felt as real as Kit had. He wiped her tears, and for the first time, he noticed how young she was. She was maybe only ten years older than him. Why had he thought she was old?

"*That girl, Kit, lost everything. Everyone she loved and she still got off the floor.*" Miss Penelope pulled away to say, "*How did she find the strength?*"

"My best guess is revenge." She was right, though. Russ would have gone home with Pa and to hell with revenge. Yet that rage pushed her off the floor and into action and well…her strength impressed him because if he lost Isabelle, he didn't know if he could find that type of will inside him. Other than Isabelle, he didn't know anyone else that strong.

Miss Penelope Jack lifted her chin. *"Revenge? Can you help me?"*

"Come on. You can't sit here crying for the rest of your afterlife. We're going to Regina, maybe you can show me around. Weren't you from there?"

Much to his surprise, she stood, pulling herself together, and she gave him a smile as she walked past. She led Russ back to the room.

Pa was there.

"Hey, did you see Kit leave?" Russ wondered.

"I did," Pa said. "She didn't want to bother you. Said she had to stop believing in a foolish dream. I imagine she'll be by our place soon enough because she mentioned something to that effect."

That was good enough for him. Russ couldn't wait to show her around and introduce her to Isabelle.

"Russ…" Pa cleared his throat. "Have a seat, son. I have a story to share with you. Perhaps I should have told you sooner, but these are the types of things a father likes to put off, in case they never come up."

Russ sat on the bed by Miss Penelope.

"Some *Cîpay* legends are like prophecies, since they speak of things yet to come and not things that have passed. I mean, I suppose one day they'll pass, but some haven't yet."

Russ glared at Pa, wondering where he went with this. He wasn't used to him babbling.

"They speak of destruction of six of the seven tribes and how the tribals survive by becoming *Cîpay*. Each time a tribe is destroyed, warriors are sent to protect the remaining tribes. Six prophecies. Many warriors. Many have visions that support these stories. What Kit shared was the loss of the sixth tribe. One tribe remains. Ours. Which means this warrior who Mother will call on to protect The Ghosts of the Earth is already walking among us. Maybe this warrior is one of us."

Russ nodded. "Guys like Montague and Cal will be busy.

Probably Kit, too."

"I suppose. Guys like us, too." He looked sadly at his hands. "The last story is about brothers born at the heart of Sacred Land. One will be a ghost hunter. The other will be a teacher."

Russ listened closely.

"They will be family to the last warrior, Uncle Alex, Antoine's father, and will use his teachings to hide the last tribe."

"What did your uncle do?"

"He taught us to blend in. Hide in plain sight."

Didn't seem like a hard thing to teach someone, but he could see warriors like Silver and Montague being a bit stubborn. "Where you going with this?"

"Legends…" Pa fell silent.

Russ said, "Some say Silver is a legend, but we both know he isn't. He's cursed. And now I am, too. When I die, what makes me so immune to this curse? I'll be sucked down with the rest of them and trapped underground until I find someone to latch onto and drive them mad." Russ sighed.

"It's not that. You see these legends… What if…" He stared at Russ.

"I see what you're trying to say. You're worried we might be these guys from the legends. Well, sure Cal might be a warrior, but I'm anything but. So maybe the hero you want is Sammy or something."

"The Ghosts Tribes believe in these prophecies or legends because they have visions that support them. These images nag at them. Give them a sense of purpose. Respect that, Russ, because you might not believe and you might not have visions but theirs are still real."

Russ glanced at Miss Penelope. She was real, beside him, listening to Pa tie into him in his calm way.

"Did I offend you in some way?" Russ wondered.

"I don't know what happened between you and Kit, but I expect better of you."

"Me? What did she say I did?"

"She didn't, but I know a broken heart when I see one."

"I didn't break her heart, Pa. She lost the man she planned to marry. Her leader."

"She said you didn't believe in visions or legends. Is this true? Did I not raise you to respect the beliefs of others even if you think them foolish?"

"Oh." Russ thought about this. "I see. You mean to say she thought the man she planned to marry was the one to fulfill these legends and I disgraced him when I told her only fools made decisions based on legends and visions. I should find her and apologize."

"It's for the best if you leave Kit alone. She's angry at the world. Until you reset the path of your destiny, she doesn't need you confusing her."

"*I agree with him*," Miss Penelope said, but Russ ignored her because what did she know?

"Yeah. I can't imagine having a vision I put all my faith in only to discover it was hopeless. I'm sorry I said those things to her. I should have been more thoughtful of her feelings. You ever have a vision, Pa?"

"With all these voices in my head, the last thing I need is a vision. Besides, when I see how deep those who have visions believe, I don't need one. The truth speaks clearly."

"So you believe two warriors will save the tribes? Save us? Even if Julien is gone?"

"It is a truth so real, this action is already done." He smiled proudly at his son.

"Maybe we'll figure out what to do without Julien." Russ pulled the flyer from his pocket and read it aloud, "'*Losing your son to drugs and booze? We can help.*' What the heck does that mean? How will they help when half of them we meet are strung up on something weird?"

Pa shook his head. "It's always another cause like that. They're constantly trying to recruit a new group of people by playing on their weaknesses and fears. Hoolie says if you respond, they give you a job to do like search our tunnels for a plant or run parcels for them through our tunnels. Then they invite you to meetings and get you fired up about this or that so you don't ask questions, and when you do, well then they bring out the drugs and call it a cleansing or a ritual."

Russ glanced at Old Cracker Jack in case she knew something. "*He's right. Those flyers are their lure. How they get new recruits.*"

Russ thought about this. "I guess it's an easy way to build an army. Say I was doing drugs or you're afraid I might be. You go to them. They talk to me to find out what I want or how I think, then they give me a job. Next thing I know, I'm in their tribe, wearing a sheet and doing things like starting Isabelle on fire. I have a new family who saved me and all I have to do is help them save others."

Pa frowned. "Wish they'd just leave us alone. We're not hurting anyone."

No, they weren't. But they did have a few things others might want like tunnels to hide out in and plants that might be more useful than they knew. "We don't find the things they want important because Sacred Land or even the Cursed Lands, well, they have an entire different value, don't they? Not really one I can explain to a guy who doesn't see what I see." He thought about the tribe living on Sacred Land, and the spirits coming and going on the Cursed Lands. "Silver spoke to Cal and me, and Kit I guess, about protecting Sacred Land. Doesn't really matter from what, does it? We're not gonna let Julien's death stop us from following the law of the land."

–SEVENTEEN–

If Russ thought Moose Jaw was a new world, he was even more shocked by Regina. He saw a woman with short hair, a short skirt, and high shoes. He thought their boldness was neat as heck to see. Sure some gals dressed like the ones in Moose Jaw, but they were few.

People didn't stare at them in Regina. The city was full of hustle and bustle, making Russ long for the quiet of his farm. He took many mental pictures, because Isabelle would be excited to hear about this place and he didn't want to return.

~~

Later that night, Russ sat by Isabelle and showed her the land Pa helped him buy. "Getting land was easy. They're practically giving sections away. What we did is, Pa bought more and I bought this parcel between your farm and ours from him. He figured it would be best. I have to help him though, 'cause he has more land than he can farm, so in a way we're sharing. He plans to get Cal to help, too, even if he never said that. And I have to get a house built on this parcel."

Russ showed her where he planned to build their house, by the haystack—his happiest place on earth.

He told her about Kit.

She sat with her hands on her lap, listening to every word. Her eyes straight ahead she asked, "Kit got off the floor on her own after having lost everyone she loved?"

Russ nodded.

"She must be brave." She never said the words, but he knew the look; she thought about when her ma had died and how hard that was. Russ waited for her to sort through her grief.

"Did you hold her hand?" she asked with a slight anger to her voice.

"Whose?"

"This brave Kit you slept with. Did you hold her hand?"

Russ shook his head. He hadn't held her hand once. "I stitched her. Pa held her hand, when she let him. She isn't a big fan of men in general."

"Yet she let *you* touch her?"

"Yeah, she thought I was a boy. I mean really, you should see her. I'm not much of a threat to a warrior."

"She was in rough shape?"

"Pa invited her here. If she shows, ask her these questions yourself."

Her jaw tightened and she glanced off at the fields instead of at him and Russ wondered what she thought. Surely, she wasn't jealous of Kit.

"Francis likes this Kit."

"He does? She never mentioned him." He thought about Kit with Francis and couldn't see them together. "I don't know. They don't fit together."

"So you know her well?"

"No. I guess we talked a bit." He thought about how comfortable he was with her. As if they were old friends, only more so. "I just don't see it, is all. But she was pretty upset when I sat with her, so maybe if she cleaned up they would be good together."

"He'll be pleased to hear you helped her. And if we're to marry one day, you should be making my brothers happy."

"I do find life easier when they aren't beating on me. Is that all you're thinking? Because, Isabelle, no one compares to you in my eyes."

"Do you ever think about me out of my clothes?"

"Yeah," Russ answered much too quickly.

"Wanna swim in the creek?" she asked, taking out her napkin of cookies.

He sat taller and bit into one. "Cal says we shouldn't." He blamed him. "That's how Desire ended up pregnant and I'm not so sure we're ready to have a baby yet. One day sure, but now? Pa said God would punish me for getting out of my pants before we married, and the minute we did, the storm showed up. Plus, every time I get naked with you, Thomas gets to beat on me. The arrangement was clear and I'm already homely enough, I don't need my face rearranged."

"Oh."

Russ finished his cookie and flopped back into the haystack, at peace with the world. She rested against his chest and all was right.

"But you want to?" she asked.

"Yup." Russ caressed her hair gently. "I dream about us together every night. But I want to have a future with you more, so we'll wait. We have forever."

"Roussel, one day will we get married?"

"Of course we will." Russ smirked, trying to act smart but feeling like a goofball. "If you want to marry me, that is."

"Remember how your ma taught me to sew?"

Russ nodded.

"Well, she talks a lot when she sews. She told us how babies are made and ways we could mess around without getting a baby made."

Russ shot up. "Holy dirt, woman! She talked to you about things like that?" What the heck, Ma!

"Yup. She said a baby couldn't be made while we had our monthlies and we could count ten days later as safe as well. She said if we missed our monthlies, we were to see her. Especially me. To Desire, she said no more monthlies."

"What the hell is a monthly?"

"When we bleed each month. She said if Desire notices any blood to see her 'cause she was different now that she carried life inside her."

Russ paced in front of the haystack, dizzy. She told him something important, but he needed to hear her say the words before he could believe them.

"Your ma, she said a bunch of other things. She talks like you: clear and smart."

He was smart like Ma? That was the weirdest thing anyone ever said to him. Russ shook his head, not able to figure that one out.

On his knees, Russ held both her hands, lost in her eyes. He had a bunch of questions he wanted answers to but was too chicken to ask. So he blurted out, "Is it painful when you get your monthlies?" So not what he wanted to say.

"It hurts in my stomach as if it's ripping itself out. Sometimes my legs hurt, too, like the blood is draining from them and my bones are thirsty."

Russ thought about the days she couldn't come see him 'cause of tummy aches and that made sense. She was in pain a lot.

"So…" He took a minute to find the right words. He had a hard time saying them but they needed to be said. "So asking me to swim with you means we can mess around because you had a tummy ache a few days back, and one day we'll get married?"

She nodded.

"What else should I know?" What else should he ask? The questions were too many.

She glanced down. "Your mama was calm. I like how your mama is always calm. Mine was never that way."

"Yeah, but what did she say about us messing around after she knew that horrible story of what happened to you the last time those jerks came by, because you told her, didn't ya?"

"She said things wouldn't be like that with you. That I'd be in control and you would be gentle and us getting together would be pleasurable. She told me to do it when I was ready, so I wasn't scared no more. But she told me to be sure the timing was safe so not to scare you. Then she told me to marry you right away so we didn't have to worry about those things and she could rest easy."

Russ nodded. That answered the questions that mattered. She wanted to do this. He was seventeen. A man with land. Swimming naked with his girl held a new meaning. A grownup one. Even though Pa said to keep his pecker in his pants, he knew Russ wouldn't, and that's why he helped him buy land. Ma expected the worst from him and took a different approach. She gave him a solution.

"You're sure it's safe?" he asked again.

She nodded. "We have days of safe left."

Damn. Russ couldn't wait to tell Cal this.

Russ walked her to the creek. They were alone. Not even a mosquito bugged them.

He figured they'd get naked and splash around in the water. But she stood, pleading him with those magical eyes to undress her, and so Russ took his time. One button and the next. He had her dress undone and an arm around her waist and was lost in her lips when his new suspenders slipped down. Her chest heaved up toward him and Russ was a puddle, melting into the dirt with her.

He never felt as vulnerable as he did in that moment. He flowed with her into the mud, so bloody hot the cold ground gave him a jolt, which somehow made her crazier. The mud oozed cold against their bodies but he slopped it on her warm skin, making them one with the earth.

Russ lost track of their clothes but they weren't on them.

They made love in the mud, along the creek, not far from where he planned to build their house. She snuggled warm against him. They were one with the earth and for a moment, he was who he wanted to be.

Russ forgot about Thomas and Cal. He forgot about how Ma said he should be gentle. He was too eager, too rough. This beast he didn't know how to contain erupted in him and she urged him on. Her body begged him to do things to her they'd never done until then.

Time stopped and started again while he rested, spent, with her against him.

Russ glanced at the water they never made it to and at their entwined bodies. Blood smeared on her leg and his stomach. Not much, but in moments like that, any amount of blood freaks a guy out. "Dang, did I hurt you?"

"I'm fine, that was..." She beamed. "Fun."

Fun? Wow. Yeah. That was the definition of fun and thinking about it got him excited enough to leap up.

"We'll clean up in the creek." He carried her into the water with him but she didn't splash around as she usually did, she rubbed against him, teasing. He was hot despite the cold water. "Isabelle?"

She nodded, dancing around him in the water.

He couldn't move a muscle. "May we do that again?"

"We better."

~~

Later that afternoon they snuggled in the haystack, dressed. She said to him, "It's my birthday tomorrow."

"I wanted to get you a dog, but I never found one. So, well, sorry."

"I got what I wanted." She fell asleep against him and Russ was so tired he slept with her, only to wake to a growling dog. He shot up and scanned the fields for Kit because this was her black monster.

"Oh my gosh, he's beautiful." Isabelle jumped up and dived for Fangs. "Thank you." She glanced at Russ with the biggest grin.

Fangs loved her. He licked her and drooled all over her like she was his sweetheart.

"He's not yours. That's Fangs. He belongs to Kit. I told you she'd come."

Her eyes swept the prairies for Kit. "Where is she?" Her words were snappy, unlike her. "Do you see her?"

Russ scanned the area, but she wasn't here. "Maybe she brought you this dog as a thank you because I stitched her?" Where the heck was she? Russ wanted her to meet Isabelle.

Isabelle ran off with Fangs and Russ watched her play with him. Not sure what was happening but grateful just the same. She smiled and that's what mattered, always.

Those next days blurred. They fell together everywhere they could. The first unsafe day reality sank in. Sure, he had plenty of her to explore, but she never gave him the chance. When Russ sneaked into her room, he discovered she could get him hopping even with his pants on. She had one hell of an imagination, his girl. He sadly never explored her that night. He was too busy recovering from the shock of what she'd done to him. Russ didn't ask where she found her ideas 'cause if she said Ma he'd probably kill himself.

~~

One day in July, they arranged rocks in a square to outline their house. Silver watched from a distance, and Isabelle asked how soon they could move in. As if he hid a house in his back pocket he could pop out for them.

They had time, but when she asked questions like that, the

only time they had was now.

Russ waved to Silver but he crossed his arms, reminding him to get back to work. So he did.

Still, her question nagged at him all day until Russ asked Pa later that night while they read the old newspapers.

"So Pa, how old should I be before I ask her to marry me?"

He didn't even glance up. "Older."

"Regardless, I started our house." Russ pretended to read the paper.

Pa folded the flap of the paper and peered at him. "Didn't I tell you to keep your pants on?"

Russ pretended to read. "Sure ya did, but then Ma told her a bunch of stuff, and you're smart and all, but I like Ma's way better. So anyway, you gonna help me build a house or not? 'Cause we'll marry soon."

"Your mother!" He folded the paper in a wild fury, but then he sat staring at Russ and a small grin crept on his lips. "What did she say?"

Russ leaned in. "Let me put it this way. I need a house 'cause if she keeps giving Isabelle ideas, I'm not only gonna cave, I'll give you my pants to hold until I die."

"Yeah, them gals are nasty. We'll start tomorrow. If we work on the frame every chance we get, you could be in a house by the time you're twenty. Means you'd have time for college, to earn yourself a decent education."

Russ winced. "I ain't gonna make twenty, Pa."

"I want you in school." It wasn't an order, just him sharing what he wanted. Well, that's how Russ saw it because he never handled it well when others told him what to do.

"Nothing saying I won't go to school but she wants a house now. And she doesn't ask for much. I think I should at the very least do this for her."

"I'm sure Cal will help, and if I get her brothers in on building duty, we could have something decent put together by the time you come home from college for Christmas. You could move in next summer, I guess." He squinted, seeing Russ' life as he planned it out.

Russ let it go, because Pa offered to help him build a house.

Later that night, he sneaked out while Cal and Desire crept in. Sammy saw Cal climb in and rushed to crash with the girls. Poor boy. Russ wouldn't do that for Cal.

Desire slipped off, probably to find something to eat since she was always hungry. Russ was left alone with Cal towering over him. Russ' foot was half out the window when Cal stopped him. "What's with you and that weird gal anyway?"

Russ smoked him one, but Cal watched his puny fist hit him as if a fly annoyed him.

"I always imagined you'd attend college and be one of them professors or something."

"Nothing saying I can't do that. Piss off."

"A man doesn't leave his wife to go to school. If you have a wife and house, moron, you can't be at a college three hours away. You need to make a choice."

Russ glared at him. Why couldn't he have both?

"Pa says you're talking like a man all of a sudden. If we're building you a house, I want to live there, too. Not in a room in the back. I want to actually live there with my family but you can't tell anyone we live there, not even Isabelle."

Isabelle wasn't stupid and she'd figure things out on her own, so Russ nodded.

That's how his house became Cal's, even if they always called the place Russ' house.

–EIGHTEEN–

It wasn't long after, Isabelle and Russ cuddled outside by the haystack. Her brothers weren't home and they would have the place to themselves once her pa fell asleep.

Russ told her what Pa said about their house as he pulled her hand out of his pants. Man, ending things was harder than pulling any trigger. "Behave for a minute, I'm thinking."

She snuggled against his chest. "Yes, it's not a good week."

They were silent for a long while.

"I have to quit school," she said. "I can't go back this fall."

He'd been avoiding this conversation.

Really, he didn't expect her to go back last year so this wasn't a surprise, but the disappointment in her voice was.

"Why?" Russ played in her hair lightly, enjoying the stars overhead, debating if he could sneak under her blouse and end the touching. Sometimes he was weak when she was around, and this moment was one of them weak moments so he stuck to her hair.

"It won't be the same without you," she said.

"I never said I was leaving."

"Papa tells me you'll leave for college and I can't go."

Russ swallowed the lump that formed in his throat. He'd put off thinking about this because he wasn't ready to leave. Really, all he ever wanted was a simple life, but something always got in the way of that. "Pa says college is a possibility. He's said that for four years. This is my last chance to go. So he says. The college is by Moose Jaw. I've been waiting, because...well...if you could get in Normal School, we could see each other often enough."

"I don't want to be a teacher. I want to be the mother of

your children. I want you to go to college, but I want to be where you are so we'll be together," she said.

They stayed silent again. Really, that's what he wanted, too.

"Girls can't go," Russ finally said. "I mean, they just can't. It's a French college, too. When he talks about all the things I could do there and learn, I want to go. It would be great, but..." The thought of leaving her, the farm, and his friends... "I'll be back and all smarter in a couple years."

She didn't ask him to stay. Francis was still at home and they got along fine, yet since her ma died, a fear lived in her that she'd never be free of the house. Made him think of Ma and her eighteen then some family she had to raise after her ma died. Not that Isabelle's family was that big, and her brothers were older, but she was the only gal in a house of tall gangly freaks.

Still, he had a choice to make. Since she was for him going to college, he leaned that way. It felt right. Problem was that leaving Isabelle felt wrong and he wasn't even sure he could.

Russ ran a hand along her arm to comfort her but she winced. "What's wrong?" he demanded, sitting her up so he could get a good look. She'd come to him bruised up before, said her mama had hit her 'cause she didn't take the cake out of the oven on time, and dirt like that. Of course, they took that from the woman of the house. Pa said you respected the woman of the house or you cooked your own meals and sewed your own buttons in a hole you dug yourself, and on top of that, you'd get a whopping from him until you got smarter.

Now that her ma was gone, no one in the house should be as much as questioning Isabelle. She was the woman of the house. Russ wasn't tolerating that, even if he didn't live with her.

"I hurt my arm against the pigpen, is all."

He studied the bruise again. It was possible that she got the mark from the pigpen. "What were you doing there? Did someone push you into the sides?" Rage blackened him.

"I'm feeding the pigs this week for my brothers. When I told Francis about Kit, he went to find her. Thomas figured he might need a hand if she hunted not-good people so he went, too."

Now they dug around for trouble. Why hadn't Cal gone with them?

Russ studied her arm under the stars. "That means only your pa is home? Did he do this?"

"I slipped when I ran away from him. He was mad at me and..." she checked the bruise. "It was my fault."

"Why would your pa be mad at you? 'Cause you asked him about Normal School? Was your fight about me?"

"I don't like repeating myself." She wouldn't either.

Russ thought back to their conversation. He wanted her to go to Normal School but this wasn't what she wanted. *I want to be a mother.* Doom washed over him, because he trusted her when she said such and such a day was safe, but really, he wasn't keeping track. Isabelle wasn't the lying type, but she knew damn well that if she got pregnant, he wouldn't go to college.

He checked the bruise.

Had she told old Skinny that they were messing around? Russ didn't see him taking the news well. Isabelle was old enough to be a mother if she wanted, but what did he want? By caving, he agreed they were ready.

He grabbed the last cookie.

She was pretty clear what days weren't safe, and sometimes she attacked him anyway after telling him... It'd be his fault if she was pregnant, and really, did he care? He wanted to have a bunch of babies with her. He lay back dreamily with cookie crumbs on his shirt.

He couldn't see himself leaving her so he decided he'd marry her for sure. Hell with college. He wouldn't make a great father like Pa, or be some fearless protector like Cal, but he could love her and respect her as she damn well deserved.

"I'll talk to the priest tomorrow about marrying us. See what he says 'cause Pa didn't give me a straight answer. I don't like you in that house anymore."

She never once told him living there was hell, but she nodded and said, "If we married, could I keep going to school? Regular school in Eau Claire?"

Like him, she needed to know where she stood before she made a decision. He could have said no or yes, his answer wouldn't have changed her mind about marrying him, it would only make it clear what her place was. So he answered honestly. "I ain't the boss of you. I don't see why we can't go to school and have our own place. Hell, you're a woman running an entire farm, and you still come to school with me at least three days a week." He shook his head. "I don't deserve a gal like you, but if you'll have me, I'll marry you tonight."

"Let me know how long I have to wait, 'cause tonight feels like forever."

Funny how waiting when you're seventeen is worse than eating a cold meal. He was sure they didn't have any kind of time to wait and so he talked to the priest the next day while at his Latin lesson with Miss Penelope sitting beside him, not saying anything. Cal didn't come this time. He took the summer off for hunting.

This priest had shot a man while protecting his church not that long ago. Russ figured this wouldn't be an issue, but he sure had questions. "Does your Pa know you're talking marriage?"

"A man doesn't have to ask his pa for permission."

"I see. And why can't you wait?"

"What would I be waiting for? I'm gonna marry her."

He could have pointed out that Russ wasn't a man, but he studied him and maybe he saw a man in front of him.

"Aren't you going to college? Your pa told me you were."

"What Pa wants and what I want aren't the same. He can go to college if he's so horny for it."

The priest sighed at Russ' choice of words and he regretted picking horny when Cracker Jack snickered.

"She pregnant?"

"Heck no. We ain't married. I ain't some fool." Russ might have been lying to a priest, 'cause for all he knew, she could be pregnant. He had no idea anymore what days were safe or not and when or where his pants were off. He was a lost cause when it came to her, surviving the cave-ins. All he saw in his mind were her panicked brown eyes asking him how long they had to wait as if two minutes were too long.

"Who will cook for Monsieur Dubois if she's off cooking for you?"

Leave it to a priest to reason with something so stupid.

Russ didn't much care, but he understood what he implied. Monsieur Dubois wouldn't let him waltz off with his daughter. So the plan was settled. He had to talk to her old man, not pa, not the priest. Made sense but that sounded like the last thing he wanted to do.

Father didn't have a great deal to say other than that.

"I'll be back," Russ said, determined to make this simple.

Miss Penelope walked beside him on their way back to the farm. *"He's not really teaching you Latin."*

"What?"

"That wasn't Latin. Sounded like gibberish to me."

Russ frowned. He wasn't a big fan of Miss Penelope, but what if she was right? He needed to talk to Hoolie, see what the heck he spoke. But first things first.

~~

Russ was alone when he found Skinny chopping wood out by his place. The pile of timber sheltered them from the rest of the world.

"We have a problem, Monsieur Dubois," he said, in the most grownup voice he could muster.

"Oh we do, do we?"

Russ took a real risk approaching him this way, yet he did because an axe to the head sounded like a better way to die than being choked to death.

"'Cause way I see things, I'm the one with the problem. Yup. You're the bloody problem. I saw you sneaking out of my house this morning. I should line your pecker up on this block and chop it off."

Russ ignored the remark, because he hadn't considered him using the axe on other body parts and he'd grown kinda fond of that one.

"You need a cook and asked her to quit school when she doesn't want to."

"That what she tell you?" Bam! He smashed another log to bits and Russ handed him a new one to vent on. Then Russ picked up the old axe and broke up a few logs with him. So they looked like equals and not like Russ begging him to see things his way.

"She doesn't need to tell me. I have a brain. You need help around here and asked her to quit school. You didn't like the fact that she don't want to quit so you tossed her into the pigpen." His words slipped when Skinny dropped the axe and stepped toward him, yet Russ pretended he wasn't about to be smashed like a bug. "I don't like you treating her that way. She's the woman of this house and demands your respect." Russ pulled up the axe and brought it down. He sighed when the piece didn't break. "She should finish school, and maybe, just maybe if you didn't give her so much bloody work to do she could do better in school and could go to Normal School while I head for college." Russ swung again, putting his muscles into each swing and much to his relief, the log split.

"My dear boy, kiss your dreams of college good-bye. For a bright lad, you're about the stupidest thing walking these prairies." He crossed his arms and glared at Russ, but he was the first one who knew Russ wasn't going to college and for some reason, he felt like they were on the same side—apart from Skinny looking like he wanted to chop off all his body parts.

Russ slammed the axe down. "You tossing her into the pen ends today." He didn't say it like a threat, 'cause Russ liked to tell things how they were. Things were easier if everyone understood. The words poured out of him and he wondered if Pa was dumb enough to talk to Grandpapa while standing near the axes.

Skinny rubbed his lips and if Russ wasn't mistaken, he tried damn hard not to smile.

"I won't leave her with you if you plan to treat her that way. So you see my problem? 'Cause everyone keeps telling me what they want, but a man who slits a throat for his gal, thinks for himself. I'm here to tell you the new rules around here because I won't have anyone hurting her."

"I know what you did for her and I appreciate your dedication. Any other fool would have been out on his ass at *Monsieur Dubois*. I keep you around because I respect your pa, and I'd started to respect you."

"I'm learning how to build a house. I ride and I bought land. We'll be fine."

"I doubt that."

"Then I'll move in here and help you instead of Pa. I'll prove that I belong with her to you." Russ was calm, but his biggest flaw was that he didn't know when to shut up. He had a dozen solutions figured out and prepared to share them until one got him what he wanted. Isabelle would have probably shut him up a moment ago, so he could have avoided Skinny picking him up by the scruff of his neck and hauling him to the gate like a stray cat he didn't appreciate hanging around his good girl.

"Really? You tell your pa this brilliant plan?" He dropped Russ like a sack of potatoes and rubbed his bare foot in the dust as if he might charge. "What makes you so sure I'll allow any of this? That he'll allow any of this? Because you forget, young man, we think for ourselves, too. You think you're special because you slit a man's throat to protect her? You can't even imagine what I've done for her."

Russ stared at him for a long time while he picked the right words, but he couldn't say any of them.

Skinny softened and leaned on the fence to glare toward town. "All these years she begged me to let her go to school. I asked myself what the heck does she need school for? She should have quit years ago when the witch Penelope wouldn't give her the grades, yet anyone who wants to go that badly, well it has to be a good thing. Then she tells me this week her wanting to go has nothing to do with learning. She's hot and heavy for you, not school and she went because she wants to prove to you that she can finish." His jaw clenched. "I told your pa I won't let her go to school without you looking out for her, but he says he can't justify you going any longer. You have to get to college. So if you're done, so is she. She's old enough, doesn't matter if she didn't make the grades."

"This what you told her? That she was too stupid to finish properly?" Russ clenched his fists.

"She thinks if she goes, you'll stay, and that's all she wants. She'll do whatever it takes to get you to stay. 'Whatever it takes', her exact words. So best make up your mind and stick to your decision because she'll be carrying your baby in no time. You hear me, boy? Am I speaking clear enough for that stubborn brain of yours?"

Oh. The anger deflated. He was right. That's exactly how Isabelle thought. Still, Russ said, "She wanted to prove Miss Penelope wrong. She's smart you know. You don't give her a chance to prove what she knows."

"This that important to you?"

"What do I care if she goes to school? Miss Penelope was so stupid we weren't learning anything useful anyway. I know more by going to the city with Pa than she could ever teach."

"Then why did you go? You should be in college."

"'Cause I couldn't leave Isabelle."

Skinny glanced his way, confused. "So if you're not leaving for college, then why come annoy me? Just walk her to school and give her one more year to be innocent. I don't like her talking about being a mother at her age."

"I want to see her happy."

"All I want, too. And just so you know, I didn't toss her in the pen. That girl is my world." Just like that, they were on the same page in the same book and their relationship was good after that. Skinny told him she could stay in school until she was done, but meant Russ had to walk her there and pick her up every day. Russ had to chop the wood around his place until he was strong enough to break a log in one swing. Then he could marry her. Apparently, he thought being a man took muscles and not brains, but a smart guy knows when to let things go, so even though they were rules Russ didn't like, he agreed.

~~

Russ read in the haystack later that day when Isabelle stopped by with cookies.

"He says I get to stay in school and you aren't leaving. Is that true?"

Russ nodded, eating a cookie. Damn, they were probably the best cookies in the world. He would never get sick of them.

"He says you can stay the night if you stay in the guest room. He said a lot of nice things and even asked me to read him a story." Isabelle was so excited. "He said he'd help me study so I could make all my grades this year."

"Glad he came to his senses," Russ said, snagging the last cookie, he politely offered it to Isabelle but she never ate any so he wasn't worried about her wanting a bite. When she shook her head, he bit into it.

"He told me that we couldn't get married until next fall. When we're eighteen."

It actually sounded real and made more sense than waiting until Russ grew muscles, 'cause that might not happen.

Her eyes were alive with energy that made him proud. Russ fished in his pocket for the ring. "Here. It's for you." He didn't tell her how he ended up with the wedding band. Pa pulled the ring off her mother before he buried her and told Russ to give it to Monsieur Dubois, but Russ figured Isabelle's ma's ring belonged to her so he held on to it for her. She slipped the band in her apron without glancing at it.

"I want you to wear the ring, as a promise that no matter what we'll be together."

She studied him for a long time and he thought she might ignore him. "You're leaving?"

Dizzy, he lay back. "No. I have a house to build and I have to prove to your pa that I'm worthy of you."

She slipped the ring out of her apron and handed it back as she had the book years ago, as if such a thing might get them in serious trouble. "You are so smart, you should be in college. Forget about me and go."

He slipped the band on her finger, pulling her beside him so they could cuddle properly. "I'm exactly where I want to be." Russ saw their future like a brilliant story about to unfold.

She finally checked out her new ring, studying the earth symbols edged into the gold. "This is Mama's." Her eyes gave away her happiness. In them, Russ saw his entire future. They were gonna be happy. Yes, they were.

-Nineteen-

September 1928—

In the early fall, when Russ walked Isabelle to school, he figured he might as well help the new teacher, Miss Huney. She took him up on his offer without batting an eye. "Russ will bring you all on an adventure today," she promised the class and let him go off with them so she could have time to bring Isabelle's teaching up to snuff. She had hard problems for Isabelle to solve while he taught her students real things they'd need to know; like how to shoot an arrow, how to find good drinking water, how to dig a well, and he planned to even show them how to build a canoe.

Much to his amusement, Miss Huney hid French books in every desk, and lied to the superintendent, saying everyone excelled at their English studies. They didn't but they knew how to read.

On the second day of his adventure teachings, Miss Huney asked if Russ could add. He was prepared to leave with Isabelle but paused in the doorway. "I add just fine, thank you very much." Maybe she needed to learn? He stayed back and waited, in case.

"I found it curious that none of the students knew what a number looked like."

"A number?" Russ studied Miss Huney. She was twenty and Thomas was taken with her, which pleased Russ because he was busy, and not always glaring at Russ. "I can't say I know what one looks like myself."

She placed the books in a pile and leaned against her desk, her shawl draped over her shoulders. "Will you have good crops this year?"

He scratched his head, no idea what she was about to show him. "The crops suck, but we'll be fine."

"How do you know this?"

"Pa says so."

"Wouldn't it be nice if you could calculate that on your own?" She smirked.

He stepped in, intrigued. "Yeah."

"Do you have a loan to pay?"

"Pa says I can pay my debt back if I don't pay him for the expenses he put out." He frowned, not sure how that made sense. Wouldn't Pa be out the money?

"That means we'll be fine." Isabelle got ready to leave but Russ wasn't ready yet. Miss Huney knew something important and he wanted to know what.

"Can you show me how paying a loan works?"

Miss Huney squinted at him as if she might squeak into his brain and see the mess. She went to the chalkboard and wrote squiggles down. He'd seen them before. "These are numbers and I've arranged them in a problem. What is the answer?" They were linked with weird symbols like crosses and lines.

Russ studied her problem hard, glanced at Isabelle for help, then just about said sixteen but then he answered truthfully, "Gibberish." Still, sixteen felt right, but he didn't want Miss Huney to think he was a fool after she trusted him with her students.

"How did you pass your tests if you don't know this?"

"Dunno. Write those squiggles out in French. No one knows what that crap means but you."

She wrote TEN PLUS SIX EQUALS WHAT.

"Sixteen," Russ answered 'cause everyone knew ten plus six was sixteen.

She squiggled under the problem: 10+6=16. "That's the same thing. Think about these numbers like another language. Once you know these numbers and how they work together, I can show you how your loan works and how even bad crops will pay the debt down and allow you to buy supplies for next year."

Russ stared at Isabelle. Damn. Numbers. Why hadn't Old Cracker Jack ever taught them this? "She showing you this stuff?"

Isabelle nodded. "It's an adding language but I can use them in my recipes, too."

Russ sat at the desk and after all the kids were gone. He stayed late with Isabelle once a week to learn how to use numbers instead of writing out the entire word and memorizing the answer. Numbers actually made sense. And he could do a hell of a lot more than add with them. Numbers worked so well, he could see right out that Pa helped him pay for his crops and took nothing for that help, and that wasn't gonna fly.

~~

A few weeks later, Russ stacked stokes in the field alone because Cal hadn't come home all summer.

Russ explained numbers to Silver and how they added, subtracted, and multiplied, while he worked. Dust blew down the road, headed to town, by Dubois Farm, throwing off his count. He thought about following the wagon, to see where it headed so fast, but he had a dirt load of work to do in his field if he planned to prove to Pa that he was a man. Plus, a ghost is hard to ditch and curiosity isn't an excuse Silver goes for. He took learning seriously and knelt, writing his numbers in the dirt as if his afterlife depended on them. When he made it to ten he lay on his back to watch the clouds while Russ corrected them.

"Your four is upside down. It's not a chair, it's a man reaching to the heavens for salvation."

Silver groaned, wiped them out, and restarted.

Russ smirked, watching him, finding it hard to believe this guy was his grandpa, considering he looked about thirty.

"How long have you been dead?" Russ had wanted to ask him that since forever.

The hardness in his jaw vanished and Silver relaxed. He was almost real. *"Not dead, tied to that moron. The world has gotten so noisy I barely hear the earth talk."* He sighed. *"Russ, I saw my boy grow into a man and now I get to see my grandson do so. It's a blessing."* He bowed his head. *"I also saw my wife, sister, and best friends move on without me, and so it is a curse."*

The wind warmed Russ. He had his shirt off to enjoy the heat. Doing all the work sucked and Isabelle hadn't been by with water. "What does the earth say when it talks to you?" Russ asked, building another pile for the thresher.

Silver invited him to sit by him. "*Dig your fingers in the soil and listen.*"

It came off a challenge and Russ wasn't one for letting a challenge go unmet. He needed a break anyway. He touched the ground over his numbers. The topsoil was dry, but deeper he found a cool and moist spot. He dug around some roots, not sure what Silver expected him to feel.

"As fun as it is to dig with you, I should get back to work."

"*Just wait for it.*" Silver lay back.

Russ knelt with his hands in the soil, wondering where everyone got off to. He hadn't seen Isabelle's brothers in weeks. Which was why he was bitter while tossing his earnings into stokes. He had so much work to do and these arseholes were off on their own adventures while he did all the work. Didn't they know harvest season was important and hard work? Didn't they bloody care? Was he the only grownup around here?

Russ watched for Isabelle, for any action from her place. He didn't have time to walk her to school today, so she was home and promised to bring him lunch. His stomach grumbled. She usually brought him water every couple of hours, too. She didn't show though, which happened sometimes. She had mats to beat and dirt crept up that she forgot about. Once a horse foaled and she stayed to help 'cause that happens. Well, not at this time of year. Russ wondered what could be keeping her this time.

Silver ordered, "*Stop thinking for a minute and breathe.*"

Russ cleared his head and focused on his breath. An overwhelming fear brushed into him. He yanked his hands out of the soil, picked up straw, and piled it.

"*So? Did you hear it?*"

Russ rubbed the flying ants off the back of his neck with his new blue hanky—a gift from Isabelle. "I felt fear. If that's all you wanted to show me, why don't you piss off?"

Silver chuckled. "*Oh boy, you are a stubborn one. I see why Bernoit hesitates to teach you the truth. Come with me,*" *you taught me, now I teach you."*

Silver vanished into the earth. Funny guy. Russ shook his head when Silver reappeared.

"Oh yeah, forgot you have to take the long way around. Go in under the haystack."

"I don't have time for messing around underground."

"If you want to be a man and defend this land, you'd better learn to listen to what Mother says. I'm not giving you an option, come on."

Russ did want to be a man, so he made his way into the tunnels. He hadn't slipped in them since the tornado but they hadn't changed at all. The lantern hung by the entrance and Russ lit it, following Silver in silence.

They arrived in an empty room and Silver waited, arms crossed.

Russ glanced around.

"And?" Russ asked.

"We're starting easy. Do you see them?"

Russ saw earth walls. He ran his hand over them. Silver sat in the middle of the room cross-legged so Russ sat across from him, since he'd seen Cal and Pa do this many times when Pa taught Cal something. Russ placed the lantern beside them. It occurred to him that Pa raised his oldest sons differently even though they were close in age. Pa was always torn between two worlds, and Russ belonged to the above-ground one, Cal this hidden one. Now Grandpa planned to give him a crash course on something Russ wasn't sure he wanted to learn.

The humid air left a film of musty dust in his mouth. He moved his tongue around to get a proper taste, because there was something special about tasting the earth that fed you. *Another breath.* This one had a sweet smell and Russ closed his eyes. This was the perfect place to think.

Yet, he didn't have a thought.

The silence settled on them peacefully.

Something touched his back. Russ jumped, ready to kick some ass but no one appeared, not even Silver. He returned to the ground and sat perfectly still because even if he saw nothing, someone haunted this chamber.

On his knees, Russ ran his fingers through the soil, finding the dirt warmer than soil should be. Something brushed against his cheek. Startled, he shot up, but the lantern blew out and Russ was too shocked to feel around.

The room exploded with spirits.

Dozens of 'em.

They had no faces, only screaming sheet-like souls that swept into the earth then ran into each other and howled some more.

They flung themselves toward him. Russ held up his wrist to protect himself, and the spectres were repelled as if his tattoo were a shield.

He backed out of the room slowly and weaseled through the tunnels, lost. Russ wasn't sure how to get out, but if Cal could find his way around down here, so could he. He ran his hands over the walls and closed his eyes. The screaming was contained to certain spots. Russ followed the walls. When he found a spot without the pain, he moved toward it. Walking with his eyes closed until he stumbled in the mud by the creek with no clue how he escaped those tunnels but happy to be free of them and their ghosts.

He rushed back to the haystack.

Silver waited for him in the sunlight, sitting on the haystack, his bare feet dangling. *"By the looks of ya, you saw them."* His smile made him shimmer brighter.

"What were those things?"

"Cursed souls."

"Will I end up like that?"

"I want you to end that. Stop them from returning to the ground and help them move on."

"Well, if you started this curse, it can be ended. We need to share everything. What is the white horse you have in your soul? How did you do that? Did you kill a horse?"

Silver peered off at the prairies. *"I saw her. She stood there, this beautiful, sad woman. When I approached, she shifted into a horse and charged for me. I relive her pain daily. She chose me. I have no idea why. She suffers because a greedy man exchanged her happiness for his own."*

Russ bowed his head. "Kinda like what happened to Miss Penelope. Stupid Kaplain wasn't very nice to her."

"Oh? You're starting to like your shadow, are you?"

Russ ignored him. "Why don't those spirits have a face? You have a face."

"*The first soul I cursed did. His name was Edgar.*"

"Why didn't they leech onto me?"

"*Every year on the last day of October the earth weakens and the cursed find a new host.*"

Russ squinted. "What's so special about that day?"

Silver shrugged. "*It's the day Mother allows them a second chance to live again. The cursed souls are free to pick a warrior on Cursed Land. Only, well…it's not only warriors walking these lands anymore. Over the years, the cursed have chosen settlers and driven them mad. When they die, they drag them down with them instead of moving on. They lose their identity and become faceless. This is why I believe they enjoy hiding under sheets.*"

Russ shivered. That would be hell. "So I can move on, or Miss Penelope can drag me down there, but it's my choice, right?"

"*I know only what I see. Those cursed by those spectres like to be covered when they come to Cursed Lands. They suck their new hosts down with them when the host dies. A shadow like you have is different. She is not evil, she's curious. I spoke at length with Hoolie about what might have happened. He thinks maybe she's a spirit with unfinished business.*"

"You sound upset by this, Silver, but when Monsieur Bellecoeur passes on, will you let him move on or will he be bound to the earth with you?"

Silver considered this. "*I imagine he'll be bound to me, but I am Cîpay, not some lost soul.*"

"Still, sounds like his plight sucks." Russ sat on the haystack beside him. "You see my soul?"

"*I have the Sight. A rare gift that allows me to see your soul. The boy I see before me is not the man your soul wishes to be. You fight your destiny and this has changed the course of many lives.*"

"What do you see in Isabelle's soul?"

"*The witch?*" Silver studied him.

"Take that back." Russ punched him but his fist went through him, even if he looked solid.

"*I will not tell you what you already know.*" He walked toward the setting sun before Russ could ask what the heck that meant. Much to his surprise, he passed Cal who appeared by the creek. They chatted and Cal bowed to him.

"Where you been?" Russ hollered at Cal, excited to see him. He ran toward his brother, not able to contain his grin. But like a scene from his worst bloody nightmare, Cal raised his arrow and yelled for Russ to duck.

Duck?

-Twenty-

When Cal shot his arrow, Russ dropped, peeking over his shoulder to see what happened. To his horror, a wagon drove down the road in broad daylight with men wearing sheets.

What if they'd left Dubois'? Isabelle was home alone. Russ leapt to his feet and headed toward her place. A bullet broke up the air around him as it whipped by. He ran, because the wagon moved fast and taking a shot at him wasn't easy if he moved faster. Cal's arrows flung one of them off the cart, then another.

Then much to his dismay, Cal shot toward the bloody horses. They reared up and the wagon smacked into them causing a real mess. Russ left Cal to that hell 'cause he had to make sure Isabelle was all right. Which wasn't a brotherly thing to do, but knowing his brother was Cal, he made the right choice. He'd seen him survive worse.

Russ told himself that Isabelle knew how to hide and Fangs would tear apart anyone who went near her, but sometimes dread makes a guy run like his bloody pants are missing and Thomas is looking to make his pecker-kicking a reality.

Russ glanced down the road as he crossed it, 'cause even though he trusted Cal to take care of himself, he was worried about him. In broad daylight, Cal and a couple of his friends hauled the men off the wagon and dragged them to the creek. Then Cal and his crew vanished faster than Russ could run like a mad fool across the road and down Isabelle's lane and through her gate.

He ran smack into Pa. "What are you doing here? Get."

"Where is Isabelle?" Russ demanded.

"I thought she was with you. Dammit." His voice shook with panic. "She's not here."

Cal would have told him if she was in the wagon. The dog wasn't around the yard either.

Russ shoved past Pa. He had to see everything they did to her place—every last detail. He wanted to look away, but he couldn't. He stared, intently. Anything he saw would be bad, but he couldn't not see this.

Monsieur Dubois was hanging lifeless. A man Russ respected, feared, and told he wanted to marry his daughter while he wielded an axe, hanged from the stoop by the neck. Things were thrown around him. His gun was there, but he didn't get a shot off or Russ would have heard. Why for the love of these prairies didn't he get even one shot off? Russ had a decent imagination, but he couldn't phantom a guess. This was Isabelle's pa. The only parent she had left.

A message singed on the lawn. Pa put the smoldering fire out before anyone saw.

Pa mumbled. Russ saw more. This visit wasn't by some cursed freaks storming in and going crazy. Silver might be right, but Russ wouldn't ignore what he saw. This was real, and real men did this. He'd figure out why later.

The only question that mattered in the moment was, "Where is Isabelle?" He didn't want her to see her pa and Russ was prepared to cut him down himself, but first he had to find her.

"Where is she?" he demanded from Pa as if he knew and wasn't telling.

"I'll help you search. Let me cut him down first."

Russ should have helped Pa cut his best friend down, but he wasn't thinking straight.

She hadn't left her farm and headed his way or he'd have seen her. Russ started in the house and searched every hiding spot, calling out her name. "Isabelle, it's me. Please make a sound. I have to find you."

The dog scratches on the door to her room gave Russ chills right down his legs. He wiped the blood off the doorknob and went in.

The open window let in a cool wind that danced her curtains around. She'd scrambled over the bed, smearing blood on the sheets. Not hers, he promised himself, even if he had no clue.

Feathers from the pillow were everywhere. The blanket he gave her was slashed.

They'd spent too much time in her room. He didn't like this. They'd ripped the only picture of her ma. Russ placed the frame face down. The woven basket where she collected the things she stole had spilt. He stared numbly at the things that were important to her. They didn't make sense to anyone but her. These things strewn across the floor made him want to puke. He saw the nickel he'd given her, a hawk feather they'd found together, and the book they were reading. His life was scattered on the floor.

On the wall, they'd written in blood, "Die witch". He rubbed at the mess with his bare hands, so she wouldn't see what they'd written, smearing the blood around.

She didn't own much, but everything she loved was ruined. Why would they do this to her? What had Isabelle ever done to anyone? She was the type who helped people who hurt her.

Russ followed the blood out the window. A piece of her sleeve blew in the grass behind the house. He told himself that if she were dead, she'd be there, 'cause these arseholes wanted to make a scene. He promised himself he'd find her and she'd be fine.

When he found her knickers by the barn with blood on them, he wasn't feeling the promise. The dirt had tracks that proved she'd struggled, fought.

Russ threw up. Intense fear rang loud around him as he rested his head against the side of the barn and hurled his cookies until nothing was left.

He was sick from searching, but he looked harder.

He found Thomas in the barn. Dead. And like with Monsieur Dubois, they'd made a statement. They'd nailed him to the door of the barn his arms out like on a cross. Someone who couldn't spell wrote letters across his chest in white paint. It said WHICH.

Silver could say cursed fools did this. Cal could go on about how drugs were involved. But this was hate. What would drive someone to hate another so deeply that they would disgrace him in death?

Russ called for Pa and he helped get him down and wash

the paint off. Russ didn't want anyone else to see this. Knowing evil existed this profound would make it hard for him to sleep at night.

Thomas was too big for them to carry, but they rested him by the barn and Pa signalled to Cal to look after him.

They didn't exchange thoughts, but Russ knew Pa understood, too. This wasn't a few men scaring them off the land or hoping to steal drugs. These guys were angry and only blood would do.

Russ combed the barn. He told Pa, "If Thomas had headed out here, he'd planned to protect Isabelle."

"Or the Healing Chamber," Pa offered. "You see the warnings they're writing? They think Dubois cursed them. They've brought Eastern beliefs of witchcraft to the prairies. Russ, these people are scared. Acting out of fear."

Russ thought about what Pa said while he rifled through every place they'd ever hid. He called for her dog. Fangs would know where she was. Yet he was missing. "How do I get in the Healing Chamber? Maybe she's there?"

"She's not," Cal said, approaching. His hair blew around in the wind and his face smeared with blood as if he'd been through a war himself. Russ told him they weren't giving up until she was found.

Cal made signals to the empty field and vanished in his way.

–Twenty-One–

They searched late into the evening for Isabelle and came up empty. Darkness fell heavy on the fields, but Russ wanted to search them anyway. Every minute counted.

It didn't make sense. If she was in danger, she knew where he worked. Why hadn't she run to him? Cal didn't have anything useful to say. Pa looked like death was due any moment.

Ma sent the girls and Samuel to bed, but Samuel peeked around the corner. "Sammy? You know where she went?" Russ demanded from him, sure Sammy wouldn't disobey Ma unless he wanted to help. What if he knew something?

Sammy nodded and rushed to his room. Russ raced after him, but Pa grabbed his arm and pulled him back. "Let Cal talk to your brother. You need to sit and calm yourself."

"Calm myself? All those witch hunters in the wagon better be dead."

"What wagon?" Cal asked as he vanished around the corner. "I ain't seen any wagons."

Good. No. Not good. If what Silver said was true, now those spectres were back in that chamber, ready to join with someone else or they were all latched onto Cal and going to drive him mad. Argh. Russ threw his knife at the wall and the blade sank deep in the wood. Pa retrieved it before Ma saw and he slipped the knife in his pocket with a glare at Russ that said he better pull his shit together and fast.

"I want Isabelle back."

Cal bounded down the steps. "Samuel saw the dog chasing a man in a sheet through the field north of here."

"How?" Russ demanded.

"He climbed on the roof of the barn."

Ma wrung her hands in her apron. "He knows he's not allowed up there."

Cal spoke softly to her, "I promised he wouldn't get a smack since his observations might be helpful. But if I catch him up there again, I'll turn him in straight away."

Ma nodded, "Go, find that dear child."

Russ flipped his shotgun open, loaded it in the house even though Ma had strict rules about that, and he stormed out. Others followed but they didn't get far down the lane because Kika appeared with Fangs in his arms.

He didn't say a word. He wore suspenders, dressed like Russ, except he wore his hair in a braid that fell down to the middle of his back, which was how he wore his hair while hunting.

Russ studied the limp dog he held to see what had killed him. He pulled away with a new fear. "Cougar." He'd forgotten all about her and this reminder sent shivers down his back.

Pa ran for the horses and Russ started out on foot toward the cougar den. Dammit. What if Isabelle ran into the cougar?

Pa met up with Russ, gave him a horse to ride, and they raced toward The Cliffs, where they let the horses go so they could explore the area on foot.

When Russ faced one of the cougar cubs, it occurred to him that this probably wasn't the brightest idea. This was the biggest, baddest cat in the area. The one that had torn a mare to shreds. And they faced her cub in the dark.

"She had two cubs," Russ told Pa.

Pa used the lantern to peer around the corner, to the face of the cliff. "Looks like the den caved in, one was probably lost." The creek rushed below adding a chill to the night air.

The cougar was the hunter. They wouldn't see her until she pounced. She'd fight for this cub to the death.

The cub hissed out a low growl.

Her eyes sparkled in the dark night by a large rock. At her feet laid the body of a man, highlighted by the full moon.

"Betcha Fangs brought him down and the cougar killed him."

He was nothing but a mangled bloody mess. Pa held the

back of his hand to his face. "That was the banker from Moose Jaw. He gave you the loan for your land. What the hell is going on? Is everyone out to get us?"

Russ ignored his fit. He didn't trust anyone anymore yet if someone had told him the banker would end up in a sheet eaten by a cougar he'd have laughed his ass off. Seeing it now though, wasn't so funny.

Russ kept his gun on the cub, not sure why he hadn't shot the cat yet, but the moment it leapt, Russ pulled the trigger. So did Pa. Being young, this cub wouldn't do them much damage on its own but they shot out of fear.

"Isabelle, are you here?" They hadn't moved while they faced off with the cub. Really, Isabelle handled animals well, Russ promised himself, even though she wouldn't survive a cougar. Still, sometimes, if they had larger prey, they might let her run off. Russ told himself things like this. Yet where was the cougar tonight? She had food here.

Funny how hope gripped him even though he knew the situation was hopeless. He saw little things as huge possibilities. He hated that, 'cause then when he'd find her mangled, the loss would suck the life from him. Yet he couldn't see such a thing. He couldn't imagine her dead.

A small movement caught his attention by one of the maple trees. It could have been anything, even the cougar, but this hope drove him forward, and the small movement is where he rushed, almost tripping over the cub.

Pa had taken the path to the den and he hollered, "Mud is oozing out of the den and sliding to the creek. Weird but the creek is flowing hard. We haven't had a decent rain since the tornado back in June. What's going on? It's almost like a dam broke up creek."

"Isabelle?" Russ called.

He walked up to the first tree and waved the lantern around. Isabelle was knee deep in mud, standing perfectly still, staring at him with sheer horror on her face. "Don't move," she whispered. "It's sucking me in every time I move."

Russ lifted the lantern around in case the cougar lurked, but Isabelle pointed to the mud at her feet.

Needing to get a closer look, Russ stepped toward her. The

ground moved under him, tumbling him back. He dropped the lantern and didn't bother reaching for the light. Isabelle screamed as a roaring sucked her down. Russ scrambled on the roots of the closest maple tree and blindly reached for her.

He caught her hand, the one with the ring and held her.

Where was the rest of her? The lantern vanished in the mud, drowning them in darkness.

"Holy dirts, Pa! It's a bloody sinkhole. Get us out of here."

Pa signalled the others with a shot. They had a drop off the cliff to one side, the trees and boulders were around them so he couldn't see anyone.

"Isabelle?"

She squeezed his hand.

Russ pulled her. The ground collapsed around him and the root dropped underneath him. "Pa, get a rope, the ground moved, and I am not letting her go."

"I don't have a rope. Get the hell out of there."

"She's alive. I'm not leaving her." Russ couldn't see her face but she gripped his hand with both her hands. He slipped his feet around the root. The mud slopped around her arm. Any movement on his part made the root sink lower. "It's like a giant mud bog's sucking us down. Pa?"

"Get her face next to yours. I'm coming." Pa's voice came from the other side, under another of the maple trees. He held a lantern and stared Russ square in the eyes. His voice came off soothing, as if he knew they wouldn't survive this. "Imagine the earth is alive. She's stronger than you. She feeds you. She knows all you know and all you want."

"So she's like Ma?"

"Sure like Ma. Can you fight Ma?"

"No. It's best to go along with her."

"Will she hurt you?"

"No." The panic vanished. Russ knew how to get what he wanted from Ma.

"The earth is up to something, and we'll slowly and respectfully get out of Her way." Pa lay like Russ on the root of the other tree. His hands slid around Isabelle's waist. The mud made a weird sucking sound as she moved against it. When the earth relaxed around them, they pulled. Her face was even with Russ'. Isabelle gasped rapidly, coughing. Pa shifted and held his arms under her armpits. Russ did the same with one hand and used the other to wipe her lips. He needed more light so he could see her.

"We gotcha," Pa said. "Don't struggle. Let us do the wiggling for you."

A low growl made them freeze.

Russ said, "Don't suppose you have the shotgun handy, eh Pa?"

His grip on her never changed, but when Russ glanced up, the cougar dug a paw in Pa's leg. Russ was never this close to a cougar in his life and for some reason, he wasn't afraid. He was mesmerized. She was beautiful. Monstrous. She moved her shoulders one at a time like a hero ready to kick his ass as she walked over Pa. He grunted from her weight.

The cougar slashed and Pa sucked in a deep breath but didn't let go. Could Russ watch his pa be eaten by a cougar? He couldn't let Isabelle go. Where was the gun? Pa had Russ' knife. These thoughts flashed through his mind and it felt like hours that they stayed frozen in the moment, but the moment lasted a second, a quick flash and an arrow caught in the cougar's throat as she prepared to attack. She fell and the tree Pa used for support wavered with the extra weight. He let Isabelle go as mud sucked him backward, taking the light.

"Roll this way," Cal yelled.

Russ had no clue where Pa had ended up. He shouted to Pa, "You alive? Say something." Of all the things Russ had faced in his life, his fear was never as deep as it was in this moment. "Pa?"

Pa's voice was muffled, but the comfort of hearing his pa relieved him just the same. "I'm fine. Happy to see Cal and his arrows. There's a ledge here. Someone pull me up."

Shadows moved where the tree had been.

"What the heck?" Cal assessed the situation. "Someone tell me why the tree slid over the edge. What is the ground saying? It's like an oozing mud hole. Desire, I need a rope. There are two on my horse, but get me more. I don't trust these trees. Strap a line to the horse and pass the rope here. You with me, Russ?"

"Get us out of here."

Lanterns were suddenly on them.

"I'm working on it. The tree you're on… Has anything moved?"

"Yes." Russ saw Isabelle. From the ledge, a crack had formed and she was wedged between it, the ground oozing inward as the dirt slowly turned to mud, burying her alive.

"She's in mud up to her neck and the mud monster is eating her."

"There's no such thing, Russ. Calm yourself. You got an arm around her?" Cal asked.

"Yeah. I ain't letting her go. I don't care if this goes over the edge. I won't let go."

"Neither will I." Cal gripped his ankle and ran a rope around Russ. He tossed the line up the tree overhead. Another hit Russ' shoulder. "Tie that around her but not to you. I don't want any more weight on this ledge. If this thing goes we'll be buried in mud as it slides down the bank."

"Cal, for once in your goddamn life can't you say something hopeful?"

"Why say things when I can do them. Now tie."

The mud oozed cold around them, but Russ slipped closer to Isabelle and wrapped an arm around her, under her armpits. It meant the only thing free of mud was the bottom parts of his legs. Russ sank but his feet twisted around the root, and despite the things Cal did, he held his ankle. Worst part was that his feet itched. Probably fleas from the stupid cougar den under them.

"Can you feel your feet?" Russ asked her.

She shook her head, shivering. Her fingers dug into his arm. Russ held the root with his entire body.

"Mine are itchy," Russ told her as he wound a rope under her armpits. The mud pulled her heavy skirt, sucking her in deeper. He needed to get her out of her clothes. She owned two skirts. Both had buttons he knew exactly how to undo, but undoing them meant shoving his head in the crack and the mud was expanding.

"I'm sinking, Cal," Russ warned him. "The rope is around her but I can't tie a knot."

"Pass the line here," Pa ordered from limbo above him.

Russ tossed the end over his shoulder and gripped her better.

They pulled on the hoist. Isabelle screamed but hardly moved.

"I need more light," Pa demanded. Light shone around them in all directions.

Russ was sprawled out with his arms deep in the mud. The rope clung around her. Her arms wound around his, her face in line with his.

"We're in this together," Russ promised.

What had Cal said about a mudslide? Would they survive?

Isabelle struggled to breathe. She hadn't said a word but air went in. She was alive.

"I won't let you go, Isabelle," he promised her.

Pa talked and they listened carefully, Russ the most. "Russ, loosen the mud around her and get her out of her skirt or dress, her clothes weigh her down. Hold the rope, Isabelle. Hold tight. Cal, you get up on the branch overhead and pull Russ straight up. No matter how much Russ screams you haul him up."

That was a risk. If the tree went over so did Cal, yet he said, "Done." He'd assessed the situation as fast as Pa had and sped up the branch, ready before Russ was. Someone still held his ankle. Russ glanced over his shoulder. Desire gripped him. She had a rope around her and was elbow deep in the mud. *Shit.*

"Damn, Pa, what if I ain't strong enough to haul 'em up?" It sent shivers down Russ' entire body to hear Cal doubt himself.

"I know you are. Straight up."

Pa didn't say going down arms first against her skin would break up the mud sucking her in. He didn't tell Russ that he wouldn't be able to breathe or if Cal failed, they were dead. He didn't say Cal was heavy and his added weight to the tree might push them in deeper.

Pa didn't have to say any of that because what he'd said was that they stood a chance and Russ focused on the hope. He glanced up. Pa clung to the branch with Cal and they were stupid enough to tie the ropes holding Isabelle and him around their own waists. Damn. If Russ was lost, so were they. Even though the light was dim, the moon shone on them. Pa gripped the ropes. They were gonna pull. Russ nodded, ready.

Isabelle shook. Her frozen skin terrified him. Russ kissed her muddy lips. "I love you, Isabelle, and there ain't another soul on these prairies I'd do this for. Maybe sometimes, love keeps those we care about safe for a while longer." He plunged into the mud.

Now, it sounded like a great idea in his brain before this moment, but plunging head first in freezing mud that wanted to ooze him into hell, well, he realized the plan lacked brilliance. He slid his hands along her body, undoing the buttons and pushing her skirt outwards to give her room to move. He needed to breathe.

Stop thinking for a minute.

The panic stopped and he used his soul to breathe. The earth around him shifted. He became one with the movement. A snake slithering to free Isabelle.

She held tight to the rope around him. The rope around her was the last safety if he failed and they were sucked into the mud hole.

She slipped down a bit but his diving in loosened the mud around her for a moment. He jiggled her frozen legs. If he died, he vowed to haunt these prairies like Silver. They could watch clouds float by together.

The mud let her go to get a new grip, giving him the break they needed. Russ wrapped his arms around her waist wondering how long a guy could go without air because air didn't matter anymore. Maybe he was already dead.

Cal tugged at the rope around him with a force that broke a rib.

Russ screamed, sucking in mud and real air all at once. Isabelle was one with him and she came up, too.

Cal and Pa grunted so hard they didn't hear Russ cry out as the ropes ate through his skin. Of all the days not to wear a shirt. He buried his head against Isabelle, holding her by the waist.

They dangled by the rope over the hole. It gurgled and ate up her skirt and the lantern like a hungry mud monster.

The tree shifted and Cal and Pa jumped.

Russ landed on hard ground with Isabelle on top of him and probably more broken ribs making it harder to breathe.

Pa cried out and Antoine announced that Pa's leg was

broken. Many had gathered to help. Desire brought them a blanket. Ma had clothes for them. Where the heck had she come from? The rest blurred around him. Someone doing this or saying that.

Russ held Isabelle. "Are you alive?"

"I am," she said so simply as if they'd gone for a walk and a bit of rain spattered on them.

Russ washed her and cleaned himself up. Someone started a fire and it burned wild, yet she remained cold.

Ma told her to drink tea, healing tea. Russ had no idea such a thing existed but she drank eagerly. At one point, Russ counted the warriors because he'd never seen so many together. He lost count at thirty. For some reason that gave him a hopeful feeling inside.

He shivered. The cold mud caked on his skin. How long was she in the mud? The idea was enough to keep him awake forever.

Ma checked his ribs and wrapped cloths around him that made it easier to breathe.

"There are stories about these holes, but this was the first one I ever saw," Desire said as they warmed around the fire late into the night. "They say from these holes spirits arise to protect Sacred Land. All who disrespect Mother will be consumed by her energy. All suffering from pain will find peace in her embrace."

"Could be," Pa said. His eyes were glossy and he was too relaxed, even for Pa. He was strung up on something. Ma snuggled against him as if she belonged out here on the prairies in the dark by a cougar den. Pa was too comfortable for a guy who'd snapped his leg. Gerard the pharmacist was still setting it.

"What did you give Pa?" Russ demanded from the pharmacist.

Cal answered for him, "Let the Medicine Man do his thing."

"Medicine Man?" Russ couldn't hide his confusion. "That ain't no Medicine Man. That's old Gerard, the pharmacist from town." Gerard was even dressed in what he normally wore at the store. His belt shone, catching the light from the fire. His grey hair was slicked back. He didn't look like he belonged with the locals any more than Ma did, but he ignored Russ and kept working on Pa.

Cal said, "Yup, he's the Medicine Man for the Ghosts of the Earth. Trained under a Healing Ghost, he's very good." Cal sat calmly, not at all bothered.

Russ shook his head, amazed that he thought their pharmacist being a Medicine Man was normal. It was weird and Russ didn't like him working on Pa as if he were a healer. Worlds were crossing and things were getting confusing.

"You're just like him," Cal said.

"What does that mean?"

"You act innocent and stupid. I see people talking down to you all the time like you're the village idiot, then I hear you're the one smothering our biggest enemies. I'm on to you."

Russ didn't explain how these things happened to him and he really wasn't doing anything special. Instead, he sat and listened to Pa talk. He blabbered about nothing. His words slurred as he watched what Gerard did to his leg. "Yup, could be spirits warning us. Or maybe the tunnels, the water from the creek, and unstable soil from the roots made a sinkhole." Leave it to Pa to hope for a logical explanation where there was none. For once, they had to accept the fact that a mud monster tried to eat them. Plain and simple.

Silver sat by Pa and he smacked his son on the back of the head. Pa rubbed his neck but didn't glance at Silver when he said, "Just saying, sometimes legends and fact intermix."

Cal chuckled. "You sure do like to suck the magic out of everything, Pa. I like your story, Desire. Maybe these spirits protect the land from evil spirits. God knows, we sure could use a hand."

Silver mumbled beside Pa, "*Cal, careful what you wish for, not all spirits are friendly.*"

Everyone stayed quiet after that, as if they'd heard Silver's warning and were worried.

Isabelle slept in his arms but Russ held a stranger. She didn't talk to him or acknowledge him. Her leg throbbed above the ankle. She didn't let anyone else touch her, so while she slept the Medicine Man Drug Store Owner Gerard ran his hands over her ankle to check the injury. Russ couldn't help but notice how smooth his hands were. They weren't worn away like Pa's. They were gentle hands. Maybe he had a healing touch, after all. Russ watched what he did, prepared to ask questions but he remained so calm, and Isabelle didn't show any signs of distress while she slept, so Russ relaxed. Maybe he'd given them something in the tea. Something that made him sleep so hard, he wouldn't wake up if someone tried to smother him.

–Twenty-Two–

"Isabelle?" Russ asked the next day.

She stared at the field, not moving.

"Isabelle? We're going home."

She didn't move, didn't give him her beautiful half smile. He watched her chest, making sure she breathed. Air went in and out, but he wasn't so sure she was alive.

She's alive, he promised himself. She'd laugh again and be herself again, it would take time. He'd felt death tease them and knew they didn't have forever. If the earth wanted her, it would win.

"Say something, anything."

She wouldn't look at him.

"Cal, give us a few minutes."

Cal and Desire waited for him to get her on the horse but Russ couldn't rush her. The images of her journey to this stupid cougar den flashed up at him as if he read her thoughts.

Cal shook his head and left him a horse. Russ didn't care what Cal thought. If she needed a moment, she'd get one.

"Do you know about your pa?"

She nodded.

"And Thomas?"

She nodded again. "I disrupted the energy, changed destinies and Mother has shown me the price." She kept her eyes on the field, mumbling gibberish like that. "I can't go back in that house, Russ."

How much had she seen? Had she witnessed them being tortured? Was she snapped?

"Pa says you live with us for now," he promised her, even though Pa hadn't said anything of the sort. "We'll get your fields down. Francis was in Moose Jaw with Kit but Cal will get him."

She nodded.

"You ready to ride?"

"This was my fault. I didn't get away fast enough." She frowned, meeting his eyes. "I'm sorry." She glanced at their feet. "Why am I so stupid? Why do I have to love you so?" She sounded truly crushed, and to anyone listening, it probably sounded like she didn't want to love him, but he knew how she was and that wasn't it at all. She called herself stupid 'cause if she loved someone she'd lose them, yet she loved him anyway. She was upset 'cause of what happened and she thought this would come between them.

He'd seen the wounds on her thighs when he'd washed her last night. He'd seen the bruises on her chest and understood why she'd cried out when they hoisted her out. She'd taken a beating.

Every breath hurt him, but whatever Ma and Gerard had slapped on his chest helped a lot. Russ was impressed. Then again, maybe he hadn't broken a rib and the pressure from his injury felt worse than it was.

Silver appeared about ten minutes into their slow walk home and strolled beside Russ.

"Why didn't you say something?" Russ asked him.

"*About what?*"

"About them coming for Isabelle?"

"*How would I know something like that? I was with you.*"

Russ was ready to tell him to find a hole to spend his afterlife in and leave him alone, but Isabelle asked, "Who are you talking to?"

"Silver."

"Oh." She held her chin up. "Why can I never see him? Is he real or have you gone mad?" Her question wasn't a judgement, and Russ supposed that if he had gone mad, she'd love him the same.

"Are you real?" Russ asked him.

"*Yeah.*" Silver sighed. "*I'm sorry, Russ. What I see in her soul is worrisome. You shouldn't be near her.*" Silver left, head down.

Isabelle asked, "What did he say?"

"He's stupid. Forget him." Why would Silver say that?

"It's not a good week."

Russ rubbed her leg while they walked and she pushed his hand off her, which was something she'd never done before. Russ examined his hand, shocked, as if it failed him somehow.

"Isabelle? We'll be fine. Won't we?"

She didn't answer so Russ told her about what Silver had taught him. Then he told her about Bellecoeur so that she understood the different types of curses. He worried that Cracker Jack might start infecting his thoughts, but he couldn't tell her that. "How do we break the cycle and get those spectres out of that chamber for good?"

"Is this important to you?"

"Yes."

She thought for a spell, then said, "The curse means evil spirits pair up with those living on Cursed Land. Yet they didn't pair up with you because you're protected from evil things by your tattoo."

He contemplated his markings. If she was right, it meant Cracker Jack wasn't evil. Silver had called her curious. He relaxed a bit.

She continued, "The curse is not meant to destroy Sacred Land but protect it. These troubled souls are supposed to pair up with *Cîpay* for guidance but the lands were taken over by souls who cannot stand the burden and go mad." Her jaw tightened. "I don't have a tattoo."

"I don't know how to give you a tattoo, but I'll ask Pa who gave us ours."

"No. When I die, I'll take as many with me as I can. This will reset the balance." She looked relieved so he didn't tell her that he wouldn't let her do that.

"Well, it's settled then. You just have to die when these spirits are searching for hosts and suck them all up. But, Isabelle. I saw what these men did to your family. They could have swung by our place but twice they picked you. These were real live men, not ghosts, and cursed or not, I'd like to know why they're picking on you."

"Because Francis was chosen to protect our Healing Chamber. It's the most sacred of Healing Chambers."

"They wouldn't know or care about that." Russ frowned. "Does your family protect something else?"

She sat a bit taller, and pulled the blanket over her so no one could see her. She looked much like Isabelle in the moment. Proud, yet silly. Her jaw remained firm and he wondered why she wouldn't tell him.

"We shouldn't have secrets."

"This is not my secret to share. When it is, I will tell you."

He nodded. "So we have two problems, one feels real world and one feels slightly realer."

She nodded. "So let's find two solutions. What we need is a powerful tattoo to stop the cursed from returning, taking their new hosts back to the earth. As for what Francis protects, he will die protecting his secret, then it'll be my turn. This is how our destiny works."

"I won't let that happen, Isabelle."

She glanced down at Russ. "You don't get a choice in this, Russ. Sorry."

–Twenty-Three–

October 1928—

She missed her monthly. Isabelle hadn't told Russ. Nope. Pa did. So Russ got a smack with the news. Pa told him while they walked the horses to the barn and Russ finished his job before he said a word.

Pa had plenty enough to say for the both of them.

He said she went to Ma in a panic, but Pa looked calm about this as he stood on his makeshift crutches. "It's not a problem, son. She might get it, but it's best if you married her right away so to avoid this in the future." He stayed silent for a long time. "Something you want to say to me?"

"Nope."

"Not even an apology for disappointing me? I mean, you know better. Cal I messed up on, but I made things clear for you. Hell, I even involved your ma, and you have no idea how hard talking about these things can be for her."

Russ walked away.

Isabelle had already told him, but he hadn't listened. Russ reheard her saying, 'It's not a good week'. She hadn't said, 'This week sucks'. No. She'd said, *'It's not a good week'*. That was what she always said when they wanted to mess around but shouldn't. Russ tried remembering how many times they'd ignored that warning before that horrible day… Not many. Maybe once. But he was too upset to remember because all he could see was her pulling away from him over and over since the attack.

He'd hoped to forget the pains of her attack, but now all he saw were her knickers in the dirt covered in blood and dizziness almost pushed him down. Russ threw up along the side of the chicken coop and pulled himself together.

A wave of dates poured at him as he counted the last time she'd let him touch her.

Trouble was, even if he did add right this wasn't normal math and he guessed at best. Relying on her telling him when she had her monthly. Had she even had one *last* month? His brain wanted to say no, but then she would have freaked last month…

Things never did add right for him. What he did know was that it was over a month since they spent any time together alone. And there was a damn good chance that at least one of them pricks had attacked her and what if they'd raped her?

But who knew if she counted right before that?

Dammit. *What if?*

Russ needed to face Pa and tell him, 'So what? We were gonna get married anyway.' He needed to talk to her and promise her that he'd be the best pa ever, no matter what. She'd made her wishes to mother his children clear and that's what they'd focus on.

If she was pregnant, no matter what happened to get that baby inside her, Russ promised himself he would be a good pa. Him. He desperately wanted to share this bond with her. He had no idea he wanted this until someone might have stolen it from him.

Anger flared up inside him. He never did take it well when others robbed him of things.

Russ shook those selfish thoughts away, because if he was this upset about it, he couldn't imagine how she must feel. The thought made a shiver pass over him. How was she feeling? No wonder the happy left her. No wonder she didn't want him touching her.

There were too many problems.

He leaned his head against the chicken coop. Then he wailed on the old wood until his fists bled. Sometimes, there was no point in thinking. So he prepared to face her, with no clue what he'd say.

Pa was in his face when he spun around. Who knew how long he'd been there? Russ couldn't shove him away because he was a cripple. "I'm sorry they put their filthy paws on her."

How did Pa know now and not a moment ago? Maybe Russ wasn't acting like a man about to marry his best friend and start a family with her. And Pa, well, he was smart. Russ met Pa's eyes, his jaw firm. "Any baby she has will be ours, and if you say anything else I will beat the lies out of you."

He nodded, but the pain in his eyes troubled Russ. "That's damn near what Cal said, so think about that."

Russ' head pounded with the impossibility of it all.

Isabelle was sewing when he found her. Her ankle had healed but Doc wanted her to stay off her foot for another week and he'd see then how things looked. He was being a moron and saying dirt like that because he didn't like Gerard stealing his thunder. Russ asked Cal what he thought, and he said to let it play out, Isabelle would walk on her foot when she felt like it, despite what anyone said. So Russ bit his tongue.

When he saw her sitting like an angel, he softened. None of this was her fault and she was scared as hell. She needed him strong enough for both of them.

Russ sat beside her, bringing in the chair real close.

"You know?" she breathed the words with a heavy breath, setting the knickers she made aside.

"I do."

"Your ma says I shouldn't panic, we have to wait for two monthlies to pass. But I never miss one, you know."

Russ nodded even if he had no clue. "Why would we panic?" He acted calm, like the change of plans was no big deal.

Why wouldn't she meet his eyes? Did she hate him for not protecting her?

Russ placed a hand on her cheek to turn her toward him. His knuckles hurt when he opened his hand, and he pulled away, shocked by her tears. He never saw her cry before. Those tears blew the common sense right out of him.

She needed him to say something. Anything. He thought about what Cal might say and went with that. "You'll make an excellent mother."

"Do you still want to marry me?"

"Nothing will ever change that, but I desperately need to kiss you, 'cause I'm terrified you don't want to marry me."

The brown in her eyes sparkled from the tears but she nodded quickly.

"You want to talk about what happened that night?" Their foreheads touched. Their cheeks brushed. He needed to think with her again. Thinking alone wasn't working.

"You saved me."

"I didn't let go. Pa and Cal saved you. Those men, they touched...your things. That bother you?"

"Yes."

"I picked them up and packed things up. Is it fine that I touched your things?"

"They're yours, too." She pulled away. He was used to that, but her fear of him had to end.

"Isabelle? I can't think as only me anymore. Be with me again."

She glanced at him in a panic and he didn't let her recoil. She always had a hard time refusing his kisses so Russ teased them on her lips, his hand against her cheek, the other slipped not so innocently up her skirt. She melted into him as if she couldn't believe he waited this long to do something they needed so desperately.

Russ pulled her onto his lap, his hands frantically consuming her. He'd meant the touch to be a kiss but his brain lost smarts and he dived to undo her blouse, right there in Ma's sewing room.

She pulled away to breathe, her head against his. Russ' hands rested on her breasts and he waited for her to say something but she gulped with her eyes closed. She whispered, "I like how you touch me, yet each touch makes knots in my stomach."

"Let's focus on now," he told her. "The dreams we got coming."

"What if this baby isn't—"

He refused to let her say that aloud. Never. He kissed her. Cutting her off. When he pulled away, Russ whispered, "I'll tell you a story, and every time you're scared I want you to think about the possibility until it's a true story, because in my mind, this is exactly how I remember things on that day."

Her eyes were huge as she waited for him to create a happy memory for them to grasp.

"You see, I worked the field all by myself with nothing but skeeters bugging me and I was so tired of straw. And out you came with a tall glass of water for me and a bunch of cookies—"

"No more cookies," she cut him off with a frantic snap. "Just me and the water."

"Fine. When I went to grab the cup; you poured the water down your dress and gave me a tease of a smile as you started to unbutton."

She rubbed the blood off his knuckles while Russ invented a story that might have been true had their day gone differently.

"I didn't even bother to check if we were alone or count back days, I tore into that dress to lick the water off your skin as if I was parched and you were covered in the only water left on the planet. That was a good day for us, and I can't wait to have that kind of fun with you again."

He nuzzled her neck with his lips. "Gosh. I love you, Isabelle. I don't give two dirts how young we are. I want to spend forever licking water off you like that."

She nodded, wiped her tears, and shoved them in her apron; like she did with everything else she didn't want him to worry about but that was just for them.

"I'm going to the priest," he lied while he did her blouse up. "I can't wait another moment. Do you need a dress to wear for our wedding?"

She glanced at herself. "I...I have my mother's, but I..."

Russ set her back on her own chair so he could get up. "Sounds perfect. I'll get the dress for you and bring it here." She couldn't go back in the house. He couldn't go back in her house, and it was too bad because they were wasting a good house.

Russ left her to her sewing and found Ma outside the door. She grabbed his arm and studied him for a long while. "Silver upset your pa when he told him she wasn't the one for you."

"He told Pa that?"

"He said your souls didn't line up, or weren't linked...but it's because she's so worried about your reaction. A woman should never go through that. Her fears should be fine now that you talked to her."

Ma always made him feel better, and she was always honest with him. "Ma, you ever been through that?"

"Heavens no. But you're good with her," she blurted out.

"Probably 'cause she's good with me." His stupid answer made Ma nod in her curt way as if he'd told her this situation was none of her damned business. Maybe to her that was what he'd said. Russ never understood his ma, but when she slipped back into the room, he stood where she'd been to listen. He wanted to be sure she wasn't telling Isabelle crap that'd make her feel worse.

It occurred to him that she talked to her differently than Desire or even the girls. She was always yelling at the girls, and she was right blunt with Desire, but to Isabelle she talked as if Isabelle was a frightened rabbit who might run away.

Russ wanted to tell her she didn't have to talk to her like that, but when he stepped in the doorway, Isabelle cried against her. And well, maybe she needed a good cry after all she'd been through so he kinda thought this plan was a right old good idea. Maybe he'd get Ma alone one day and have a cry on her shoulder, too.

Well. There was only one thing he could do when he felt this upset so Russ left them and went to find a shovel.

–Twenty-four–

Russ tossed another scoop of dirt into a pail when Cal found him.

Cal peered in the freshly dug hole.

Only Russ' head showed and he stared at Cal's feet.

"Is this your burial hole?" Cal asked. "Sammy found me this morning and said Pa mentioned killing ya."

Russ kept digging. He needed to have a grownup conversation with him. If he planned to act like a brat, he could bugger off.

Cal jumped into the hole with him. He filled the pail and hauled dirt out without a word.

Russ kept digging, filling the pail. They worked until the hole loomed over their heads. He'd have to get out and make a ladder before he went any deeper. He had about another ten feet to go.

Cal leaned against the wall and stared at him. "Nice hole. Got Silver excited, you did, but you can't dig deeper than another five feet. There's a water pocket under us."

"This hole will be a well," Russ said. "Pa's is too far and I don't want Isabelle trucking water back and forth this winter if she's pregnant and I get too busy."

The news about her being pregnant didn't surprise him. "You know there's water here?" Cal looked at his feet. "How?"

Russ shrugged. "Same way you do, I guess."

"You're more in touch with the land than you let on," Cal said as he crossed his arms. "I talked to the priest for you, and I need your thoughts on things."

"Did you know he's not really teaching us Latin? It's gibberish." Russ pounded the shovel into the dirt, ticked off.

"I don't want a jerk like him marrying us, but who the heck am I gonna get? Nothing is going the way I want. Nothing." As he stewed about the priest, Russ thought about how he'd vanished along the side of the church the night Isabelle was taken. What if the priest had helped Eric Kaplain escape?

"I knew about the Latin but until I understood why I didn't want you digging him a burial hole, so I didn't tell you."

Russ thought about dropping Cal in one. "When did you find out?"

"The priest told us not to speak it until we were good enough, but I figured we were getting good, so I tried to have a conversation with Hoolie about three months ago and he just about fell over with how good I spoke the Language of the Dead."

Russ frowned, not sure what that was. "A white priest is teaching us how to speak something called the Language of the Dead? How did Hoolie learn it?" Skeptical, Russ frowned.

"From the ceremonial chambers. He talks to spirits there all the time. I went with him and sure some of these spirits speak French and such but all of 'em speak a very old language that was born with Mother. I understood everything they said. They called me a *Cîpay* warrior." He grinned but Russ wasn't happy about any of this.

"And?" Russ snapped. "Why not tell me?"

Cal hauled himself out of the hole. "*Cîpay* learn when ready."

"Cut the crap, Cal. I need to know what's going on."

"Well…I hoped you'd tell me. When I went to the priest to ask him if he'd marry you and Isabelle, he asked me for a favour." He offered Russ a hand and pulled him out of the hole. Russ stood so they were eye to eye. "Wants me to convince you to go to Normal School."

"So he won't marry us?"

"He never said that, but I got thinking, there is a better way." Cal smirked. "I mean, you could have a tribal wedding." Cal rubbed his wrist, ignoring him and Russ wondered if he'd been set up, but he was curious what a tribal wedding meant, just the same. "I get that you're not into the mysteries of the earth, especially since mud tried to eat your gal, but it's fun and you might discover something about yourself you didn't know."

"What does that mean?"

"It's not like those weddings up at the church. This ceremony starts with many. We will help you find ways to get in touch with who you are inside."

"How?"

"We use the connection we share with the earth."

It sounded like they might be digging another hole. "I know who I am."

Cal let out a long breath as if he knew Russ wouldn't get how deep this ceremony would be, but he continued, "It's supposed to teach your wife who you are…inside. So she can decide if you are the one she chooses."

"She already chooses me."

"The you standing here, maybe, if you should be so lucky. What if you show her the real you and she changes her mind?" He raised an eyebrow as if Russ hid things from Isabelle. "Once she decides, she announces to the many that she sees the real you. That you are the one she wishes to raise her children with, to teach her boys to be men, and to protect her girls from whatever she fears, and that you are the one she chooses to love at night. She also tells the men of the tribe that if you screw up she will send you packing and they better support her decision and ban you."

Russ smirked. That was better than any wedding he'd witnessed. Getting married in front of Silver's ghostly tribe was genius. He was sold on the idea, but then Cal said something even better.

"She says this to everyone with a dance meant to seduce you. As the dance continues, you get worn into submission and slowly the many leave until you are just the two and your bodies bond in harmony in the earth that joins us all. If she chooses you, you will not be able to refuse and in the last moment when she breaks you, you will get to see the real her."

"So how does this bond to each other through the earth work? We gonna stand in a hole or something?"

Cal smiled. "Sure, why not?"

Russ gave him a doubtful look and Cal chuckled.

"Ever have Samuel walk by and your feet get warm and full of happiness?"

Russ nodded. He felt that all the time.

"That's his energy touching yours through your connection with the earth," he explained. "People forget we have this link to each other, or such things bother them, so they wear shoes to block the energy, but I like to be connected to Mother. It helps me know what to say."

Russ stopped pacing so he could think. He rubbed his feet in the earth as Monsieur Dubois had done that day he didn't kill him for telling him about wanting to be with Isabelle.

His feet itched. A terrified itch that made him want to run away. "What are you scared of?" Russ asked Cal in case the feeling came from his brother.

"Everything. I'm scared of every little bloody thing. Mostly, I hate that they all believe we're some legend. Look at us, Russ. How the hell are we gonna end this curse?"

Russ shrugged. "Maybe they need hope. Nothing wrong with that. You don't act scared."

"Of course not. No one can know. I have to be brave. But in the moment while she dances, she'll see the real you through this link. You stand here and say she knows who you are but the innocent boy staring back at me is not the same as the beast I sense clawing frantically at the soil." Cal planted his feet. "You'll release the beast and tear her to pieces, and everyone will know you ain't a hero."

"They already know that, Cal, they're just fighting for hope and since they lost Julien, they need a new hero. When we die they'll find other brothers to harass."

Cal turned and walked away.

"Cal? Will you set this up for me? For real?" Russ wanted to see her dance more than anything.

"Yeah. I'll set it up but I have one rule." Cal turned around and his left foot rubbed the ground. "No sex for forty-four days before these things. This is important, 'cause this energy I talked about needs to be focused and pure, not tainted by hers."

Russ calculated fast. The dates were close, so what if he was off by a few days? "Done," he said much too quickly, and should have thought for a moment if what Cal said even made a lick of sense. "We better do this 'cause I don't want to do another forty-four anytime soon." Russ realized his mistake too late.

"Figured as much." Cal walked away with his secret, leaving Russ with a deep understanding of just how smart Cal really was.

~~

Russ told Isabelle they were getting married by the light of the moon and he wasn't waiting another day. She sent him off so she could get ready.

Later, Cal invited him to smoke a pipe with him with the promise of it helping him relax and get in touch with the earth. This was apparently important, so Russ agreed, even if Pa had told them not to smoke.

Cal filled the weird pipe with herbs he took from his satchel. The pipe looked more like an old stick. Touching it felt like something they shouldn't be doing but they sat by the haystack and passed the relic back and forth, smoking.

When Pa showed up, Russ thought he'd smack them, but his eyes lit up. He glanced around like a boy about to steal a cookie and got in on their fun. He tossed his crutches aside and sat with them. "Haven't seen the pipe since my wedding." His smile was wide as he puffed on the pipe. "At least I get to smoke with one of my sons."

Cal winced as if Pa had slapped him. "I will only say sorry so many times without punching you, so get over it."

Russ copied Cal but he was sure he smoked it wrong because the smoke made him dizzy. He didn't correct him though and when Silver appeared, Cal passed the cylinder to him and the smoke swirled inside him taking on the shape of the white horse.

It relaxed him and Russ rested back in the straw wondering if the earth would talk to him or if he wasn't worthy.

Russ shot to his feet when Isabelle appeared beside him. He hadn't seen her or heard her, he'd felt her. The earth exploded with happiness just for him and couldn't contain the joy so it rained on him in air that danced. The stuff in that pipe made him ponder things like that.

She wore her mother's dress. Cal brought the gown over for her so Russ hadn't seen it. Turns out Cal put the empty house to good use with Desire since Francis didn't need a house, but his uncle was going to take it over shortly.

The dress was red. A delicious red. *This red looked good enough to lick off her.* Lick. He wanted to rip a tiny piece off her dress and lick the skin underneath, then rip off another, exploring her forever.

Russ almost ran toward her, his entire body craved her so wildly, as he tried not to count the days since they'd touched with all their skin. Yet his soul wanted to touch hers through the earth. His words wanted to mingle with hers in the air. Even his thoughts yearned for a moment of silence only she knew how to experience with him. A wild hungry, like a famished man devouring her cookies, erupted to life in him.

Her hair was up and looked like something Ma did for her, all tied in a fancy bun with curls wild and free flowing around. Nothing like Russ was used to seeing her wear. Kinda neat and he wanted a better look, yet he wanted to get further away to see it all together.

Her eyelashes moved so slowly, even as he ran, Russ was sure he could count each one.

She was beautiful and there in the field where he started to build a house by a haystack that saved their lives, she stood on her ankle without any help, which meant Cal was right.

Russ ran to her, yet he realized he wasn't even moving. He stood still with her already in his arms. Time was weird, spotty. He twirled her around and around, his hands held her and she giggled. Yet Russ watched himself do these things.

When he glanced back at himself, he was shocked to see Kit with him. She turned her back on him and crossed her arms, searing a fire between them. Neat that he was divided.

Russ set Isabelle down, and meant to show her how he was divided but her red dress blew in the wind and he fell to his knees in front of her. Russ rested his head against her belly and cried. He cried like a fool all over her belly and couldn't stop. Tears slid down his cheek and hit the ground making life blossom into flower babies.

What the heck? Russ glanced at Cal, shocked. He raised his eyebrows, a gloss to his grey eyes that promised fun. '*She sees the real you,'* he mouthed so slowly, his invisible words hit Russ. *'Feel the earth talk to you.'* He pointed to his feet.

Isabelle and Russ stood for real in the earth, bare feet. She stood closer to Russ and he had no idea which one of them had moved.

He glanced back to see if he was still divided and he was. It made sense, really, he always felt torn between worlds.

Isabelle raised her left lip a touch in the hint of a smirk he found amusing. This time he didn't smile back 'cause behind her was Thomas. Russ knew he was a ghost, 'cause he'd pulled his lifeless body from the barn door. Yet he charged for Russ, and dang, he sure did look real for a ghost.

Russ stood his ground in front of her, ready to take each blow. Thomas vanished when Silver stepped in front of him and her ma was to the right. A ghost pinned her. Russ glanced to his left and grabbed the shotgun that appeared and he blew the ghost in two.

Monsieur Dubois nodded proudly to his left but then he threw mud at the other Russ and he felt himself shift to that Russ so he could protect Kit from the flying mud.

Silver whispered that the Dubois girl was the wrong gal for him, but no one heard except Kit.

Men wearing sheets arrived. Russ wasn't gonna run from them, not today, not on his wedding day, not ever. But they forced him back to the Russ crying on Isabelle.

Happiness could be found with Isabelle and he'd cry all over her until he found it and none of them could stop him. Not even himself.

A low drum beat in his chest. No. Not his chest—underground. Under his feet. The earth spoke to them.

The images faded and Isabelle and Russ stood again, studying each other, only she was beautiful and he kept crying.

Cal twirled between them before he could touch her and Desire followed and grabbed Isabelle's hand to pull her into the dance, so Isabelle hauled him in. Russ reached for anyone to save him, pulling Ma into the dance. The love in her grip remained strong. Russ was happy she was his ma 'cause any other would have given up on him long before today.

Cal ran them through the other Russ and Russ felt himself become one, the boundaries of each world were clear in his mind. The movements were freeing like the wind, swaying one way and the other, pulling and being pulled into a snake-like dance that went above ground and underground in a quick breath.

They splashed through the sides of the creek and each step made the air around him come to life with an explosion of tears Russ couldn't catch because his hands were full of dancing.

The strange dream caused him to forget about the priest and the cursed. He danced like a winding snake. They pulled Isabelle and Russ into a circle and danced around them. Pounding their feet into the ground. Faces he knew yet each one offered a smile he couldn't grab.

Then the drums stopped and they ended the pounding. Russ stood like a fool wondering what was next.

Isabelle danced in her red dress that was too tight in the hips and much too loose in the chest. A dress he needed to desperately rip into bits so he could lick the skin underneath one piece at a time.

Smoke curled around her. Russ couldn't search for the source 'cause his eyes were tied to her movements. Bubbling energy pushed from everyone as they pounded it toward them. She channelled the energy in a sway meant only for him and the others were gone. Russ saw nothing but her calling him, teasing him in a dreamy smoke.

Her hips, her chest, her entire being crippled him.

She whispered things he couldn't do but he wanted to. She rubbed against him as she'd done in the water the first time they'd made love. Slithering higher and higher until she was a giant snake dancing for him in the smoke. Her apron was around her and she picked him up and dropped him inside.

Was the smoke coming from him? Russ glanced at his hands as he tumbled into her apron with a nickel and a book, and so many tears he might drown. The clay pipe was there, smoking. He blew the smoke out of the apron so she could dance in the light fog he created, 'cause nothing else existed except the dance.

When he glanced up, she became Isabelle again and not the snake. He stood before her wondering if he was strong enough to rip a piece of her dress so he could taste the skin underneath. He planned to try.

Russ stopped living in his body and left as a spirit, so he could dance with her in her magical tease. Other spirits joined them, when the drumming started again and Russ longed to touch her but couldn't. He was a man without touch. He was a ghost.

If vows or promises were made before God, they weren't spoken aloud; they pounded them into the ground, first with the feet of others then with their bodies sinking into the haystack.

Russ woke in the haystack with her naked in his arms, her red dress in pieces around them. They were buried in the blanket from his bed, but he didn't remember going for it. He actually didn't remember much. Things blurred and melted together in that crazy dream he'd had.

Toward the end of October, nights were cold and they had no business in the straw, naked with her dress in pieces, but he was hot against her, his body ready to satisfy her all day.

Russ sighed, content. She was his wife. She chose him despite the torn crying fool inside him.

"Gosh, did you see any of that?" Russ asked, hoping to hell she hadn't seen him loopy.

"I saw you."

"Did you see me smart?"

She shook her head. "I saw two yous. You were happy and I wasn't there. But when you were sad I was there." She brushed his chest with her fingertips. "Do I make you cry?"

"Those were tears because I wanted in your dress and couldn't find a way in. You take the things I showed you last night and shove them in that magical apron of yours so no one knows I'm a stupid horny fool."

She giggled but Russ cut off those giggles with lips on hers.

Cal tossed him pants. "Yuck. Enough of that, lover boy, we have work to do."

"What?" Groggy, Russ wondered where he came from.

"Your house, we need to build it."

Twenty men surrounded them. Shit. Russ pulled the blanket over them to protect her. "Damn, Cal, she's naked. Why did you bring everyone out here?"

"That ain't my fault. Blame the beast inside you for that one." He had a silly grin. "Cover your wife up and let's move. Ma wants her in the house. She has curtains to make or some bloody hell like that. Oh and you're supposed to sign this marriage certificate. Pa needs to run it to the courthouse to make it legal with the higher powers who mustn't know about what happened last night. That was between you, your wife, and the earth you pounded her into. Then get your sorry ass over to the pile of lumber Pa brought over."

Isabelle shot off toward the house, wrapped in the blanket. Russ could still taste her. He didn't want this moment to ever end but Cal shoved his pants against his chest. "Dress."

Russ signed his paper. Isabelle already had and so had the old priest across the border who Pa liked to visit which Russ found interesting and was about to point out when the certificate vanished in Cal's pocket. He never saw that paper again, but Russ assumed Pa filed it.

"But the fields?" Russ asked Cal, not sure why he argued. If Desire's family wanted to help build a house, really, he should shut up and get to work.

"What more can we do to them until the thresher comes?"

Cal was right of course. No one knew when the thresher would come through but they should know by now. What if they were missed and never got their crops threshed?

Russ did up his pants and glanced around.

"What you searching for?" Cal demanded, and Russ' feet grew warm with Cal's annoyance.

"I lost the pipe." Everything blurred, but he imagined the relic was special to Cal.

"What pipe?" Cal shrugged, genuinely confused.

"The one we smoked with Pa. You know, the sacred earth pipe with carvings along the side."

"No idea what you're ragging on now."

Russ sobered as he watched Isabelle walk to the house. "I didn't tear her dress apart in front of you idiots, did I?"

Cal didn't have to answer. When the teasing began moments later, Russ promised himself never to smoke an imaginary pipe again. The effects were worse than the whiskey. Some type of drug that made his brain turn to smoke and smear into everyone else's.

–Twenty-five–

On the last day of October, Kit leaned against the livery barn in Eau Claire. Francis loomed over her and playfully rubbed the scar on her chin. His eyes gobbled her up. In the cold air, she made a circle with her breath and watched the cloud blow back at her.

"I'm frozen," Kit complained.

"I need to talk to my sister." Francis' eyes sparkled in the cold and the gleam reminded her of how the sun danced off the skiff of snow making twinkles like magical sparkles. She smiled, despite the cold, because Francis was magical and she loved being a part of his life.

He pulled her into a hug. Kit rested against his chest, a sadness filling her. She enjoyed her time with Francis but, like a heavy curse, sorrow would always be around them. "Do you believe in curses, Francis?"

"I'm a Ghost of the Earth, grew up on the Cursed Lands. I have studied every type of curse possible and know nothing about them." Francis grinned the foolish smirk she grew fond of. "Some curses are tough to break, but I imagine mud and naked bodies could do the trick." He nibbled her neck. "I am destined to make you fall madly in love with me."

Kit chuckled, glad that he didn't hate her for her foul moods.

Francis grabbed her hand. "Whatever your destiny, your fate will come to term when it must. Until then, I know a place we can hide and make out. I'll be gone for a few minutes, Isabelle promised to meet me out back. Then I need to talk to Cal."

Francis' grip was warm on her hand and he pulled away reluctantly.

Gosh. Was it possible to love him, even with this ache inside her that promised another life was her destiny?

He winked as he backed up and she decided she could take any path she chose. "I love you," she promised him. He grinned and ran off.

Kit was daydreaming when out of nowhere Isabelle appeared. She leaned against the barn with her.

Kit faced her but Isabelle stared straight ahead.

"Isabelle, how are you? Francis is searching for you."

"He found me. He won't help me. So I come to you."

Kit frowned. "What do you need from me?"

Isabelle studied Kit, her eyes peering into her soul and Kit stepped back in case she could see in her soul. "I'm pregnant."

Kit swallowed a lump in her throat. "That's good news." She wanted to be happy for her but a heavy weight fell on her shoulders and she slumped forward, despite the happy news. The healer in Moose Jaw said children would not be in her future since that blade had pierced her stomach. And until Isabelle stood in front of her carrying Russ' child, she hadn't realized this was something she might ever want.

Isabelle's shoulders sagged, too. "I fear I won't make this pregnancy. I need you to perform a ritual in the Healing Chamber."

Kit was at attention. "What's wrong?" Everything in her searched for signs that Isabelle needed her help. Her eyes were clear. Her skin was shiny. Glowing. She stood tall and strong. Her breath smelled sweet. Kit ran a hand along her neck and found her temperature perfect. "You look fine."

"I have a spirit haunting me. I stole his life when he attacked me. I can't see him, but I feel his presence. He is a weight on my every thought." She gripped Kit's arm. "Francis put his shadows in an amulet, said you helped him. I want you to put my shadow's soul in this." She dangled a gold cross in front of her.

"Where did you get this, Isabelle?" The *Cipay* symbols on the cross weren't used in rituals anymore. Well, not by healers.

"Charlie told me this cross would protect me from spirits. He's Russ' cousin. He gave me the chain and everything after

Hoolie told him I had a nasty shadow. He's such a good boy."

Kit nodded. "It doesn't always work."

Isabelle put out her jaw. "Then nothing changes, right?"

She could try. They sneaked away to the Healing Chamber. The only entrance was on Dubois Farm, in the pigsty by the woodpile. Before performing the ritual she'd used on Francis she'd sought out many counsellors and teachers to prepare. Silver had even studied his shadows carefully. Rushing this didn't feel right, but who was left to ask for guidance? Besides, she didn't want to wait on this. If this spirit infected Russ' child, she would never forgive herself for not helping.

To see in the dark chamber, she lit a candle by the altar carved into the wall. The sacred plants lined the wall, even without light.

"Sit," she instructed Isabelle. "What is your shadow's name?"

"Jessie Kaplain."

She stared at the girl. She'd killed Jessie Kaplain? Eric Kaplain was tearing the countryside apart searching for Francis. Eric said Francis was to blame and Francis never once said otherwise.

"Russ know this?"

"If you ask my husband, he will tell you he did it." The way she stretched the word husband was a warning.

Kit nodded. "You know, Isabelle, I don't want to feel the way I do about him. I can't control it. It's why I stay away. I won't ever tell him. Francis and I are happy."

"Ever is a long time, Kit. We both know better."

"Then we'll focus on the now. Put the necklace on. I'll call the spirit, so I can see it."

On her knees, Kit said a prayer and drew a few symbols in the dirt. The motions were to relax Isabelle. She didn't need to say a prayer or even draw in the dirt, this connection was simply a part of every healer and she'd long ago discovered how to tap into the spiritual world with nothing but an open mind. She faced Isabelle and summoned him.

He appeared by Isabelle, relaxed. Taken in his prime. Very good-looking. Kit nodded to him. Then she spoke to him as she would anyone else. If he was a good spirit, he'd help her, if he was not, she would have to summon powers from the earth to contain him. "You're shadowing Isabelle, and while she carries life, she needs relief. Enter her necklace and allow her to enjoy this sacred time without the burden of your soul. I will call on you once the child is born."

"*Not my soul that'll be the problem.*" He laughed and the light blew out.

Something bumped into her.

Kit jumped to her feet as faceless spectres entered the Healing Chamber and dived for Jessie. "*Ah. Power,*" he breathed. "*I feel so alive.*"

Isabelle lit the candle and glanced up. "Is everything all right? Did the ritual work? Do you have to draw symbols or anything?"

Jessie glowed a fiery orange.

"How do you feel?" Kit demanded.

Isabelle smiled. "Great. This is working."

Kit's hand shook. "Jessie called in a bunch of spirits, he's powerful and…"

Isabelle got to her feet. A slow smile spread to her lips as darkness corrupted her. "With the necklace on, I control him. There are no more spirits in the earth. Jessie has taken them all in and now he's tied to me. Russ' mother will give me a tattoo and they will all die with me."

Kit's hands went to her mouth. She'd done this on purpose? "You can't contain that many spirits. They'll drive you mad. Let me remove them and curse them back to the earth. It's a simple ritual."

"You just take care of Russ when I'm gone." Isabelle stormed out. "But you keep your paws off him until then."

Kit sat against the wall in tears. What had she done?

–TWENTY-SIX–

Pa was furious when he found out they'd be last to see the thresher and they were a month behind. Meant their crops would be under snow. At least he was off the crutches and able to kick at the dirt in his anger.

"Someone has to be last," Russ pointed out while he chopped another log. One swing and the log split in two. He was impressed with himself.

"There'll be snow on the ground," Pa grumbled.

"There already is. We'll be fine. It's only November."

Desire walked by and, despite the cold, she only wore a shawl over her shoulder. Her tummy showed. Russ counted back. She should be about six months, but she was ready to pop. Isabelle's dress was tight across her stomach, but she didn't have a belly yet, and really, if Russ wasn't so obsessed with her, he probably wouldn't have noticed how tight her dress was getting.

"Where's Cal?"

"He said Francis is home and he's gone to see him. He'll keep an eye on the Healing Chamber for him for a spell."

"Isabelle will be thrilled her brother's home. Glad to hear Cal plans to stick around, his wife explodes with life."

Pa nodded. "Mine, too."

"Yours 'too' what?"

"Your ma, she's pregnant." Pa didn't look happy with the news.

Russ wasn't sure what to say. "Well, good for you."

"Yeah." He took a deep breath. "I'm terrified."

"Why?" Russ laughed. "You're already a pa. I should be the wreck."

"When Samuel was born, your ma just about died." He

studied his hands. "I never saw so much blood. I have no idea how I'd breathe without her keeping the voices calm."

"You mean a woman can *die* giving life?" As if they didn't have enough problems. "That's something you should have mentioned. I mean damn, Pa, if you wanted me to keep my pecker in my pants, information like that would have done the trick."

"It's not a secret. That's how her mother died." He nodded, serious, but Russ drowned in this news.

Nothing made sense. "So if you didn't want to get Ma pregnant why did you?"

"I caved." He shrugged. Russ suddenly understood how much caving went on in the world.

~~

Francis arrived with Cal around lunch and Ma set them out plates as if she expected them.

"Hey! It's my brother!" Francis grinned at Russ. "Sorry I missed the wedding. Here, a wedding gift." He handed Russ papers.

Russ glanced at them. "These are the titles to your land."

"Yup. I protect that land, and the best way to protect it is to hand the ownership over to someone else. It's not all of it. I gave your brother some, my uncle, and your Pa, too, but the rest is yours."

He was giving Russ land? "Can I pay you for it?"

"There is no value to Cursed Lands that you can pay with cash. The debt is paid with your life, so I curse you with such a burden, but I trust no one else. Isabelle will explain to you the significance of what you protect." He grabbed Russ' shoulder. "You're family. They have me in the crosshairs so I'm going down, but it'll take them a while to figure out what I did with the land and who owns it now. By then, hopefully the curse will be over."

Russ was about to go into what happened with Thomas and his pa when Desire walked into the house with a baby in her arms.

Ma dropped the bowl of buns she carried and grabbed the chair. Desire picked one off the floor and walked off to the sitting room as if nothing had happened.

Cal chased after her and Russ sat back and chuckled, relieved. If Desire could give birth without a hiccup, he had nothing to worry about for Isabelle.

"Congratulations, Ma, you're a grandmaman."

She stared at Russ as if he could explain what had happened. "She was walking the yard this morning," Ma stammered.

"Yup, I saw her. And now she holds her baby. Best get in there and see." Russ was teasing of course, but Ma dropped everything and rushed to the sitting room.

The baby was all they talked about all afternoon. Cal was a pa to a beautiful baby girl who looked like him. Russ handed her to Pa since everyone got to hold her until someone blurted out her name and the father approved it.

Pa handed her to Isabelle. She gasped. "Echa. Look, Russ, she's like Echa from the story we're reading."

Cal took his daughter from Isabelle. "The saviour. Welcome Echa. That's the perfect name for our daughter."

Russ was thrilled that Isabelle got to name her and grabbed her hand to sneak off with her before supper. Everyone was so caught up in the baby they didn't notice them slip on their jackets and head out.

They ran to the haystack in their heavy boots.

"Something bothering you?" Isabelle asked, her breath forming a white puff. Her smiles were an effort these days, so he should have asked her that question.

He wondered where Kit was and why she hadn't come with Francis. He'd assumed they were together. Before he could share his thoughts on the subject, a bunch of wagons drove by and into the farmyard. A Mountie led the pack. Russ had seen pictures of them in the newspapers but this was the first one he'd ever seen in real life. He sat tall on his horse with his strange looking hat.

Isabelle crouched behind the haystack and Russ joined her. "What does he want with Pa?" Russ asked.

Pa rushed out of the house alone, slipping on his jacket. The Mountie met him, taking long strides. He looked so important; Russ wasn't paying attention to the rest of the crew. Pa spoke to the Mountie. Then he hollered good and loud to someone in the wagon, "Liar."

"Can you see who Pa is mad at?"

The wagon was closed in but the driver yelled back at Pa. He was about to get off the wagon but the Mountie lifted a hand and everyone calmed.

Isabelle whispered, "Jessie's pa."

Russ shot up and was about to help Pa but Silver blocked his path. *"They're searching for you. Hide."*

"Me?"

"Eric Kaplain says his son went missing months ago, and he's got proof you killed him. He found his body in a field with your hanky on his arm. Has your name ticked on it."

"Didn't they burn the bodies?"

"They did. He must have run by the wagon and taken it off him before."

"Shit. They'll take me to prison for murder."

"Russ." Isabelle grabbed his hand. "You can't leave me. I can't do like Desire. I can't."

"I can't let Pa take the blame."

Silver wouldn't let him by. *"You get your ass in that tunnel and stay there until I come for you. Is that clear?"*

"But Pa can't take the—"

"No one has to take the blame. Your pa is gonna say your hanky was stolen."

That didn't sound like much of an argument. "My future is in the hands of a guy who can't lie worth shit?"

"Just stay low."

Russ had read enough crime stories; he knew the Mountie always got his man. He waited in the tunnel with Isabelle for a good hour. Being underground was much warmer and Russ was curious why. It had been cooler in the summer. He thought about that when Cal slipped in the tunnel and sat quietly in front of them.

"Well?" Russ demanded. "What happened?"

Cal grabbed Isabelle's hands, which was weird. "They took Francis away. When they searched the house, Kaplain pointed a finger at Francis, saying he did Jessie in. Francis said, he did. Said Jessie had your hanky because you'd helped him, not killed him."

"But that ain't true at all," Russ snapped.

"Francis don't want to see you hauled off, Russ, so he's gonna take the blame for this."

"Like hell he is."

"It's already done. He told me to make sure you stayed here with Isabelle. She needs you."

Russ felt his entire body tense.

"Francis is a good boy," Isabelle whispered which settled the debate for Russ—he would do whatever he could to get him out.

–Twenty-Seven–

The next week—

Pa rented the same room in Moose Jaw and was at the first trial for Francis with Isabelle. Russ paced the hotel room while Kika and Silver watched. Kika didn't pay Silver any attention so Russ pretended he wasn't staring him down, too.

He needed to do something. "Blowing Francis out of that prison sounds like a righto plan to me."

"Your pa wants you to stay," Kika reminded him.

Silver said, *"Anything you do will make things worse for Francis. They have a system that proves—"*

Russ cut him off. "I understand how the law works. But this is bullshit. They're taking Kaplain's word against ours."

"No, Francis is admitting to this crime," Kika pointed out.

"Francis didn't kill Jessie, and that is a fact. I was there."

"So who did?" Kika asked.

Russ went to tell him he did, but Silver spoke before him. *"The girl. The witch."*

Russ clenched his fists and went to smoke him but Silver wisped out.

Kika jumped up, ready to fight in response to his anger. They stared at each other and finally, Kika turned the knob on the handle to his blade. He dumped out a bunch of bills on the bed. "Fine, don't tell me. Your pa told you to stay, but your ma gave me all these bills in case you didn't."

Silver roared with laughter as he materialized again. Russ felt a bit of a smirk coming to his lips. What did Ma think he'd do? Russ shoved a bill in his pocket and slid the rest back in Kika's blade. "Good. Let's go exploring. Someone around here might know what we can do to get him out of this mess. We'll use the monies to buy us information. That'll work."

They moved the dresser ahead. "Where did Ma get the money?" Russ whispered to Silver as they accessed the hidden entrance.

Silver smirked but didn't answer. He led the way in the passage and Russ felt better doing something, even if he wasn't sure what the plan was yet.

"So where do we go from here?" Kika checked out the cement wall, both hands flat against it. "This leads underground to blessed tunnels." He faced Russ excited and rushed down the steps.

"Can you lead us around these tunnels?"

"Of course." Kika beamed, proud. "But what are we searching for?"

He just about blurted out "Kit". Would she know someone who could help them get Francis out of prison?

"We need to find a tunnel runner, I guess. Kit told me they work down in the tunnels. They might know people, things." Russ acted as if he were an expert when he had no clue what he was doing. Isabelle said acting like he knew things would make him look smart, and so he tried.

At the bottom of the steps, they faced three doors in a dimly lit square area, the staircase hid a gloomy area along the forth wall. Russ peeked in each one but shut the doors, not sure which one to take. A soft sound behind the steps caught his attention. It could have been a sigh, a yawn, a deep breath, heck, it could have been one of them *squats* Cracker Jack had gone on about.

He motioned for Kika and Silver to wait in the shadows. Russ leaned against the steps so he was vulnerable and an easy target. People thought he was a dummy and took a chance when they normally wouldn't.

A subtle hand slipped in Russ' front pant pocket for the dollar he had peeking out. If he wouldn't have been so bloody jumpy, he might not have noticed, but as it was, he felt like that hand had jolted life into him.

Russ let him steal the dollar. To the air in front of him he said, "There's only one, 'cause I only have one problem. If you listen to it, you can keep it. If you have a solution, I double it. Help me with the solution and you get another bill."

Russ blocked the way out of the gloomy corner. So whoever was under them steps was trapped.

He'd been standing for about five minutes, with Kika pacing and peeking in the doors like a caged rat when along his ear came a soft whisper, "I heard they arrested Francis and have my own plan. If I show you…"

"Kit?" Russ stepped into the dark with her. Without a thought, he threw his arms around her and twirled her about. "You're alive."

"Barely." As she got her footing again, Kit leaned into him, her hands on his chest. She raised her head, grazing along his jaw and pushed away from him.

"Damn, Kit. You smell like the earth after I run the plough over it. So you heard about Isabelle's brother?" He had a hand along her waist and couldn't help but wonder why the heck the earthy fragrance came off her.

"I…" She pushed him off her, stepping into the light. "How is Isabelle?"

He smirked. "Great. I'm gonna be a pa." He couldn't help it, his smile grew to impossible widths.

When she'd stepped out of the shadows, Kika leapt up as if his pants had exploded in flames. Russ pulled him back 'cause he knew how nervous she was around guys.

She wore the same type of clothes as him. He glanced at the suspenders and cap. Her shirt was even half tucked in as he liked to wear it.

Kit explained, "We were making Kaplain's life hell. We had us some fun but things crashed around us. Francis is a good friend. I should have been with him."

Silver mumbled, *"She has revenge eyes, Russ, be careful you don't fall in that trap."*

"Shut up," she snapped at him. "Where the hell were you when I needed you?"

Kika peered over his shoulder. "Who's she talking to?"

Russ glanced at Silver leaning against the far door with his arms crossed, looking mighty bored.

"Silver," she spat the word at Kika.

Kika dropped to his knees. He always did weird things. So

Russ waited in case he was praying. Silver stepped forward and knelt beside Kika. They were silent and suddenly Kika pulled his blade out, leapt to his feet, and was behind Kit faster than Russ could sigh.

Russ pushed his blade down. "Enough of that you two."

"She lies. I feel nothing. Only the hope Russ offers."

"Silver is here. He knelt by you and everything." Russ pulled his blade away from Kit. "He's the hope you feel. He's always with me. I thought you knew that. Who the heck do you think I'm always talking to?"

"You see him?"

"Of course. I thought you could, too."

Kika pursed his lips and stored his blade away.

"Done now? Think we could hear Kit's plan?" Russ asked, opening his hanky and taking out a cookie Isabelle had made. He offered the treat to Kit since he had this urge to take care of her that he couldn't explain.

Her filthy hands reached for it. First, she sniffed it. Studied it. "This is just a cookie."

"Yeah. Isabelle made them. They don't taste as good as they used to, but she's a good cook."

Glaring at Kika, she bit into it. Her eyes darted over them and Kika stayed behind Russ as if she were deadly.

"I saw you with her... Her playing with Fangs. I...didn't want to bother you, but I wanted to thank you for giving me the push I needed to get off the tunnel floor." She shared a half smirk. Russ had forgotten how much he enjoyed talking to her.

Seeing Kit smile gave him a warm feeling inside.

"My plan means stealing something," she said.

Silver studied her intently. *"Yes, Russ, that will help."*

He knew she'd help.

"Wait here." She vanished under the steps.

"That's Kit. I told you about her," Russ explained to Kika.

Kika whispered, "You didn't tell me she was a warrior of the earth." He stood a bit taller.

"Probably because I have no idea what that is. Just be nice, she's scared. And stop acting weird."

She returned in a second and slipped through the door to their right.

They followed as fast as rabbits. The air reeked like a familiar mix of dirt, dust, and mildew.

Knowing this wasn't a place for a woman; Russ asked her, "Are you hurt? Do you need me to get you out of here safely?"

"She's fine on her own," Kika snapped as if Russ annoyed him and should leave him be with her or something.

She glared at each of them with her intense stare but she stood taller. Kika had the right approach with her. She wanted to prove she could survive on her own. Russ let him slip in behind her and followed from further back. "I'm Kika. You ever hear of me?"

"No," she told him and he glanced at Russ as if he should have told her about him.

Russ remembered what Cal had said about a woman picking a warrior and added for him, "Kika is studying to be a *Cîpay* warrior from Sacred Land. He taught me everything fun about the earth. He's not married if ever you're searching for a husband. I mean, you could do worse. He's smart, he's fast, he reads, and he shoots a nice arrow."

She stopped walking and glared at Russ so he stopped talking.

Kika grinned, though.

These tunnels were more mysterious than the ones on Sacred Land. Some were neat and clean, then unexpectedly they'd lead off into a rat hole for them to wriggle through. Lanterns lined the corridors, but she never reached for one. Kika used his lantern more to check her out than to give them light. Not sure why, but that annoyed Russ a wee bit.

"You and Francis together?" Russ asked. "Isabelle said you are, yet you didn't come by for lunch with him so I wondered what's going on."

"I am not leaving him," she promised.

Kika marked the walls with his free hand every now and again with the symbols they used in the tunnels. They were always in a specific order with variations: bird, rock, water, sky, earth. So it read: Where the Eagle Soars, Small Rock, Running Water, Sunny Skies, and Sacred Earth or it could read: Humming Bird, Crooked Rock, Standing Water, Windy Skies, and Blessed Earth... The combinations were endless, but the order was always the same.

Kika stopped and pulled Kit into his arms. The lantern was at his feet and he had a knife to her throat. It happened in an instant, 'cause well, Kika moved liked that: faster than Russ could think.

"What now?" Was he searching for a reason to act tough? Holding a knife to her throat wasn't that brilliant, even for Kika.

"She's taking us in circles." Kika motioned with his chin at the mark he'd made earlier and he was right, this particular area felt familiar. The rocks were cut with axes, which was different from the other tunnels, which were worked smooth. Why keep bringing them to this tunnel?

A man in a sheet appeared before them, a gun in his hands. He shot and the echo resonated through the tunnel, shaking them.

Russ threw his blade.

Silver smacked into Kika as he pulled his soul to the earth and the dim lantern light was enough for Russ to see the blood on Kika's shoulder as Kit stumbled away from him.

Kit dropped to all fours so she could steal the light. She scrambled away from the sheet as he fell and she rounded the corner. Russ let her go because Cracker Jack stood before him.

She hadn't shown herself in a bit, and seeing her in the tunnel shocked the dirt right off Russ. He stepped back and almost ran the other way. It was just like her to scare the dirt right off him, so he fought the fear and ignored her. If she watched, he couldn't very well kill a man who had killed his friend. Well…he wouldn't assume Kika was dead yet. Shot didn't mean dead, he promised himself.

Russ approached the sheet carefully but Cal was before him, appearing out of nowhere. With his face painted like a warrior and his arrow necklace resting on his bare chest in the dead of winter, he looked like a monster. More so than Cracker Jack hovering beside them, freaking Russ out with her clean shoes and perfect hair tied in a bun as if she wasn't dead but ready to tattle on him to Jesus.

"Leave this guy to me," Cal said, setting his lantern on the ground. The light danced around them, making shadows.

"Aren't you supposed to be in the hotel room? Pa is gonna–"

Russ took Cal's knife from him. "Pa is used to me ignoring him. Don't kill this guy," Russ ordered and left Cal to deal with the jerk. He rushed to check on Kika, in case.

He was dead.

Russ said a prayer over his body and pulled his grief in. Pain trickled out in anger and tears. He faced the wall and wiped his hurt on his sleeve. This was his fault. They should have stayed in the room and waited for Pa and…and what? Be victims in another way.

Frustrated, Russ watched Cal press his knuckles into the guy's vocal cords and he pulled Russ' knife out of his arm so he'd bleed out. The conscious man tried to break free, but with a quick slice, Cal cut the tendons in his ankles and he dropped in a pile. Cal proceeded to tie him up and hang him upside down on the lantern hook. He hung the sheet in front of him and made him face the wall so they didn't have to look at him. "There, not dead. Happy now? He can hang out for a spell, and if God wants him to live, He'll save him."

"You have to mark the back of his hand," Russ said with a shake to his voice that made Cal glance his way.

Cal squinted. "What for?"

"So he doesn't get cursed back to the earth when he dies."

"I don't carry around a tattoo making kit, moron, and rituals like that don't exist or I'd know about 'em."

Russ fell to his knees. "Who taught you to make a tattoo?"

"Ma. Who else?"

"Ma?" Russ gaped, shocked. "Well, I can't ask Ma to show me how to mark this guy up. Maybe we could make a deep scar or something." Using Cal's knife, he made two deep cuts on the back of the guy's hand in the shape of a cross. The only symbol he could think of that would ensure a good eternal life. He took the sheet off and spread the white cloth on the ground so he wouldn't die in it. Then Russ knelt beside him, gathered loose dirt off the floor, and built the soil into a pile. "We'll create a ritual. None exist because this is a curse our family made and we'll end it."

"Since when do you believe in curses?" Cal knelt by him and watched as he drew symbols in the dirt. He used the symbols from the gold cross Charlie had given Isabelle.

"I ain't taking chances. These guys are hurting people I care about. Our only other option is to take these souls in ours and move on with them, but they wouldn't even look at me." Russ' voice shook again.

"Me neither. They're terrified of me." Cal glanced at Kika. "Desire will be crushed."

"We can fight them like Pa by going to trials. We can stop them from getting in our tunnels as Skinny did. We can forbid them to use our tunnels as Antoine does. But what if Silver is right and there is more to it? What if we're fighting a bunch of maleficent spirits who can't move on and make their hosts nutso? All that won't help. It's like fighting a giant fire with a small bucket of dirt."

Cal nodded and scooped up the bit of dirt. He blew the dust gently on the guy he'd strung up and said a prayer to Mother to free his soul and take theirs in place of his.

"So if we take their place, what we gonna do cursed to the earth, Cal?"

Cal got to his feet. "Protect it. You sure I can't kill him? I'd like to tell Desire I killed him."

"Tell her what you want. He doesn't die by our hands."

Cracker Jack melted into the wall and Russ could breathe easy again.

"I need to find Kit. She had a plan."

"You're with Kit? Her bright idea was to blow Francis out of there. We ain't doing that."

"Explosives?" Russ had thought that earlier. "No, but explosions do make nice distractions."

"You plan to steal explosives from these idiots?" Cal asked.

"Why not? They take things from us."

When Cal smiled, Russ saw his French Savage brother. He returned to his stone warrior face, the face—he told Russ later—that kept him alive when he hunted.

"This way," Kit called from around the corner. "Hurry."

Cal had already vanished, leaving Russ in the dark.

–Twenty-Eight–

"Wow," Russ stammered. The room housed more explosives than a guy could dream up. Crates and crates full of 'em.

"Think we could use 'em?" Kit asked. She'd placed the lantern on one of the crates and the flames danced dangerously, casting shadows around the room.

"No idea how. But we should probably store a few of these crates until I come up with a plan." He opened a crate marked 'Nobels' along the side, to peek inside.

"I'm sorry about your friend." Her voice was sincere.

Russ was sorry, too.

"If it helps, when I lost everyone I loved, I held onto one hope." She never told him what her hope was.

"He's safe, watching over us. That's my hope. Sorrow shouldn't be felt when someone dies a brave death. We must let them continue their journey." Isabelle had told him this, and over time, Russ believed her, 'cause letting them go on adventures alone made more sense than crying over someone he couldn't go on adventures with again.

Kit grabbed an entire crate and brought it to the tunnel they'd come from. Russ was about to follow her with a second crate when a voice drifted into the room.

"Take these babies to the tracks," the voice said in an unfamiliar accent, like he over bit his A's. "Load them from there."

Russ ducked behind a stack of crates, but Kit walked in at the same moment as the men did.

"Oh what do we have here? A dame. A pretty little Coolie. What you doing on this side of the tunnels, Shela? Ya lost?"

She babbled in Chinese about not knowing where she was. Russ peeked as a man in a suit dragged Kit by the arm and hauled her out. His hair was slicked back. He held a weapon Russ had never seen before, but he thought that maybe the strange device was a modified gun.

Were they government?

Russ followed them out 'cause he wouldn't let these guys hurt Kit.

Their light shone bright down the long corridor and if they glanced back, they'd see him. An arrow would be nice right about now. He was a good thrower but he only had one knife.

Best he could do was slip along the wall, following at a distance. If they attacked her, he'd intervene.

They dragged her through a door and Russ slipped closer. He stood in the open. The dark tunnel felt like a trap. If they came out, where would he go? Russ searched for Cal. Even if he were in a side tunnel, he'd never see him. He was good at hiding.

"What ya have in here, Coolie?"

Something metal hit the ground. Dammit. Russ opened the door and slipped in the room.

He didn't exhale.

One had Kit bent against a wooden table with a knife to her throat, the other went through her bag. The room was well lit. A fishy aroma hung in the makeshift kitchen.

Russ sneaked behind the one pinning her and whispered, "Freeze or I slice." He pulled him off Kit.

His pal dropped Kit's things and stared ahead. Kit pulled a shoelace from her back pocket and tied his hands behind his back while Russ kept his bloke still. She got in his face when he was secured, "Tell me what you're doing with the explosives."

"Hauling them out. All I know."

Kit got to her feet and helped Russ secure the other one. They tied their feet, too. These guys didn't put up a fight, which made Russ nervous. Either they were super confident or didn't know how to fight and were just goons sent in to do some dirty work.

She sighed, glaring at them. "Shipping explosives to where?"

They were silent. Russ didn't really care, they had one crate, probably all they needed for a distraction, so he searched the room for a way out, but Kit had a knife to the one's privates, and she repeated her question with a crazy look to her.

Russ found an exit leading to another hallway. He prepared to leave when the man said, "Eau Claire. Eau Claire. A town no one cares about."

Russ turned around. He cared about Eau Claire. He knew a whack of people who cared a whole bunch. "Why?"

He shrugged. "We haul the crates there safely. All I know."

"If that's all he knows, you might as well kill them, Kit."

"My pleasure."

"No, wait." The other took a deep breath. "We're using tunnels from Eau Claire that go to the border. It's how we plan to haul these explosives to the States."

These idiots were not the freaks who'd tried to burn Isabelle. "They're smugglers, Kit. These aren't the guys we're looking for."

Kit didn't give up. "Do you know Francis? Do you know what he protects?"

One of the blokes answered, real calm, "We all stand to make a fortune, all I know."

"We can't let them ship those crates," Russ pointed out. "We can't have explosives travelling under Sacred Land."

Kit nodded in agreement. "Leave the shipment to me, Russ, because Kaplain won't like these boys on his turf." She ran off the way they'd come, leaving Russ feeling like they'd somehow made a silent deal: she'd keep them from shipping the explosives while he found a way to use them to get Francis out of this mess.

PART THREE

SPRING

"What good is being dead if all I do is watch you suffer?"

–Silver

–Twenty-Nine–

The shipment of explosives never did make it to Eau Claire, and Russ was proud of Kit for however she'd kept them safe. He was thinking about making a trip to Moose Jaw to see her while he walked home from town, the mail in hand, when he noticed Ma stumble toward the house, her arms against the barn for support. She rested against the water barrel and slowly collapsed to the grass.

Russ ran to her, shocked at the blood streaming down her leg. She wasn't a light woman so he shouted for help and Pa ran from the fields where he planted crops and helped him carry her in the house.

~~

Two days later, Antoine and Hoolie were out planting Pa's crops and Doc had left. Cal and Russ paced in front of the house, waiting to find out what the heck was wrong with Ma.

Pa walked out with a bundle in his arms, but the sorrow on his face spoke volumes. He sat on the steps with his oldest sons on either side of him. "Your ma is doing better, but your brother didn't make it." He wept over his baby and Russ leaned on him and cried with Pa.

"Why?" Russ asked when Pa finally pulled his emotions together.

"His soul wasn't ready. Perhaps next time. I miss him, yet I didn't even know him."

Silver appeared and knelt in front of Pa. He bowed his head. *"Your son is safe. He could not find the strength for the journey he was to endure. He has chosen another path that will touch your lives, soon. This is all I know."*

"Can I hold him?" Cal took the baby from Pa and they were silent for a bit, thinking. At some point Sammy joined them and snuggled on Russ' lap.

"Xavier," Cal said, naming the baby. "He looks so strong. I'll dig him a burial hole by the oak trees."

Pa stared at the oak trees lining the creek, far off in the distance, on Antoine's land. "He'll need a bed, to rest in," he finally mumbled.

Their custom was to return the body in the dirt they came from, but Russ agreed, Ma would want to see her baby in a bed of some sort and not in the dirt. He shot up, taking Sammy by the hand. "We'll make it. Right, Sammy?"

~~

Russ was alone with Ma in the barn, checking her mare. A week passed since the funeral on Antoine's land. Pa told Russ not to talk about the death of his brother but he was troubled because on top of everything else, this was a new worry he hadn't considered for Isabelle.

"Ma? How did Xavier die? Pa talks of spirits and journeys, but I want to know what really happened."

"You are the first one to ask."

"I didn't mean to pry… I just need to know."

"I fell." She kept working.

"Was there something…anything I could have done?"

"No. Pass me the brush." She grabbed it from him. "I'm older; it's not as easy to carry a child. My balance isn't as good." She stared at the horse. "I fell, Russ. I was chosen to protect my child while he grew and I fell. He died because I am old and I fell. This is how life really works."

She wasn't that old. "Ma?" He hadn't ever seen her cry and her lack of emotions about this bothered him. "How can you be so strong?"

She stopped working and faced him.

He wanted to say he was scared. That he was sorry. That he hurt with her. All those words were lost on his lips as she glared at him with her thinking eyes. Finally, he bent and grabbed another brush from the bucket so he didn't have to look at her anymore.

She walked up to him, placed her hand on his chin, and squeezed. "You have one job in this life; be strong for those who don't ask what really transpired. No matter what accidents occur, and they will happen. You won't be able to protect everyone or even this land. But you have to stay strong because there are moments when you can do something. Moments when you can protect. And if you're all sad and feeling sorry for yourself, you're useless in those moments and that isn't an accident; that is you being weak. If you can't take it, if you feel like breaking down then you come out here and brush this mare until you feel better, but you stay alert and you be ready."

Russ nodded and had to confess everything he hid this past week, "Francis will be taken to Regina and executed. It's final."

"How did Isabelle take this news?"

Russ rested his head against the horse. "I haven't told her. I can't tell her. I haven't told anyone. They can't take any more bad news." Russ tossed the brush in the bucket and sighed. He stared out at the field through the open barn door. A cold spring rain fell but the barn stayed warm.

Ma whispered something and Russ glanced her way. "What did you say?"

"I said, 'it's a long way from Moose Jaw to Regina'."

"What does that mean?"

She glanced up from where she worked. "You said he is to be executed in Regina. But his trial was in Moose Jaw. They'll have to bring him there. Cross roads, tracks, probably even cross the blessed lands. You'd think, anyhow."

"You saying I should go make an accident along that journey?"

She stared at him. "I never said that. Now you're searching for trouble." She worked some more. "Accidents happen all the time, though." She shrugged. "Some we can't help and others we can. Now you run along and tell Isabelle I am sorry to hear about her brother. He's a good boy."

Russ stared at her, not moving.

"Get on now."

He didn't move.

"Worrying about Isabelle will do no good. That is

something you can't control. Focus on things you can."

"Like that trip from Moose Jaw to Regina?"

"Get."

He ran off, no idea what Ma had said to trigger the perfect plan, but damn, they were going to bring Francis home.

–THIRTY–

The next month—

Kit studied the map Russ had laid out on the hotel floor and she glanced up at him. Gosh, she found it impossible to believe he married someone else. She was so sure he was the one. What a stupid idea, really. Why would she think that about him anyway? Because of some vision? Because Silver said she belonged with him? What did he know?

Russ brushed the hair off his forehead and pointed again. She watched him, distracted. Why did he make her feel this way? She had a good man...one Russ was here to help her rescue.

She swallowed the lump in her throat and glanced down. He handed her the pencil and she expertly traced the tunnels over the map, marking the entrances with little x's. "Memorize them because I have to burn this before you leave. Many of these tunnels could be collapsed. I haven't been in them since the night you..." She wanted to say, "Held me" but his brother squinted and Cal made her nervous. "Since the night I lost everything."

"What do you see, Cal?" Russ asked.

"So the tracks and roads all meet here before Regina." He pointed to the place on the map. "This is our best place to ambush them. We'll walk the area to be sure."

"It's a two-day walk," Kit said. "Trust me. The tunnels aren't far from here. We have a chamber with a large entrance that allows even a horse to walk down. We could use it to hide, ride out."

Russ took out his pocket watch and let out a long sigh. "We have a couple days to get things ready." He was pale.

"We'll get you home before Isabelle goes into labour." She knew how he wanted to be there for his wife and Kit was about to send him off. She opened her mouth to say the words but he smiled at her and she quickly glanced away. *Damn it.* He saw things so clearly, she wasn't sure they could even do this without him.

"Ma's with her." Russ sighed. "No matter what we do now, everyone I love has a big target painted on them."

Kit frowned. "How so?"

"Francis didn't kill Jessie."

Kit kept perfectly still.

"They were coming for me, but Francis took the heat and they let him because they really wanted him. They were coming for me to flush him out." Russ studied her. "Everyone is afraid to think of why, but I do all the time. Now that his pa and older brother are dead, he owns the land they want. Well, he did. After he's out of the way, they'll be coming for Isabelle and I suppose me. Nothing we can do to stop that now that they sentenced Francis to death. He can't go home." He stared at Cal. "Sometimes, I think it'd be easier to protect our land if I knew what they wanted. Is it to use the tunnels? Is it for some drug that grows there? Or is there something else?"

Cal said, "Never mind all that. Don't you get it? Someone always wants Sacred Land for something else. We're here to say no. Plain and simple. Now your plan will get one of our warriors back. We have nothing to lose anymore, Russ. He's a dead man regardless and we're next on the list anyhow. Sorry, Kit, I didn't mean to be insensitive. I know how much he means to you."

She bowed her head. She knew the choice Francis had made and understood his sacrifice. All this was a distraction to get them away from Cursed Land.

"I have everything to lose." Russ reached for Kit's hand. "Tell me, Kit. Were you and Francis to be married?"

Kit drew in a deep breath, not looking at his hand, wondering why he felt so compelled to touch her all the time. Did he even notice when he did things like that?

"Our last words were in anger." She couldn't glance at Russ. "He went home for good and I didn't want to go with him."

She asked, "Russ, do you know who killed Jessie?" Should she tell him what Isabelle did? Would he know how to help her?

Russ swallowed so loud she heard him struggle with it. "A lot happened that night. A lot of bad guys died."

Cal sat back, watching them. "Could we focus on the task at hand? You two have a weird energy around you." He picked his brother's hand off Kit and shook his head. "I'm scared, too, but let's at least pretend we're not a bunch of cowards."

Russ tightened his fist and placed it on his lap, studying the map.

~~

They travelled by wagon and Kit snuggled under the covers watching the grey sky. This spring was the coldest she'd ever lived.

"You cold?" Russ asked.

Cal drove and stopped to point out where they'd placed warriors.

"I'm fine," she lied. If he sat by her she'd just die.

Russ slid in beside her. "It'll be warmer if we share blankets." He grinned and she couldn't help herself she smiled back. "You have a beautiful smile, Kit. You really should flash it more."

"Not much to smile about." She leaned on him. "You scared about being a pa?" she asked, to remind him of his family waiting for him.

He smirked, always so relaxed and happy to talk about Isabelle. She clearly meant everything to him. "Terrified, but Isabelle is great. I can do anything as long as I have her by my side."

Kit had to wonder if their connection was only in her head. He clearly didn't think about her that way. Yet, it wasn't Isabelle by his side, it was her. She was about to point that out then decided to let him be happy.

"So, you gonna fess up and tell me how you kept the explosives from going to Eau Claire?"

She pulled away to glance at him. "Well, I did store a few

for us before I wet the others. Then I played them boys against each other. Smugglers against Kaplain's crew. Now there are no more smugglers in Moose Jaw and Kaplain's men lost a lot of ground to cave-ins when they tried to haul unstable crates out."

"I was watching the newspapers, but we don't always get them all and they arrive a few weeks late. Think the explosions that made these cave-ins got in the papers?"

She shrugged. She couldn't read and never thought about it. Sometimes she felt like Russ lived in a very different world than her. "Probably not. Those who know about the tunnels like to keep them secret so they can do their business down there without idiots trying to cash in on their turf." She yawned, snuggling against him.

"Rest," he said. "It'll be crazy and you look so tired. We'll have Francis back with you soon."

–THIRTY-ONE–

Cal walked the tunnel in front of Russ. "What's going on with you two?" he demanded of Russ.

"Us two who?"

"You and Kit." He glanced over his shoulder with a worried frown. Darkness filled the rest of the tunnel, but the light from the lantern danced over his frown.

Kit had stayed by the church to unpack the explosives. Russ rubbed his gut, hoping to clear out the knots. "She's upset and missing Francis and I'm worried about Isabelle. The faster we get out of this mess, the happier we'll both be. Why?"

He really stared at Russ, up and down. "You haven't been messing around with her?"

"No!" Russ lifted the lantern to see his brother's face. Why would he think that? "What's wrong with you? She's my friend. I think of her like…Kika." He thought about that, because it wasn't entirely true. She was a friend, sure, but not like any other friend he'd had. Knowing she was around kept him grounded when he freaked the hell out like this. "I have to know your secret, Cal. You told me you were scared of everything…how do you stand so strong all by yourself? I need some of your not-freaking-the-hell-out attitude. I feel like throwing up. I can't leave Isabelle's brother to die, but I don't want to leave Isabelle when she's this close to labouring." Breathing was hard. He needed Kit to smack him or something so he calmed.

Cal touched the wall. His pants were filthy. He stood silently and mumbled something in the Language of the Dead. When he pulled away, Silver was with them.

"I have the wisdom of our ancestors with me. All I have to

do is touch the earth and I feel them. Their knowledge and courage flows through the earth. When I have an entire tribe believing in me, past, present, and future, my fear seems small."

Silver placed a hand on Russ' shoulder and the maps Kit had drawn exploded in his mind as if they were right in front of him. He knew exactly where he was, where the exits were, and what was overhead.

"This way." Russ took the tunnel to the right even though this path wasn't as big as the tunnel they'd turned off. Cal and Silver followed.

They walked in silence for over an hour before they reached a dead end.

"We have to clear away this debris," Russ told them. The air had a strange taste to it, as if thick and dusty.

"Isn't there an easier way?" Cal complained as he pulled a large chunk from the collapse and stacked the debris along the wall.

"Nope. The entrance we need is close to here, probably on the other side of this rubble. I feel it."

Cal didn't ask how, just cleared the mess.

"This is the spot," Russ confirmed, seeing the area so clearly in his mind, both underground and above. "The road is to the right, the tracks where you'll make the diversion are to the left. This comes up by a clump of bushes. Silver, check things out, make sure I'm right."

Silver left.

Cal sighed. "Pa says we shouldn't get him to do things for us."

"So? He's here, he can help."

"I agree with Pa on this one. Silver is getting too solid, he needs to let go of his life, not grip it tighter. What is going to happen when old Bellecoeur kicks the bucket? Silver needs to move on, Russ."

Russ climbed the mess to check how deep the debris ran, ignoring his brother. He didn't want Silver to move on.

Russ could actually see the exit. "I can fit through here. This will work. Silver can let me know when they're close and I'll come up and get Francis once you have the wagon secured."

Cal nodded. "I'll create the diversion and make sure he's there for you to grab."

It sounded easy, but a good plan always did.

–Thirty-Two–

Russ waited underground. He lay on the debris, listening. When a wagon ran overhead, dirt crumbled on him. Russ peered out of the hole at Silver who lay in the grass, his link to the world above. "*Not them,*" Silver said, bored.

Russ sighed deeply.

"*What troubles you?*" Silver asked.

"What if they see Cal? Or you? What if Cal blows himself up?"

"*He's fine. I'd tell you if anything went wrong with him.*"

"Tell me before things go wrong. What good is being dead if you're useless when I need you?"

"*Thanks, Roussel, glad you understand how hard this is for me.*" His sarcasm annoyed Russ. "*I can't see the future, only souls, dead or alive, that's all I got.*"

Russ stared at his grandpa, seeing his comforting grey eyes. "Why did Miss Penelope leech onto me and why didn't Jessie? I want to get rid of her."

"*We both know why Jessie didn't latch onto you.*"

"He's following Isabelle?" A bit of vomit lurched up the back of his throat. "I have to get him off her."

"*Your shadow appears stronger every time you're afraid and weakens when you're relaxed. She doesn't want to do you harm, but Isabelle's is sucking her into the earth.*"

"Damn it. You can't let him do that."

"*I don't know how to stop him.*"

"Just…don't let him. Find your own spirits to help you."

Russ stayed quiet, lost in thoughts about how to ditch Cracker Jack and wondering if maybe he could offer her a deal that involved her punishing him then leaving. Of course, the only punishment worse than her popping up in his life at bad times was losing Isabelle, so he didn't offer her the deal.

Silver leapt up. "*This is them.*" He vanished. An explosion shook the ground and Russ waited for him to return.

"Miss Penelope? Can you tell me when to head up?" He didn't trust her, but he thought it might be worth a try to put her to good use, show her he was the boss of things. She didn't show herself, though.

Russ was ready to slide out of the hole when Cracker Jack whispered by his ear, "*This is probably the dumbest idea you've had yet.*"

A shiver passed over him as he slipped out. Daylight smacked into him, making it hard to focus.

The prison wagon was stopped on the tracks, alone. A group of warriors were riding off on horses. Probably part of Cal's diversion. Russ' job was to get Francis out and safe, so he ignored the fire at the front of the van and the arrow through the driver's head, which Cal was trying to remove.

He flung the back door open. Francis shook his head as if to clear it. "Russ?" His hands were shackled to the bench. Russ had a bunch of tools in his pack and he took out what he needed to break him free. "What are you doing?"

"I will not let them kill you for something you didn't do."

He helped Francis out of the van. Cal threw a body in the back of the van and tied the corpse where Francis had been. Russ didn't have time to watch them follow through with his plan, but Kit did nod to them as she set the explosives by the gas tank.

A train was coming in the distance.

Russ led Francis to the hole and they dived in as the explosion lit the skies around them, ringing his ears. The earth shook so they moved over the debris quickly. It didn't ease up as the train passed overhead.

Fallen rocks scratched their legs and hands. Russ had gone down the hole the wrong way and couldn't get turned around. So he had to shimmy backwards until he dropped into the main tunnel with Francis.

Then he felt around for the lantern and got a good look at Francis. He was skinnier than usual and his eyes were caved in. In this dim light, they were even glossy, but he was alive. Russ planned to keep him that way.

The ground shook. Debris fell on them.

Russ dived for cover as darkness surrounded them.

He coughed, tasting the dust.

"Francis? Francis?" Russ felt around for him. He dug through his pack and found a candle. He lit it and checked the mess. "Francis, I'm trapped. How are you?"

No answer.

How would he get out of here?

"Francis?"

–Thirty-Three–

With the lantern, Kit headed down the tunnel toward the water. She grew up in these tunnels but they were no longer home. She touched the wall for a marker and chose the path to the river. From the water, she had a good view of the road. The train had stopped a ways off and men were out looking at what they'd hit or what had caused the explosion.

She scanned the area to make sure everything was fine. Someone crawled out of the hole Russ had brought Francis down.

Francis? What was he doing? He looked lost, confused. Her heart sped because something was wrong. He should be headed underground to the church.

He saw her. She pointed out the men looking at the debris so Francis dropped and crawled in the bushes. Kit rushed to the tunnel she'd left. It came up on the other side of the tracks. She had to get over there and see what was wrong with Francis and Russ.

When she came to her side of the tracks, Francis was already there, slipping in the hole carefully. "Shh," he said. "They're getting close. There was a collapse on the other side. I lost Russ and hit my head. I have such a bad headache I can't even think."

Without hesitation, she grabbed his hand and ran toward the church. They could go in from the other side to dig Russ out.

"He might not be alive," Francis whispered.

"He is. I feel it," she promised herself, gripping his hand tighter.

–THIRTY-FOUR–

Cracker Jack appeared. She leaned against the wall, her arms crossed.

Russ stared at her. "What do you want?"

"*It stinks in here*," she complained.

"You don't have to follow me around."

"*You might want to follow me, though.*" She sounded smug. Russ lifted the candle to get a better look at her. The sadness in her annoyed him. She made all her own problems, what the heck had her upset now?

"*I make my own problems?*" she snapped, reading his mind. "*Your explosives quaked the unstable ground and look at this mess.*" She shook her head. "*Now what will you do, smarty-pants?*"

They were in a tight area, with about enough room to sneeze.

"Might look like a trap to you, but digging's in my blood and I ain't afraid of nothing down here," he lied, because he was afraid of her. He blew out the candle so he didn't have to stare at her, then he removed his shoes so he could feel for a draught of any sort. There had to be another way out.

He leaned against the wall, wondering where Silver was and if Francis was alive on the other side of the rubble. Kit would never forgive him if he got Francis dead and Russ didn't like the idea of her upset.

Miss Penelope stood beside him in the dark and their shoulders rubbed. "Will I die down here?" Russ asked her.

"*If you want to, I guess.*"

"I don't."

"*I never knew you for not doing what you wanted, despite what anyone said.*"

She was right. He could do this. In the Language of the Dead, he prayed for his ancestors to guide him. He waited for the enlightenment he'd gotten earlier when Silver had touched him but the wisdom never came. Cracker Jack sniffled beside him.

Was she crying again? "Miss Penelope, could you stop feeling sorry for yourself for one moment and maybe find me another way out?"

She sighed. "*I could.*"

He lit his candle to get a better look at her. She wiped her tears and stood, pretending she hadn't been crying.

"Will you help me get out of here?"

"*Only if you stop calling me Old Cracker Jack in your mind.*"

"You hear all my thoughts?" His mouth fell open, horrified.

"*Yeah and I don't like this connection any more than you. Why do you hate me so?*"

"Because you're mean," he stated the obvious.

"*You're the mean one. I was protecting myself from you. You turned everyone against me.*"

They stayed like that, and Russ thought about Silver attaching himself to Bellecoeur. He had a strong will to live, which kept Silver alive. Russ didn't want to be like Bellecoeur, but he suddenly felt that way because what she said was true. He'd told Pa she was a horrible teacher. Russ always put her down, and he guessed if he had someone like him in his face all the time, he'd be annoyed with the world, too.

"I'm sorry, but my regret doesn't make how you treated us right. You should be sorry, too."

"*I am, Roussel. If I could go back, I would change that first day we met.*"

Russ didn't even remember the day they'd met. He must have been young.

"*You were teaching your sister to read and I pulled the book from you, and told you that my job was to teach. We were told in Normal School to establish who was the teacher with the older students. And I did what I thought best.*"

Her words brought the memory to life for him and he saw

the book clearly. The one Isabelle had stolen off her desk not long after.

"Back then, I had no idea what a Cîpay was, or how deep your beliefs in teaching and learning were rooted. I'd given you the greatest insult possible without meaning to and you made my life hell for it. If I could go back and tell you that you were a good teacher, I would, because you are."

Russ sat up prouder, her words had a deep impact on him, and he realized that he could teach. He should teach. Why wasn't he teaching? He liked to farm, but his heart was in teaching and when he got home, he'd tell Isabelle this and see what she thought.

Miss Penelope got to her feet and pointed to an entrance that was high in the wall. The hinges on the door made it open upwards. He would have missed this way out completely. This type of exit was for coming into the tunnel and not getting into from this end, but he could make anything work.

He scrambled through it, trusting her because he had no other choice. The passageway grew smaller then bigger, keeping him on his knees the entire way. He felt ground wearing through his pants. With the candle in front of him, he moved much slower than he wanted to, but patience was always his strongest quality and he took his time. Strange bugs ignored him and the soil had an orange tint that made him nervous. Russ even took out his hanky and covered his mouth so as not to breathe in any of the dust. Time disappeared until he wondered if he'd travelled for hours. It wouldn't have surprised him if he crawled out into night-time. But the day greeted him when he pushed up a board and popped up into a cemetery like a lost gopher.

The place was desolate and he glanced around the stones, lost in a field. No buildings, no life surrounded them.

He was lost but didn't have time to think his next actions through. He needed to get back to Francis. He might be hurt in that collapse from the other side. Russ headed out of the graveyard. His knees ached. When the church came into view, Russ just about died. How the heck had he made it back?

"Thanks, Miss Penelope."

He sneaked into the church in case someone else had returned.

The place was quiet.

Where was Cal? Or Kit?

Thirsty, Russ opened his pack for his water but found the flask empty. He'd have to head to the back of the church and see if the priest had anything to drink before he started the search for Francis. Francis might be hurt and they'd need supplies. He was in the back, filling his flask from a pitcher when the church door flew open and a shadow rushed in. Another held the door.

What was going on?

Russ peeked out and quickly ducked back in when a strong aroma of gasoline wafted through the area.

His pack rested on the pew in the back, hiding his knife. Still, he couldn't let them burn a church.

Russ sneaked out, but they were already heading out the door, tossing a torch to light the back.

Russ grabbed a drape from the side window and tossed the heavy fabric on the fire to smother the flames but they must have sprayed the drapes too because they exploded. He was cut off from the front door and the area grew smoky.

What was happening? Why burn a church? He rushed to the altar so he could get in the tunnel. The thick smoke disoriented him and Russ ran into the priest, knocking the man in his sleeping garments off his feet.

"Sorry," Russ mumbled, helping him up. "Two guys did this. We have to get out of here."

"We have to put this fire out." The priest tried to break free from his grip, but the only way out was the tunnel so Russ dragged him to the entrance and shoved the altar aside.

"Help me, we have to save the Saint Sacrament," the priest was trying to lift the tabernacle by himself, like a madman.

Russ placed a firm hand on his shoulder. "We have to get out. Your church is lost."

He followed Russ, heat rushing over them in the thick smoke. Once in the tunnels, they hurried until Russ felt they were safe, then he stopped and turned the lantern on the priest. "You hurt?"

"Just shaken up," he admitted.

"What the hell? Why did they burn your church?"

The priest closed his eyes and leaned against the dirt wall as if the weight of the world rested on his shoulders. He was around Pa's age. "Who are you?" he demanded.

"Russ from Sacred Land."

He stood up taller and followed Russ as they kept walking. "You're real? I grew up with stories of *Cîpay* but they were just that, stories. Legends."

"I'm real all right. Real tired of this shit. Come on." Russ headed toward where Cal would be.

The priest started talking, interrupting his thoughts. "A man paid me a visit last week, said I'd do things his way or lose my church. I'd read about them harassing guys in the south, and sent word to the warriors that we need help. I never expected they'd send a boy. Thank you for saving me, but losing that church…"

"Their way?"

"They demanded a bunch of things from me, but mostly, they wanted to store crates and barrels. A few nights and they'd be out of my hair and they'd even leave cash for my trouble."

Russ glanced over his shoulder at him. "Did you?"

"A man can do a lot of things, young *Cîpay,* but the day he compromises his beliefs, is the day he sells his soul to the devil."

Russ thought about what he meant. "So you knew they were up to no good and wanted you by the neck. You're smart." Still, he wasn't so sure this wasn't related to them coming for Francis. Maybe they knew his way out was this church or something.

Russ held a lantern up and almost kissed the mark on the wall that promised they were close.

They turned right and ran into Francis and Kit. He had a hand resting on her hip and pulled her in closer when he rounded the corner. Russ was so happy to see him; he threw his arms around him. "I thought you were buried so I was going back for you."

"We were going back for you," Kit told him. "You hurt?"

"I'll live."

Cal stood behind them.

"Where's Silver?" Russ asked Cal.

"He went to check on things at home and never came back," Cal mumbled, glancing at the priest in his nightwear. "Why's he here?"

"Church is burning."

Cal dropped his pack and pulled out water and food. "Seems we ain't the only guys with troubles. Rest. You're safe here." Then he headed back down the tunnel, probably to take care of things above ground.

"There were two of them," Russ called after him. Kit wiggled out of Francis' grip and went with Cal, leaving Russ alone with Francis who closed his eyes, beat, and the priest in his nightwear who frowned, worried.

"Damn, Francis," Russ said. "Am I ever happy to see you."

"Isabelle?"

"Come home, see her for yourself. She misses you," Russ told him. "You and Kit can settle…"

Francis opened his eyes. "Russ, you know I can't go home. Tell Kit…" He sighed and ran off down a side tunnel.

Russ thought about following him, but the priest put a firm hand on his shoulder to stop him. Yeah, he couldn't really leave the guy alone down here. Why was he always the responsible one?

–THIRTY-FIVE–

The trip home was long and Russ felt like he ran the entire way. Nothing happened fast enough.

His house reeked like mustard seeds when he walked in. Russ glanced around confused. A yellow powder sprinkled on the doorframe. What was going on?

The weight of what he had to tell Isabelle made Russ take the steps one at a time as opposed to the wild way he normally dashed up them. Francis was alive but would they see him again? He needed to tell her everything and see if she had a better solution for them. Thinking alone was hard.

When he saw Isabelle in bed, helpless, Russ thought for a moment that Miss Penelope took him up on his silent deal and he cursed himself for even thinking it.

Ma sat with Isabelle with a cold cloth on Isabelle's head. Russ hurried to his wife's side.

"What's that smell?" he asked, recognizing ammonia and boiled wheat mixed into the stench of death.

"Isabelle?"

She didn't move.

Ma explained, "The last few days she had labour pains. They stopped all of a sudden and I'm nervous."

"She's labouring? Isn't it too early for that?" He grabbed her hand and almost climbed on the bed with her, no idea what to do. Cal and Pa had explained all the details but this was like nothing they'd said.

"She's too weak, Roussel. The pains are in and out and she's too weak to push if they get stronger. She needs to eat. She needs water. She needs sleep, but this fever..."

Russ sat up straighter, hearing what she wasn't saying.

"So what do we do if she goes into labour?" Soup and

water were on the nightstand. By the looks of the strange tin case with medicine and the poultice, he guessed that Gerard had been by.

"Ma? How long has Isabelle been sick?"

Ma wouldn't face him. "Since you left. She'll get better. We need to give her strength to labour. I sent Pa for Doc several times, but he didn't show yet. Gerard was good with her and he'd gone to talk to Doc to be sure they didn't miss anything. He'll be back. I've done everything I could think of."

"Then what's wrong?"

"Her fever won't break."

Isabelle opened her eyes and studied him with those telling brown eyes. She raised the right side of her lip into a tease of a smile and the action gave him hope. "You're home. Francis?"

Russ crawled right in bed with her and held her. "Oh my gosh, I missed you, Isabelle." He kissed her hand. She burned up. "Francis is fine, but he's not coming home. We'll meet up with him somewhere else. I have so much to tell you, but first you have to get better."

She nodded and sipped a spoonful of the soup Ma offered her. Then she snuggled against him and fell back asleep. Russ rested for a bit, thinking.

He touched Isabelle's belly gently as he sat beside her.

"We'll save this one." Ma was determined and her optimism took Russ off guard. "I had Pa chip ice from the ice block. She likes the cold along her gums, so I'll bring you more. On the back of her neck and on the bottom of her feet is the hottest so keep a cold pack there. I left wheat in a bag on the ice and we'll use that when the pack cools. It'll last longer. Bernadette killed one of her chickens and is boiling the hen into a soup. She needs fat."

The haunting possibility that Isabelle might not survive weighed on him. Russ thought about how she'd killed Jessie and he might be sucking her to hell. "Ma, could you make her a tattoo on the back of her hand? Like ours. Make her one with a cross, too. And anything else you think might help."

"Russ…" Ma looked ready to tell him that was a stupid idea, but then she studied her own tattoo. "Couldn't hurt now, could it? You believe hard enough, it might help."

She went to get a few things then Russ watched her shove grey soot under Isabelle's skin with a fine needle, to give her a silver arrow like his.

It was weird to see Isabelle so tired. She always bustled with happy innocence.

Later that night, the contractions started. Ma had Russ climb behind her, holding her against his chest so he could feel the contractions for her and encourage her to push when needed, when each effort would count. By this time, she'd eaten the chicken soup, one sip at a time.

Her fever wasn't as high.

Gerard brought her all sorts of things. He'd rubbed mud on the soles of her feet that she said tickled. He'd made her swallow a pill Russ bet came from his store and not the Medicine Man world. Russ didn't complain. If Gerard used magic that might help her even a bit, Russ was game.

Russ sent Desire to find Kit, since she grew up among Healing Ghosts and might know ways to help. Russ asked Pa where Doc was, and he said tending to calls in hell. He looked right calm about it, but Russ worried he might have done him in. Strange what goes on in a man's world.

Isabelle gripped his hand with each contraction. Russ wished there was a way to relieve her of this pain, but Ma said if she were stronger, this type of suffering wouldn't be so hard on her.

Desire said things differently when she showed up with Kit. "We need to take her to the Healing Chamber."

—Thirty-Six—

Kit knew Isabelle was dying when she walked into the room. No amount of Healing Chamber would cure this. She knelt beside her and prayed for her soul to find peace quickly.

"Kit. Do something," Russ ordered her. The anger in his voice was intense. How could she tell him that the spirits were killing her?

"This is beyond what I can help, Russ." She refused to watch him. He sat behind Isabelle, cradling her in his arms.

Isabelle's chilled fingers brushed Kit's tear-stained cheek. "My baby."

The baby. Kit leapt up. She had to protect the child from these spirits. "Isabelle, do you have anise?"

Weakly she pointed to the drawer. Kit flung it open. Much to her shock there wasn't only leaves but seeds. She even pulled out dill. She handed the dill to Desire. "Get me more of this. Francis keeps a pile in the Healing Chamber. We need the entire plant, pile them around the bed."

Desire ran out.

She'd used these to help keep the evil spirits away. How bad had their assault gotten these past few months?

Kit tossed the seeds in a bowl with water and set to burning them over a candle. "Get her out from under the blankets I want to make a circle around her with these leaves."

Russ' mother set to work quickly.

Kit grabbed Russ' mother's hand that gripped the sheet. "I'm Kit."

"I know who you are. My husband talks highly of you and your healing skills. You can call me Ma, like all the others do."

Kit warmed up to her. She was skilled and open to

learning. The spirits around Isabelle felt much calmer when Ma was in the room, so she kept her working near Isabelle.

When Desire returned with the dill, Russ had questions that interrupted them. "What's wrong with her? What are you doing? How will this help?"

Desire placed a hand on his shoulder. "She can explain later, for now, we trust a healer. She is the last and knows something we do not."

"Isabelle, what else helped ease the burden? Do you hear them talking to you yet?" That was Russ' pa's biggest complaint. Of course, *Cîpay* burdened him and not evil spirits, but Kit planned to treat Isabelle the same and adjust when things helped.

Isabelle touched the chain around her neck.

Kit nodded. She had no one to explain the importance of the relic, but if it came from Russ' family she understood the sacred value. She wasn't above thinking anything was possible when dealing with malicious spirits. "I will make sure the talisman goes around the child's neck the moment he or she is born." Kit faced Russ' mother. "Will the birth be soon?"

"Yes, she has to push, but where will she find the strength?"

"Silver," Russ called. "Silver, we need you."

Silver stood by him. He was usually with Russ, so this didn't surprise her. He stood between Jessie and Isabelle, his arms crossed. Silver glanced over his shoulder at Russ, but to Kit, he explained, *"When he clings to the new world, he cannot see me. He is close to losing his vision of the old ways. I'm used to being ignored by him. Kit, the child's soul is strong, but this fool is after her. I will have to call on Cîpay to protect her."*

"What do I do?" she asked Silver. Russ glanced up at her and noticed she focused on the wall.

He squinted, trying to see what she saw.

Kit glanced away.

"Who are you talking to?" Russ demanded.

"Shh. *Cîpay.* I need one to protect your baby."

Russ nodded. "Yeah, you find one. I'll do whatever they want."

Silver called a woman to him. She appeared at his side, his height, soft brown curls highlighted her pale skin. Her gown flowed around her, gorgeous. She sat by Isabelle and met Kit's eyes. *"I'm Marie."* Golden eyes seared into her.

Kit pulled away. How was this pale woman *Cîpay?*

"Isabelle, push with me." Ma held her legs up. "You're so close, Isabelle. One more time. I see the baby's head. Bunches of brown wavy hair like Roussel's."

Now, of the things that happened to Isabelle, the treatments, and the kisses Russ poured on her, that one thing gave her the most energy. She opened her eyes. Her smile brightened the room and made the panic vanish.

Russ grinned at his ma.

Isabelle didn't push, though. She rubbed her face against Russ'. Kit held her hot hand. Too hot, but now was not the time to cool her down.

Isabelle shivered. "You hear that, Roussel? Our baby will look like you." She relaxed against him, but her next words were whispered to Kit, "I trust you to be there when I can't."

A scream broke through her lips and Isabelle bore down, pushing with her everything.

A girl broke into the light of the world with a strange tearing sound that alarmed Kit. The *Cîpay,* Marie, had a type of light shield around the child and when the wild spectres dived for her they bounced off and back into Jessie. Silver kept his hand on Jessie.

His ma said everything was fine. But she meant the baby. Isabelle's spirit lingered out of her body. Russ held her empty body, talking to her, but her breath left her.

Silver reached for her hand, his other gripped Jessie firmly. *"Ready?"* he asked her.

Much to Kit's shock, Russ split in two. A see-through Russ stood with Isabelle, holding her other hand. "I'm going with her."

Silver sighed.

"Russ?" Kit glanced at him on the bed.

He cried. "She's not breathing. Kit." His pleads broke her heart.

"Russ, stay with me."

He dropped his head on Isabelle's shoulder and held her

with a moan that pained her. His love was so deep, a piece of him died with her and she physically saw him leaving.

The baby cried and the see-through Russ shimmered but still walked with Isabelle, Silver, and Jessie.

As they strolled off into a strange glowing field that appeared where the wall had been, the real Russ glanced up. He wiped his tears and stared at his ma for answers. She asked him if he wanted to see his daughter but he shook his head.

"Maybe give him a moment," Desire offered, taking the baby. She watched the spirit Russ walk off.

The tribe's Medicine Man arrived in this moment. He bowed, respecting the *Cîpay* in the room. Cal and Bernoit followed him in and did the same.

Russ stared ahead, holding Isabelle. "All of you get out."

They all left. Kit went to follow them but decided that maybe someone should stay with him. Kit worked quietly, gathering the leaves and placing them back in the nightstand.

"She didn't glance back, not a good-bye or nothing. I watched her walk off." His jaw firmed as anger settled on him of how unfair life was.

"That's because a part of you went with her," Kit promised him quickly. "You will have to pull that part back, Russ."

"I can't. Thinking hurts." He kept his eyes closed, not moving. "Why did they kneel to my baby?"

"Respect. *Cîpay* protect her."

She gathered the towels off the floor and piled them. There was hardly any blood.

"Did Jessie kill her?"

Kit kept cleaning.

"Did he?" he demanded.

"She did something that upset Mother and to balance this disrespect out, she sacrificed her soul. The spectres from Cursed Land were in Jessie, corrupting him." She sat and told him everything about the ritual she unknowingly helped her do. About how Silver protected her and called on *Cîpay* to guard his daughter. "You're a father now, Russ. You can't sit here and feel sorry for yourself, that girl needs you."

He thought about this. "So what did Isabelle do? She was kind. She cared about everyone."

"It doesn't matter, that is between her and Mother."

"But you know?"

"Yeah. I do."

"Was it really so bad?" He rested his head against Isabelle.

"No. It wasn't. In fact, what she did might have been a good thing." She gently placed her hands on his. "I'm sorry, Russ. I know how much you love her."

"I shouldn't have left her."

"She died knowing you were here and her brother was safe. That's a good thing."

Kit said a few prayers and Russ watched, holding Isabelle against his chest.

Doc came in. Kit shot up and nodded to him. He was tall and covered in mud with fine orange dust that was vaguely familiar. He spoke to Russ but Russ stared ahead and didn't answer.

"I want the baby brought in here, so I can check her. He needs to see her."

–Thirty-Seven–

Dead.

Isabelle was dead.

Doc checked the baby and told him she was a healthy baby girl. She was early, but doing fine. And she was lucky because the fever should have killed her.

Russ watched this unfold while he sat quietly with Isabelle, as they always did, and thought.

He watched Kit move around the room. She had Isabelle's secrets. How? When had they met? He wanted to know everything. Yet he didn't. Why would Isabelle keep this from him?

When Desire told him to let Isabelle go, he glanced at Kit. Her chest moved up with a big breath and she whispered, "It's time."

He did. He let Isabelle go. Not because he wanted to, but because Kit knew loss and if she thought he should face the world, he didn't want her telling Pa he'd gone crackers.

Russ left her on the bed. No one moved to touch her. Her hair was a mess on the sheet as if she slept. Just sleeping. An angel.

She was gone off with Silver, leaving Russ broken inside. Shattered.

He wanted everything ruined like him. He tossed the lantern at the wall. Glass shattered into a million pieces and he scrutinised the mess of glass and goop wondering what else he could break when Cracker Jack—Miss Penelope—all prim and proper appeared, her pretty shoes hovering over the mess. She looked mighty sad, as usual, and her stupid face annoyed him.

Russ snagged the glass on the nightstand and pitched it at

her. And the bowl. And the notebook—

He stopped himself. The notebook was Isabelle's.

Russ turned his back on Miss Penelope and brought the notebook with him to the haystack to think.

He curled up in the chilly night, clutching the notebook. He must have passed out because when he woke, Kit held him. It seemed fitting that she'd stayed. He'd held her when she lost her husband and now she held him. Still. She'd somehow gotten up and moved on after. Could he?

Russ forced himself to his feet and watched her sleep. If she could walk away from the comfort, from the moment of untroubled peace, so could he. He glanced over at his house. Isabelle stood in the window watching him in the haystack with Kit. Shit.

–Thirty-Eight–

Russ flew into his sitting room.

Isabelle wasn't at the window, Ma was.

He looked around frantic. Ma ignored him.

"I saw Isabelle at the window."

Ma turned around and studied him. He thought for a moment that she'd tell him he was nuts, but as usual, she surprised him. "I was talking to her, promising her you'd bounce back from this, maybe I summoned her. Sit. We need to talk."

He saw no way out of this, and always had a hard time saying no to Ma, so he sat on the floor 'cause they couldn't afford a sofa. He fought the urge to cry as he stared at Kit in the haystack. Crying for Isabelle felt like the worst sin of all. He held every tear in as he sat there, but he was sure if anyone saw his soul, it'd be a stormy mess.

From his window, Russ watched Kit sleep peacefully. The sun cast a soft pinkish glow on her as it rose for the day. Silver joined her. Cloud watching, he enjoyed his afterlife the best he could. When she woke and stretched, he talked to her. She glanced at Russ and ran off with Silver.

Ma watched all this without a word. Suddenly, she said, "Pain means you're alive. If you're alive, you have to live. You have responsibilities and others depend on you."

"Can you summon her again?"

"Just think about her really hard. She's with you all the time now."

Russ saw the future he'd planned for them. Just him contemplating the freshly seeded field. He had no desire to farm, to live here, or to live. This responsibility Ma spoke of, he didn't want it.

His daughter cried and he heard Desire tend to her. "At least she can feed her," Ma said as if reporting the weather.

"I have no idea how to raise a baby," he admitted. Hell, he had his life all figured out until that point. He really did. And now what? He saw no future without her.

"I have to show you something." Ma looked around as if someone might bust her doing something illegal. She grabbed his hand and brought him outside to the burning barrel. She glanced around again and dug in, pulling out a rumpled paper.

He pulled the mess from her hands and rolled it flat on the ground. Pa's poster of Louis Riel had a fist size hole in it. "Did Pa do this?"

"Put a hole right through the wall, too."

Russ had never seen Pa lose his temper. He'd never seen him make a fist.

Russ dropped the poster back in the barrel.

"We all miss her, Russ. No one has any clue how to handle this." She placed a hand on his shoulder and pulled him into a hug. He hadn't been crushed against her in years and he was much too tall but she smelled like baby powder which made him wonder if maybe he should go see his daughter. Isabelle would want him to shape up. She sure wouldn't understand him acting like a flake.

When she pulled away she said, "Not once has anyone thought you wouldn't be able to raise that child. So you get back in there and be strong so the others see how it's done."

He nodded.

When he opened the door, Desire and Cal were arguing in their room in the back of his house. A house, he realized, he didn't even pay for. Who had? Maybe the place belonged to Cal and he'd told Desire the house was Russ' so she wouldn't think about him owning things. Or maybe Pa used his secret stash of cash and liked to own buildings he didn't live in.

Russ returned to the window and looked out at the haystack. Kit was gone. So was Silver.

Russ sat on the floor and rested his head against the cold window.

"His soul is gone," Desire snapped at Cal, interrupting Russ' thoughts. "He left with Isabelle. I watched his soul walk off with Silver, holding her hand. He should have stayed."

"A part of him left. The rest of him stayed." Cal's voice was firm. "He won't abandon his baby. Just give him a minute to ground himself again. He's weird like that, but he'll hear this angel needing his help and come for her. He never once let Isabelle down. He won't fail either of them. Just let him say good-bye."

"And if he doesn't?"

"He will. Enough with that."

Were they talking about Russ? He checked to his right and jumped when Isabelle materialized out of thin air.

She was there, so quiet, looking at the haystack with him, thinking.

He didn't move, praying that if he didn't even breathe she might stay.

"*You know,*" she said suddenly. "*I read the paper you brought back from Moose Jaw and they charge a fee—*"

Cal stormed through her. Her image vanished into a wisp.

"Cal, what the heck? Can't you see I'm thinking?"

"You're done thinking. Your baby needs you." Cal plunked the baby beside him, where Isabelle had been, and he vanished in the way he did.

This baby needed her mother. Russ was about to point that out to Cal and tell him not to bother him while he thought with Isabelle, but the baby made a yawning sound.

Isabelle used to do that.

"Just waking up?" Russ asked the baby, a habit he used to do with Isabelle.

She'd say, '*Oh yes, I had a wonderful sleep*'.

The baby kicked the blankets off and Russ made the mistake of glancing at her. Something he promised himself he wouldn't do, because looking at her meant he was ready to see her yet he wasn't...

She batted her eyes.

Her long eyelashes were exactly like Isabelle's. Russ even peeked up to tell Isabelle this, forgetting she was gone.

He understood what Pa meant now. What Ma had meant. He had a destiny he couldn't escape and raising this baby so she grew up properly wasn't a choice he could make. He had a sense of duty to her and this responsibility pushed him off the floor.

He walked around her, mesmerized. Wondering if he could count those eyelashes. Isabelle was happy to hear she had hair like his, but other than the light hair, this was Isabelle's daughter. Her skin was dark, her eyes full of wonder. He smiled at his little girl, eager to show everyone how perfect she was, but no one was around.

Desire had wrapped her in a pink blanket, but like her baby, she hadn't dressed her. She needed clothes, 'cause Russ wasn't raising a naked little girl. He had no idea where Isabelle had stored the things she made, but he bet he'd find her clothes somewhere. As he watched her, she reached for him. Just a hand waving wildly in front of her but the movement was the first time anyone asked him for help with such a simple gesture.

Russ forgot about the clothes and sat beside her, offering her a finger to hold. She grabbed the finger and blabbered something. Not words or anything, but the sounds meant, *join me, I want to lie here for a minute and think*. He gave her a minute, sitting beside her on the draughty floor of a house he owned but hadn't paid for, wondering if he could really raise her to be as good and wonderful as her mother was…or had been…

They stayed, the two of them, sharing silent thoughts. Then the baby lifted the right corner of her mouth into a tease of a smile and the innocence to the gesture made Russ smile back. He'd forgotten how nice it felt to just sit and think with someone, no real worries.

"You're right, Isabelle, souls do come back," he said as if she watched their daughter with him. "When you tried to save her, you must have left an imprint of your own soul on hers." This was how he saw it. Isabelle was with him, just in a new way. This thought helped him survive and forced him to breathe alone again. Only he wasn't alone.

The baby's eyes moved up and she studied his face, mesmerized. Then she glanced off over his shoulder. Russ looked, too, and was shocked to see a woman in a fancy dress standing there. She appeared like Silver; a ghost, only more solid, so real he could smell her lavender scent. Her eyes were the colour of a field of wheat, like his cousin Antoine's.

"Who are you?" he demanded, protecting his daughter.

"*Marie. Do not fear me. I won't let harm come to this child.*" She sighed peacefully as she smiled at his daughter.

"I protect her." Russ rested her against his chest. She was tiny but filled the huge void in his life. When the ghost didn't challenge him, he lay with her on his chest and breathed. In and out. He could do this.

"You feeling better?" Cal rested beside him and the woman stepped back when Cal walked in. He never paid her attention so Russ ignored her, too.

"Name that squirt yet?" He had his girl with him and she slept against his naked chest.

"She kinda looks like a Bella."

Cal chuckled. "Perfect. So listen, we ran into a bit of a problem. I need your help. Montague has vanished. I sent out word that Isabelle was in labour and he should be here to bless your child. No one's seen him. What if he's dead?"

"You brag you're all linked through the soil. If the leader of our people is dead, shouldn't you know?"

"Yeah. I guess. But where is he?"

He'd turn up. "Maybe we should send one of these ghosts haunting us to find out," Russ said bitterly and Marie faded out.

Russ didn't want to talk about Cal's problems, so he shared his own. "You know, of all the ways I thought I might lose her, I never thought God would pluck her from my life like a flower."

Cal stayed on the floor with him so they could stare at the ceiling with their daughters on them.

Cal said, "It's kind of a lesson on how quickly life changes, eh? A slap to your face you won't ever forget."

Cal liked to talk, so he let him.

"One evening, I hunted that cougar 'cause I wanted to see if I could, and I found Desire. She was new to the area and I'd spent a bit of time with her, ya know, messing around, having fun, but there she was in the mud, hardly alive. Maybe she was even dead and I breathed life back into her, hard to say. I carried her to Kika and he helped me with her. Months passed before she was back on her feet, but the scar of that night will be with her forever."

Why hadn't Cal come to him? "Who attacked her?"

He didn't answer.

They stared at the ceiling, secrets looming between them. "Cal? Why do they force themselves on our gals?"

"You're the only one who knows."

"So you married her 'cause she was pregnant but you weren't to blame?"

"Well, no. Clearly, she's mine. Like I said, we'd messed around a bit before that and Echa is a mini-me." He smirked. "But I couldn't know that at the time…"

"How did Desire feel about what happened to her?"

"Well, things are different for her," he explained. "She believes like the others of her tribe, that children belong to their mothers and are given to her by the powers of the earth. The same force that grows crops and trees. I explained the mechanics of life to her. She said this might be true but as the mother she chooses me to protect her child."

"Her child? You mean yours."

"I explained this to you before your wedding vows. She chooses the father. If I screw up or she sees someone better, I'm out, he's in. Those squirts become his to protect and I can't say a thing but bye 'cause that's what a loser pa says."

Explained why he worked so hard to please her.

Did others believe this? Russ thought about them lords in their fancy dresses in Moose Jaw. This type of belief was smart, really. Giving women this power meant their men couldn't flake out.

"Things weren't like that for us," Russ told him. "We just were. I used to give her things like coins and she'd store them for us. These things weren't a gift to her, they were just ours, and she kept our things safe."

Bella squirmed on his chest and her tiny fist banged into him. "I have so many things going through my mind at the moment. I need someone to talk them through with." He needed to talk to Kit. She knew loss. She knew how to get off the floor and move. She knew things about Isabelle that he didn't. Yet he couldn't bring himself to tell his brother that.

"You have to pick one to focus on when you're in a crowd. Remember?"

"Which one?"

"The one that gives you hope. Isabelle chose you to protect her daughter. You gonna man-up?" Cal cut himself off but Russ could tell he had much more to say.

"I don't know how to raise her."

"You're not alone. There are things though that only you can do for her."

"I need a bit of time to think, Cal."

"I'll give you time every now and again, but if you flake out on your daughter, that I won't understand."

He was right; Russ had things to share with Bella.

Cal broke the silence with a horrible sigh that almost made Russ cry.

"What are you thinking, Cal?"

"Why do men rape women?" He bit his words and Russ bet the next ten fools in sheets he ran into he'd demand an answer from before he buried them alive.

Before Russ could answer, Marie did. Russ wasn't sure when she reappeared but he repeated what she'd said in case Cal hadn't heard it, "Disgrace and power."

"So they get on top of 'em and tell them they belong under 'em?" Russ was used to Cal. These thoughts he should keep in his mind, but he didn't know how. "Why? I mean why the hell would they do that, Russ? I can't imagine the hate actions like that would take, not only of yourself, but of others." He sighed. "I mean, when I'm with her, damn, it's the best moments I get. I probably don't deserve how incredible she makes me feel. It sickens me that someone would ruin a moment like that."

"These men come covered. Clearly they're afraid of something." Russ winced not sure why fear would drive them to that point.

"Cowards," Cal cursed the word out.

"When I'm afraid, I like to know I control something. Maybe this gives them power," Russ said, thinking out loud because Isabelle wasn't there to filter these thoughts to. "They slink back to their worlds with this sense of power over others."

"Yeah, well, power is a matter of opinion. I can take that power from them as fast as they stole it from Desire. We need a way to track 'em. Any ideas?"

Something he said made sense but Russ drowned in pain and couldn't see his logic in the fog of thoughts crowding him. He hated crowds. Russ waited for Isabelle to share her thoughts, 'cause whatever he missed, she'd see.

She was gone.

Bella wiggled.

"You know, sometimes when Isabelle and I sat together thinking, she'd blurt out something brilliant, and just now, I thought you were gonna do that. Not sure why, but you were close to finding me an answer to a question I've been tossing around." Without Isabelle, Russ had no idea what he missed.

No, he knew. He missed her.

"Pa went nuts," Cal said. "Silver had to get Kit to calm the spirits in him. He's sleeping now. She'll leave, return to Moose Jaw for a spell. I asked her to look around for Montague and to give Francis the message about his sister."

Russ nodded.

"It terrifies me that I could be you," Cal admitted. "I'm sorry, Russ. I really truly am."

-Thirty-Nine-

October 1929—

Today was their wedding anniversary. Their first one. The bleak day brought light snow that hopefully wouldn't last.

The house was quiet. Bella played on the bed and Russ planned to read her a story 'cause neither of them could sleep. Those evenings were common. Russ worked extra hard during the day so he could sleep without thoughts haunting him at night, but they found him anyway. Thankfully, the late hours meant no one except Bella was awake to witness him going insane. Bella looked ready to play so Russ promised her a story, only he couldn't find Isabelle's notebook.

Bella tugged at her feet, which was cute as heck but wasn't much help. She probably didn't care about the story at her age, but he needed Isabelle with him tonight.

Russ snooped around the room he slept in. Ma had been by to tidy things up. Where had she hidden Isabelle's things?

At the foot of the bed was a large wooden trunk. Russ flipped the lid off feeling like a thief in his own house.

Isabelle's fragrance dropped him to his knees. Isabelle's things, her notebook on top, were all stored so neatly. That night, he pulled out the notebook, but over the years, Bella and Russ grew familiar with everything in the trunk. He loved it tucked away at the end of his bed, and he was thankful to Ma for doing something so genius.

"Found it," he told Bella, glancing at her.

Marie stood over her.

Bella mumbled to her in her strange language. Marie opened her hand and Bella studied it as if the ghostly hand was neat as heck. "You visit her often?" Russ asked.

"*I won't ever leave her. I tried to visit my nephew and niece but I can only go so far from her. Perhaps this is my punishment for the wrong I did in my last life.*"

"You're a shadow?"

"*In a way, I'm hers.*"

"How can she be cursed, she's a baby?" Russ grumbled. He didn't want this strange woman shadowing his daughter all her life.

"*I'm cursed for things I did in my life. In my last life, Bella was to be my child but wasn't born yet. I was chosen to protect her and failed. A part of me died with her. That part now needs to live.*" Bella tried to grab her hand but her tiny fingers went right through and Marie sighed. "*I was to be her mother and I made poor choices. She was given a new journey. I am bound to her soul until we teach each other what we were destined to learn. Then I can return to protecting the lands as Cîpay do.*"

Russ frowned, if that was the rule, Miss Penelope might be with him for a bit, because there wasn't anything he wanted to learn from her.

"How come I can see you sometimes?"

She shrugged. "*Must be moments where you're open to the spiritual world. Your soul is very torn. You have trouble grounding yourself. Some souls give to the earth, others take from it. You do both.*"

Seeing ghosts hovering around his daughter made him nervous, yet proud. "Well, you can stay as long as you don't freak her out."

"*You amuse me, Russ. I see much of your father in you, but more of your mother.*"

"You know Pa and Ma?"

"*I grew up with Bernoit. Your mother is a rare gem with Bella.*" She faded out.

Russ cuddled up beside Bella and held the notebook unable to open it. "You ready? Your ma wrote stories on her own at the end, you know. I'm not even sure what the last one was about."

She pulled on the notebook and Russ gave her the paper that peeked out so she was busy while he read.

That night was the first time he'd read to her from the

notebook but, over the years, their time with the stories turned into a weekly thing. She'd come in, stand by his bed with her sleepy eyes, staring until he caved and let her cuddle beside him, reading her stories from the notebook. Then they'd think together until they fell asleep. Those were the best sleeps.

That first night was no different 'cept she gripped the paper. Russ relaxed and enjoyed the quiet, curious why the world was suddenly so silent.

A strange sound brought his attention to the window. He sat up when a shadow tumbled through his window and landed on the floor. Russ hurried to the crumpled man, greeting Montague.

Russ was about to call Cal for help but Montague shushed him. "I need to talk to you."

Russ sat on the floor and got a good look at him. His skin was weathered and covered with a light orange dust. "Where you been? Everyone thought you died."

"Death would be a nice break, but my journey is not complete." He sat back, eyes closed, and took slow breaths. Russ thought he slept and left him to stay by Bella when Montague caught his arm.

Russ studied the hand holding him. Such a tough hand claimed he'd lived a hard life, but he was no older than Pa.

"Tunnels are no longer safe off Sacred Land. Silver said you would teach me how to save our people, and so I am here. You are the last." He opened his eyes and Russ was amazed at how blue they were. Almost like water. They reminded him of Bernadette's and for some reason, those blue eyes made Russ feel as if Montague was family. Maybe he was.

"The last what?"

"The last teacher I will have."

"What could I teach you?"

Montague pointed to Bella on the bed, sleeping like an angel. "When I was born," he said. "Your grandfather told the tribe I was their leader. I was a baby, like her. A baby was their leader. I was born to a young woman with no husband. Yet Silver called me a brother." He smiled proudly. "I should have been outcast, disgraced, yet thanks to Silver every warrior taught me. What could I do but trust in their faith? They believed so strongly… I could not fail my people." Montague sat, a beaten, tired man on Russ' floor and Russ joined him. "It is a curse and a blessing to have a destiny others wish to see fulfilled."

"Well. That I understand. People say Cal and I will end this curse."

"The curse is almost over. Silver tells me Isabelle brought many of the souls with her and Cal has marked many others so they move on. Kaplain remains but he eludes us. Still, Francis is determined to find him. Maybe the stories are wrong and they were not brothers, but a brother and a sister?"

Russ liked that. Meant Isabelle was a hero.

"Talk to Francis, he should teach you things. I know nothing."

Montague studied him with those blue eyes. "Each thing I am taught made me who I am, just like each thing you did has helped us end this curse. I hold within me the wisdom of all our warriors, and you will be the last to bless me with your knowledge. Then I will be free to merge my soul with Sacred Land and protect it as an eternal leader. An ancient. It will be safe for eternity. I will then be *Cîpay*."

He seemed so sure, Russ didn't want to disappoint him, but what could he teach a warrior? Maybe he needed to see Cal. "I can get Cal—"

Montague raised a hand. "Listen." Unusual silence surrounded Montague. As if the world bowed in respect to him. He stared at Russ, his blue eyes digging into him. "Do you hear the world dying?"

Russ shook his head. "No, but I'm probably not the best guy to ask."

"Why not?"

"I have a heavy heart." Russ stood and took the paper from Bella. He shoved the flyer back in the notebook, feeling so empty inside. "Today should be my first wedding anniversary, and I spent this unhappy day with my daughter who never met her mother," Russ admitted.

Montague sat on the edge of the bed to study Bella. "You're a good father and teacher. The Dubois girl selected wisely."

Russ felt stronger, braver when Montague spoke, and understood why Cal was so taken with him. This guy knew things. Maybe he was here to teach Russ?

"I'm teaching at the school in Eau Claire. If you want to come, you're welcome anytime. The children would love it if you stopped in to share a story."

"A school?" Montague tilted his head, curious, and again, his gesture reminded Russ of how Bernadette moved. "You want me to go to school?"

"If you've never been, a little time there might be well spent. You can't spend the night on this floor like an animal. Across the hall, Bella has a bed she isn't using. You're welcome to crash there. She shares the room with my niece so be quiet and expect Cal to stop you when you sneak in."

He rubbed his chin, thoughtful. "My warriors live here?"

"Nope, they just tumble in the windows and I find them beds."

Montague's laughter filled the house and Cal was at the door with his knife almost instantly.

"Montague." Cal considered the knife he held then put the blade away, giving Montague a questioning look. "What are you doing here in my...brother's house?"

"Apparently, learning to be civilized from your brother so I can better understand how to protect Sacred Land." He smirked. "Already he's taught me many valuable things. I have to think as both a man of a modern world that is changing and a soul of an ancient one that will never change." His smile grew. "I was so focused on the ancient ways, I forgot that our future is not in our past but from it. Thank you, wise teacher."

Russ hadn't said anything even close to that, but Cal nodded as if that made sense and went back to bed. Montague followed, and Russ assumed he found a place to sleep because he was still there, ready for school in the morning.

PART FOUR

TWO YEARS LATER

"Freedom is one breath that never ends."

–Silver

–FORTY–

June 1931—

Francis was filthy. "I haven't been home in two years," he told Kit. She hadn't seen him in as long and she couldn't look at him. She knew he left to remain safe, but his disregard for her irritated her. He could have invited her along. What was she supposed to do while he was gone? Where had he gone? What had he done? Had he met another? All these questions stirred her anger and silenced her tongue.

He studied the ground, then met her eyes, like the shy boy he'd been the first time he'd sought her out. The gentle caring man she grew to love was still there and she softened a touch.

Why was he here?

"What's the story with the boys?" he asked, pointing to the young ones camping on the floor of her chamber. Since Francis walked in they were silent, but they normally talked her ear off.

Kit glanced at Souris and Squirt. They were nine and five and living in the tunnels wasn't a good fit for them. She was thinking about bringing them to a woman who had helped her once, Mable. But Kit kept putting it off because truth was, she liked having the boys around. They brought purpose to her dark existence, and she'd been running from many things lately, running from them when they needed her was proving to be hard.

"Their pa went crackers in the head and touched them the wrong way. I was there because I did favours for cash." She actually hadn't done the favours, but she wanted to spite Francis a bit so she let him believe it.

"You what? Favours better mean you did his blasted dishes." Francis looked disgusted, and she was irritated that he still felt the need to protect her.

"I needed to eat. I was alone," she reminded him. "You left me." Her voice softened and she whispered so only he could hear, "I killed their pa before anything happened."

Francis got to his feet and pretended to wipe the memory from her with his fingers. She pushed his hands away. "Don't touch me, Francis. You lost that right when you walked away from me. You know damn well I would have gone with you."

When she raised her voice, the boys leapt to their feet. Souris had his fists tightened, ready to tackle Francis.

"And what?" Francis' voice was soft. "Lived in the shadows? I've been watching Kaplain, but he was surprisingly quiet this last bit." He stepped closer to her.

"Yeah, getting his plans blown all over the prairies does that to a guy."

"He's planning something else. Something to draw me out." His jaw tightened. "Promise me you won't do favours for cash anymore."

"I can't. I can't even look at a man. I brought these boys to the tunnels, but they can't run for cash 'cause they're terrified of men. I sat with them and drew pictures, using stories to teach them about good men like you. I told them how Russ had helped me. How deeply he loved his family." She bowed her head and whispered, "I have so much to teach them, but this is not the place. They need a home, a family."

Francis browsed her notebook. He paused at the picture she'd drawn of him, then kept flipping to the newer ones of Russ. He stared at each one for a long time.

"I can't just dump them off somewhere. What do I do?"

"Antoine would probably take them in."

Kit sighed. "I thought so, too, but turns out their father...um...has them afraid of coloured folks. When I brought them there, they took one look at Emma and fled. I'm surprised they even stayed here when you walked in."

Francis glanced at them, cowering in the corner. He knelt and opened his pack.

They stared at him, silent.

He pulled a shiny apple from his pack. Squirt edged out of

the corner but Souris hauled him back.

"They stayed, because these are warriors. They want to learn to protect you. Right?" he asked.

"I wanna be a warrior," Squirt said.

"I'll set this target up. First one to hit it, gets to eat the apple. I have a bunch more targets like this one and I'll show you how to never miss your mark."

Souris jumped up, excited and much to her relief, they forgot their fears and took the knife from Francis. He patiently taught them to throw it.

~~

The boys were sleeping in the corner. Francis had taught them to throw knives for two hours. He'd fed them and sat with Kit watching them sleep.

"It would be nice if we could raise them. Wouldn't it?" Francis sighed, content. "Did you ask Isabelle and Russ? Maybe we could hide out there for a bit."

Kit froze. He didn't know his sister had died? She reached for his hand. "I tried to find you. So I could tell you. Isabelle died in childbirth. I'm sorry. I was with her. Russ held her. She had spirits and family around her and she'd just found out you were free."

Francis took a deep breath and turned away from her.

Touched by his pain, Kit placed a hand on his shoulder. "I'm sorry. Russ had your niece dressed in blue the last time I saw her." She glanced at the boys. "She looks so much like Isabelle."

Francis kept his back to her. "So you and Russ?"

"No. He relives that moment she died every time he sees me. It's best if I stay away."

He faced her again, tears stained his cheek and she quickly wiped at them. Her touch lingering too long.

"I'll see if Cal can take them in. I brought Cal a wanted flyer I wanted to show him anyhow. Thought he'd get a kick out of it." Francis opened his pack and pulled out the wanted flyers he had.

Kit grabbed his arm to stop him and took the one on top from the pile. His skin warmed under her fingers and she regretted touching him when he looked up with his loving eyes.

Francis glanced at it. "I kept that one because it's a baby, and she reminded me of my sister—"

"This is her. Your niece."

"Damn." He stared at the wanted flyer. "Kit. I left because I wanted to marry you and I'm a man on the run. But I can't take this longing I have for you anymore. Everyone I meet, I find myself comparing to you." He dropped the flyer and grabbed her hand. "Seeing you with these boys today only confirms it for me. Marry me. Let's raise these boys ourselves."

Something in her wanted to say yes, but he was right. What kind of life would they have? What kind of life did she want? She closed her eyes, convincing herself that she'd be happy with Francis.

She pulled away.

"I know I did you wrong." Francis stood and strolled to the door. "But we can make this work. I'll be ba—" His voice caught and he grabbed for the wall. "Run," he mouthed and a fine line of blood trickled from his mouth. A knife was in his gut. How? Who?

"Boys, hide."

Kaplain shoved him into the wall and pulled his knife out. "Stay away from me." He pulled Francis in his fists and tossed him at Kit. "Creepy annoying mutts. Took you long enough to come for her."

Kit caught Francis in her arms. The boys scrambled into a crack, but Kaplain ran off.

Francis was still alive. She could help him. Frantic, she ordered the boys to get her sacred dirt.

"Boys!" They were pushed into the corner, terrified. "Souris, get my pack. We have to save him." He was all she had left. Much to her surprise, he bravely brought her the bag and knelt by Francis with her.

Francis grabbed her wrist. "Kit."

"I need help. Help!" She hollered down the dark tunnel.

She held Francis' face in her hands. He studied her, his face soft and caring. "Gosh, I missed you. Thank you for the bit of happiness you gave me." He closed his eyes.

"No!" She shook him, demanding he stay with her.

A hand caught hers and Kit looked up into comforting blue eyes. "Montague?"

"We can heal him. Fetch me the sacred plant."

"I have none left."

"Go get some." He opened the satchel around his belt and pulled out supplies. "Go."

"Kit?" A child's voice pulled her from her grief and she checked on the boys. They were afraid again. Their happiness from earlier forgotten.

"It was Kaplain," she told Montague.

"Matters not who or why, only that we do all we can to save my warrior."

She didn't correct him, but that attitude would kill his people.

Air went in to Francis' lungs and Kit focused on that as she escorted the boys out. She needed to find them a safe place while she went for help.

—FORTY-ONE—

Pa met Russ by the stable. Bella played in the straw with the kittens while Marie watched her.

Russ debated what to do with Bella since his horse was sick and he'd probably be out here all day.

"Antoine says all his horses are sick, too. Something's weird. I checked with all the neighbours and they're all looking like ours. You coming to church?" Pa rubbed his fingers together in that way that meant he was about to lie about something.

"I can't leave these horses. Ma stayed up with them all night. The least I can do is put them down if they don't improve."

"Antoine says to wait the illness out. He's trying a few things." Pa shifted, his fingers rubbing his pants. "I have something to tell you." His voice shook and Russ glanced up.

Pa had been acting strange since Russ got back from college a few weeks ago. "Spit it out, and whatever lie you're thinking up, forget it. Just tell me straight."

"It's time."

"Time for what?"

"I mean all the horses...the dark skies, and Silver won't answer me. What if Silver is dying?" He winced. Marie left Bella to stand closer to Pa. Bella followed. "I have to make sure Bellecoeur's body returns. Silver wants him placed in his burial hole with him."

Russ stared at him. He felt the lack suddenly. Silver wasn't dying. He was gone. Missing from the energy of the world.

Silver had moved on. *To where?* He had no idea.

Of course, this was what he wanted Miss Penelope to do, even Marie, but a heaviness fell on him and Russ missed him already. "We have enough ghosts in our lives, letting a few go probably isn't a bad idea." Russ felt himself shut down so nothing else could hurt him.

Marie gasped. "*Russ!*"

Pa was gentle. "You'll be troubled by this, so know I'm here for you."

"Silver's been dead for a while, Pa. I get it."

Pa winced. "Not to me, he hasn't. He was always there for me, Russ. He was there for you, too. It's fine to be angry or upset, but I need your help."

"I'll go with you." They glanced at the horses, and Russ knew he couldn't up and leave their livestock if a virus spread. "I'll deal with them first. Is Ma going?"

"She doesn't have time to get ready. The train will be here in twenty minutes. With the horses down, I have no choice but to be on that train or wait until tonight's. She hoped you could bring her up this afternoon, after church, but I couldn't find anyone with horses that weren't sick." He sighed. "Keep an eye on her, since Xavier died, she spends a lot of time at church."

"Yeah, that's fine, I'll get her there. Is Silver scared? Are you?"

Marie snorted. "*Uncle Silver ain't scared of squat.*"

Pa glanced around. "Did you hear that? Marie? Are you here?" He stared right at her.

"She follows Bella around. She said you grew up together."

"Antoine's sister is here? Do you see her spirit?"

"Sometimes." He hadn't realized Marie was his cousin. She dressed much too fancy for farming and looked nothing like Antoine. And apart from her golden eyes, she looked nothing like any of them. "She's right beside you. Worried about you," Russ reassured his father.

"It's nice to know." Pa accepted her presence that easily and didn't look worried about her haunting Bella so Russ relaxed about her hanging around.

"I called him this morning, to talk. Like I do every day. He didn't appear." Pa's voice showed his distress. "What if he's already dead and I didn't say good-bye? I spent so many years ignoring his teachings… What if I need him?"

He wanted to say '*You're a grown man. Figure your shit*

out yourself.' But Russ thought about what Ma might say and instead, he said, "Just ask me. You're not alone." Russ grabbed a horse blanket and went to wrap one of the mares. He didn't want Pa alone. "Take Sammy and the girls."

"Russ." He opened his mouth but said nothing.

"You better be going. I'll handle things here. Where's Cal?"

Bella pulled on Pa's pant leg. Pa scooped her up. "Desire says he's missing since this morning. Maybe he felt Silver leaving and went in. Cal is very in touch with these things."

Russ doubted that very much. "He would have told you, besides, ain't a horse in the area he could have taken. Take Bella to Ma, tell her I'll finish up with the horses, and we can catch the train tonight. Same hotel?"

Pa nodded. "Bye Marie. Nice to know you're close."

"Tell him..." Marie stared at Pa but she never finished the thought.

Russ gave Bella a kiss on the forehead. "You be a good girl for Grandmama at church and no saying those bad words in front of her or the priest."

Her eyes sparkled when she glanced at Russ and she giggled. Marie sighed, watching them go.

He stood by her. "Tell him what?"

"When I was alive, I moved parcels, pretending to be my dead husband and misplaced a few."

Russ glanced at her. What the heck was she telling him? Once Bella reached the house, Marie faded out and he never got the full story.

Russ sat by his horse and watched her breathe. He'd have to put her down soon. She suffered and he couldn't see any reason for it. She snapped her belly again.

Russ got to his feet and cleared out the food and dumped the water troughs. He planned to start fresh in case a bug contaminated their food and water. Halfway in, he heard the train leaving and saw Ma walking to church with Bella, Desire, and the other girls. Sammy must have left with Pa. He was thankful to Desire and Ma for looking after Bella while he was at college.

When he was done clearing the old food and water out, he boiled water and washed everything down, even the horses. While he worked restocking their food, someone walked into the barn and he jumped to his feet. "Who's here?"

"It's me." A woman whispered from the shadows and for a moment, Russ thought maybe everything would be perfect, that God had sent Isabelle back. It took him a moment to register that she was gone and this was someone else.

"Kit? What are you doing here?"

She stepped from the shadows and he studied her. She had short hair and wore pants with suspenders as if she were a boy. But she so wasn't. Her dainty face had full lips and for the first time, he noticed how her body curved. He placed these thoughts away, returning to the comfort of her presence.

Russ held a bucket, not sure when he'd picked it up, but he dropped it, making a clanging sound that echoed through the barn.

She stepped forward. Light bounced off her features and like him, she looked like she'd aged in her soul over these last few years. Kit knelt by his horse and the mare rested her head on Kit's lap. "She been down long?"

"They're all down. Even Ma's best bred. Won't get up. Won't eat. Watch, she snaps at her belly like it's something she ate. I cleaned everything out and just finished putting them new stock, but they still need fresh water. I boiled some to be safe and it's cooling."

Kit pulled her satchel out. "I agree. Looks like she ate something not for her. Boil these and we'll add the medicine to their water and see if we can fix your team."

Russ had the stove in the corner going and added the leaves to the water.

Kit paced in front of the horses, tilting her head as she studied them.

Russ stopped her from pacing by grabbing her shoulder. She considered his hand as if his touch shocked her. Kit was frail under his fingers so he loosened his grip a bit in case he hurt her. His hand slid on its own up her shoulder to the warmth of her neck and she pushed her face into it.

Russ needed to hold her. The sudden desire shocked him and he pulled away.

Kit let out a long breath. "Gosh, I forgot how healing your touch was."

Russ swallowed a lump. He'd forgotten how easy touching her was. He glanced at his hand as if it was guilty.

"Russ, I will show you something, but you have to stay calm." She pulled out her notebook from a backpack. Out flew the book he'd given her to keep her hand steady a few years back.

He picked it up. "You kept my book?" he asked.

"I... Can I keep it? I'm learning to read with some young boys."

He held it. "This is the first thing Isabelle gave me." He smiled, remembering her stealing the childish book off the desk, but it didn't bring her closer to him. His ma was wrong, she wasn't with him all the time now, he almost never felt her around anymore and the panic this should create in him was suddenly calm and accepting. He had fond memories of every moment they spent together and in them he could recapture his happy moments, but they didn't bring her closer and this was a cold truth he was learning to live with.

As for the book, the binding wasn't holding any better than he held to his life. Kit had clearly read this old book a few times, fallen asleep on it, and by the mud smeared on the cover, she either buried it or cried on it. Possibly both. Russ had books that looked like this, and he knew exactly how they ended up in this shape. Holding it, he felt her story imprinting itself on it. "I gave it to you. It's yours." Parting with the book was surprisingly easy.

They were silent, studying each other for a long while, each of them lost in their own thoughts.

"Here." She filed through the notebook and grabbed a flyer. Russ ignored it and snagged the notebook. He could have sworn she'd passed a picture of Cal. He opened the notebook, flipping through the drawings. A few pages were torn out. "This my brother?" Why was she drawing pictures of Cal?

"Yes. The Ghost Hunter, I had to draw him for some... I was telling stories to some boys and they like me to draw pictures of the heroes in those stories." Her eyes were golden laced with brown. They were full of pain as she studied his face. A woman like this had protected herself all her life and she'd suffered for it. She needed Ma to let her cry on her shoulder.

Russ studied the drawing from different angles. "It's good. His eyes are perfect." Even on paper, they laughed with him. "You have a gift for storytelling in pictures."

"His eyes are easy to draw. Others, not so much. *You*, not so much."

"You drew me?" He stared at her.

She shifted uncomfortable then removed the medicated water from the stove and added it to the water Russ had cooling. After filling the troughs, she cupped some and treated the horses, one by one, ignoring his stare.

Russ turned the pages to see what else she kept in her notebook. There were many pictures: one of his farm, Francis staring at a fire, Russ' house, Francis laughing, their church, Francis sleeping, the haystack, lips.

Bella. On a Wanted Flyer… "What the heck is going on?" Russ dropped the notebook, clutching the flyer. "My Bella? She's a baby. What the heck do they want with a baby?"

His hand shook when he showed her the flyer in disbelief.

Kit stayed silent, watching him freak out. Finally, she said, "Can you read what it says?"

Russ contemplated her, mystified. "I read in three languages, but never in my life have I seen words so horrifying. I wish I didn't know what they meant. I don't... I mean what the heck, Kit?" Losing Bella was not an option. He would invoke Marie's help if he had to. He wasn't sure how much protection a ghost could offer but he'd push the limits.

"I doubt they'll attack today," she said. "I stumbled on this last night. Came here immediately."

Russ grabbed the shotgun, took one last look at the horses, and headed into town. Kit ran after him.

"How are you involved in this?" Russ demanded, glaring at her.

"Francis showed last night. I haven't seen him in two years."

"Really? He doing good?"

"He was breathing when I left him with Montague, but he's been hurt and needs healing plants from the Healing Chamber. I thought I'd grab a few leaves, snag a horse and head back. Now I have to wait for tonight's train. Figured I might as well stop in and show you that flyer while I wait."

"Any idea what they want with Bella?"

She grabbed his hand and Russ was so shocked by the warmth to her touch that he pulled away.

"Don't pull away from me, Russ." She stopped walking and he faced her, clutching the shotgun. She studied his face and gently placed her hand in front of his eyes, but she didn't dare touch them. "Your eyes always captivate me."

Russ closed his eyes, his anger vanishing in her imaginary touch. What would it be like to have her hands run down his face? It was a long time since he'd been touched by a woman, he had no idea if it would be a welcomed comfort or worrisome effort.

"You're storming off for no reason. It's not like they have plans to steal her..." Her voice trailed off and they stared at each other as the truth sunk in.

Russ caught her wrist because the idea terrified him. "Every damn horse in the area is sick. They're here, and they got us exactly where they want us. What I don't get is why the hell do they want Bella?"

She bowed her head. "Maybe a trade?"

It didn't matter if they were after drugs, or revenge, or to make a statement or even some parcel Marie might have hidden away years ago. Bella was in trouble and she was his only focus. Russ picked up the pace. He had to get to her before these creeps did.

As he walked, he grabbed Kit's hand, not looking at her. "Sorry about Francis."

Kit studied him. "Do you know how to unleash the curse?"

"From what I understood, from what you told me, the curse ended with Isabelle. She gave her life to end it." His words were bitter and she flinched as if he'd hit her. "Isabelle took those evil souls in hers—to contain it. No way in hell am I unleashing anything like that again. Her efforts will not be lost. Every day I suffer her sacrifice. Her daughter suffers for it. No." Not that he knew how casting a curse would work anyway. "We keep Bella safe and make a clear statement that no one messes with my family. We don't need a curse, I am wild enough."

When they arrived in town, church was already over. Like

usual, a crowd gathered outside, talking. Russ found Ma with Cal's girls against her while she chatted in a group of women, discussing the situation with the horses in case someone had an idea how to save their teams.

"Where is Bella?" Russ demanded.

"In the church." She followed him in. "The priest likes to read her a story after mass..." Ma's voice trailed off when she saw Kit following him.

Russ tossed open the doors to the church. "Father?" his voice shook as Russ tried not to panic. Where was the priest? Russ stormed to the side and swung open the doors. The place was empty. Ma stood in the entry with Cal's girls. Kit searched the confessional.

"He's not here," Russ told her.

"Maybe he took the tunnels?" Kit asked.

Russ knew a tunnel existed from the confessional to the livery barn. It had caved in a long time ago, but Antoine and Hoolie had cleaned that mess up. Kika had said they were boring so he'd never cared to explore them but clearly Kit had.

Desire flew in. She checked her girls. "Cal signaled me. There's a crew in town, keeping to the shadows. We have to get out of here," she told Ma.

"They're here for the money," Ma said.

"Money? What money?" Russ stammered. Kit looked just as confused so he didn't feel like a lost idiot.

"They have Bella." Ma grabbed the shotgun from Russ. "Get your girls out of here, Desire. I'm going after that priest."

"Maybe the priest hid her someplace safe. Let's not go killing a priest, Ma." Russ had no idea how he was the voice of reason here, but his thoughts were coming at him clearly.

"If the priest stole her, they bought him off with a promise. He'd clearly been planning this, earning my trust." She stared at him. "Russ, do you remember Antoine's sister, Marie? She dropped off parcels at our place not long before she was murdered. I was to hide them, keep them safe. I took out the cash and left it for your father to find, but some packages had these bonds in them. Isabelle's father needed cash and so I gave him one, in case it could help. He brought one of the bonds in that package to the priest figuring he'd know if it was worth something. He told the priest that he'd found them in a tunnel under his farm." She kept her eyes on him, steady and firm as if her eyes told him things her even voice would never say. "Trouble started soon after and they were the target."

Russ prepared to argue with her that the priest probably wasn't involved and no one would care about bonds, yet the odds were about as possible as Silver believing these men were cursed or Cal thinking they wanted a drug of some sorts, besides arguing with Ma was about as useful as arguing with Silver.

They were here and they had Bella. If they asked him for bonds in exchange for her, he would give them. If they asked for anything in exchange for her, it was theirs. Once she was safe with him again, well…then he'd set the debts straight.

Russ quickly ordered everyone to work so they were covering more ground. "Only ways out are the back, the front, and the tunnels. I'll check the town with Ma. Kit can check the tunnels."

"I'm going with Kit," Ma snapped and there was never any use arguing with her, so Russ let her go. Even though Ma hated guns she checked to see if the chamber was loaded, looking like she handled guns all the time. Then she went to the confessional, without him showing her where the entrance to the tunnel was.

Russ stormed out but ran smack into Cal.

"Bella's missing." Russ felt the realness of those words as panic settled on him. The world suddenly felt too big. Bella could be anywhere.

Cal remained calm. "Call Silver, he'll let us know where she is and take care of it."

"Pa said he wasn't answering."

"What? Why not?" He knelt, with his hands in the dirt. "Silver." He paled. "He's one with the earth. Feel this."

Russ didn't bother; he knew he wouldn't feel anything anyway. "Marie?" he called, no idea if that would work.

"Who? We can't do this without him." Cal looked ready to puke. "I can't do this without Silver."

"Bella is missing. You have to focus. Where do the tunnels from the church come up?"

"Antoine's."

Russ said, "I'm going there. You search for signs. They don't leave here with her." Once again, he called, "Marie!" She'd said she could only go so far from Bella. Meant Bella was too far from him.

Russ ran toward Antoine's. A strange foreboding washed over him. The prairies were peaceful as he ran, which conflicted with the knots ripping inside him. Russ only had his knife, and the blade would have to do if he ran into trouble in the tunnels. Logic told him that he'd find the priest reading to Bella, afraid and hiding...yet this priest had fired when Isabelle was tied to that cross. This was not a coward. He wouldn't be hiding.

The thought of him being captive terrified Russ. Anyone who could manhandle a priest would be hard to face.

Russ tossed open the cellar door at Antoine's and rushed down the steps. He pushed the walls until he found the fake one.

Russ lit the lantern and started down the tunnel. He over-focused, as if his eyes might notice something his ears couldn't. "Marie?"

She blew into him, almost knocking him out. *"Hurry!"*

Russ followed her.

A gunshot exploded to his right.

Russ moved the lantern around to get a better look at the tunnel wall. Marie was gone.

He ran his fingers over the wall. The shot had come from the other side so he walked several feet, hoping to find a path leading...

Kit stumbled in front of him. "Did anyone come this way? They can't be far." She pushed past him.

"Where's Ma?"

"Dealing with the priest. He handed Bella off to them."

A shot rang to his right again. Russ dashed through the tunnel. He stumbled into a room with an impossible scene.

Ma stood against the wall. She sucked in a quick double breath and walked up to Russ. She handed him the gun and strolled out into the dark. It enveloped her as she left the lantern by the priest. He knelt, face against the wall, the back of his head shot off.

"Oh Ma."

Kit appeared beside him and gripped his shoulders. "Russ, you look at me. No one ever needs to know what happened. As far as you know, the priest was attacked and they stole Bella. You hear me? He was one of us, and we can't let on that they are dividing us."

He just wanted Bella.

He stumbled back, in a fog. Kit's terror etched on her face in thin lines around her eyes.

Somewhere in this moment, their breathing became one. They shared the same rhythm, their natural connection stronger in moments like this. In and out. And the link made so their thoughts were one as they planned their next move. The air went in smoothly. His fears vanished.

Russ didn't ever remember breathing this easily. "Would people really risk hurting my little girl for bonds?" He rubbed his forehead, the stress of his plight settled between his eyes.

Marie appeared. "*They have a car. Hurry.*" She vanished as if sucked backwards.

"Marie! Show me where."

Kit grabbed his shoulder. "Russ?"

"Bella has a shadow who follows her. I'm trying to see her."

"We'll get her back. They can't be far."

Far enough or Marie would be here.

-FORTY-TWO-

Russ ran to his house. In his room, he hid a handgun. They'd left Isabelle's notebook on the bed, the paper Bella liked to play with was crumpled beside it.

He grabbed it, promising her he was coming for her.

Without meaning to, Russ read the flyer he'd brought home from Moose Jaw for Isabelle to decipher years ago. One line jumped out at him, '*Membership ten dollars*'.

Damn. That's what Isabelle had tried to tell him the day Cal walked through her ghost. A membership meant a list. If he had names and wasn't chasing ghosts, once he got Bella safe, he could end this. Didn't matter if they wanted drugs or land or even bonds. Kaplain wouldn't have a hope of getting anything if he lost his warriors. Now that Bellecoeur was dead, they wouldn't have anyone to organize them or give them ideas… It would end with this membership list.

He needed to think straight because losing Bella was not an option.

He needed Silver to tell him she was fine.

Banging downstairs made him rush down the steps. Kit was in the kitchen cooking.

"What are you doing?" Russ stared at her, shocked.

"I have to make your ma something. She was hurt." Kit moved things around on the shelves, so the herbs Desire kept were in a different order. "Cal brought her to his room."

Russ refused to take the blame for her messing up Desire's cupboards. He grabbed her hand to stop her. "Go home, this isn't your fight. Take Francis his medicine. We've seen enough death, I won't have his on my head, too."

Kit stood taller, so her forehead was even with his lips. The oddest sensation rushed over him to kiss it. The desire burst

in him, a frantic need, as if he might never get a chance again. He ignored the strange longing he suddenly had, pushed the distraction aside, and focused on the list they needed to find. But he saw nothing else and finally placed his lips on her forehead softly. All his fears became hers and without meaning to, his hand slipped around her, holding her against him. He pulled away, and rested his cheek against her skin, content by such a simple touch.

"I'm not leaving," she promised, pushing him away. "You didn't leave me." She pulled down a glass jar and shook the dried flowers it contained. She was close to him, yet he needed to keep her in his arms. "I sent Cal to the Healing Chamber. He bled all over the place, but he wants to head to Moose Jaw. He thinks whoever stole Bella got away. He knows of a doctor with an automobile in a town nearby and plans to borrow it. I'll send the plants with him."

"I'm going, too. I'll take Ma with us. You get everyone else and head to Antoine's, get on the train tonight. I agree with Cal; they got away. With no horses to chase them..." Damn it. They must have given them something. Russ pulled down the tea. "Just make her a tea. So...where would this healing room be? I have to talk to Cal."

She raised an eyebrow. "If you don't know, you don't go."

Helpful. "Since when don't you trust me?" He stood too close to her, again.

She touched his face, her hand lingering on his cheek. "It's not a question of trust, but place. *Cîpay* see when ready."

Would he ever know what it meant to be *Cîpay?* Some days he thought of it as a journey to becoming a spirit, but now he felt as if Kit expected him to be one.

Russ ran to the haystack and rolled underneath. In the dark, he felt to the south for the lantern. Sure enough, the old lantern hung there. He lit it and moved it around the chamber. The room only had one exit which lead to a corridor with various veins leading off. Russ took the first exit that would lead toward Dubois farm.

A weed along the left side of the tunnel glowed in the darkness ahead. Russ went toward the strange shining plant. Another was up ahead so he continued down the path. It led to a chamber. Russ walked in but the room was empty. He touched the glowing plants that grew out of the walls. They sprouted toward the thin light, filtering in from the holes overhead. Russ slid his fingers in one of the holes. These plants were surviving on very little light, amazing.

"Leave it to you to walk into a Healing Chamber and touch a hole." Cal walked in. He had bandages on his neck.

"The priest is dead," Russ told him.

"Surprised he lasted this long. I'm not in good enough shape to deal with that mess. Give me a few hours. I had to get stitches and Ma was too upset to do it. I won't trust Kit after what she did so I had to run to town and get Doc to fix me."

"What do you mean 'what Kit did'?"

"I can't prove it, but she killed the priest, not saying he didn't deserve to have his double crossing brains blown out but still…that was our priest just the same, and I was handling the situation."

"Maybe she didn't do it."

"She claims the crew did it, but the fools I saw didn't have a shotgun on 'em and she did. She didn't deny it. Which means, I no longer trust her. I mean, why not tell me the truth?"

"Kit…" Russ was at a loss for words. She took the blame for Ma? "You saw them?"

"Yeah, riding off. Not a blasted thing I could do. Bella was fine. She waved and everything."

Russ placed the lantern on a ledge. "Silver thinks it's a curse he caused, but it's more. These people are real. We'll steal their list, find every single one of the pricks on it, and end this." He shoved the flyer at Cal so he could see how serious this was. "I want Kaplain first."

Cal dismissed the flyer. "You can't pay attention to these flyers. They change every day. This one is old. Now they're more about elections and political issues. Whatever it takes to get people fired up about a cause. Garbage. They have no vision. Sometimes, I see messages in them if I read them backwards that say, 'Die Ghost Hunter', but Desire says that's my imagination." He lay on the ground as if he was about to have a nap in the dirt chamber.

"What I see, is that they have a list." Russ showed him the

flyer again. "Bellecoeur wanted a crew he could trust. Maybe it grew into something else when they discovered these plants or these bonds Pa and Skinny had."

Cal's eyes shot open. "What do you know, Russ?"

Russ checked the plants along the wall. "Do the plants always glow? They are so weird. What are they?"

"They don't glow."

"They're glowing. Like Silver does, or did."

Cal squinted. "You're seeing a soul in a plant? Are you serious?"

Was he? "I didn't know a plant had a soul." Russ passed his hand over the glowing light coming off it. He had a giddy feeling. "How does it grow down here?"

"They're the sacred plants. We use them for rituals, bonding ceremonies, coming of age visions, healing. You smoked it the night you married. Basically, we can't get in touch with the spiritual world without them. They don't have much value except to us. But if you move those rocks, you'll find a metal container, in it are a bunch of papers. Those have value out there in the fake world. They increase in value the longer we hold onto them, too. And someone knows we're hiding them, they just can't figure out where. Someone is determined to tear every inch of our land apart to find them. Someone who was bribing our priest and turned him against us."

Russ was still checking out the plants, not interested in papers. Papers were easy to hide or hand over. He had no attachment to them. His big worry was the curse Silver had told them about, because if there was a chance Silver was right, these plants meant Isabelle's sacrifice was useless and he refused to let that happen. "So if others used these plants to get in touch with spirits, could they accidently activate the curse?" He was tempted to rip out every plant. "I think about Silver wanting us to end the curse, but even if we get all the cursed souls to move on, there could be more if these plants got in the wrong hands."

"Yup. Never ending."

Russ thought about the smoke from his wedding. He knew the effect of these plants all too well. He touched the leaves of the plant. "You better yet? I want to get going. After we find Bella I'll tear down this list..."

Cal had his eyes closed. "They ask for ten bucks. That's a lot of cash because they are searching for certain types of people to hide among. The list is pointless. Do ya have any idea who is on this list you rant about? I do. Bankers, priests, teachers, farmers, entire towns... I'd tell you it's a good plan, but some of the swanks on the list don't even know what they're doing on it."

"Then why they signing up?"

"They were sweet talked. Made to feel important. This group pays them attention. They promised them things they want and get them wild enough about things. Only a few know they stole Bella and plan to exchange her for...whatever."

"I keep saying it doesn't matter, I'll just hand it over. But if I hand over this plant, I'm possibly restarting the curse and Isabelle's sacrifice is pointless, so I can't. And as for these papers or bonds, they were given to Ma by Antoine's sister Marie. She took them and hid them here for us, so we could afford to protect Sacred Land. We might need them. There is nothing for us to give. It means we have to eliminate the threat. Those few will be on the list."

"And the others? They don't know squat about Cursed Land that grows drugs they like or bonds that went missing years ago resurfacing. They'd see ya coming for them and think you were Satan himself."

"I'm not that scary looking, am I?" Russ asked. "I want to know who this 'they' are because that's where the rest of the lost souls will be. I won't let Isabelle's death be in vain. And I sure as hell won't let them hurt my daughter for a few bucks."

"Kaplain is in on it, but I can't get him alone anymore. I agree, harmless or not...if I have a cougar in the area, I don't have to kill it, but I do need to know where it hunts."

"No." Russ's voice remained firm. "You have to kill it. I can't take that chance again."

"You sure the priest gave her up? I saw him help you save her mother," Cal reminded him.

"Yeah. Twisted."

"Think they threatened him?"

Russ said, "It's like they're turning us against ourselves or want us not thinking straight. They're grouped together and this unity makes the pricks stronger. It's what we need to do."

"I need sleep so this can heal."

Russ nodded. He could always count on Cal.

–Forty-Three–

It took them forever to get to Moose Jaw. Russ and Cal jogged seven miles to the next town. Once there, the doctor was out on a call so they waited for him to get back. Doc decided, after listening to their story, to drive them to Moose Jaw and Russ swore he'd never been in a buggy that moved so blasted slow.

Well. He was here now, but the hours ticked by and he was still without a clue as to how to find Bella. Moose Jaw was endless faces Russ couldn't focus around. They'd hit a night with a celebration of some sorts.

Cal knew how Russ couldn't handle crowds. The minute the doc dropped them off, he brought Russ to a back alley. In the quiet and dark they could think.

He gave Russ a job more his speed. "Find Montague." The simple order came with no other instructions. Russ glanced around for Miss Penelope but she didn't appear so he focused on the plan, sure it was a good one.

"Hey," someone called. Cal stepped forward. Two men glared from the alleyway.

One shoved the guy who'd called. "Let's hit the dust, it's nothing but smoked Indians not worth the lead."

It was like when Bella babbled. Words that made sense to them, but the meaning was a bloody mystery to Russ.

Still, he stepped behind Cal because Cal was ready to toss his knife. The strangers stared Cal down. Then one made a weird sound like an AHHHHH while he batted his hand in front of his mouth. They walked off together, making other weird gestures.

"What the heck was that about?" Russ asked Cal. "They sure are weird in this city."

"Nothing."

"Felt like something. What's an Indian and what does smoked mean?"

"They call locals that and they think we're blasted."

"Us?" Russ wanted to laugh. Then again, Cal looked more and more like a local these days but Russ didn't recall ever seeing him drink anything since they got into Monsieur Dubois' whiskey when they were pretending to be men but ended up puking their brains out instead.

"Why do they think we're blasted? We're minding our own."

"Watch your back. Trust no one but me."

"You be careful, too."

"No one will even know I'm here. I'm following you so you don't get killed with your dumb idea. Just give me a name, but not Kaplain, since he's buried in gold I can't penetrate." Cal slapped his back, bringing him back to attention. "Snap to it, warrior." Cal pointed him toward the far cement wall in the alley. Russ didn't question him. He checked it out. Sure enough to the right was a door hidden in the shadows. The metal door didn't have a handle and when Russ pushed on it, the door didn't move. He asked Cal what this was, but he'd vanished.

How could he get in? Russ examined the bricks. One had the marking Cal wore on his upper arm carved into it, some type of flower, like the one Louis Riel used. Just a tiny mark on the left side of the brick. Russ pushed on it and the wall pushed in, just enough for him to enter.

~~

Like rats, the tunnel runners had multiplied under the city, and even though they were dirty, not one of 'em looked starved or beat on. They ran a business under the city and were good businessmen even if Russ found them somewhat arrogant. One nudged his friend and rolled his eyes calling him a Blasted Lost Frenchman to his face. Another told him to return to the creek he'd crawled out of. They were in shoes and slacks, making him feel underdressed in his farm clothes and bare feet. Talking to these young men with attitude was hard. Russ wanted to smack them on the back of the head. Was he that stupid when he was their age? Probably. He didn't feel any smarter right about now, but at least he respected those around him.

After the fourth one turned up his nose at the nickel Russ offered, he tried a different approach and went exploring by himself.

He stayed to the side of the main tunnel, searching for the stairway where he'd met Kit when he noticed a shadow. When he glanced that way, the shadow vanished.

The main tunnel hid all sorts of secret exits. The air changed announcing them, but taking one without any clue as to where the passage might dump him was a huge risk. Not because Russ thought he might get lost, but because someone might trap him in a collapse and he felt rushed. Bella was with them for eight hours. He rubbed his bare feet on the cement floor hoping to sense something. Anything.

Being back in these tunnels felt strange. They had a more lived-in odour to them, making him wonder how much business went on down here. The rocks were cold to the touch and the beams had carvings to serve as markers. Overall, the atmosphere was different. Russ felt like he was in the stuffy bank, watched by gods who could decide his fate at any moment. He hated the feeling. He liked being in control.

Russ wasn't as good as Cal at sensing things with his feet, but as fate would have it, he didn't have to be, a tiny cough to his right was all he needed. "Did you see him?" A tiny voice asked. "It was him. I saw him."

Russ stepped back and over, curious what a child did in these tunnels.

"Shh. He'll hear you."

The tunnel had a slim crack in the wall and four eyes peered at him from the dark. Russ lifted his lantern to see them but they slunk back until they were out of the light. These brats were around Samuel's age. He leaned against the cold wall. Russ wouldn't fit in the opening. He was much too broad, but he planned to talk to them just the same.

"You gentlemen wanna make a few coins? I could use eyes while I go off exploring these tunnels 'cause I'd rather not die down here. Ya know?"

Silence.

"You have a name?"

"S-s-souris and my brother is S-s-squirt."

"Do you speak French?"

"*Ouais, Monsieur.*" Souris stepped forward. He had a bit of a mousy look to him. "We ain't allowed to s-s-speak French. Kit s-s-says only English if we 'pect to eat." He curved his shoulders in and rubbed his nose. His beady eyes didn't hold one spot for long and he kept flicking his wrist.

The young one stepped into his light and Russ caught his breath. He looked to be five, if that. His blond hair stuck up with filth. His clothes fell around him loosely, too big. His bare feet were covered in dust, and his dirty face blended him into the wall, all except his eyes, which stood out, watching Russ as if he were his hero.

"You know Kit?"

They both nodded.

"She said we had to hide until she got back for us. Did you come for us?" Squirt had a happy breath to his words. "We gonna all live with you? We heard her talking to the warrior and we ready."

"I could use a hand. Do you know your way around these tunnels? I need to find my daughter. A guy name Kaplain might have taken her. He runs with a rough crowd. They like to hold meetings and such."

The boys slunk back into the dark.

"I don't feel a draught coming from this slit you gentlemen are in. If you want me to let you out, you're gonna have to prove braver than this."

"I'm brave." Souris stepped forward again.

Squirt whispered, "We can go home with you?"

"Shh." Souris silenced him. "It don't work that way. Kit s-s-says we wait for her."

"Who's watching you?"

"No one no more. We ran away from Mable's and back here s-s-since we don't want Kit to leave us when s-s-she goes into hiding at your place."

"Do you guys know me?"

Squirt pulled out a paper from his pocket. "We gots pictures."

After a long silence, Russ pulled out his hanky and unwrapped a cookie. "These are my daughter's favourite. My wife used to make them for me, and after she died, I learnt to make them myself. They aren't half as good as hers."

"You for real?" Souris stayed tight against him.

Russ didn't hand the food over, just studied it.

"How big's your little girl?" Squirt asked.

"Smaller than you. She repeats the swears I say which gets me in trouble with Ma, and she steals my coins 'cause she likes shiny things. She giggles like a fool when I tell her to hide and she thinks it's the end of the world when I give her a bath. She likes to beat on my brother and she giggles when my pa kisses her cheek."

"You have a nice Pa?"

Russ nodded and glanced at the cookie like a tease.

Souris spilled what he knew. "They meet under the s-s-shoe repair s-s-shop. I can take you there, but you gotta promise to take us to Kit."

"Can we go home with you, Mister? We can meet your Ma? Will she like us? I can wash up first. I don't mind a bath, not at all."

Souris nodded, as if this is what he'd wanted to say but chickened out.

Russ exchanged the drawing Squirt held for the cookie. He studied the page in the dim light.

Souris said, "S-s-she tried to draw ya s-s-several times, but could never get the eyes right."

Instead of eyes, images clustered together, reminding Russ of the scribbles Bella drew. It made sense, but only to her.

Russ stared at Souris confused. Souris' eyes grew huge as he shoved half the cookie in his mouth. The other half he handed to Squirt.

What were these boys doing here? His gut tightened, because the idea of Bella ending up here terrified him. Maybe Kit was right and he'd take them home.

"My brother," Souris told him. "He's too young to run these tunnels, but he s-s-sticks with me s-s-so he learns. I keep him s-s-safe. I'm a trained warrior." His grin grew as his head jerked several times to the same motion as his wrist.

"Your mother knows you're down here?"

"She's gone. Sleeping forever," Squirt said quickly.

"Where is your pa?"

Souris shied away but Squirt said, "You could be our pa. Kit says your ma makes real good cakes."

Why would Kit tell these boys such a thing? Russ was stumped. "So you live here?"

"It's warm, clean enough."

"Show me where the men who scare you hang out. I have to pay them a visit before we head home."

The younger brother grabbed Souris by the arm and peeked at Russ. "He said home."

What would Pa say to him bringing two tunnel-rats home? He didn't care, he needed their help and they needed his.

The main tunnel led to another staircase. They crept under the steps. A trapdoor was at their feet and Souris opened it. "This will take us to a passageway they don't know about and you can watch them without going in. Kit s-s-says it's s-s-safer to know what they need before they ask."

They dropped into the hole.

The other Moose Jaw tunnels were manmade and most of them were nicer than Russ' house. Walls were made with cement, held up by support beams. They were built to last. The tunnel they dropped into was a blessed tunnel made by Mother Herself. The passageway reminded Russ of home. The walls were jagged with small beams holding an edge to them that screamed, "*If God wants you dead, He'll do it now.*" These were the runners' secret tunnels. The places where they vanished when things grew too hot.

The tunnel was short and slanted upward. Several draughts slipped from the right side of the tunnel. Through this short tunnel, anyone could access a bunch of places.

The passage slowly grew bigger and a draught of freedom was in front of them. Souris dimmed the lantern. "Wait here, when you s-s-see their s-s-shoes pass, you crawl out. We'll go pack up."

–FORTY-FOUR–

Russ expected all sorts of people to pass but the only feet that crossed his line of view were those of a barefooted woman. "Kit?" he whispered and crawled out of the passageway.

She raised her lantern to get a better look at him.

"What are you doing here?" he stammered. "Is it already that late?"

She nodded. "I went straight to my friend Mable's just outside of town, but the boys I was telling you about ran away, so I'm looking for them." She looked sick.

"They are apparently packing up. Got it in their heads they're moving in with me."

She smirked. "Sorry, they must have heard Francis telling me we could hide out at your place."

"Did you see Francis yet?"

"No. On my way, I just got here."

A man cleared his throat nearby. Kit stepped back and raised her hand, warning Russ to stay back.

No one was around, but men spoke low.

"Ahhshhit." It was the first time Russ heard a woman swear, but he understood Kit's terror in those two simple words she spoke as one. Yet she stood her ground and something in him was excited to know a woman so bold, so courageous. Standing with her made this easier, as if she shouldered half his fear. This gal was the strength he needed and he found himself reaching out to her despite everything.

She dimmed the lantern, pulled him into the dark corner with her, and whispered, "We're by the Meeting Room. The entrance is four feet to your left. When you go in, closets line the far side. Several trunks, a table…" Russ had no idea what she said after that. Her lips brushed his and her hand slid under his shirt. Her fingers magically shooting life into him.

He froze against the wall, forgetting to breathe or think as her lips stopped talking and danced against his. His hands slipped around her, needing to melt into the rest of her. They were as tight as they could get, locked in a kiss and he had no idea how she'd vanished the fear, the ache that sucked him in daily. He melted into it, finally sure of who he was. Their tongues danced, teased. Lips so soft against each other, then firm. Her hands pulled him toward her.

He was alive, ready to take on the world. She fed the strength he needed to breathe. He didn't need air anymore. He needed her soul against his.

She rested her head against his. "Sorry. I waited forever to do that and if we're to get dead today, I just had to."

He breathed, his hands frozen on her.

"I'll be a minute. I know a few of these blokes. Stay."

Stay? He couldn't move. He felt too much.

She peeled his fingers off her and pushed the wall about four feet from him. It moved, revealing a room. She opened the door slowly.

He was still recovering when a thin light escaped the room and a pistol greeted her.

Russ stepped forward, ready to help, but she waved him off and arranged the lantern on the hook by the door. "Put that thing away before you blow your dick off, love." Her voice purred in an unfamiliar way that made Russ uncomfortable.

The man holding the gun had a shake to his index finger. He was more terrified than she was.

"Look what the cat dragged in," someone joked from inside the room.

"Not funny." Kit pushed the gun aside. "I'm searching for my mark. Ya see him? Tall, skinny bloke. He owes me but hit the fields before he'd paid up. I thought that maybe he stumbled in on you boys. What y'all doing tonight? Any jobs?"

The door shut.

Russ leaned against the wall to hear but they were entombed and only a muffling echoed against his ear.

–FORTY-FIVE–

Kit sat on the edge of the table and lazily turned a few pages of the book on it. The ledger contained names and money paid. Some had stars beside them, others were stroked out.

She crossed her legs, letting them dangle playfully, very aware that all eyes were on her.

"Yeah, I have a big job you could do," someone said.

"Shut up, maybe she'll help us." Arnold pulled his sheet off and stepped up to her, too close but she lured him, teasing. Doing what she had to survive, until she had all these guys right where she wanted them. "You truck those two brats around. You must be good with little ones."

"I can be very motherly if that's what you want."

He smiled. "Don't I know it," he said to the others around him as if he were a big stud. Then to Kit he explained, "We have to look after a baby for Kaplain and we don't know squat about babies."

Kit kept her face blank. "Babies are not my strong suit, but I guess I could do this, for a price. Show me. I'll see what I can do to help, but I want my cash up front. I'm tired of you boys not delivering."

Arnold slid a bill up her leg and she met his hand and pulled the bill from it. A ten. He thought this was worth ten dollars? Her hand shook when she slid it up her sleeve. She could buy those boys enough food for the month with a ten!

"Come on, we have to meet Kaplain here in ten minutes, so we have to hurry. She's in the shoe repair shop."

Her heart skipped a beat. She was this close. She thought about going to tell Russ, but anything unusual would set them off. Arnold was very bright and he liked her because she didn't make him feel threatened. She grabbed his hand and followed him up the staircase and into the shoe repair shop.

–Forty-Six–

Russ fought the urge to rush in after Kit. He needed a way to get in there to make sure she was safe without having a dozen men coming down on him. He lit the lantern. Beside the door was a hook with several sheets. He took one off and held it. Could he slip one on? The idea terrified him. Not a breath in him could do it. Isabelle would never forgive him if he…

He touched his lips and the memory of Kit's kiss gave him determination. He had to slip this sheet on for Bella.

He pulled the sheet over his head without a second thought and pushed into the room.

It was empty except for a guy standing at the far door with a pistol. He glanced at Russ in the sheet, his eyes running up and down him. "Jesus Christ, Peter, you lost your goddamn shoes?" He chuckled. "Only asshole I know who has to take his shoes off to screw a whore. Took ya long enough. The others left without us. I told them you were finding a pencil. Ready?"

Russ sighed.

"Come on. Grab the book." He pointed to the table where a notebook with a heavy leather padding waited. Russ walked up to the notebook and flipped it open.

He almost fell over.

This was the list! Under his fingers.

He snagged the ledger and prepared to run but the guy sidled up to him, "So? How was she?"

Russ grabbed the pencil he handed him.

"Good, eh?"

Russ considered killing this guy. The moment the thought entered his mind, Penelope Jack appeared. She snooped in the lockers and paused to grin at Russ.

"Come on, I told you everything. Did she do that thing with her tongue?"

Russ cleared his throat and the guy laughed full-hearted. He slapped Russ on the back. "Come on. I told you she was outta your league."

Russ followed him out of the cellar and into an empty shoe repair shop. They slunk through the business. Powerful smells made his stomach turn. Finally, they were out the back door that led to an open field. Russ felt like a fraud, like a sinner.

The scene before him gave him pause. Crowds always made him snaky, but this was worse because the crowd fed the earth a crippling energy of...*hate*. No goodness lay here and the hate created a fear.

Russ wanted to run.

Faces blended one on top of the other. Some were covered in cloaks, bandanas shielding their faces, sheets, or other types of veils. They could stand beside their best friend and he wouldn't know.

No one laughed.

Russ needed to sit or run. Both.

He stood before a desk, facing a line up. His hands were sweating. Despite the late hour, the sun shone.

Russ studied the crowd, hoping to see one face at a time and not the collective. Impossible. They were a clump to him. He let his eyes wander to the fields in the distance. Someone rode a horse pretty fast...

Dang. Kit was on the run.

He snapped the pencil in half.

Russ ran. He ran through the shoe repair shop and to the cellar that led to the tunnel. His running was cut short when someone pounced on him from above and scared the dirt right off him. Cal rolled him to the ground, a knife against his throat.

"It's me, Cal." Russ choked out from under the sheet and Cal flew off.

Russ was tied up in the sheet and wriggled it off before Cal killed him. "Kit is on the run." Russ dived for the tunnels.

"Did she have Bella?"

"Why else would she be running?" Russ could think of a dozen other possibilities, but that was the only one he was prepared to accept.

"Maybe she robbed them. I don't trust her, Russ. She killed the priest."

"I trust her. So what if she killed the priest? He exchanged Bella for something." Russ stormed to the tunnel.

"Not that tunnel. I have guys tied up in that one. Some idiot messed with a dame. Easy target. Up, come on."

Up? Russ glanced up. A trapdoor led to a crawlspace above them.

Cal said, "I searched everywhere for the book, but this list you want doesn't exist."

Russ slapped the ledger into his chest. "I got it. And they marked certain people with stars...those are the first crew we'll visit. But Kit first. In case she has Bella."

"No way." Cal glared at him in disbelief.

Russ didn't care about the list anymore.

Cal shoved the notebook back at him and hoisted him up. Russ noticed his shoulder bled. "You're still hurt? I thought the Healing Chamber fixes those things."

"I got in a fight on my way here. Not sure how you missed the mess these tunnels are in."

The boys! Dang it. Russ crawled ahead. "You put a dent in their number, I'm sure."

"Well, this is true, but I got cut. And you know how I hate that."

"We need Silver, he'll know..." Russ felt stupid saying it. Silver was gone. A strange sadness fell on him. He had no idea how much he'd relied on him, and thought maybe Pa was right about asking him to do things for them, because now that he was gone, what were they gonna do?

Cal stood behind Russ. "Don't move," he mouthed and turned his small lantern off. They waited. They could hear them under them, running around like fools. When all was quiet, Russ followed Cal. They shimmied through the tight crawlspace for about twenty feet. Then the passage dropped into another tunnel.

Montague helped Russ out of the tight hole.

"What are you doing here?" Russ asked him.

"Keeping watch on my warriors."

"Francis?" Russ asked.

"His lung was punctured, he stood no chance."

"But Kit said—" Russ pulled the plant out of his pocket and offered the leaves to him as if it might magically help.

"I set her on a mission. Her soul couldn't bear the grief of losing another she cares for and she needed a moment to deal with the possibility."

Russ' soul sank. Francis was gone.

Montague was probably right, giving her a task had helped. "She might be pissed she wasn't there for him."

"I was. She will find comfort in that."

Grief washed over Russ that cut through him so deep he couldn't feel anything else.

"He is one with the earth, a *Cîpay*. You will tell her this."

Russ mumbled, "It would help if I knew what that meant."

Montague's blue eyes pierced into Russ. Cal crawled out behind Russ and stood, waiting with him for Montague to explain. "It means she will find comfort in that."

"As will we," Cal agreed. "He died protecting Cursed Lands. Now the duty falls to us."

"Yeah, whatever." It frustrated Russ that they never explained to him exactly what they protected or what *Cîpay* were. Maybe none of them knew, and they just pretended so they didn't look like a fool. "I have young boys down here I need to find," Russ told them. Suddenly everything crashed on him.

"Russ, head down this path and turn right," Cal ordered. "You'll come to a staircase, take it. The stairway leads to the hotel room Pa likes to rent. I'll meet you back there. If you can't wait to chase after Kit, make sure you leave the list in that room."

"Where are you going?"

"To keep them from chasing after you. Coming Montague? I could use a hand."

Russ hurried off. He found the steps easily and started up them. Squirt and Souris stepped out of the shadows. "Wait for us, Mister." They were pulling a backpack behind them that was too heavy for them.

Russ stared at them, no idea what to do. He couldn't leave them. He picked up the pack and rustled Squirt's hair. "Keep up."

He led him to the hotel room. Pa already had the dresser moved ahead and he sat on the bed, talking to Ma who sat in the rocking chair in the corner. She shot to her feet when Russ stumbled in with the boys. They were quick to rush to her and avoid Pa.

"Where did these young men come from?" Ma brought them to her. "What kind of trouble are you in now?"

"Sorry, Ma. They need a home and I couldn't leave 'em. Kit is on the run. I'm going after her in case she has Bella."

"You young men come here. I have to clean you up." She brought them to the basin. They glanced at Russ who smiled and encouraged them to listen to her.

Pa got to his feet. His eyes were red. Russ couldn't imagine how hard losing a father twice in a lifetime would be. Russ tossed his arms around him. Pa gripped his dirty work shirt and cried against his shoulder.

"How old were you, Pa? The first time he died?"

Pa pulled out his hanky and wiped his eyes. "This is the first time."

Russ wanted to correct him, but the boys pulled away from Ma to watch, stepping closer together as if Russ was in danger, so he decided to finish this conversation another time.

"I got the list," Russ whispered. "A membership list. It's over. If Bella isn't with Kit, she might be with one of these guys, so you start looking. Now, we know whom we're fighting. I'll leave this ledger with you, but I have to go, Pa. In case."

Pa pulled away and stared at him in disbelief. "What list?"

Russ shoved the ledger at Pa. He glanced in it and quickly wrote a few names down. "We need to get this ledger to Antoine and Hoolie," Pa said which made sense since Hoolie had the gift of Sight and could pick out which one of the guys on this list was shadowed by a cursed spirit.

"If you're sending Bellecoeur home, hide this book with his body. We'll mark every one of them with a tattoo on their hand that stops them from returning to the earth and forces them to move on," Russ told him. "It worked for Isabelle. I saw her leave with Silver."

Pa shut the ledger and sucked in a quick breath. "Russ.

This is… How did you get this?"

"I'll take this book to the priest," Ma offered. "I have to find these young men food anyhow, they're skin and bones." She was dressed in her Sunday best with a new hat. She wore strange boots, too.

Russ pried the notebook from Pa's hands and brought it to her. "You look beautiful, Ma." He held her hands on the book and met her eyes. She was the strongest, bravest woman he knew. This woman would cry with his gal and kill anyone who hurt his daughter. "You are the best ma."

She squinted as if expecting his compliment to come with a list of things he did wrong. Then she glanced at the boys. "You are a good father, teacher, and son." She stole a long look at Russ and wiped something off his chin. She stared at the invisible culprit on her fingers. "Kit?"

Russ felt his face flush. How did she know?

He rubbed his chin, wondering what was on it to give him away.

She glanced at Pa, shocked.

"Silver is never wrong about these things," he told her. "Or rather he never was."

"Can't escape your destiny, after all." Ma prepared to leave. "You can try, but your path is always before you. Walk out with me, Russ. You young men stay, and behave until I return."

Russ added, "You don't have to be afraid of my pa. Call him Bernoit. He'll teach you how to write your names until Ma gets in. He's an excellent teacher."

Ma strolled out with the ledger in her hands as if the book belonged to her. She nodded to everyone she passed and not one person even glanced at it.

Russ walked her to the church down the street. With so much he wanted to say to his ma, he almost said nothing.

"You mentioned bonds, which is a bit of a different problem. I fought curses and drugs and people just wanting our land…" He sighed. "I'm running around hoping to stop all these problems in case one is right." He hated this and just wanted Bella home with him.

"Now why would you worry about that?" She peered into him, probably sure he'd fail anyway.

"If I knew what they wanted I could give it to them and they'd leave us alone."

Her fingers curled around the ledger as she brought it in front of her. "So when a swarm of mosquitos attacks you for blood, you allow them to take their fill and expect no others to return?"

He frowned understanding better why she shot the priest. Ma didn't see hope in anyone, they were all bloodthirsty skeeters to her.

"Well…no."

Before he left her, he had one last thing to ask. The one question no one else could answer for him. "Do you know what a *Cîpay* is?"

"A *Cîpay* wouldn't waste time worrying about what they want and would simply give them what they need."

What they needed was a good bullet to the brain for taking his little girl. "Have you met a *Cîpay*?"

She stared at the church door, as they stood at the bottom of the steps. "I have met many."

"Is Cal one?"

She looked confused for a moment. "Does Bernoit know what you need?"

"Well, no. No one usually has the answers I need. I met one, Marie. She watches over Bella. She's nothing like Cal. Still, I'd like to meet a real live one."

She looked at him seriously. "What do you really want to say? I doubt we should talk about things neither of us needs explained."

She was right, of course. What he really wanted to learn was hard to say, "Miss Penelope is shadowing me. No one knows why."

"I was told she died in her sleep."

"Well. Truth that I found out from her was that she was drunk and had drugged herself because she wanted to forget her pain. I was with her when she died. Now she shadows me."

"She found someone with answers she wants and latched on. Makes sense. When she has what she needs, she will move on."

What did she need? "Maybe she's to blame for Kaplain

thinking our land is worth more than it is," Russ shared his thoughts. "She wants to make that right, and she needs me to help her get revenge on him."

Ma sighed, as if she expected this stupidity from him and it was about time he came clean. "No one needs revenge, Roussel. Give her what she really needs. Why are you telling me this?"

"I understand how it feels to have someone you trust betray you then have them shadow you. She appears in all my weakest moments and it terrifies me. I just wanted you to know, because if that priest is shadowing you, I figured you might need to hear that others are afraid, too."

Ma pulled on the church door, and for a moment, Russ wasn't sure his ma knew fear. "If she appears when you're weak, then make all your moments strong. *Cîpay* live their beliefs, Roussel, they don't let the beliefs of others cause them to lose focus."

Really, things were that simple.

She shut the door and Russ stood for a moment wondering if his ma was *Cîpay*.

–FORTY-SEVEN–

If this was Cal's story, Russ figured he'd already have the girl saved and Bella would be giggling in his arms. Cal was strong in every way Russ needed to be. Russ stormed past the crowd chanting mob-like. They had him terrified and he wished for a quiet place. One moment of peace so he could think.

As he walked, the crowd thinned out, yet someone walking by pushed Russ. He knocked into someone else. They shoved him and he flew face first into the dirt. He tasted the dust from the earth that fed him. Remembering what Silver had taught him, Russ dug his fingers into the dirt and closed his eyes without a thought.

He took a deep breath.

He waited for the promise of the earth to share Her secrets. A strange pull teased at him from the south and Russ assumed the call of home pulled at him, but he couldn't be sure. He opened his eyes, expecting the bustle around him to consume him again but much to his horror, Miss Penelope stood in front of him. Her fancy shoes were in his line of view and the last thing he wanted to see. Movement happened around him, but it annoyed him that she appeared when he hoped to commune with his ancestors, searching for an answer.

"Talk to me." Russ scrambled to his feet, sick of her appearing at his weakest moments to mock him.

A man walking by shook his head as if Russ had gone mad.

Warmth grew between them and Russ didn't feel hate coming from her. It occurred to him that she might be appearing at his weakest moments to help him or because she was afraid. Or maybe like Marie, she was always there and he only saw her when he needed strength.

He met her eyes firmly.

"*You need a horse*," she pointed out and she was right of course, he was just too terrified to think straight.

The livery barn was several blocks away and Russ ran to it. He didn't know the owner since they'd come by automobile. But Russ found him on the ground when he arrived. He helped him to his feet. "You see who did this to you, sir?" Russ asked.

"He stole two horses." He looked dazed. "What a day. First this woman storms through—"

"Did she have a girl with her?"

"Yeah, a little Black girl."

Relief washed over Russ. "I'll get those horses back, but I need one that rides fast and hard."

"Why would you do that?"

"Because you gave me hope that my daughter might actually be alive."

"They stole your daughter? Dirty buggers. I knew something was wrong with that gal when she stormed in here. I'd go with ya, son, but I can't ride no more." He brought Russ to a mare. "She's my best."

Russ met his eyes and pulled a few coins from his pocket. "This is all I got, but I'll bring you more."

"Just bring my horses back and you keep that."

Kit had headed south so Russ went that way. He rode the horse hard and stopped about thirteen miles out of town by a white two-storey house. Someone watching from the second floor window closed the blinds. He smelled lavender and sure enough, Marie appeared on the front steps.

"Is Bella safe?" he demanded, scrambling from the horse.

Marie nodded and ran toward him but halfway down the path, an invisible force yanked her back and Marie fell on her ass. "*She's fine here, but Kit isn't. She went to lead them off Bella's trail and ran that way.*" She pointed south.

Russ was torn. He wanted to see Bella, but he trusted Marie. She'd never given him any reason not to. "I'll be right back."

He looked at the horse tracks by the gate. They led off so he kept riding.

The sun set when he caught sight of three horses in the field. He rode toward them.

Kit was pinned to the ground by two men. One held her shoulders and the other undid her pants.

Russ didn't bother slowing down. He dived from his horse, landing on the jerk fumbling with her pants. While he dropped on him, he kicked the other directly in the face. His head snapped back from the force of his descent and Russ heard his neck crack.

Great. More shadows.

Russ slit the throat of the one he'd landed on and pushed him off her.

"You hurt?"

Before she could answer, out of nowhere came one of them fancy automobiles.

Russ turned to defend.

"I got Bella out of there." Kit breathed as she scrambled to her feet, ready to fight by his side. "I had to run. Sorry."

Russ never got a chance to thank her. One of them lassoed him. It was the last bloody thing he expected, but they swung a lasso and yanked him forward by the neck. Russ kept his hands around the rope to stop it from tightening around, which meant he couldn't fight. Just like that, he was hauled off for a lynching.

These guys weren't wearing sheets, sure enough, Jessie Kaplain's pa was with them. His jaw was steady as he watched them string Russ up. Russ kept his eyes on him, watching the determination in his stance. Kaplain was prepared to watch every one of them die and Russ had no idea why. Maybe Pa was right and he just hated them. A strange madness haunted his eyes, making Russ think about Isabelle and how she'd have asked, "Has he gone mad?" and this time Russ would have said, "Yes, evil spirits cursed him."

These men had done this before. No talking. No cheering. Russ was gonna die and when Cal found him he'd get the message loud and clear to mind his business.

They flung the rope around the tree branch and hauled him up. Russ understood why Skinny never got a shot off. To remove his hands from the rope meant instant death. Yet the cord wore away at his fingers and already the air wasn't going down the way he wanted.

Russ kicked, but they weren't beside him, which meant he wasted energy kicking at nothing. They pulled him up higher.

One handed a cloak to Kaplain but he shoved the robe away, yet they insisted and he finally snapped it from them. He looked drugged when he spoke to the air, instead of his friends.

When another started praying and chanting, Russ got the impression this was a ritual. What kinda tribe hanged guys as part of a ceremony?

The field loomed before Russ, empty. Strange not seeing Silver with his bow, ready to protect him. Russ was never afraid to die because he always thought Silver would be with him as he found his final breath, yet he was alone. The sun was partway vanished for the day. The moon struggled for presence, blooming onto the sky as if painted into the grey. For once, even the wind stood still. He'd never noticed the silence before, but the peace was comforting. As if the world was ready to welcome him.

Isabelle appeared, far away, playing in the field. A happy energy around her as she chased a couple dogs, Beast and Fangs. They bounced, in love with her. The fun made Russ smile and he hoped she didn't look his way and see him. She'd seen enough bad things in her life, he wanted her to forget about him and have fun.

Miss Penelope appeared beside him, watching Isabelle with him. She had nothing to say.

Isabelle ran off with the dogs, so happy and free while he hanged, feeling more alive than he ever did…as he died.

He fell. His feet touched the ground and Russ gasped for life as sound rushed at him.

Russ was yanked back up in an instant, but he twirled to see Kit and she was a better sight than Miss Penelope so he kept his eyes on her.

Kit picked up his knife. Russ didn't even remember dropping it. She was ready to use it, when Miss Penelope stopped her with a hand on her shoulder. Kit jumped and turned around shocked. The pause put her in jeopardy and they tackled Kit.

"Stop," Russ tried to yell, but only air escaped. The rope loosened and he landed on the ground again. Russ glanced up to see why he was free, and in the tree was an arrow. It had sliced clean through the rope. Russ scanned the area for Silver but Montague and Cal stood in the field.

Russ wiggled out of the noose and tackled the man closest to him, fighting his way to Kit.

He snapped him in a headlock and was about to snap his neck. Miss Penelope's fancy shoes appeared in his line of sight and Russ stopped, because he did not need another ghost haunting him, wanting him to teach something impossible. Russ dropped him when he passed out.

Cal took the man from him. Jessie's pa, Kaplain. Cal wrapped the lasso around his neck. Kaplain's head flopped forward.

"Mark his hand, Russ, so he goes straight to hell."

Russ glanced up. Since when did Cal believe in heaven and hell? Yet Russ carved a bloody ghost on the back of his hand, disgracing him and marking him for judgment. Then he left Cal to handle him. Meanwhile, Montague had dished out his own vengeance on the other guys.

Russ pulled Kit to her feet and kissed her cheek. She clasped onto him for dear life. Their lips locked in a desperate kiss.

"I thought I lost you," she said between breaths, as if she'd had him to begin with. Maybe she did. A part of him, anyway.

She pushed past Russ and looked smugly at Kaplain. "We got 'em." She was ready to stab him when Francis appeared at his side.

Russ grabbed her shoulders, pulled her into his arms, and kissed her until Francis vanished.

When she pulled away, Kit said, "This man killed my family. I have to kill him."

"We were fighting ghosts as men, when really, we should be spirits. Francis is his shadow. We cannot kill a man who has a *Cîpay* tied to his soul. We trust that Francis will keep him in line. The curse will end if a warrior spirit latches on to each troubled soul and is strong enough to bring all the cursed souls tied to him with him to afterlife." Russ rubbed his neck. That had been close.

"Do you see him?" Kit asked looking around. "Do you see Francis? Tell him…tell him…"

"He knows," Russ promised her.

"I don't have to see to believe," Cal assured her.

"We have others to visit, in case others spectres haunt other good souls," Russ told Montague. "The list has names of people we'll mark. We'll pay them visits and summon *Cîpay* to protect them."

Montague thanked him for teaching him and turned to leave.

"Montague, thank you for being there when I needed you," Russ said.

He nodded. "Thank Francis, he came for me." He faced Russ. "Silver is not gone. He is a part of the earth we use to nourish us. In every breath we take, in every action we make." He extended his arms. "My brother is free as one day we shall all be."

That was a nice thought, and exactly what Russ needed to hear.

He watched Montague run off. Feeling safe, knowing he was out there.

"How is that warrior related to us?" Russ wondered.

Cal said quickly, "His sister was Grandma Lacey, but he grew up with Pa. All Pa told me."

Kit said, "I left Bella with a woman who was always very kind to me. Her name is Mable. She lives back a ways, in a white house."

Russ rode back with Kit and Cal. When he took Bella from Mable, he noticed a mark on the back of her hand like Charlie had. A *Cîpay* mark of judgement. Her green eyes pierced into him but she didn't say a word.

Marie watched him settle Bella on his horse. *"They didn't hurt her,"* Marie assured him and Russ noticed she shimmered when she said it. What had she done to keep her safe?

"Just curious, Marie, how does a ghost keep a girl safe?"

She smiled. *"I am Cîpay. Never ask where I have been, or where I am going. For each of us has a journey no one else can understand."*

–FORTY-EIGHT–

The next morning, as Pa bought the train tickets for home, Russ stood by the tracks with Bella in his arms, making out the shadow in the field. He squinted. "Do you see that silver streak over there, Bella?" He pointed and she looked. "Can you see what it is?"

She slapped his face and kissed it leaving behind a wet spot.

Kit sidled up to him. The boys followed her closely. They were dressed in new clothes and were washed, courtesy of his ma. "Rumours are that leaders stole the cash and the membership list and headed to the States with it."

"They blame us for everything else, but this they let go," Russ said. "I guess without Kaplain or Bellecoeur leading them, they won't have us as a specific target. Most of the guys on that list wanted to be part of something bigger than them. Fancy rituals and good drugs, maybe even those bonds Ma mentioned. They wanted something to fight for so they added causes to the mix."

Still, Russ was taking his duty to protect Sacred Land seriously.

"I am the last of the Ghost Healers. This is a heavy burden for me to bear. What do I do, Russ? All my life I thought I had this big destiny that would reveal itself to me if I got together with you, but that proved to be impossible. So I took your advice and pushed these feelings down and enjoyed what life delivered even if it never felt right. Now here I am. And I don't know which way to turn."

Russ knelt and set Bella down. He dug up a flower that grew wild in the grass and presented the flower, root and all, to Kit in a silly gesture, symbolic of the story Silver had told them many years ago. "There are no divisions between the tribes. There never were. We are the Ghosts Tribes. We are all, each of us, in our own way *Cipay*. We teach, we find comfort in each other, and we are never alone. Come home with us and teach us how to heal. We will teach you how to protect."

She took the flower from him, and much to his shock, she was in tears.

Quick to his feet, he wiped them gently and whispered, "I was wrong, Kit, when I told you to enjoy what was in front of you. Always go for more, this way, when you lose everything in front of you, you have so much more around you."

–FORTY-NINE–

June 1936—

They were together like every night eating supper at their long family table—the one Pa made so they could eat together as often as possible. He was still weird about his meals, yet there was a comfort in knowing they'd always be welcome at his table. They were a big group: Ma, Pa, Bernadette, her husband, and their son Xavier, the younger girls and Samuel, Cal, Desire and their three girls. Souris and Squirt were there, too. So was Russ' wife Kit, and Bella of course.

They cracked jokes and laughed.

Russ was enjoying the evening when he heard it. It wasn't a noise; more like the lack of noise. A silence that fell on the farm through the open window. The chickens stopped clucking, the horses waited, even the air ceased blowing for one second. Total silence meant nature respected *Cîpay*. And the only one who stopped by these days was Montague.

"He'll wait," Russ told Cal and Pa when they started to get up.

"Anyone at this table know why Montague might be out waiting for us while we're enjoying a good meal?" Russ asked.

Souris shifted in his chair. He hadn't eaten much and his tics were suddenly worse than usual. Russ gave Cal a look.

Russ said, "Hope no one at this table got dirty with them locals by the creek, 'cause Montague, he don't like that."

"He don't?" Souris' eyes grew huge. "We was just talking." He glanced at Ma and back at his plate.

Russ smirked, knowing that guilty look all too well. He

was proud of Souris. He grew into a fine young man. He'd taken a liking to languages so he learnt fake-Latin, too.

Pa shook his head and pointed to Souris. "You and me will be having a long talk later about *talking* to girls."

"Then I get a turn." Cal ground his fist into his palm and Souris was ready to run.

Much to everyone's shock, Ma said, "You boys stop picking on Souris. He's a good young man. Russ and Kit are raising him to be a man I'm proud of."

Souris relaxed his shoulders when he saw whatever secret he kept was safe with Ma.

Pa laughed. "Montague is here to talk to me about the tunnel collapse from last week. He wants help to clear the rubble out. It'll take wagons. Sounds like a job for strong young men. Right, Souris?"

Souris nodded. "Yes, Ssssir."

"Tomorrow sounds perfect," Russ offered. "After church." They had a new priest and Ma loved him, but she never went to church with them anymore. Russ didn't blame her. If he had a priest haunting him, it might be hard to go in. Still, he appreciated what she did for Bella. She was a good mother so he prayed extra hard for God to forgive her and free her. Russ knew He had a soft spot for mothers so he played on that. To be extra sure, when they got home every Sunday, Kit and Russ went out to pray in the field with their hands in the earth, because Mother would understand and might be able to convince this other God. Russ didn't know how the gods worked, but covering them all was best.

Things weren't quiet or anything after that and grain prices dropped on crops that sucked, but they settled into a happy life just the same, and they never went without. Kit said Pa hid a stash of money in the storm cellar. Kit found it and counted it. She said they could rest easy.

As for the bonds Ma had mentioned and the metal box Cal had told him about, they vanished.

The curse was contained by warriors Montague dispatched. They made a few house visits. Hoolie went with them, since he could see souls and he pointed out which ones had shadows they had to worry about.

Kit and Russ never had children together and God knows

they should have. Ma said that sometimes God chooses certain people to raise others who need raising. That's what they did. Raising Souris, Squirt, and Bella was enough. They were each a handful in their own way.

After supper that night, Russ found himself out at the haystack, cuddled in with Isabelle's notebook. The pages were full of new stories and drawings.

Miss Penelope was the first one to join him. She sat beside him in the straw and fell back. She was relaxed these days, for a ghost. *"You're doing a good job teaching, Russ."*

Russ opened the notebook to the first page. He liked teaching at the school and was happy he'd taken his certification.

She said, *"It's a beautiful night. What are you thinking about?"*

"Not much. Just enjoying the quiet."

They got along better, and having her shadow his life didn't seem so weird now. He didn't look at her company as a curse, but more like a learning opportunity, because once he gave her a chance, Penelope actually knew neat things and he grew to enjoy her friendship. *"This is my last night here. Silver is coming to help me move on."* She spoke his name with a great deal of respect that made the longing he had for his grandpa a touch deeper.

"It was nice getting to know you," he said, not sure why she was suddenly moving on. "When Silver shows, say hi for me."

She vanished.

Kit joined them and he snuggled with her, his hand under her blouse. He stared at her. "It's stupid, Kit, Miss Penelope just mentioned Silver, and now I miss him. I never got to say good-bye."

"Put your hands in the dirt and close your eyes."

He glared at her. "That never works. You'll just have your way with me." He brushed her lips. "It's nice to see these lips so happy."

She touched his eyes. "Relax."

He raised an eyebrow. He was far too relaxed these days. Russ dived for her neck but Silver appeared beside her and Russ jumped back as if caught doing something wrong. Kit glanced over, but he was already gone.

"Damn. Grandpa scared the dirt right off me."

His warm laughter echoed over the prairies and Russ smiled. "Jerk."

"I have something to show ya," Kit pulled a drawing out of the notebook.

It was...well him. Russ' eyes were serious, yet they sparkled with a playful look. They were happy grey like Pa's eyes, and kinda dangerous dark like Cal's, but more heroic like that big ass poster of Louis Riel.

"You finished it."

"You stopped thinking."

She was right of course; he had everything he needed, except a quiet place to think.

Elsewhen Press

an independent publisher specialising in Speculative Fiction

Visit the Elsewhen Press website at elsewhen.co.uk for the latest information on all of our titles, authors and events; to read our blog; find out where to buy our books and ebooks; or to place an order.

Sign up for the Elsewhen Press InFlight Newsletter at elsewhen.co.uk/newsletter

Sacred Land Stories
Alternate history infused with magical reality

Legends on the Prairies

"Don't you believe in legends?" Such a simple question, yet what Sacri really wants Alex to believe is that he is the hero from her legends, meant to save land sacred to her tribe. Alex is a lot of things: a painter, a sculptor, a dreamer. Fired from a good job, grieving for a woman he hoped to marry, he is the local drunk. He is a lot of things, but hero isn't one of them.

In the heart of the lonesome prairies in 1892, Sacri's determination entrances Alex. Despite everything, Alex finds himself praying to a God that he thought had abandoned him, in the hope that just maybe there is some truth to Sacri's stories. To add to Alex's unease is the certainty that Sacri's brother, Silver, often merely glimpsed as a shadow riding his horse across the horizon, will happily kill Alex if he turns out not to be the man that Sacri thinks he is.

ISBN: 9781908168122 (epub, kindle) / ISBN: 9781908168023 (352pp paperback)
Visit bit.ly/LegendsPrairies

Ghosts on the Prairies

Some things are worth a fight. Strong words that Antoine's father drilled into him. After his father mysteriously vanishes one night, Antoine must find another income or he risks losing the Sacred Land that his father swore to protect.

On a well-paying ranch, Antoine meets Emma, a victim of underground slavery. Fighting for her freedom costs him his home, his sister, his best friend, and puts in question all of his values. If he succeeds, will she and her son fit into his world?

The prairies of 1916-19 come alive with bootleggers, slavery, fools in sheets, haunting spirits, shifty tunnel runners, and even exploding churches.

ISBN: 9781908168535 (epub, kindle) / ISBN: 9781908168436 (384pp paperback)
Visit bit.ly/GhostsPrairies

Cursed on the Prairies

Russ has the perfect life planned: go to college, marry Isabelle, farm with his father and brothers. But then Isabelle is snatched by a bunch of men dressed like ghosts.

Who are these men terrorising them and trying to burn his gal for being a witch? His father thinks they're acting out to scare them off the land. His brother wonders if they're wanting a sacred plant that grows in the tunnels. His ma knows of other secrets haunting them… While those things might be true, his ghostly grandpa, Silver, shows Russ something he can't ignore: a curse summoned years ago that may doom them all.

With lingering spirits, a troubled girl shadowing his destiny, dark rituals, a love potion, cursed men plaguing their lands, a prison break that takes him away from home when his wife needs him the most, and the earth itself trying to suck them in, *Cursed on the Prairies* proves that, in 1928 the prairies are still a place full of secrets that even a ghost can't bury.

ISBN: 9781911409144 (epub, kindle) / ISBN: 9781911409045 (336pp paperback)
Visit bit.ly/CursedPrairies

CAN'T DREAM WITHOUT YOU

FROM THE DARK CHRONICLES

Legends say that tens of thousands of years ago, Whisperers were banished from the heavens, torn in half, and dumped on a mortal realm they didn't understand. Longing for their other half, they went from being powerful immortals to lonely leeches relying on humans to survive. Over the years, they earnt magic from demons, they left themselves Notebooks with hints, and by pairing up with human souls, they eventually found their other halves. Humbled by their experiences, they discovered the true purpose of life and many were worthy of returning to the heavens. But many were not.

The Dark Chronicles are stories that share the heartache of select unworthy Whisperers on their journey to immortality after The War of 2019. *Can't Dream Without You* is one of those stories, in which we meet Steve and Julia, two such heroes.

Steve isn't a normal boy. He plays with demons, his soul travels to a dream realm at night using mystical butterflies, and soon he'll earn the power to raise the dead. Al thinks that destroying him would do the world a favour, yet he just can't kill his own son. Wanting to acquire the power that raises the dead before Steve does, Al performs a ritual on Steve's sixteenth birthday. He transfers Steve's dark magic to Julia, an innocent girl he plans to kill. But Steve is determined to save Julia and sucks her soul to Dreamland. From the dream world, he invokes the help of her brother to keep her safe.

Five years later, Steve can't tell what's real or what's a nightmare. Julia's brother wants to kill him, a strange bald eagle is erasing memories, and Steve's caught in some bizarre bullfight on another realm with a cop hot on his trail looking to be Julia's hero. All the while, Steve and Julia must fight the desperate need to make their steamy dreams a reality.

ISBN: 9781908168924 (epub, kindle)
ISBN: 9781908168825 (288pp paperback)

Visit bit.ly/CantDream

BLUEPRINT TRILOGY
KATRINA MOUNTFORT

The *Blueprint* trilogy takes us to a future in which men and women are almost identical, and personal relationships are forbidden. Following a bio-terrorist attack, the population now lives within comfortable Citidomes. MindValues advocate acceptance and non-attachment. The BodyPerfect cult encourages a tall thin androgynous appearance, and looks are everything.

In *Future Perfect* we are introduced to Caia, an intelligent and highly educated young woman. In spite of severe governmental and societal strictures, Caia finds herself attracted to her co-worker, Mac, a rebel whose questioning of their so-called utopian society both adds to his allure and encourages her own questioning of the status quo. As Mac introduces her to illegal and subversive information she is drawn into a forbidden, dangerous world, alienated from her other co-workers and the companions with whom she shares her residence. In a society where every thought and action is controlled, informers are everywhere; whom can she trust? Katrina's story examines the enforcement of conformity through fear, the fostering of distorted and damaging attitudes towards forbidden love, manipulation of appearance and even the definition of beauty.

In *Forbidden Alliance* we return to Caia and Mac some sixteen years later in a story that poses questions of leadership, family loyalties and whether it is possible to justify the sacrifice of human lives for the greater good.

In *Freedom's Prisoners* tensions have escalated. The rebels may have won the first battle in their fight against the Citidome authorities, but can they win a war? The Citidomes are fighting back and no-one is safe any more as RotorFighters rain down fire on defenceless villages destroying them and their inhabitants. Katrina explores betrayal, guilt, hope and endurance in an explosive conclusion to the *Blueprint* trilogy.

The *Blueprint* trilogy is a thought-provoking series with a dark undercurrent that will appeal to both an adult and young adult audience.

Katrina Mountfort was born in Leeds. After a degree in Biochemistry and a PhD in Food Science, she started work as a scientist. Since then, she's had a varied career having been a homeopath and forensic science researcher, and currently works as a freelance medical writer. She now lives in Saffron Walden with her husband and two dogs. When she hit forty, she decided it was time to fulfil her childhood dream of writing a novel!

Book 1: *Future Perfect*
ISBN: 9781908168559 (epub, kindle) / 9781908168450 (288pp paperback)

Book 2: *Forbidden Alliance*
ISBN: 9781908168900 (epub, kindle) / 9781908168801 (288pp paperback)

Book 3: *Freedom's Prisoners*
ISBN: 9781911409120 (epub, kindle) / 9781911409021 (288pp paperback)

Visit bit.ly/BlueprintTrilogy

THE SYMPHONY OF THE CURSED TRILOGY

REBECCA HALL

INSTRUMENT OF PEACE

Raised in the world-leading Academy of magic rather than by his absentee parents, Mitch has come to see it as his home. He's spent more time with his friends than his family and the opinion of his maths teacher matters far more than that of his parents. His peaceful life is shattered when a devastating earthquake strikes and almost claims his little brother's life. But this earthquake is no natural phenomenon, it's a result of the ongoing war between Heaven and Hell. To protect the Academy, one of the teachers makes an ill-advised contract with a fallen angel, unwittingly bringing down The Twisted Curse on staff and students.

Even as they struggle to rebuild the school, things begin to go wrong. The curse starts small, with truancy, incomplete assignments, and negligent teachers over-reacting to minor transgressions, but it isn't long before the bad behaviour escalates to vandalism, rioting and attempted murder. As they succumb to the influence of the curse, Mitch's friends drift away and his girlfriend cheats on him. When the first death comes, Mitch unites with the only other students who, like him, appear to be immune to the curse; together they are determined to find the cause of the problem and stop it.

INSTRUMENT OF WAR

The Angels are coming.

The Host wants to know what the Academy was trying to hide and why the Fallen agreed to it. They want the Instrument of War, the one thing that can tip the Eternity War in their favour and put an end to the stalemate. Any impact on the Academy staff, students or buildings is just collateral damage.

Mitch would like to forget that the last year ever happened, but that doesn't seem likely with Little Red Riding Hood now teaching Teratology. The vampire isn't quite as terrifying as he first thought, but she's not the only monster at the Academy. The Fallen are spying on everyone, the new Principal is an angel and there's an enchanting exchange student with Faerie blood.

Angry and nervous of the angels surrounding him, Mitch tries to put the pieces together. He knows that Hayley is the Archangel Gabriel. He knows that she can determine the course of the Eternity War. He also knows that the Fallen will do anything to hide Gabriel from the Host – even allowing an innocent girl to be kidnapped.

INSTRUMENT OF CHAOS

The long hidden heart of the Twisted Curse had been found, concealed in a realm that no angel can enter, where magic runs wild and time is just another direction. The Twisted Curse is the key to ending the Eternity War and it can only be broken by someone willing to traverse the depths of Faerie.

Unfortunately, Mitch has other things on his mind. For reasons that currently escape him he's going to university, making regular trips to the Netherworld and hunting down a demon. The Academy might have prepared him for university but Netherworlds and demons were inexplicably left off the curriculum, not to mention curse breaking.

And then the Angels return, and this time they're hunting his best friend.

Visit bit.ly/SymphonyCursed

SmartYellow™
J.A. Christy

SmartYellow™ is the story of a young girl, Katrina Williams, who finds herself on the wrong side of social services. After becoming pregnant with only a slight notion of the father's identity, she is disowned by her parents and goes to live on a social housing estate. Before long she is being bullied by a gang involved in criminal activity and anti-social behaviour. Seeking help from the authorities she is persuaded to return to the estate to work as part of Operation Schrödinger, alongside a surveillance specialist. But she soon realises that Operation Schrödinger is not what it seems.

Exploring themes of social inequity and scientific responsibility, J.A. Christy's first speculative fiction novel leads her heroine Katrina to understand how probability, hope and empathy play a huge part in the flow of life and are absent in the stagnation of mere survival. As readers we also start to question how we would know if the power of the State to support and care for the weak had become corrupted into the oppression of all those who do not fit society's norms.

SmartYellow™ offers a worryingly plausible and chilling glimpse into an alternate Britain. For the sake of order and for the benefit of more fortunate members of society, those seen as socially undesirable are marked with SmartYellow™, making it easier for them to be controlled and maintained in a state of fruitless inactivity. Writer, J.A. Christy, turns an understanding and honest eye not only onto the weak, who have failed to cope with life, but also onto those who ruthlessly exploit them for their own ends. At times tense and threatening, at times tender and insightful, *SmartYellow*™ is a rewarding and thought-provoking read.

J.A. Christy's writing career began in infant school at the age of seven when she won best poetry prize with her poem '*Winter*'. Since then she has been writing short stories and has had several published in magazines and anthologies.

She holds a PhD in which she explores the stories we use in everyday life to construct our identities. Working in high hazard safety, she is a Chartered Psychologist and Scientist and writes to apply her knowledge to cross the boundaries between science and art, in particular in the crime, speculative and science-fiction genres.

She lives in Oldham with her partner and their dog.

ISBN: 9781908168788 (epub, kindle)
ISBN: 9781908168689 (320pp paperback)

Visit bit.ly/SmartYellow

Urban fantasy from Tej Turner

The Janus Cycle

The Janus Cycle can best be described as gritty, surreal, urban fantasy. The over-arching story revolves around a nightclub called Janus, which is not merely a location but virtually a character in its own right. On the surface it appears to be a subcultural hub where the strange and disillusioned who feel alienated and oppressed by society escape to be free from convention; but underneath that façade is a surreal space in time where the very foundations of reality are twisted and distorted. But the special unique vibe of Janus is hijacked by a bandwagon of people who choose to conform to alternative lifestyles simply because it has become fashionable to be 'different', and this causes many of its original occupants to feel lost and disenchanted. We see the story of Janus unfold through the eyes of eight narrators, each with their own perspective and their own personal journey. A story in which the nightclub itself goes on a journey. But throughout, one character, a strange girl, briefly appears and reappears warning the narrators that their individual journeys are going to collide in a cataclysmic event. Is she just another one of the nightclub's denizens, a cynical mischief-maker out to create havoc or a time-traveller trying to prevent an impending disaster?

ISBN: 9781908168566 (epub, kindle) / ISBN: 9781908168467 (224pp paperback)
Visit bit.ly/JanusCycle

Dinnusos Rises

The vibe has soured somewhat after a violent clash in the Janus nightclub a few months ago, and since then Neal has opened a new establishment called 'Dinnusos'. Located on a derelict and forgotten side of town, it is not the sort of place you stumble upon by accident, but over time it enchants people, and soon becomes a nucleus for urban bohemians and a refuge for the city's lost souls. Rumour has it that it was once a grand hotel, many years ago, but no one is quite sure. Whilst mingling in the bar downstairs you might find yourself in the company of poets, dreamers, outsiders, and all manner of misfits and rebels. And if you're daring enough to explore its ghostly halls, there's a whole labyrinth of rooms on the upper floors to get lost in...

Now it seems that not just Neal's clientele, but the entire population of the city, begin to go crazy when beings, once thought mythological, enter the mortal realm to stir chaos as they sow the seeds of militancy.

Eight characters. Most of them friends, some of them strangers. Each with their own story to tell. All of them destined to cross paths in a surreal sequence of events which will change them forever.

ISBN: 9781911409137 (epub, kindle) / ISBN: 9781911409038 (280pp paperback)
visit bit.ly/DinnusosRises

About the Author

Born and raised in Saskatchewan, Tanya Reimer enjoys using the tranquil prairies as a setting to her not-so-peaceful speculative fiction.

She is married with two children which means among her accomplishments are the necessary magical abilities to find a lost tooth in a park of sand and whisper away monsters from under the bed.

As director of a non-profit Francophone community center, Tanya offers programming and services in French for all ages to ensure the lasting imprint and growth of the Francophone community in which she was raised. What she enjoys the most about her job is teaching social media safety for teens and offering one-on-one technology classes for seniors.

Tanya was fifteen when she wrote her first column. She has a diploma in Journalism/Short Story Writing. Today, she actively submits to various newspapers, writes and publishes the local Francophone newsletter for her community, and maintains a blog at *Life's Like That*.

Cursed on the Prairies, is her third *Sacred Land Story* for adults and her fourth novel published by Elsewhen Press.